W

Some

Love

Some

Anne Marie Forrest

POOLBEG

Published 2009
by Poolbeg Press Ltd.
123 Grange Hill, Baldoyle,
Dublin 13, Ireland
Email: poolbeg@poolbeg.com

13 5 7 9 10 8 6 4 2

A catalogue record for this book is available from the British Library.

ISBN 978-1-84223-350-4

Typeset by Patricia Hope in Bembo 11.3/14.5
Printed by
Litografia Rosés S.A., Spain

www.poolbeg.com

Note on the Author

After many years spent in Wicklow, Dublin and Melbourne, Anne Marie now lives in her native Cork with her husband, Robert Plant, and daughters, Lucy and Sylvie. These days she divides her time between her family, writing, and making a home out of the old church they bought on their return to Cork.

Her first published novel was the bestselling *Who Will Love Polly Odlum?* Anne Marie's novels have been translated into French, German, Spanish and Latvian.

website: annemarieforrest.com

Also by Anne Marie Forrest

Who Will Love Polly Odlum?
Dancing Days
Something Sensational
The Love Detective
Love Potions

Published by Poolbeg

Acknowledgements

Thanks so much to everyone in Poolbeg and to my agents Ros Edwards and Helenka Fuglewicz who helped me turn my idea into book form. Thanks also to all the booksellers who stock my books on their shelves. Thanks too to all the readers who take my books down from those shelves and carry them home.

And, of course, thanks, as always, to my truly wonderful family and to all my friends who probably won't need to read this book to find out what happens as they've already had to suffer hearing me banging on so much about it.

Dedicated to the memory of Peter Twomey

'Death leaves a heartache no one can heal,
love leaves a memory no one can steal.'

How it all started . . .

"So, which one of us is going to do it then?" I ask.

Dana, who's sitting at the other side of the kitchen table, doesn't answer straight off but takes a breath so deep I can actually see her chest rise and fall.

"Well?" I press.

"You," answers Dana emphatically. "You'll have to, Rosie. I just couldn't."

"Okay." I pull the phone towards me. "Well, here goes." My stomach is churning. All day, ever since this morning, I've been near sick with excitement. But now I feel really nervous too. I'm all jittery.

"Go on!" urges Dana.

"All right, all right." I pick up the receiver.

"Hang on a minute!" she cries.

"What?"

"What are you going to tell her?"

"What do you mean, what am I going to tell her? I'm just going to – you know – tell her."

"Maybe you should prepare her first. Maybe you should

say something like, 'Caroline, you'd better sit down because I have some news to tell you'."

"Okay, I can start with that."

"No, no, hold on. That sounds like you're about to tell her some bad news."

"I'll leave it out then."

"Or . . ."

"Or?"

"Or you could say, 'Caroline, you'd better sit down because I have some good news to tell you.' You know, making sure to emphasise the word 'good'."

I sigh. "Look, why don't you just make the call?"

"No, no, you do it."

"Then let me get on with it and no more interruptions."

I dial the number.

"Is it ringing?" asks Dana.

I nod.

"Put it on speaker. I want to hear her reaction."

I put it on speaker. We both listen to it ring. On and on. I glance over at Dana. I see her brow furrow. She looks as if she's about to say something but, then, we hear Caroline's cheery voice:

"G'day –"

"Caroline, it's Rosie!"

"And Dana! We're –"

"– Caroline here! Sorry I can't take your call right now but if you leave your name and number after the beep I'll get back to you!"

"Oh my God! Oh my God!" cries Dana. "What do we do now?"

"I don't know!"

"Hang up! Hang up! We can't just leave a message!"

Beep!

I hang up.

"We can try again later," I say.

"I guess. But I hate this waiting."

And it's then, at that exact moment, I have my brainwave. That's when it hits me. "Or . . ."

"Or?"

"Or we could always fly over, tell her in person."

"You're kidding!"

"I'm not sure I am."

"We can't just fly all the way to Australia!"

"Why not? What's there to stop us? Think of the surprise Caroline would get. We can bring her back with us. I've always wanted to see Australia. You know my sister lives there."

"But −"

"And it's not like we can't afford it!"

"But −"

"Think of the shock on Caroline's face if we just turn up!"

"Rosie! It's a crazy idea!"

"Oh, come on, Dana. Let's live a little. Let's just do it!"

The chance of being struck by lightning is two and a half times greater than that of winning the Irish National Lottery.

1

"Rosie, are you awake?"

"Hmm?" I open my eyes. I see Dana's face leaning over me, her big brown eyes peering at me, magnified through the lens of her glasses.

"Oh, so you are awake?"

"I am now," I grumble. Slowly I sit up. I stretch my back. I rub my neck. I yawn. I look around confused. "Are we nearly there?"

She shakes her head. "No, we've hours yet."

"Why did you wake me then?" I grumble as I give another yawn.

"I didn't mean to," she answers but I suspect she did.

"You won't mind so if I go back to sleep." I turn, shut my eyes and try to get comfortable. But then I get a nudge. "Jeez, Dana! What?"

"Rosie, please don't! I can't bear sitting here with no one to talk to. I'm going mad. I swear my head will explode! I can't stop thinking." Then suddenly she bursts out, "I mean, when you *do* think about it, about *us* of all people winning eleven million euros!"

I sit bolt upright. "Dana! Shhh! Keep your voice down!"

I quickly look around and am relieved to see that those in the seats nearby who aren't sleeping are oblivious, each absorbed in his or her own private drama. One is engaged in trying and failing to get the remote for his TV working. One is trying and failing to get the lid off her can of peanuts. And one has his head tipped right back, his face scrunched up, his eyes screwed shut, his fists clenched tight and looks as if he's desperately trying, and failing, to pretend he's elsewhere – somewhere – anywhere – but stuck for hours on end in this cramped tubular container high up in the sky with nothing between it and the vast teeming ocean below save thousands of metres of nothingness. I know the theory – sort of – but how do planes fly, really?

Enough with the aerodynamics? What's that about eleven million euros? Okay, well . . .

'It could be you,' as the ad says and it was. Or I should say us – me, Dana and Caroline – exactly five days ago. Honestly, I'm not joking. Last Saturday to be precise though we didn't find out until Sunday morning. Or rather that's when Dana and I found out, Caroline hasn't yet. So how does it feel to win eleven million euros? Hmm . . . Pretty indescribable really. But let me try. Okay, think how you would feel if the person you'd loved from afar for years upon years just turned up on your doorstep one day and declared his undying love for you. Or think of the feeling you'd get if you had just found out you'd sailed through that all-important exam or got that all-important job on which your whole future depended. Or how you'd feel if you were standing at the open door of a plane, about to do a parachute jump . . . Actually, no, none of these feelings, not even combined, comes close. Besides, you *could* expect all these things to happen. But winning the lotto? Who really expects that, *really* expects that? Sure, I've daydreamed about it – who hasn't? – but for it to actually happen, well, that's way, way, *way* beyond my wildest dreams. But it has happened to us – to me – and the feeling it generates is just so much bigger, so much more fantastic, so much scarier, so much more extraordinary than any I've ever felt. It's like – oh I don't know – no single word exists though *maybe* un-bloody-believable – comes close. Yeah, winning the lotto feels absolutely un-bloody-believable. Yet, even that's a bit like saying the world is a big place – it's still completely and utterly inadequate. But the world, *our* world at any rate, is a different place. Everything has changed. *And* we haven't even got our hands on our winnings yet.

Take this morning. Alarm clock goes: *beep! beep! beep! beep!* I wake up. I'm disorientated. Pre-dawn. Pitch dark outside. Horizontal rain sleeting against the window. For a split second I go to turn over, reluctant to face my usual workday schedule: the tiresome journey into work, work itself, that collection of random people I know as my colleagues and with whom I routinely spend so many of my waking hours. And then – wham – it hits me. That's right, I'm no longer a wage slave. I am in fact a millionaire, correction – multi-millionaire, and my alarm isn't set to propel me from my bed at such an ungodly hour to go to work but, rather, to go with Dana to the airport to fly off in order to break our most stupendous news in person to Caroline the third and, as yet, unsuspecting member of our winning syndicate who's on an extended holiday in Australia with her boyfriend, Mick.

Apart from the fact that we simply can (being multi-millionaires and all), that's the reason Dana and I are on this plane. Yes, sure we could have used the telephone, that was our original intention, but hey, millionaires are supposed to jet off at the drop of a hat, or an airplane wheel, or on a crazy whim. It's part of the job description. Don't you know that flying is like taking a bus to the wealthy? And, besides, there's been so much media speculation as to our identity it seemed like a good idea to take ourselves out of the picture for a little while, until the fuss abates. It's pretty hard to act normal enough not to arouse suspicion in such abnormal circumstances.

So how did all this come about? Well, Dana and Caroline grew up together and I've been friends with them for over five years, ever since I moved in with them in the house we rent from Caroline's older brother, Donald, and share with another friend of ours, Shane. For the past few years, even before Shane moved in, we've had this little syndicate going. Ever-dependable Dana is the organiser and every Wednesday and Saturday she's unfailingly bought a €6 Lotto Plus ticket. This is the sort of thing Dana is very good at, being the methodical kind she is. She even has this dedicated little red notebook in which she keeps tabs on how much we owe her. Every so often, when we think of it or when she thinks to pester us, we stump up whatever's outstanding. Dana even kept it going when Caroline left Dublin two months ago to travel around Australia with Mick.

Anyway, last Sunday when Dana and I were having a late leisurely breakfast she happened, as is her habit, to check our lotto numbers – 1,3,7,11,18,40 – in the newspaper. 1 – Caroline's birthday, 3 – how many of us there are, 7 – just because it's traditionally considered a lucky number, 11 – Dana's birthday, 18 – my birthday, and 40 – our house number. And there they all were. Each and every one of them. Six out of six. All sitting in a pretty row.

I can still hear Dana's scream. My eardrums have yet to recover. My ribs too – who'd have thought there was so much strength in Dana's skinny little arms but she nearly squeezed the life out of me when she lifted me up and danced me around the room – no mean feat, I have many inches in height on her. Not one of the most dignified moments of my life, but definitely amongst the happiest.

Anyway, since winning the lotto – how I love those words – *since* winning the lotto, since *winning* the lotto, since winning *the* lotto, since winning the *lotto*, Dana and I have the same conversations over and over and over, conversations about just how truly unbelievable it is (and I think part of us doesn't really quite believe it yet), conversations about what we are going to do with our money and it is a lot of money, no two ways, or even three ways, about it. €11 million split three ways is €3,666,666.66 each (we won't squabble over the final two cents). That Sunday was spent in a daze but we did make the decision not to tell anyone, not a soul, not our families, not my boyfriend Finn, not Dana's boyfriend Doug, nobody – *not* until we'd first told Caroline. Sure, this secrecy is only temporary yet I feel bad. I've never had to tell so many lies. My boss thinks I'm in bed with the flu while Finn and Mum and Dad think I've been sent to London by my boss. At least I didn't have to lie to them face to face (which I'm not sure I'd have managed) but could hide behind the telephone. My parents live on the outskirts of Dublin so I don't see them all that often and Finn – who's a musician (and, I might mention, the best thing that's ever happened to me and yes, that does include winning the lotto) – is up the country playing a string of gigs.

So, anyway, Monday saw us ringing in sick and maxing out my already over-stretched credit card to book our flights. Tuesday was dedicated to getting our visas. Which brings us to today – Wednesday – which sees us in the air, winging our way to an unsuspecting Caroline to tell her news that will change her life forever, news that came at a particularly fortuitous time in the wake of all our recent bad luck, of which there has been much. Not least the failure of Love Potions, the shop we three put our blood, sweat and tears into setting up and for which we shed even more tears when it closed down again. But – hey! – these are happier times. It's time to look forward.

"Rosie?"

"Yeah?"

"Caroline is going to get *such* a surprise, isn't she?" Dana speculates. Since she's been speculating in this fashion since we got our plane tickets, and before, all I do now is make vague agreeing noises but that's encouragement enough for Dana. She goes on. "Such a land. I can't wait to see her face!" She falls silent. For a moment. "Rosie?"

"Yeah?"

"Are you *sure* we shouldn't have told her we were coming?"

Again, this is not the first time Dana's asked this question and again I answer as I did every other time.

"Yes."

"You're absolutely sure?"

"Absolutely sure."

"Maybe we should have emailed her?"

"Maybe, but we didn't and, anyway, I'm not sure she even reads all her emails. She hardly ever replies to any I send, too busy having the time of her life with Mick."

"But what if we can't find her?" worries Dana, as is her way.

Again I answer as I've already answered before. "We have her address from the last email, don't we?"

"I know, but what if she's moved on?" worries Dana.

"Then we'll give her a ring. Stop worrying. Look, if we'd told her we were coming it would have been impossible not to tell her why. She'd have started with all the questions, wormed it out of us – me at any rate, and then what would be the point in coming at all? No, no, it's better to wait until we get there, until we're face to face and just imagine the look on hers."

Dana laughs. "I can't wait!"

Now Dana falls silent again. I glance over at her. As is often the case of late, I see she has this great big happy-to-the-point-of-goofiness smile on her face to which the only possible response is to grin back.

"You know," she says, still beaming, "any moment now I think I'm going to wake up and find it's all a dream." She lays her head back on the headrest. "It is though. It is un-bloody-believable." There, that word again. "One minute we're going about our everyday ho-hum, humdrum, regular boring old lives, worrying about how we're going to make next month's rent and, the next – wham, bam – our lives are turned upside down and we're rich beyond our wildest dreams. Just like that!"

She clicks her fingers and gives a happy sigh.

Studies show that the euphoria evaporates within a year of a lottery win, upon which people return to their previous level of contentment.

2

Since we've both brought just one small bag each as hand luggage we get through Melbourne Airport without the hassle of baggage reclaim. Then, once outside, we head for the taxi rank, join the queue and, when we reach the top, we hop into the next available taxi, sit back, relax, and let the driver take us into the city centre, to where Caroline is staying.

Within half an hour, we reach the city proper and, just as I'm thinking what a pleasant, vibrant and thoroughly modern city the Melbourne I'm seeing through my window is, we take a sudden, sharp right turn and, just as suddenly and sharply, the scene changes and we swap the prosperous, tree-lined, generously wide boulevard with its up-to-the-minute glass architecture for something else entirely. Now we're driving at speed down a narrow decrepit back street flanked on either side by the steep, dreary, blank rears of buildings so high and so close together that they block out all sunlight. Down the bumpy, pot-holed road, barely wider than our car we go at what does feel like an alarming speed. We pass under a railway bridge, past an upturned, abandoned, rusting supermarket trolley, past an overflowing dumpster and, just as I'm seriously beginning to worry what's with this crazy driver and his crazy driving, and worry just how this trip is going to end, we pull up abruptly outside the jewel in the crown of these back alleys, or whatever is the very opposite of that – a building that is the seemingly impossible, that is even more dilapidated than its counterparts. From the taxi I stare out, taking in every dingy detail – the peeling paint, the graffiti, the broken downpipe, and the five or so rough-looking females hanging out on the steps – each and every one of whom wouldn't look out of place in a police line-up. I give Dana a quizzical look. She returns it. Why is our driver stopping here? And then I notice the sign over the door – The Bourke – the name of the place Caroline said she was staying in the latest of the sporadic, short-as-a-telegraph emails we've received from her. But, no, this can't be right. What Caroline loves is hotels with grand entrances, canopies, red carpets, six-foot-high potted palms, brass luggage trolleys and doormen in swanky uniforms, all shiny buttons and enough gold braid to put a general to shame. What Caroline does not love, has never loved, is run down, cockroach-infested-looking buildings. Sure she's travelling with Mick who, despite having made pots of money from his role in *Fate Farm* though it's yet to hit the screens, would probably be happy to rough it, would probably thrive on roughing it. But still, I can't believe even he could have persuaded Caroline to stay in such a place.

"Here we are," calls the driver, oblivious to our confusion.

"There must be some mistake," Dana says to me, evidently having not yet noticed the name sign with its rivulets of rust tracking down the wall. Then she calls out to the taxi-driver: "Are you sure this is it? That this is The Bourke?"

"Yep, sure am."

"The Bourke Hotel?"

"Y'mean the Bourke Hostel?" he clarifies.

"Hostel?"

"Ah, yeah."

"Hostel?" Dana repeats like it's a word she's unfamiliar with. She eyes up the loiterers. "Hostel?" she repeats. "You mean like a backpackers' hostel?" she asks somewhat optimistically. Considering . . .

Certainly, backpackers aren't renowned for their finesse but these loitering women are just about as rough as any I've seen. I doubt there's a full set of teeth between them. Nor do they fit the typical backpacker age profile – at least two of them must be hitting fifty. Sure, backpackers might be expected to experiment – to drink more than is wise perhaps, to even smoke a little pot – but you don't expect to see them down an alley, swigging from a bottle wrapped in a brown paper bag, or drunkenly squabbling over such a bottle in the middle of the day.

"Backpackers?" The driver laughs. "Nah! Bourke's a hostel for deros."

"Deros?"

"Y'know, down-and-outs."

"Down-and-outs?"

"Too right." The driver glances in the rear-view mirror and eyes us up, like – for the first time – he's wondering just what two green, pommy types, raw off the plane, might want with a place like this. We may have spent the last twenty-four hours travelling, we may look far from our best, but I'd like to think he can't believe we might be in need of emergency accommodation. Then again, maybe he's simply wondering if English is our first language given how Dana's taken to repeating his every word.

"Look," says Dana now, "can you hold on while we go in and check if our friend is here?"

I see the driver is still studying us in his mirror, like he's now weighing us and the situation up. Perhaps deciding we've come all this way to bail out some friend who's down on her luck and, not wanting to get involved in some potentially messy situation, he shakes his head and answers, "Sorry. That'll be thirty-seven dollars and ten cents."

Since Dana is the one who took out Australian dollars from the cash machine in the airport, I nudge her now. "Pay the man."

Still staring pessimistically out the window, Dana reaches into her bag and takes out her wallet. She looks down, takes out four crisp tens, and hands them over to the driver. "Keep the change," she tells him.

I climb out on my side and wait for Dana but she doesn't budge.

I stoop down and call into her, "Come on," I urge.

She gets out reluctantly. I pull the bags from the boot promptly. The driver pulls away speedily.

Leaving us in a dirty, dingy back alley, in a strange country, just about as far away as we can get from home, all alone, with night soon to fall.

The most anyone's won? Ever?
Unnamed 25-year-old woman – €163 million – Spain

3

Up the rough-hewn steps, warily edging past the watchful loiterers we go, and into the Bourke Hostel to find it as bleak, bare and as unappealing as only an institution can be. The lights are harsh fluorescent. The walls are an especially ugly shade of mustard. There's a random scattering of mismatched furniture, scruffy armchairs mostly – none of which is occupied.

"Gulp!" says Dana, jokingly, but only half-jokingly I think, as she looks around, taking it all in with her big brown, worried-looking eyes.

The one person we do see, even if it is just the top of her bent head as she pores over a magazine, is a woman sitting behind a counter protected by a security window that extends right to the ceiling.

Dana grabs my arm. "There's no way we're going to find Caroline here," she hisses. "Think about it. We must have got it wrong."

I pull my arm free. "Look! Since we're here we may as well ask!"

I start walking over to the woman with Dana following so closely behind that she's almost treading on my heels.

"Hello," I say through the little circular hole in the glass screen but the woman continues reading her magazine, engrossed in the horoscope page, seemingly unaware of our presence. "Ahem," I cough for attention and, perhaps, finally having established what the stars via some antipodean Mystic Meg have in store for her, she looks up.

"Yeah?" Straight away it's clear she's not the smiling kind.

"We're looking for a friend of ours, Caroline Connolly?"

I guess I'm expecting her to draw a blank but, instead, she picks up a phone and presses some numbers. "Who'll I say is looking for her?" she asks.

"Rosie Kiely and Dana Vaughan."

She listens for a few moments, then puts down the receiver. "No answer." Then a thought strikes her. "Ah, hang about, that's right, I saw her go out this arvo. Said she wouldn't be back 'til late."

"Excuse me," Dana pipes up, "what exactly is Caroline doing here?"

"How d'ya mean?"

"She's not . . . ah . . . like . . . a resident, is she?" Dana asks.

"Caroline? Strewth, no. She works here as a volunteer."

"As a volunteer?" I echo. As a volunteer? Caroline? This is just as unlikely a scenario as her being a resident, possibly more so. One would be the result of bad luck and, like good, that can happen to anyone; the other of good intention and the Caroline I know was never too big on those. Maybe, somehow, we have our wires crossed. I begin to describe her; "Blonde bob, well-dressed, perfect make-up . . ." I point to my shoulder ". . . and so high."

"That's our Caroline all right." The woman gives an unexpected fond grin.

Our Caroline? Excuse me? How long can she even know her? She's not their Caroline, she's ours. As for working here as a volunteer? I mean, come on! That just can't be.

"You can wait for her here if you want," the woman nods in the direction of the busted armchairs, two of which are now occupied by a duo of rough-looking Sheilas, to use the vernacular. I wonder if Australians actually use that expression. Maybe not, maybe it's like, 'Top o' the morning,' and its utterance only serves to mark the user out as a misguided foreigner trying too hard to please.

"We'll come back," I hear Dana telling the woman.

"Whatever." The woman has lost interest in us already and is flicking through the pages of her magazine.

"Why don't we try ringing her on her mobile?" suggests Dana.

"Good idea." I take out mine, bring Caroline's number up on speed dial, press the button, then listen, but the tone I get is an unfamiliar one. I shake my head. "I don't think my phone is working here."

Dana turns to the woman. "Could you ring Caroline's mobile for us?"

"I guess," she says, in not a particularly obliging way but she picks up the receiver again. "What's the number?"

I call it out and the woman dials. Then she listens for a moment. "Are you sure you've the right number?"

"Yes, sure."

"Well, I'm not getting a proper tone." She shrugs and puts the phone back down.

"Can we leave a note for her?" I ask.

"If you want."

"Have you a piece of paper?"

She sighs, glances around, finds a notebook, tears out a page and passes it to me.

"And a pen, if you have one?"

She sighs again, searches her desk once more, finds a pen under her magazine and hands it to me. I begin to scrawl out a note. "*Surprise! Surprise! It's us – Rosie and Dana. We're here.*" I pause. I think about telling her, or at least hinting at our lotto news, but decide not to. We didn't come all the way out here just to write it in a note. I think about asking what she, of all people, is doing volunteering in a place like this. Again I decide not to. Who's to say our lady behind the desk won't take a peep? I keep it to a minimum. "*Gone to find somewhere to stay. Can't get you on your phone but will be back in an hour or two – it's 5.30pm now.*"

I fold the note, write Caroline's name on the outside and hand it back.

"Would you mind calling us a taxi?" I ask.

The woman sighs, again, but she does however disobligingly, oblige.

When the taxi pulls up, we load our bags into the boot, then quickly clamber in.

"Thank goodness!" Dana flops back in her seat and gives a loud sigh of relief.

"G'day," says the driver like he's Crocodile Dundee but there the similarity ends; he's sallow-skinned, wears a turban and must weigh – oh – about twenty stone, give or take a burger. "So where are you girls off to then?"

"The nearest good hotel," I tell him.

"How good do you want to go?"

"How good have you got?"

"There's a five-star not far from here, fronting onto the

23

park, but rooms there will cost you," he warns, conscious perhaps of where he picked us up.

"Perfect," I say.

"Hang on a second," whispers Dana, "how are we going to pay for it exactly?"

I look at her, then nod in the direction of the taxi-driver indicating that I can't exactly say in front of, or rather, behind him.

"You *know*," I say meaningfully and I begin humming the tune from the lotto ad.

She hushes me.

"What?" I whisper. "They don't get Irish television here. He doesn't know what I mean."

"One small thing, we don't actually have that money yet. You haven't a penny left after paying for the flights and I cleared out my account at the cash machine in the airport. Until we meet Caroline all we have is exactly one-hundred-and-ninety Australian dollars – minus whatever this taxi is going to cost us."

"Oh! So what are we going to do?"

"What can we do but go back and wait for Caroline and get some money from her?" Then she calls out, "Driver, can you turn around and bring us back to where you picked us up?"

He throws a disgruntled look over his shoulder, growls, "Bloody time-wasters," then does a dramatic, but well-executed U-turn in the narrow alleyway.

Once again, we find ourselves pulling up outside The Bourke and, second time around, it looks no more inviting.

Ensconced on a shabby couch, we wait. Apart from our magazine-reading friend, there's no one else in the lobby now but from unseen parts of the building an array of noises emanate. There's the low-key sound of television coming from somewhere, upstairs, I think. From somewhere else there's the clang of pots, and there's the chink of knives and forks too, and the muted sound of people talking. I've never been in a place like this before. Where do all these people come from? Apart from Seán I've never known anyone homeless. I wonder how he's doing these days. I haven't seen him in a while.

Dana has fallen asleep now with her head on my shoulder and, trying not to wake her, I shift in my seat – my leg has gone dead. When will Caroline get here? Where is she anyway? My eyelids begin to get heavy. This place is very warm. I try to stay awake but . . .

Suddenly I'm awoken by someone shaking my shoulder. I open my eyes.

"Caroline!"

"What on earth are you two doing here?" she asks, looking at me in total bewilderment.

I look around, befuddled from sleep, trying to get my bearings and when I recollect exactly where 'here' is and just why I am here, I leap up and give Caroline a great big bear hug. "Oh Caroline, it is so good to see you!"

"You too!" she says in a voice muffled against my shoulder. She pulls away. "Mind, you'll suffocate me." Now she laughs. "But I don't understand. Why didn't you tell me you were coming? And why did you come? What on earth is going on?"

"You are not going to believe this. We have something extraordinary to tell you!"

"You came all the way here just to tell me something! What?" A worried look crosses her face. "Everyone is okay back home, aren't they? It's not something bad, is it?"

"No, no – it's great news, the best!"

"So what is it?"

I glance around. A woman is now sitting in an armchair opposite us. In her late fifties, I'm guessing, she's a bird-like little thing with wild hair, clad in an ill-fitting sweater and pants. Her face is weather-beaten and dirt-entrenched, her fingers nicotine-stained. On her lap sits a plastic shopping bag the contents of which she seems to be in the middle of sorting through. Spread out on the low table between us is her stuff, daily necessities I suppose in her transient life: some more shabby clothes, a battered A4 folder stuffed full of papers and held together with an elastic band and, incongruously, a hairbrush and a grubby vanity bag. But this woman has abandoned her task for now and is sitting back, observing us with keen interest.

"So, go on, what's this news then?" repeats Caroline.

"Is there somewhere we can go?" I ask.

Dana stirs now. She opens her eyes. "Caroline!" She shrieks in excitement. She quickly gets to her feet and immediately enfolds Caroline in a hug. "Oh, it is so good to see you!" She gives her an enormous kiss on one cheek, then on the other, and then the other again, and then another hug. "Oh, I've missed you!"

"Steady on!" cries Caroline and gives one of her loud raucous laughs. I'm momentarily startled. I'd forgotten how very loud and very raucous Caroline's laugh can be. I realise just how much I've missed it, how much I've missed her. Things just aren't the same without Caroline. It's better when all three of us are together.

Dana finally lets her go. "Let me have a look at you," she says, then stands back and looks Caroline up and down. "As fabulous as ever – you've not changed, I see."

"I haven't been away *that* long."

"Well, it feels like it. It feels like you've been gone forever."

What Dana says is true, about it feeling like Caroline being gone forever but, also, about her being every bit as fabulous as usual – despite the time she's spent travelling around Australia with Mick, despite the time she's spent here in this hostel for whatever and as yet unexplained reason. But then I wouldn't expect anything less of Caroline. If she were shipwrecked, cast to sea in a lifeboat, washed up on a desert island, airlifted by helicopter and, finally – after many months – brought back home safely, I'd expect her to be miraculously still picture-perfect. In the five years I've lived with Caroline, not once have I seen her come down to breakfast in a dressing-gown or without full make-up. Heaven forbid! She'd as soon come down stark naked.

Her perfect blonde bob is as perfect as ever (though perhaps a little blonder – sun? hairdresser? – not sure). She has swapped the smart suits she favoured back in Dublin for a simple, sleeveless knee-length dress in a summery yellow. I think she's put on some weight which she's probably unhappy about but it suits her and she's as brown as a berry. Looking at her now, I don't think I've ever seen her looking quite so lovely.

"So . . ." she looks from one of us to the other expectantly ". . . go on, what's the big news then?"

"Well," I say, "how about going somewhere a little more private?"

"I regret ever winning the lottery. The money hasn't changed me but it changed everyone around me."

Michael Carroll – £9.7 million – UK

Since winning, the self-proclaimed "King of the Chavs" has clocked up more than 30 court cases, been jailed for nine months for affray, convicted of cocaine possession and banned from driving for six months after being caught at the wheel of his new £49,000 BMW without L-plates and insurance.

4

Back down the narrow alley we go, Dana and I anxiously looking about, ears pricked for the sounds of menacing footsteps following after us as we try to keep up with a remarkably unconcerned Caroline who's boldly striding out in front.

"I don't suppose this is the right place to tell her?" Dana whispers.

Uneasily I glance around. "Let's wait until we get to wherever she's taking us."

"Are you nervous?"

"About telling her?"

"No, about what might jump out of the shadows at any moment."

"Terrified!"

We turn a corner and I heave a sigh of relief – we're back again in more comfortable territory. We go past brightly illuminated shop windows, past restaurants lit with strings of fairy lights and populated with convivial patrons gathered around tables that spill out onto the pavement. Then we come to a stop outside a cool-looking bar.

"Welcome to my local," says Caroline.

We follow in after her.

In the soft lighting, my initial impression is brothel marrying Wild West saloon. I see plush red upholstery, dark patterned flock wallpaper, gold mirrors, dangling chandeliers and a crowd of *über*-trendy people – exactly Caroline's kind of people, exactly Caroline's kind of place.

But not Dana's.

"Could we not have gone somewhere more – ah – ordinary?" She calls out to Caroline. They may be the best of friends but, really, Caroline and Dana are opposites in *so* many ways.

"Hush now," says Caroline, taking no notice. "You'll love it!"

"You think?" Dana cocks an eyebrow.

"Sure."

"But we're not exactly dressed for a place like this."

I look at Dana, she's still in runners, sweat pants and top – the clothes she wore on the plane. I look down at myself – I'm wearing jeans and my most comfortable sweater. I see Dana's long brown hair is far from its best and fear mine is probably worse, probably more frizz than curls by now.

But Caroline sees none of this, or at least pretends not to. "You're fine," she reassures me, but then adds: "Besides, nobody even knows you."

It turns out they do, on the other hand, know Caroline, but no surprise there. Caroline has always had the gift of making friends easily. Straightaway, a girl in a singularly bizarre outfit – or several outfits rather – comes over. She has a layered Johnny Forty-Coats-esque thing going on and, somewhere in the city, I picture a wardrobe, empty, save for a row of dangly wire hangers. Let's see: short skirt, over longer skirt, over leggings; long skinny scarf, over military style jacket, over open-necked grandfather shirt, over vest top, over another vest top. I think I've got it all. It's a brave effort on her part. I'm not sure it quite works. Besides she must be positively roasting.

"*Caroline!*" This Jane Forty Coats squeals, then dramatically kisses her on either cheek – or the air in front of either cheek.

"Hi, Patience."

Dana and I glance at one another. Dana cocks her eyebrow again and I know she's thinking exactly what I'm thinking. Patience? Can that really be her name?

"Good to see you!" Patience tells Caroline. "You're looking fab!"

"You too. You're just in time to meet my oldest and very best friends in the world." Caroline gestures towards me. "This is Rosie."

Patience studies me for a moment, then says: "Well, hello, Rosie, how lovely to meet you." And then she makes a smacking noise in my direction.

"Hiya. Nice to meet you too," I say but hold off on the air-kissing.

Next Caroline gestures towards Dana. "And this is Dana."

"And hi, Dana." More smacking noises aimed at Dana. Then Patience turns to Caroline. "Aren't they just adorable!" Like we're puppies in a pet-shop window. "So fresh-faced and rather beautiful, both of them!" She smiles benevolently in our direction, but with a somewhat expectant air, like she's waiting for something though what I'm not sure. For us to thank her for the compliment? Or return it? I don't know. But, before the pause becomes embarrassingly long, Caroline comes in.

"Rosie and Dana have just arrived from Ireland to give me some exciting news which they haven't yet disclosed."

"Oh! Tell me more," Patience squeals in response and claps her hands repeatedly like a seal.

"Ah, we can't," I say. "We need to tell Caroline first."

"How very intriguing! How very mysterious!" She lays a hand on Caroline's arm. "You will tell me once you find out?"

"Of course you'll be the first to know."

"Fab! Now I'd better dash." More air-kissing and off she goes.

"Okay, you go and find somewhere to sit," Caroline orders, "and I'll go to the bar. What you'll have?"

"Since we're in Australia, I think I'll have one of their white wines," says Dana. "You choose."

"Same for me," I say.

We find a free couch in a corner, the seat of which is so low and so deep from front to back that it's impossible not to loll even though lolling is the last thing in the world I want to do. This couch is just too comfortable to be comfortable when I'm not relaxed enough for it. I'm too tensed up, too anxious to tell Caroline the news. I don't want to be made sit here like this, semi-recumbent, waiting for her to come back.

We wait.

"Would she ever hurry up?" Dana grumbles.

And we wait. For Caroline to get served but she seems more interested in chatting to the barman and some of her newly made friends sitting at the counter.

"Are we ever going to get to tell her?" grumbles Dana. "And who are these people? How does she even know them?"

And we wait.

"Chat! Chat! Chat! Does she ever change?"

And we wait

"*We're* her friends. None of these has flown all the way around the world to see her," Dana moans.

"Dana! Stop! You're doing my head in."

"Excuse me!"

I too wish she'd come back, but still we wait.

When Caroline does finally turn around, we see she's carrying three glasses filled with some startling blue drink.

"What on earth are those radioactive-looking concoctions?" asks Dana. "Unless things are done very differently here, they're most definitely *not* what we asked for. Do they look like wine to you?"

And we wait some more as Caroline slowly makes her way across the room, stopping for a quick word or an air-kiss with this one and that one.

"This is ridiculous! We're never going to get to tell her."

Finally Caroline reaches us. "Sorry I took so long. You know I've met some really lovely people since I've been in Oz." She puts the drinks down on the table and joins us on our low-slung couch.

"What *is* this?" Dana asks as she struggles forward and picks up her drink.

"A Blue Hawaiian."

"But I asked for wine, don't you remember?"

"I thought you might like this instead."

"But, Caroline, if I wanted this I would have asked for it."

"Yeah, but you wouldn't have known about it."

Dana is eyeing her drink suspiciously. "Blue is *not* a good colour for food or drink. Except for blue Smarties and they even banned them for a while."

"Come on," coaxes Caroline. "Can't you just try it? You'll love it."

"How come you always think you know what everyone else wants?"

"I'm usually right, aren't I?"

I notice that Dana doesn't answer and now she's holding up her glass to the light. "What's in it anyway?"

"Ah – rum, pineapple, curaçao liquor, coconut and a few other things. So, come on, spit it out!"

"I haven't even taken a sip yet."

"Very funny! No, I mean tell me what brings you here – to Australia? I mean this is just so amazing! I still can't quite believe it! To think you flew all the way out here, without a word."

Now Dana puts down her drink, looks around furtively like she's a spy in some B movie. Finally, *the* moment has come. Caroline is about to hear news that will change her life forever. I look at her expectant face. She has absolutely no idea what's coming.

Now Dana leans forward. She takes a deep breath. And then she comes out with it. "We've won the lotto."

There's a momentary pause. Caroline's initial reaction is muted, silent in fact, but then, eventually, just one word:

"Pardon?"

"We've won the lotto."

"Who?"

"We have."

"You and Rosie?"

"Yes, and you too."

Caroline is clearly puzzled. She's staring at Dana as if her marbles have all just gone tumbling out onto the floor. "You're crazy! You're winding me up, right?"

"No!"

"What lotto?"

"The Irish one."

"What? You mean the National Lottery?"

"Yes."

"But I haven't bought a ticket in I-don't-know-how-long."

"Yes, you have. I've been buying them for you as part of our syndicate."

"Is that still going?"

"Of course."

"But I haven't paid you back in ages."

"I know, but you always do in the end. That's how it works – you stump up, eventually."

"So you didn't count me out when I went away?"

"Why would I? It's not like you weren't coming back."

Suddenly I realise the enormity of what Dana is saying. Right from the very start both of us understood, assumed, that the money would be split three ways. It didn't occur to us that it could be any different but, now, I see it didn't automatically have to be like that.

"We've won the lotto?" There's a tremor of excitement in Caroline's voice.

"Yes."

Caroline looks to Dana, then to me, then to Dana again, then to me again.

"We've actually won the lotto?"

"Yes."

"You're not playing some sort of joke?"

"Come on! How sick would that be!"

"Oh my God!" She takes a drink, perhaps to steady her nerves. "So – ah – like, what are we talking about here? How much did we win?"

"Eleven million euros," Dana answers.

"What!" Caroline splutters out her drink, then starts coughing so hard it prompts Dana to stand up and thump her on her back.

"Steady on!" Caroline snaps.

"Are you okay?" asks Dana.

"Okay? I don't know." She picks up her Blue Hawaiian again and knocks three-quarters of it back. "This must be some sort of sick joke."

"No! I'm telling you, you, me and Rosie won eleven million euros in last Saturday's draw."

"Hush, Dana!" I say, "Someone will hear you."

"Eleven million euros!"

"Caroline! Shush!"

"Eleven million euros!" Caroline whistles.

"Caroline, I'm serious. Shush!"

She starts tittering like some lunatic. "Eleven million euros!!" Anxiously I look around the busy bar and am relieved to see that nobody is paying her any attention. "This is just the biggest thing ever. It's incredible! Fantastic! It's just . . . just . . ."

"Unbelievable?" I prompt.

"Yes!"

"Un-bloody-believable!?"

"Yes! Un-bloody-believable! Oh my God! I can't believe it!"

Dana and I have already been through this before and it's strange now to see Caroline experiencing it and we watch the expressions on her face flit from one to another. Utter disbelief. Dawning comprehension of what this means. Excitement. Terror even. Disbelief once again.

"Oh my God, I can't believe it! Eleven million euros!" She suddenly jumps to her feet. "This calls for a celebration.

I know – champagne! Champagne for everyone in the house!"

Dana grabs hold of her arm and pulls her back down again.

"What?" demands Caroline.

"Caroline, will you keep quiet!"

"What? Why? Keep quiet? You are joking!"

"Look, we haven't told anyone – not a soul!"

"You're kidding!"

"We're not. Nobody knows," I tell her.

But then it occurs to me. Now that we've told Caroline there's no need for secrecy any more.

But suddenly Caroline looks serious. "So you didn't even tell Doug?" she asks Dana.

"No. I don't trust him not to let it slip, like, say, to his brothers."

Caroline thinks for a second. "Nah, Doug wouldn't." Then she turns to me. "And you didn't even tell Finn or your parents?"

"No."

"And they aren't at all suspicious?"

"Finn's been up the country which is just as well – there's no way I'd have been able to keep it from him otherwise and you know how busy Mum and Dad always are, I haven't even seen them since the win."

"So you just snuck away without telling anyone?"

"Yep. We took the first flight we could," says Dana. "It cost us a fortune, or rather it cost Rosie a fortune – she paid, I didn't have enough."

"It took every penny I had. And then some. My credit card is up to its limit."

"So you haven't collected the money yet?"

"No." Dana shakes her head. "Because Saturday's jackpot was so big, there was huge hype leading up to it and, ever since, everyone is dying to find out who the winner is so we thought it best to lie low, until the fuss dies down. We didn't want to arrive at Lottery Headquarters and find a whole load of press waiting and, anyway, there was no way we'd have collected it without you. But, until we get our hands on the money, we're stony-broke." Dana laughs now and pats her breast pocket. "Let's hope this thing is real."

"Jesus!" I nearly fall off the seat. "You don't have the ticket with you, do you? We agreed you'd hide it in the house!"

"And I did, in my old copy of *Lord of the Rings* like we decided but then, at the last moment, just as we were going out the door for the airport, I began panicking. What if something were to happen to the house while we're away, what if it got burgled?"

"And what self-respecting burglar is going to target one of your old paperbacks?"

"Okay, maybe not a burglary then, but what if the house burned down? I just thought it would be safer to keep it with me."

"And you didn't tell me?"

"I didn't want to worry you."

"Well, I'm worried now – you could have lost it."

"Let me see it," says Caroline holding out a hand.

"Are you crazy?" Quickly I pull Caroline's hand away. "Not here! Not now! What if someone sees?"

"They're not going to know it's a winning ticket, are they?"

"I don't care. Just leave it where it is."

She thinks for a moment. "You're right. Of course. And

we do need to keep quiet about it, at least until we've cashed it – we don't want anyone running off with it." Then suddenly she thinks to ask. "Where are you staying?"

"Well, that's just it," says Dana. "This might sound strange in the circumstances but can you lend us some money so we can get a room somewhere? It's getting late."

Caroline gives a loud laugh. "This is surreal! You're asking me for the price of a room!"

The incongruity of the situation is not lost on Dana or me. I notice Dana is looking at Caroline sheepishly.

"Seriously, are you really that broke?" demands Caroline looking from one of us to the other.

"We have some money but not a lot. We need to keep it for taxis and the like."

Caroline laughs. "Well, I'm pretty broke too. I don't get paid much for working in the hostel, just a tiny allowance in addition to all my meals and accommodation."

"What are we going to do so?" worries Dana.

"Why don't you stay in the hostel?" suggests Caroline.

Now Dana looks uncomfortable. She shifts anxiously in her seat.

"What?" asks Caroline, noticing.

"I don't want to be odd but I'm not sure I'd feel one hundred per cent safe there."

"Safe? What do you mean? Are you worried about the lotto ticket?"

"Yes . . . but . . . I'm guessing a lot of these women have problems, don't they?"

"Of course," says Caroline. "The most obvious being the fact that they're homeless."

"I know but it's just –"

"Dana, they're people like you and me, who happen to be down on their luck."

"I know. I know. Of course I do. Look, it's just that I don't think I'd get much sleep in a dormitory. I'm not used to having so many people around me."

Caroline is annoyed. "I wasn't going to turf someone back out on the street just to give a bed over to you, there's a waiting list for them. What I meant was in my room – you can share my bed."

"Your bed? All three of us?"

"Have you a better idea?"

"What about Mick?" I ask. "Couldn't we borrow money from him?"

"No."

"Where is he anyway?" I ask.

"Is he staying with you at the hostel too?" asks Dana.

"Don't say we're going to have to share a bed with him as well?" I add.

"Don't be ridiculous!"

"So where is he?" asks Dana.

"What?" asks Caroline.

"I'm asking where he is."

"Who?"

"Mick."

"Mick?"

"Yes, Mick! Tall, fair, reddish complexion, Cork accent. Your boyfriend? Remember? Where is he?"

"Mick, well, he's . . . he's gone back up the coast. He wanted to do some more diving."

"You two haven't had another one of your fights, have you?" asks Dana.

"Of course not," snaps Caroline. "Don't be ridiculous!"

"Ridiculous? Hardly! You're like a Tom and Jerry cartoon, fighting all the time but both coming out unscathed in the end – it's what you do."

"Very funny – not!"

"Why didn't you go with him?" I ask. "You wrote in one of your emails that you loved diving."

"I do. But, you know, been there, done that, I wanted to try something else."

"Like working in the hostel? Wouldn't bungee-jumping or something like that have been more usual on a holiday such as this? No offence but working in a hostel is kind of the last thing I'd have expected."

"What do you mean?"

"Oh come on, you know. You've always been more of the capitalist kind. Money is king! Every man for himself! Eighties shoulder-pads rule!"

"Is that how you see me?"

I shrug. "I'd have thought that's how you see yourself – apart from the shoulder pads perhaps."

Now Caroline shrugs. "A trip like this is all about learning. The opportunity in the hostel came up and I decided to go for it."

"I don't get it. It's just not you."

"You don't know everything about me, Rosie."

"I do, or at least I thought I did. I've known you long enough."

"You shouldn't pigeonhole people."

"I'm not. Well, maybe I am, but with good reason. I don't understand this. You and Mick headed off on holiday together yet, when we come out, we find he's up the coast diving while you're here in Melbourne working in a hostel for the homeless. Why aren't you together? Did something happen? Why are you working in the hostel? It's just not you."

"So you keep saying."

"Hey, girls," Dana intervenes, "enough with the squabbling. Come on, remember?" She starts humming the lotto ad tune. Then she stands up. "Now if we're going to be sharing a bed together I need a couple more of those Blue Hawaiians."

Who needs enemies when you have friends and family?

William 'Bud' Post - $16.2 million - US

The lotto winner's brother hired a hitman to kill him - in order to inherit his fortune.

5

Up the lino-covered stairs we follow Caroline, every second step creaking, then down a narrow, fluorescent-lit corridor, passing doors lining either side, to the door at the very end. We wait as Caroline unlocks it.

"Home-sweet-home," she says as she steps in and flicks on the light.

Dana and I crowd in after her. We look around. There's not much to look at. A locker and a small wardrobe both in cheap white flimsy MDF. A narrow bed dressed in a cheap, flowery duvet with a single pillow, flowery too but in a different pattern. A small window flanked by curtains in a third flowery pattern. The wallpaper — flowery too — makes for a total of four clashing, busy, floral patterns.

"What do you think?" Caroline turns and asks.

"Well . . . it's quite cosy, isn't it?" I opt for diplomacy. "Ah — nice curtains."

"You think? I hate them!"

Dana's attention is focused on the bed — specifically the width. "You seriously think all three of us are going to fit in that?" she asks doubtfully.

"We're going to have to," snaps Caroline. "We've no alternative. Now go on, get changed. You must be exhausted after your flight."

That vague niggling feeling I've had on and off all evening suddenly makes sense. Now it hits me. We don't have any bags.

"Oh my God!" says Dana, struck by the very same realisation. "We left our bags in the boot of that second taxi!"

With our winning ticket stashed under that trusted and age-old repository of people's valuables – the mattress – we've been lying in bed but not sleeping for the last hour. Insomnia is the order of the night in these strange surroundings. It's too bright for one. The horrible flowery curtains are so flimsy they may as well not be there at all and the orange light they let in from the street outside has turned the flowery wallpaper a kind of weird, eerie colour. The fact that we're in a bed made for one – and not an especially big one at that – doesn't help either. I'm squashed in against the wall, lying partly on nothing as I bridge the gap between it and the bed; Caroline is piggy-in-the-middle, and, on the outside, Dana is hanging on for dear life. In lieu of pyjamas both Dana and I are in T-shirts belonging to Caroline.

"Jeez, Caroline!" Dana is groaning. "I've little enough on without you hogging all the duvet. Give it some slack! I'm freezing!"

"Freezing? How on earth could you be freezing?" demands Caroline. "Anyway, you're so tiny my T-shirt's like a nightie on you."

"She's lucky then," I moan. "The one you gave me

hardly comes to my waist. And my feet are sticking out at the end of the bed."

"It's a small price to pay for having legs as long as yours," comments Caroline. "What can you expect when you're over six foot? Anyway, I don't know how anyone can be freezing. It's roasting in here!"

"That's easy for you to say tucked in, all nice and comfortable in the middle," snaps Dana.

"Five foot ten actually," I mutter.

"Comfortable?" Caroline objects. "There's nothing comfortable about being in the middle. I've your backside sticking into me from one side and Rosie's bony knees jutting in from the other so I –"

"Hang on a minute, I don't have bony knees."

"You're kidding. You could cut someone with those. Can't you keep them to yourself?"

"Don't you think I would if I could?"

"And how come I've never noticed how much hair the pair of you have?" moans Caroline. "I swear, it's everywhere. Couldn't you have tied it up? I'll wake up choking on a hair-ball."

"Ugh! Don't be so disgusting," groans Dana.

There's a momentary silence.

Then Dana gives a heavy sigh. "This is ridiculous!"

There's further silence as we each reflect on how true this is, just how utterly ridiculous our situation is.

"Ridiculous – you've said it," agrees Caroline.

Then silence again.

"I mean, what kind of millionaires live like this?" I ask. "Seriously?"

It's Caroline who starts us off. It begins when I feel her body shaking.

"Caroline? What are you doing?"

She doesn't answer but her body continues to shake.

"Caroline, are you laughing?"

But still no answer and it dawns on me that she can't, she's laughing too much.

"Caroline! What's so funny?"

"Us! This!" she manages. "Everything! What must we look like? It's – we're – ridiculous!"

I realise that on the far side of Caroline, Dana has joined in, quietly too at least at first, but now her – their – laughter just rises and rises and it's contagious and, soon, I'm as bad as the pair of them. Soon it's bedlam in the bed – unrestrained hooting, roaring and downright screams of laughter. I'm completely powerless as wave upon wave hits me – us – the bed is positively shaking.

"Watch it!" Dana suddenly cries. "I'm going to fall out!"

I swear tears are just pouring out. I think I'm going to choke. I swear I'm going to *die* I'm laughing so hard. Because there really *is* no other word for it – our situation *is* ridiculous, totally and utterly ridiculous.

"Oh God, I think I'm going to die!"

Finally it begins to subside. Finally Dana recovers enough to speak.

"There's eleven million sitting in a bank somewhere with our name on it yet here we are, on some Melbourne backstreet, in a hostel, crammed into this tiny little bed and in danger of choking on hair-balls, in this . . . this . . . boxy little room with the *ugliest* wallpaper and curtains I've ever seen. I mean look at them."

That just sets us off again.

"Cosy! Rosie thinks the room is cosy!" laughs Caroline. "And she *loves* the curtains!"

"Hey! I was only being polite. I was trying to think of something, anything positive to say. I've never seen anything so horrible."

"Aren't they just foul?" agrees Caroline.

"If we *ever* get to sleep I'll be having nightmares about them," says Dana.

Silence falls once again, for a very short while but, then, Caroline pipes up.

"You know, we should really be staying in some penthouse suite with floor-to-ceiling windows looking out over the lights of the city, in vast beds, between sheets with a thread count of 500."

"What's that?" I ask.

"Don't you read magazines? They're what the rich and famous use – that's how they know they've made it. They'd probably come out in an itchy rash if their skin touched anything more coarse."

"I wondered why I felt itchy," laughs Dana. "Now that we're wealthy maybe my skin is suddenly too delicate for this kind of cheap stuff."

"I think there's a more likely cause," I say. "You wouldn't know what's living in this mattress."

"Oh, gross!" cries Dana. "Stop! I'm getting even itchier just thinking about it."

"Then don't," says Caroline. "Think about the money instead. Think about how, as soon as we get home and we've got our hands on our millions, we can head into Brown Thomas and buy a lorry-load of sheets all with a thread count of 500."

"Not like this one with a *head* count of 500!"

"Rosie! Stop!" cries Dana.

"You know, one lorry-load wouldn't be enough,"

Caroline thinks aloud. "Now we're rich we'll probably have to throw our sheets out after just one use, the rich never use the same stuff twice. Princess Diana never wore the same knickers a second time, at least not after she became Princess."

"Hmm," says Dana. "I bet Queen Elizabeth holds onto them longer, she probably keeps them until the elastic go. She strikes me as the thrifty kind."

"Come on, enough nonsense," admonishes Caroline. "Let's just try and get some sleep. We have a lot of decisions to make tomorrow."

We lay there in silence for five, ten minutes but, then, Dana pipes up again. "Maybe she even fits them with a new elastic."

"What?"

"The queen and her knickers."

"Don't start us off again! Seriously we need to get some sleep!"

Sleep does come soon for Dana as evidenced by her little snores. But not for me. Or Caroline, I think. I decide to check.

"Are you still awake?" I whisper.

She grunts.

"Caroline, tell me the truth, did you and Mick have another fight?"

"What? Are you still on about that!"

"It wouldn't be the first."

Caroline and Mick are an odd couple. Opposites really in most respects. They struck up a conversation and a friendship a year ago on the train from Cork to Dublin. This was before we opened our ill-fated shop and Caroline was still working as a marketing highflier, and before Mick landed his big role in *Fate Farm*. As I recall, she was returning from a business meeting while he was moving to Dublin from the country to embark on his fledging career. And though they became friendly that day on the train, and good friends in the months after, the image of the kind of man Caroline had always professed to want – high-powered, rich, well-connected – was so far removed from Mick that it took her quite some time to admit to how she felt about him. And, even when she eventually did, when they did get together, their opposite personalities meant their relationship has always been one of those passionate volatile ones (passion is one thing they do have in common) and passionate falling-outs and making-ups are very much characteristic.

"So did you have a row?" I persist. "Is that why you're here in Melbourne while he's up at the Barrier Reef?"

She sighs. "You're not going to let it go, are you?"

I don't answer.

"Okay, okay, we did have an argument."

"I knew it! What was it about this time?"

She sighs again. "God, it was all so stupid really!" She pauses for a moment to collect her thoughts. "Okay, well, what happened was this. We were outside the bus station on our way to catch a bus up to Cairns when he stopped by the main door to give this beggar, this young teenage girl sitting on the pavement, some money. After he had, I told him he was foolish, that she'd spend it on drugs. He got annoyed, said I'd no heart. Then I got annoyed. I mean, just who did he think he was, talking to me like that!"

"I can just picture it."

"So, anyway, I went storming off."

"Yes, I can picture that too."

"Then he shouted after me to come back or I'd miss the

bus, and told me he was going with or without me. I swear I was so mad at him — shouting ultimatums at me like that — so I kept on walking. I guess I expected him to come after me to try and cajole me. If he had, I'd have given in — the last thing I wanted was to be left behind. But God! I was so mad at him. Really mad. Furious."

"I get that. Now go on."

"So I had to accept he wasn't going to come after me."

"What did you do then?"

"Though I was mad, though he was in the wrong, I swallowed my pride, turned around and began heading back again but, then, this thug appeared from nowhere and tried to grab my bag."

"Crikey!"

"Well, there was no way I was letting this scumbag have it so I began struggling with him and —"

"Caroline! You should have just let it go!"

"I know but I was livid. First Mick walking off and now this fool thinking he could just take my bag. I'd had just enough."

"And then what?"

"He was way stronger than me. He'd have got the bag, no doubt, except then the young beggar from earlier came to my help and she began struggling with him too but, for her troubles, she got a fist into the side of her head. The gurrier ran off after that."

"The poor girl."

"She wasn't seriously injured, not knocked out, but I was worried she'd suffer after-effects. So, I asked her where she was staying and when she told me here, I brought her back and they checked her out and found she was fine. But, on the spur of the moment, I asked if they needed any help. They did, of course. They're always short-staffed."

"But why did you want to help?"

She doesn't answer for a while and I begin to think maybe she's drifted off. But then –

"Two reasons. First, I was sick of the way Mick always takes the moral high ground. He acts like he thinks I'm only out for myself and yes, I guess I am a little like that. But I've needed to be. Mum drummed it into me growing up, after Dad ran out on us. She always told me and Donald that we'd have to depend on ourselves if we were going to get anywhere in this life. But that doesn't mean I'm heartless. I care as must as the next person about the inequities of the world, certainly as much as Mick. I guess I figured working in this hostel would – I don't know – show him."

"How did Mick react when you told him?"

"Don't laugh. He doesn't know. He never rang."

"Really?"

"No!"

"I'm surprised."

Caroline shrugs. "Well, that's how it was."

"So why didn't you ring him?"

"Why should I be the one to give in?"

I laugh now. "So he has no idea you're working here?"

"No."

"I don't believe it."

"Rosie, stop laughing!"

"All right, sorry." Then I ask, "And what was the second reason?"

"I wanted to show Mick that I could get by on my own. I've always had my own money. Through secondary school, through college, I've always worked and, when I graduated, I started making fantastic money, way more than anyone I knew. But now, for the first time in my adult life, I was having to depend on someone else for money. The failure of our shop wiped out every penny I had so Mick paid for my flight and he was paying all our expenses – he'd made loads of money out of his role in *Fate Farm*. I was grateful to him, of course, but I *hated* having to be grateful. It was so odd to have our roles reversed. When we first met, I was the one with the money, not him. So anyway, that day, when I came back here with the young girl, I realised that staying here, helping out, meant I could survive for as long as I needed in Australia on my own even though I didn't have a work permit. And, most importantly, I didn't have to ask Mick for money." Now she laughs. "If I'm really honest, maybe that was as much the reason as any altruistic motive but, you know, I'm glad I did. The stories some of these women have to tell are heartbreaking but what's worse is that, for some of them, you just know things are never going to get better."

She falls silent again.

"Caroline?" I whisper.

There's no answer.

"Caroline?"

She's fallen asleep.

I lie awake for a long while after that. I think about how much Caroline has changed. I don't imagine Caroline would have talked like this a year ago. So what's changed her? Our shop failing and all the disappointment that went with that? Realising she's not as strong and as invincible as she once felt she was? Realising the world doesn't always bend to her wishes? Or her experiences here in this hostel? Maybe all of these. I think Mick would be proud of her. I've no doubt he loves her but she's right, he does have a tendency to take the high ground – like when we were opening Love

Potions. Instead of giving her all his support, I remember him criticising her – us – for preying on the vulnerable which was unjustified. The people who came into the shop to buy our 'love potions' did so out of fun. It was harmless. The potions were no more than fruit and vegetable drinks with some herbs and spices – anything and everything that someone, somewhere, deemed to be an aphrodisiac got thrown in.

But as I too am drifting off to sleep, a last thought occurs to me. Something about the falling-out between Mick and Caroline doesn't ring true. I can imagine them having a big bust-up just as they were getting on the bus. I can imagine Mick leaving Caroline and going off to Cairns in a temper. But, the one thing I can't believe is that he wouldn't have contacted her to make sure she was all right. He just wouldn't do that, not when he knew she didn't have any money. So what does this mean then? Either Mick is not the man I thought he was. Or Caroline isn't telling me the whole truth.

Television permanently turned off. Suspicious? Disconnecting the phone line. Suspicious? Correspondence concerning the purchase of a new home. Even more suspicious.

Arnim Ramdass - $600,000 - US

Donna Campbell's suspicions were well founded. Her husband was hiding his share of a lottery win. Then he hid himself.

6

I open my eyes but immediately close them again. That wallpaper is just too busy to face first thing. I open them a second time, more cautiously. My mouth feels dry, my head aches – those blue drinks from the night before, the jet-lag, the broken sleep. I look at my watch. 2.00pm. I blink. *2.00pm?* What? It can't be! I sit bolt upright. What am I doing still in bed? Where is everyone? And then I catch sight of Dana lying sprawled on the floor like an abandoned rag doll. I call her name.

"Dana!"

No answer.

"Dana!"

She stirs, just a little. "What?"

"Wake up!"

Groggily, eyes still shut, she sits up.

She opens her eyes to a squint and slowly begins to look around. "What am I doing here?"

"In this place or on the floor?"

"On the floor. I must have fallen out. What time is it?"

"Two in the afternoon."

"You're kidding! Where's Caroline?"

"I don't know. I just woke up too."

She stands up. "God, I ache all over." She goes to the window and throws back the curtains but it doesn't make the room any brighter so she turns on the light and then comes over to the bed and lifts up the corner of the mattress.

"Easy, Dana, you'll topple me out. What are you doing?"

"Hmm. That's strange."

"What?"

"The ticket. It's not here."

"What?"

"The ticket is gone."

"You're joking!" And for a second I think she is doing just that but the look on her face quickly convinces me otherwise. I jump from the bed and together we heave the mattress up until it's standing on its side. We stare at nothing. There's no sign of it. When the weight gets too heavy we let the mattress fall again. I tell myself not to panic.

"I'll check the bedclothes." I pull them out from where they've fallen in by the wall, shake out the sheet and then the duvet. Nothing. I check the pillow. Nothing. Dana checks the space in beside the wall. Nothing. She checks under the bed. Nothing. Okay, it's still too soon to panic.

"Hmm. Maybe Caroline took it for safety," I think aloud. "That's really the most likely scenario."

"But it's as safe here as anywhere," says Dana as she checks the bedside locker.

"Why would she take it so?" I ask.

And then a horrible thought occurs to me but I push it away. It's an unworthy thought, unworthy of me and even more unworthy of Caroline. I've known her for years. I look at Dana and at that instant I know she's thinking the same, and, by the way she's looking at me, I know she knows I know what she's thinking *and* she knows the same treacherous thought has occurred to me. Shamed, we quickly look away, our moment of horrible disloyalty going unvoiced.

"I'll try her on my mobile," I say breaking the uneasy hiatus.

"But that didn't work yesterday."

"No harm in trying again."

I find my phone, press Caroline's number on speed dial but, again, I get that unfamiliar tone. "You're right," I tell Dana. "It doesn't work."

"Look, she's bound to be back soon," answers Dana, sounding extremely calm, considering. "What don't we shower while we're waiting? By the time we're done, she'll have returned. You go first. In the meantime, I'll keep on looking."

"Dana, face it! The ticket isn't here!"

"Rosie, calm down. If it isn't here then Caroline must have it. Maybe she's gone to put it in a safety deposit box."

"Yeah," I nod. "That makes sense."

"Yes, it does. Now go and shower."

When I come out of the shower, I'm hoping I'll find Dana standing in the middle of the room, excitedly waving the ticket in her hand, but I don't. Nor is there any sign of Caroline.

"You don't think someone could have come in here in the middle of the night and stolen it?" Dana asks.

"Like who?"

"I don't know. Someone who heard us talking in the pub?"

"Nobody heard us talking in the pub. And no robber who – at random – decided to burgle this room would risk waking three unsettled people to check under a mattress on the off-chance. Look, we're worrying unnecessarily. There has to be a logical explanation. Caroline must have taken it with her. She'll be back soon with the ticket or to tell us she's lodged it somewhere safe, you'll see."

While Dana is in the shower, I get dressed, then go downstairs. The same woman who was there when we arrived yesterday is here again now.

"Excuse me," I say.

Again she has a magazine in front of her and this time it's opened on a crossword, the size of the full page. Tapping her pen against her teeth, she's deep in concentration and doesn't appear to notice me.

"Excuse me," I repeat.

She looks up. "Another word for cow?"

"Pardon?"

"Six letters. First letter B. Last letter E."

"Try bovine." If I solve the clue, perhaps I'll have more chance of engaging her attention

"Bovine?" She considers this for a second and then, tongue jutting out to one side, she begins filling in the blanks, spelling out the letters as she does: "B.O.V.I.N.E. Perfect!"

"I'm just wondering if you saw –"

"Arid place. Six letters. Beginning with D."

"Desert?"

"Desert? Let me see. D.E.S.E.R.T. Spot on."

"– if you saw Caroline?"

"Afraid not. I've just started my shift but she's usually off in the afternoons so if she's not in her room she's most likely gone out. Four letters. Putting all of these in a basket is not a good idea."

It strikes me she's not very good at crosswords and I have to wonder why she's even bothering.

"Four letters."

"Eggs. She didn't leave a message for us by any chance?"

The woman glances around her desk. "No, nothing."

"If you do see her, will you tell her that Rosie and Dana are up in her room waiting for her?"

"Sure."

I turn to go but she calls out: "Heavy rain. Six letters. First letter D, third letter L."

I think for a second. "Deluge?"

She fills in the missing letters. "Damn! You're good!"

I go back up to find Dana still in the shower. I check around for the ticket again but since I'm just looking in all the same places I'm not surprised when there's still no show. I make up the bed then sit down on it. I look at my watch. It's two forty-five. I really wish Caroline would come back. I'd go looking for her but where would I start? I don't know Melbourne. But I hate this uncertainty. I hate not knowing.

I notice a travel guide to Australia lying on the floor and, picking it up, I begin flicking through it to pass the time but my mind really isn't on it. Why didn't Caroline tell us where she was going? Maybe she thought it would be better to let us sleep through our jet-lag. Maybe she thought there was no need for a note, that she'd be back before we woke up. But just when the hell is she going to be back? And – come to think of it – what's taking Dana so long? She's been in the shower for ages. I'm starving. We haven't eaten anything decent since the plane and you couldn't really call what we had then decent. Once Dana is through with her shower we should just go and find a restaurant and blow some of Dana's Australian dollars on a huge meal, and to hell with waiting for Caroline.

I flick through some of the photos in the guidebook. Ayers Rock. The Sydney Opera House. The Twelve

Apostles. If we had the lotto money now we could stay on and take in some of these sights. Maybe we could come back sometime – together. I think how great it is that the three of us have won all this money between us. How much harder it would be to remain friends if only one of us had won: the jealousy, the inequity would have been hard to deal with. We're going to have so much fun with it. Money might change some people and the relationships they have, but I think ours will survive. The shared experience might even bring us closer. And we've gone through so much together already. We'll be okay. We're more like sisters. I'd trust Dana and Caroline with my life.

I put the book down on the bed. Is Dana *ever* going to be finished showering? And *when* will Caroline be back?

And there's that mean thought again. I would trust Caroline with my life – absolutely – but would I trust her with eleven million euros? Yes, I tell myself, yes, I would trust her. Of course I would. But that much money *can* do funny things to people. More than to me, more than to Dana, money has always been important to Caroline. True, she started going out with Mick before his big success but she'd probably have admitted to her feelings for him a lot sooner if he hadn't been a struggling actor when they first met. Yes, Caroline's always been attracted to wealth, to wealthy people. She's never made it any secret that her one over-riding ambition in life is to be rich. She was desperate for Love Potions to succeed big time; she'd plans to expand into the major cities of the world, of franchising it. Whereas we were disappointed when it folded, she was utterly devastated. Travelling around Australia, working in this hostel – both are part of a reaction, just a phase, her way of dealing with the disappointment. But, last I heard, leopards don't change their spots.

Maybe €3.6 million isn't quite enough. Not when she could have eleven million.

I notice the drawer in her locker is slightly open. I get up and go to it. I stand there for a moment. And, then, I pull out the drawer fully and take a quick peek inside. I'm not looking for the ticket, Dana already checked it for that. I hardly allow myself to think what it is I am actually looking for but, when I don't see it, I grow even more anxious. If her passport isn't here, in the most obvious place, then where could it be? Bringing her and the ticket back to Ireland, back to Lottery Headquarters?

"Rosie, what are you doing?"

I spin around. Caroline is standing in the doorway.

"Nothing."

"Why are you looking in my locker?"

"I was – ah – looking for the lotto ticket. It's missing."

"Of course it is. I put it in a safety deposit box in the bank."

"Why didn't you leave a note?"

"I didn't think I'd be gone so long. Anyway, I had my mobile with me."

"I tried it but I just got this weird tone."

"Did you think to include the Australian and the Melbourne prefix? Your calls are probably still going through Ireland."

"Oh, I didn't think of that."

Caroline takes her passport out of her bag and comes over to where I am standing.

"Excuse me," she says and when I step aside she drops the passport back into the drawer and closes it firmly.

Then she turns around. She looks at me, really looks at me. I begin to feel uneasy. I worry what she's going to say next.

"I swear you wouldn't believe the red tape involved, it's just as well I thought to bring this for identification. And the time it took! I was beginning to think I was going to be stuck there for the entire day."

I breathe a sigh of relief.

"Caroline! You're back!" Dana comes into the room, one towel wrapped around her body, the other fashioned into a turban around her wet hair. "We thought you'd run off with the ticket!"

Caroline looks from one of us to the other. "Really?"

Dana laughs. "No, course not!" Then she hesitates. "But where is it?"

"I put it in a safety deposit box in the bank."

Now Caroline eyes us up again – as if she has more to say but, before she has a chance, Dana goes on.

"Good thinking," she remarks. "So is there somewhere close by we can get something to eat? I'm starving."

As soon as Dana finishes dressing, Caroline takes us to a steakhouse ten minutes' walk away where we are served the most enormous steaks ever. We don't talk while eating – Dana and I are too preoccupied, enjoying our first decent meal in more than thirty-six hours.

Now, Dana lifts the napkin from her lap, sets it down on the table beside her cleared plate, and sits back looking a picture of absolute contentment.

"That was delicious." She pats her stomach. "God! I can't remember the last time I ate so much."

"Me neither."

Caroline looks up from her – as yet barely touched – plate and over at both of ours.

"What? You can't possibly be finished already?"

Dana shrugs. "We were famished."

As Caroline carries on eating at a more restrained pace, we sit in silence, too full, too satisfied, to bother with talk for now.

"I don't suppose you'll have room for dessert then?" Caroline asks when she's finally through.

"Well, there's no harm in at least *looking* at the menu," says Dana, as she always does, like there's even the slightest chance she's *not* going to have dessert. She looks around for the waiter, asking as she does: "What about you, Rosie? Do you think you could squeeze dessert in?"

"Hmm . . . I think I might manage."

Noticing Dana craning like a meerkat, the waiter comes over and after a thorough consideration of the menu, I opt for the cheesecake while Caroline and Dana both choose pavlova.

"You know," says Caroline, "pavlova was invented in Australia to commemorate the Russian dancer, Anna Pavlova, when she toured here."

I nod abstractedly at this piece of Australian trivia.

When our desserts arrive, we eat them in silence apart from the occasional happy, "Mmmm," emanating mainly from Dana. "I wonder if she danced as well as she tastes," she wonders aloud.

When we're through and the waiter has taken away our plates and brought us coffees, Caroline bends down, picks up a bag, and takes out a bundle of papers.

"What are those?" asks Dana.

"Well, on my way back from the bank, I dropped into an internet café and did some searches to see what advice I could find for . . ." she lowers her voice and shiftily glances around ". . . lotto winners. You know, there's a surprising amount out there. This one here is from the Irish National

Lottery Board." She holds out a copy for each of us and, as we take it, she tells us: "As might be expected, they begin by offering congratulations and by giving advice as to how to deal with the media."

I begin skimming through it.

"Why," asks Dana who is doing the same, "do they seem to assume that everyone goes public when they collect their win?"

"You noticed that too?" says Caroline. "The thing is, it's in the lottery people's interest that winners do go public. It's great publicity for them and the newspapers love it too because they get a good story. But I found an article written by this American . . ." she searches through her bundle of print-outs and pulls out another ". . . which makes for interesting reading. This guy here says that winners should never, ever go public. He says it's a lousy deal for them. He says that every single lottery winner who has done so has stories upon stories to tell of people harassing them."

"What do you think he means by going public?" I ask Caroline. "Does he mean going to the newspapers or does he mean just telling friends and family?"

"I'm not sure. I think he means the newspapers."

"Well, we're hardly going to do that."

"No, but . . ." she trails off.

"But?"

"But I've been doing a lot of thinking and to my mind the minute you start telling your nearest and dearest, then you'll have them telling their nearest and dearest, no matter that they've sworn themselves blind not to tell a soul and, then, those in turn will tell their nearest and dearest as well as those neither near or particularly dear to them and, soon, it becomes widely-known gossip that any journalist with the slightest interest can easily unearth. Next thing you know, articles and photos start appearing in the papers and, soon, you're tripping over the begging letters piled up on the mat in the hall as you go to get your early morning fix of coffee, all the while keeping your curtains pulled to shield you from the peering photographers camped in your garden."

"You don't really think it would be that bad?" I ask.

She shrugs. "The pressure people come under once it becomes known they've had a big lottery win is phenomenal. I didn't print it out but I read an article about this one guy who won millions of dollars in America and when people found out he ended up having to employ a full-time secretary *just* to open all the begging letters. And when that woman in Limerick, Dolores McNamara, won in the EuroMillions Lottery she was pestered by thousands for financial help. Her local post office had to put on two extra delivery services a day after her win because of the volume of post being sent to her. Many of them were simply addressed to Dolores McNamara, Limerick, and still they got to her. She became public property. She was hounded. She had to become a virtual recluse. I don't want to live like that."

"So what are you saying? That we should keep our win a secret?" I ask.

"Yes."

"Look, I don't want to be splashed all over the papers either and have every Tom, Dick and Harry coming to us with their hand out but, surely, it doesn't mean we have to keep it a total secret?"

"I think it does."

"From everyone?"

"Yes. Once you tell a single person, you can no longer call it a secret."

I shake my head. "There's no way I could manage not telling anyone, especially Finn!"

"But, Rosie, you've managed so far."

"Only for a few days, and only because we wanted to tell you first. There's a big difference between a few days and a lifetime. I couldn't keep something like this a secret forever, I just couldn't. Nor would I want to. Why would I?"

"Because, as well as having every Tom, Dick and Harry chasing us, there's really no knowing how even those close to us would react. Look, Rosie, it's okay for you, your family are nice and normal but mine, well, they're a different kettle of fish. Take my dad. He'd eat the money up, given a chance. He'd start on at me to invest in his latest crazy scheme or wacky invention or some racehorse he's taken a fancy to. He'd probably dump his current trophy girlfriend for an even brassier one and then want me to help him fund her upkeep."

"You can always say no."

"People don't always take 'no' very well so why put ourselves in that position? And my dad, for one, can be very persuasive."

"It runs in the family then," I mumble, but then I throw my hands up in exasperation. "Oh, I don't know!" What Caroline is saying does make some sense but I can't help feeling it's not the right thing to do.

She goes on. "There's no telling how friends and family will react but, also, how our win will impact on them."

"What do you mean?"

"A sum of money like this changes things for everyone around us, not just us."

Now Dana joins in. "Caroline has a point." She hesitates before going on. "Like my mum. Who knows what the impact on her would be?"

I look at her questioningly.

"You know she's an alcoholic," Dana explains.

"Yes, sure, but she's well now. She's had treatment. Hasn't she been doing okay since she and your dad got back together again and managed to put his affair and the baby behind them?"

"Only okay-ish. But there's always the danger she'll slip back again – she has before. I think she finds not drinking a real struggle. She hasn't really found anything to fulfil her, to engage her, since she stopped. Yes, Dad and her are back together but I don't know that she's happy in herself. Our win could have a really negative impact on her."

"So, Rosie, your family is nice and normal but mine isn't, nor Dana's. Like she says, her poor mum is probably pretty vulnerable – you don't want her hitting the bottle again."

I see Dana frown at Caroline's indelicate turn of phrase but she lets it pass. Instead she adds: "You have to see it from Caroline's point of view, Rosie. Maybe she's right. Maybe it is best to keep it secret."

I can see where Caroline and Dana are coming from, I really can, but, even so. Keeping it a secret until we told Caroline was one thing, but keeping it a secret forever is another. How would we manage that? But now it seems both of them are thinking the same way. That makes it two against one. But I really don't know if I'd be able to keep such a big secret – all that lying and pretending, it would be awful. Could telling them really be any more awful? "So you really are saying we shouldn't tell anyone?"

Caroline nods her head. "I don't think we should."

Dana too is nodding.

"But what's the point of having all this money if we can't share it with our friends and family?"

I think of my parents. I want to do something really special for them – just what, I don't know yet. And Finn. I could help him with his music. I don't know how exactly but having my financial support could only help realise his ambitions.

"I'm not saying you can't share the money if that's what we want to do but –"

"It is," I interrupt.

"And so do I. But we can be creative, we can come up with ways to help people without them knowing it's us. I want to be able to *choose* who I help and how I help them. I don't want to come under pressure from everyone I know, and from people I don't even know."

But still I'm uneasy. I feel I'm being railroaded into a decision that I'm not happy with.

Caroline taps her photocopy. "Now, come on, read the rest."

Though still full of misgivings, I turn my attention to the rest of the print-outs. For five, ten minutes, we read silently, then a worried Dana looks up: "Investment opportunities, legal considerations, wills, inheritance taxes, gift taxes. God! There's a lot to consider, isn't there?"

From what I read, it seems that the key, as far as investment goes, is to spread money over different options. I scan through the part about the importance of taking out life assurance. I know this is worthy stuff, stuff we – I – will have to consider – but later. I come to the part about the psychological consequences of winning. I read that there are going to be personal, family, and social adjustments. I read that research indicates that winners of large sums of money who make rapid changes in their jobs and lifestyles in general can sometimes pay a price in terms of increased boredom, depression, and social isolation. I read that it's wise to stay within one's comfort zone and to avoid making sudden and rash decisions in terms of employment or other significant areas. I think about this for a moment and think about how, from the moment we found out we'd won, I decided I was going to give up my job as a lab technician. I'd have handed in my resignation before we flew out only Dana warned me not to – she was worried it might arouse suspicions. I don't think it would have in my case. I think from the day I started they've been half-expecting it.

Dana must be reading the same part as me and now she announces:

"Well, I've no intention of giving up my course."

I look at her in surprise. "You're kidding!"

"No, I'm not."

"But Dana!"

"But Dana, what? Like work, studying is about all sorts of things, not least satisfaction, a feeling of self-worth."

I think about what she's saying and realise that's just not the case with me. All my job is, is a means to an end, a means of making money to live. Now I have enough money for that, why would I work in a job I don't care about?

"Well," says Caroline, "since I don't even have a job, that's one decision less I have to make."

"Yeah, but now that you have money behind you, you can think about setting up in business again." says Dana. "Knowing you, you have a couple of ideas up your sleeve."

Caroline shrugs non-committally. "Maybe."

"There *is* such a lot to think about, isn't there?" I think aloud.

Dana nods.

Caroline says: "The one bit of advice that keeps coming

up again and again is to do nothing, at least for a while. Stanford University did this study and it shows that over ninety per cent of people run through their money within five years."

"Five years?" Dana looks sceptical.

Caroline nods. "Here's another survey." She picks out a document. "It's from the Ontario Lottery and Gaming Corporation and it goes into what lotto winners do spend their money on. They found that sixty-two per cent of people bought a new car."

"A car would be handy," considers Dana.

"I'd like to replace the one I sold to clear the debts from the shop," adds Caroline.

"Of course I'd need to learn to drive first," Dana thinks aloud.

"What else did those people in the survey do with the money?" I ask.

"Thirty-four per cent bought a new house."

I think about this for a moment. "I don't know about you two but I'm quite happy with where we are. I'd like to go on living there, for now at any rate."

"Me too," says Dana. "Here's an idea. We could buy the house from your brother, Caroline. What do you think?"

Caroline nods. "As a matter of fact the same thought occurred to me. As it stands, Donald could sell it in the morning and we'd be out on our ear. But, if we bought it, it would give us security of tenure and it could be an investment in the long-term."

"But do you think Donald would sell it to us?"

"I'm sure he would. As long as the price is right."

"But he might start wondering where the money was coming from?" worries Dana.

"He wouldn't need to know we're the purchasers if that's what we want," Caroline tells her. "We could get an intermediary, a solicitor, to buy it for us."

"What about Shane?" I ask.

"You mean to negotiate the sale?" asks Caroline.

"No – though given that he's a solicitor he could. But what I meant is, should we tell him? After all, he makes up the fourth member of our household."

"No." Caroline shakes her head.

"But he lives with us! How are we meant to keep it from him?"

After Finn and the girls, Shane is my next best friend. He's also my oldest friend. I went to school with him. When a room became free in the house I knew he was looking for somewhere which is how he came to move in with us. That was after Dana started up the syndicate but he was never interested in joining it. He calls the lotto a tax on morons, and says he's already paying enough taxes without voluntarily paying that too.

"If we start making exceptions for Shane then how do we draw the line?" asks Caroline.

I shrug. "Oh, I don't know." This lotto winning does seem to bring with it an awful lot of decisions.

"So go on," says Dana. "What else did the winners spend their winnings on?"

"Seventy-five per cent shared the money with family and friends."

"Which we *are* going to do." I repeat again.

"Yeah," Caroline nods her head. "Like I said, we're just going to have to find ways of doing so without them knowing. You know the only time I ever won anything before this was at the merries."

72

"The what?" asks Dana.

"The merries. It's what we used to call the fairground when we were young. Mum was sick, I think, that's why Dad was taking Donald and me, to get us out of the house to give her a break – this was before they split up. Anyway, before we left home, I remember going up to her room and giving her a goodbye kiss and promising her that if I won on a raffle, I'd pick out something for her. As luck would have it, I did win. My raffle ticket came good but then faced with an array of shiny plastic stuff, a cheap version of a Barbie type doll caught my eye and I forgot all about Mum and I picked the doll instead. It was only when I got home again and saw Mum still in the bed, coughing and wheezing and asking us how we got on, that I remembered my promise." She thinks for a second. "But I'd like to do something for her. She's had it hard, especially after Dad left. Maybe I could go on holiday with her. She likes to travel but she's never really had the opportunity. She'd love to go to America."

"But without her knowing where the money is coming from?" I ask.

"Yes."

I sigh.

Caroline sighs at my sigh but before she can say anything, the waiter comes down to ask if we'd like anything else and Caroline tells him we don't, and asks for the bill.

I think," she says once he's gone, "that the most important bit of advice out of all this is to do nothing, at least for a while. Eleven million is a fortune. Even divided by three, it still is. But, remember, ninety per cent of winners manage to get through their fortunes in five years."

"I wish my body to be buried following a service at which I would like an announcement made regarding my lottery win."

Gail German – £1 million – UK

Only then did friends and neighbours learn of her windfall. Beneficiaries included a children's hospice, churches and hospitals.

7

How the world has got smaller! Way back in the 1700s, it took Captain Cook and his first fleet of opportunistic passengers, hapless convicts, daring marines and bewildered animals (chickens mainly – so I read in Caroline's guidebook) something like ten months to reach Botany Bay, from whence, as they said in those days, so many of them never, ever returned (well, the convicts and chickens at any rate). Could those early travellers ever have imagined just how much things would change in the future? For instance: in the 2000s, when booking our flights back in Ireland, we left a mere two days between our inward and outward journey thus possibly making us worthy contenders for the record for the shortest trip to Oz ever. When we do get home again, we'll probably still be suffering from jet-lag from our *original* trip out, on top of jet-lag from the trip back.

Extending our time here isn't an option given our financially straitened circumstances, despite our millionaire status. Besides we're rather keen – to understate it somewhat – to get our hands on our winnings, including Caroline. So, whereas there were two of us on the way out, there will be three on the way back – Caroline has brought her return flight forward and has managed to get a seat on the same plane.

But we still have one day left before we go home and I know exactly how I'm going to spend it. I'm going to visit my sister Sarah who lives on the outskirts of Melbourne. Just how I'm going to explain my short surprise visit, I haven't quite figured out.

Sarah has been living in Australia for almost twelve years. She met her now husband, Rod, when she was in her early twenties (and I was in my early teens) while backpacking here on a year out. My parents came out to see Sarah last year but I haven't seen her in over two – the last time she came home. In fact, since she settled here, I've met her a total of four times, those times she's been back – I never made it here. Lack of money or lack of time – it was always one or the other.

To the teenage me, Sarah was the cleverest, funniest, most interesting person ever born. I absolutely idolised her. I thought she was the coolest person on the planet and, since the 1990s were as anti-fashion a period in history as you could get, Sarah – in her Levis, Docs, plaid shirts and shaggy Rachel-from-*Friends* hair – was probably as cool (or in hindsight, uncool) as any of her contemporaries. When she left for Australia, I was devastated but even more so when she didn't come home after the year. Instead, she decided to get work as a nurse in Melbourne rather than return to Dublin which was her original plan – before she went to Australia, before she met Rod. Ah, yes, Rod. For years I blamed him for taking my big sister away from me and it's fair to say I was slow to give him a proper chance, maybe I still haven't. Perhaps the reason I don't like him is simply because he took Sarah away. Or maybe it's because there's never been the time and opportunity to get to know him properly. Or maybe it's because – and I don't like saying this – he's just not likable, at least I don't find him so. Sure he's handsome, very handsome. Sure he's charming, very charming. But almost *too* charming. Maybe it's just me but his effusive greetings, easy chit-chat, and over-the-top compliments have always stuck me as being somewhat fake and I can't help thinking he's not quite so benign as he makes out. I suspect my parents don't really like him either though they'd never say it. Of course I could be all wrong. After all, Sarah knows him better than anyone and she chose to stay in Australia to be with him, and chose to marry him when, really, she could probably have married anyone she wanted; she was always one of those super-popular girls.

Now Sarah's boys, well, they're a different matter. They're just the loveliest kids ever. Well, Lachlan and Kyle, the older two are – I've yet to meet baby Jack but in photos he looks absolutely adorable.

And so now, here I am, standing outside their blue clapboard bungalow in a street lined with similar homes in one of the outer suburbs of Melbourne. I feel a little anxious but excited too. As I wait for an answer to my knock I have time to look around. To be honest, it's not terribly impressive. I always pictured them living somewhere more upmarket but their street is just on the right side of respectable though their unkempt front garden isn't what's keeping it there. I'm a little surprised at how just untidy it is but maybe that's only temporary. Sarah *has* just had a baby. But what about Rod, couldn't he tackle it? I can imagine their neighbours' whispered grumblings: 'I mean, just look at those weeds!' I knock again. That there might not be anyone home never occurred to me when I had caught the tram in the city centre to this outer 'burb. Now, having come so far I realise how awfully disappointed I'm going to be if I don't get to meet Sarah and the boys. Perhaps I should have rung first but I just thought it would be easier to simply turn up than to have to go into complicated explanations over the phone. There's a car parked in the driveway. There must be someone home. I knock again, louder.

Sarah opens the door, looking a little hassled, a little annoyed perhaps by this interruption from a stranger for it's obvious that's what she thinks initially. After all, it's not like she's expecting to see me standing on her doorway. But recognition very quickly dawns as signified by a high-pitched cry: "Rosie!"

"Sarah!"

"Oh, my God!"

Even though this is her doorway and I'm expecting to see her, it still takes me a second to reconcile the reality with my expectations. She looks so different from when I saw her last. She even looks different from the photos Mum and Dad took during their trip to Australia last year. The lasting impression I have from those are of someone tanned, happy, beautiful – wide smile, hair shining, shorts showing impossibly long legs, skimpy little T-shirt over a fabulous physique.

Now, well now, the first thing I notice is she's wearing this checked, sleeveless, shapeless dress that comes to above her knees and which even Cindy Crawford (who she has been compared to on occasion by our proud mother, but others too) would have trouble pulling off. I see she's barefoot but I remind myself this is Australia; it seems things are more laid-back here. Her dark hair is carelessly tied up in a ponytail. She's still thin, thinner even than before, almost unhealthily so and, though her face is beautiful, of course, it does look drawn and weary. The honest-to-God truth is I'd almost pass her in the street.

"What on earth are you doing here?"

"Visiting?" I laugh.

"But why didn't you let me know you were coming?"

"I wanted to surprise you!"

"Surprise! Too right," she says, sounding for a moment like a proper Aussie. "Shock, more like." Suddenly she throws her arms around me and gives me a big bear hug. "I can't believe it's you," she murmurs in my ear. I think her voice is breaking a little which wouldn't surprise me. Sure Sarah's always been independent, I'd guess she's had to be having settled so far away from home but, underneath, she's quite the softie. Now this hug goes on for so long that, in the end, I'm the one who pulls away.

"It's great to see you!" I say when I do.

"And you too! Come in! Come in!"

I follow her into the house, down a long, narrow corridor running from front to back, my eyes taking time to adjust from the bright sunlight outside to the dark interior. But what I do see along the corridor – a bundle of mismatched children's sandals and slippers, a vacuum cleaner, a laundry basket piled high – makes me think housekeeping isn't exactly Sarah's forte. Glimpses of unmade beds through half-opened doors only add to the overall impression of domestic chaos. I shared a bedroom with Sarah growing up so I've first-hand experience. I know she's not the tidiest in the world; she'd much rather be out doing something than stuck inside cleaning. But I'd marked Rod down as a fastidious sort. The

79

last time they were home he was obsessive about keeping their rental car spotless according to Dad, out polishing and vacuuming it every morning. It also strikes me as odd that Mum never mentioned this messy state of affairs I see now when recounting her last stay with Sarah. Mum's low tolerance of domestic untidiness is legendary. That she's not exactly shy in expressing her thoughts is common knowledge too — so how come she never mentioned this?

We come into the kitchen and it's pretty untidy also. Okay, coping with a new baby and two small boys too is a lot to have to deal with but doesn't she have Rod to help out? Maybe Sarah sees something of what I'm thinking — she picks up an empty juice carton, looks around, looks to the overflowing bin but, then, gives a hint of a shrug, shoves a strand of hair behind her ear, and puts the carton pack down again on the table.

"I guess I've let things slide a little since the baby was born. You should have told me you were coming, I'd have tidied up."

"It was a last-minute thing," I explain. "Work sent me."

"Oh yes, your new job."

"Well, it's not exactly new."

Sarah laughs. "I told you about the day Mum rang here to tell me? She was so excited you'd swear you'd been made President."

"She was just so relieved I finally had a 'proper' job."

Again Sarah laughs. "That's more or less what she said. So, do you like it?"

"It's okay."

"Only okay? Oh dear!" But then she looks puzzled. "Why would they send a lab technician to Australia?"

"They — ah — wanted me to look into some new work practices," I answer, praying she won't delve any deeper.

She seems happy to accept what I'm saying. In fact, she's impressed. "Wow! You must be doing well if they're flying you around the world."

If she only knew. Work wouldn't send me as far as the shop at the end of the road.

She goes on, "I still think it was a pity your business didn't work out."

"It was a disappointment, all right."

"I can imagine. But at least you tried. That's the important thing."

I nod. "Yeah, that's what I think too."

"And Finn? That's still going strong?"

"Of course."

"Of course? Well, well. This must be a record for you. From what I hear he seems nice."

"Oh, he is, Sarah. He's fantastic. He's just the nicest, kindest person you could hope to meet. And he's clever too and handsome and funny and very talented."

Sarah gives a laugh. "Just look at the big smile on your face. I think my baby sister is in love."

I laugh too. "I guess I am. Oh, Sarah, you'd really like him. I wish you could meet him."

"It's a pity he didn't come with you."

"Maybe next time."

"I'm glad to hear there'll be a next time. I've been waiting long enough for the first. Anyway, why don't I call the boys in? They'll get such a land!" Sarah goes to a sliding glass door, pulls it across and gives a shout. "Lachlan! Kyle! Come and meet your Auntie Rosie!"

I follow her to the door. At first I don't see anybody, but then two white-blond heads emerge from the tall grass at the end of the garden.

"Boys, come here!"

The pair of them are standing up fully now and I see they're nearly identical except that Lachlan – who, at five, is a year older – is taller by a good few inches. Both are wearing shorts but no tops and have tanned, thin torsos. Lachlan has a cowboy hat hanging around his neck and a holster around his skinny little waist. Kyle has streaks of war paint across both cheeks, a tube of arrows across his back and he holds a bow in one hand.

They walk gingerly up the path, eyeing me carefully as they approach. As soon as the not-so-brave little warriors are within reach of their mother, they rush to her and then stare at me from their position of safety.

"Come on," coaxes Sarah, ruffling both boys' thick hair, "say hello to Rosie. She's my baby sister. You know the way Kyle is your baby brother, Lachlan? Nana and Gramps are her mum and dad too, like they're mine. You met her back in Ireland, when you were there, remember?"

"They probably don't," I laugh.

"Maybe not," Sarah concedes. "They're always a little shy at first but don't worry. They'll soon get over it."

They're both staring out at me from beneath heavy fringes. I stoop to their eye level.

"Hiya," I address Kyle first.

Kyle is looking at me with these huge blue eyes, framed with lashes so thick and long. They're beautiful little boys, both of them, but no surprise there, given their genes.

"Did you come on an airplane?" he asks finally in an accent that is decidedly Australian.

"I sure did."

"I was on an airplane, you know?"

"Is that right?"

"Yeah, lots and lots of times. A hundred times."

"A hundred! Wow!"

He nods gravely. "Do you want to hear me count to a hundred?"

"Ah yeah, sure – if you like."

"Okay. Here goes. One, two, skip a few, ninety-nine, one hundred!"

"Hey!" cries Lachlan, "That's my joke!"

I turn to Lachlan. "I bet you have lots of other jokes?"

He shrugs. "Sure I do."

"Have you any you want to tell me?"

He nods his head. "Sure."

Sarah laughs, "Oh dear, you'll regret asking that."

"Knock-knock," begins Lachlan.

"Who's there?"

"Alex."

"Alex who?"

"Alex the questions around here!"

I laugh out loud. "That's a good one."

Sarah laughs. "Don't encourage him too much or he'll never stop – seriously," she warns me. "There are millions more where that came from."

Suddenly Lachlan pipes up. "I'm five-and-a-half."

"Only five-and-a-half?" I look at him in feigned disbelief. "I'd have said you were at least six."

"Well, I am big for my age," he tells me, standing up as tall as he can. "I'm even bigger than Paul and he's six."

"Who's Paul?"

"My best friend. He lives down the street. He knows more jokes than anyone in the whole wide world."

"I like your cowboy outfit."

"Mum got it for me for being so good. Do you want to play Cowboys and Indians?"

"Ah – I guess."

"Well, you can be an Indian like Kyle and I'll come looking for you and try to capture you." He thinks for a second. "Do you want to be a boy Indian or a girl Indian?"

"I think I'd like to be a girl Indian."

"You can be a boy one if you like."

"No, I'm quite happy being a girl one."

"Are you sure?" he asks doubtfully.

I nod.

"Come on so." He takes my hand. I look at Sarah. She's smiling.

"I think I hear the baby," she says. "He's probably awake. I'll go and get him up."

Lachlan and Kyle lead me down the garden and we start our game of Cowboys and Indians. Not much is required of me really, except to dart here and there and pound my mouth and make 'Indian' sounds. It strikes me that this game is not very PC, but then, from my limited experience, it seems that's the case with most games children play.

When Lachlan has killed us for – oh – about the tenth time and I'm thinking I really need to come up with a new game, Sarah emerges from the house with her youngest, little Jack, in her arms.

"Come on," I say to Lachlan and Kyle, "I want to say hello to your new brother."

"Don't be silly!" laughs Lachlan. "Why would you want to say hello to him when he can't even talk!"

"Yeah," says Kyle. "He's only a baby!"

"Yes, but that doesn't mean I can't talk to him."

But, uninterested, the boys stay behind as I go to take a closer look at my newest nephew nestled in his mother's arms.

"Oh my God! He's just lovely!" And he is absolutely perfect, this little bundle in just a vest and nappy, with his little eyes looking around, his plump sumo-wrestler legs kicking, his miniature fists clasped.

I look and see Sarah too is gazing down at him, with boundless maternal pride. She looks like she could positively eat him up.

"How old is he now?" I ask.

"Hmm?" She manages to drag her eyes away from him. "Two months. Look, why don't you hold him and I'll go and make something to eat for everyone before I feed him? I'm going to have to go to work in an hour."

Without ceremony, she passes him over to me and I'm so distracted, afraid I'll drop him on his head or something, that I don't hear what she says, at least not immediately, but then it registers.

"What? You're going to work in an hour? You mean you're back at work already?"

"Ah, yes."

"But you've just had a baby. Who minds him when you're working?"

"Lily, the lady from next door. You've heard me talking about her. She's minded all the boys since they were born. I don't know how I'd manage without her. Her own grandchildren live up in Queensland so she hardly ever gets to see them and she's sort of adopted my boys as her own."

"Don't let Mum hear you say that!"

Sarah smiles.

"But, Sarah, if you're going to work then we're not going to get to spend any time together?"

"Sure we are. As luck would have it, it happens to be my day off tomorrow."

"But Sarah —"

"Maybe we could go somewhere. I know, I'll make a picnic. It'll be like old times — remember the trips I used to take you on when you were small and I'd just got my first car? I got a flat tyre the other day and it reminded me of the time we got one on the way back from Bettystown. I still remember you standing at the side of the road, your hair wet and bedraggled from the beach, watching as I tried to change the tyre. You kept whining, 'Can't we just ring Dad?'"

"Yeah, but you wouldn't. You had to do it yourself!"

"So tomorrow we could drive down the coast and —"

"But Sarah —"

"— maybe go as far as Lorne. It's a really lovely little town and —"

"Sarah —"

"— we could even take the tent. My shift doesn't start until the following afternoon. Oh, Rosie, it'll be great! The two of us off on a trip, just like the old days. Except we'd have the boys too. They'll be thrilled. I haven't taken them anywhere in ages."

"But, Sarah, I'm flying out first thing in the morning."

"What do you mean? Flying out where?"

"Flying out home."

"You're flying home? Tomorrow? Tell me you're joking!"

I shake my head. "I'm not."

"But when did you get here?"

"The day before yesterday."

"You travelled all this way for just two days?"

I nod my head.

"Two days!"

"It's just a fleeting visit but I will come back again — another time."

She doesn't say anything but just stands there looking completely dumbfounded.

"Soon – I promise," I quickly add.

And so disappointed.

"For a longer time."

Awfully disappointed.

"Maybe for a month. Two months even."

I notice a look of incredulity flit across her face but she doesn't say anything.

"You don't think I will? But, Sarah, I will, I promise."

"Sure. If you say so."

"I do say so."

"Okay. But please don't go telling the boys until you have it all arranged. I don't want them to be disappointed – just in case. Two months would be a lot of time to expect to get off in any job but particularly when you're relatively new."

She thinks I'm making an empty promise. And can I blame her? It probably does sound outlandish. But I do mean it. I could come back for two months. What's to stop me? Suddenly I want to tell her the truth, the whole truth, and how with all my money, I can come back again whenever I want. As often as I want. For as long as I want. Or I can fly them home – maybe for Christmas or for holidays in the summer. Or both. But then I think of Caroline and Dana, they'd murder me if I told Sarah. I hold my tongue. "I have an idea," I say instead. "Why don't you ring in sick today?"

"Ring in sick?" She doesn't look like she thinks this is such a great idea – at all. In fact she seems annoyed, very annoyed. It seems I can't say anything right. "You think I can ring in sick just like that?"

"Ah yeah," I say, a little uncertainly.

"It's not quite as easy as that, Rosie. I have to go into work. I depend on that job and, besides, they put up with me taking enough days off as it is for emergencies."

"But one more day? You can tell them your sister is here."

"Rosie, I can't," she says in a tone that allows no argument. "You really should have told me you were coming ahead of time then I could have arranged something but it's too late now." She looks at me for a second, like she's weighing me up, like she has a lot more to say but whatever it is, she lets it go. "Look, you just mind Jack and I'll go in and make us something to eat."

"Knock-knock!" says Lachlan.

Here we go again. "Who's there?" I ask.

"Jester!"

"Jester who?"

"Jester minute I'm trying to find my keys!"

"Very funny."

"Knock-knock!"

But this time I don't answer. "Lachlan, can you just hang on a minute, I'm going to look for your mum."

"Ahhh!" he says, disappointed. "Will you listen to my jokes when you come back?"

"Sure I will."

I get up, and go back inside taking baby Jack with me. On the kitchen counter, I see a tray laid out with some sandwiches, some fresh fruit, and a jug of juice. But there's no sign of Sarah.

"Sarah!" I go out into the hallway. "Sarah!"

"Coming," I hear her call from behind a closed door.

"So there you are!" I say as she emerges from the bathroom. I notice her face looks a little puffy. Like she's been crying.

"Sarah? Are you okay?"

"Of course, I'm okay. What a question!" She manages a smile but I notice she's clutching a ball of tissue in one hand. She notices me noticing. "My hay fever is playing up. Now come on," she says brightly. "Lunch is ready. Let's eat."

Still feeling somewhat puzzled, I follow after her into the kitchen where she picks up the tray and heads back out into the garden.

"Kyle! Lachlan!" she suddenly shouts. "Clear this stuff off!" She nods towards some pencils and colouring books on the table. The boys look startled, as if they're not used to their mum barking orders at them like this. "Come on, boys! Now! I mean it!"

"Mum!" says Lachlan, "Why are you cross?"

"I'm sorry. I've just got a headache."

"Well, you shouldn't shout. It'll make it worse. Would a kiss make it better?"

"I think it would." Sarah smiles now and Lachlan comes over and gives her a hug and a kiss.

"Hey! Don't leave me out," says Kyle and he hurries over to her too and grabs her around the waist.

I pick up the pencils and other stuff and, still carrying the baby in one arm, I take them back into the kitchen.

Despite what Sarah may say, that nothing's the matter, our lunch is rather strained. Maybe it's just because Sarah is annoyed that I'm only here for such a short time and I didn't give her notice I was coming but my attempts to figure out if this is so, or if it's something else, are deflected by her falsely cheerful but stubbornly evasive answers. Mindful that the boys are listening, I don't press the issue. Our conversation moves on to other topics.

"So work is going well?" I ask.

"It's fine. I'm a ward sister now, did I tell you that? Lachlan, come on. Have another bite. You're not eating anything!"

"It must be hard to juggle everything."

"Oh you know, I manage, I have to. And Lily's a great help. I can always call on her. Kyle, how many times do I have to tell you to stay in your seat?"

"Is Rod still away a lot?" Rod is a rep for a big company that manufactures Australian souvenirs in China and sells them to tourist outlets around the whole of Victoria and New South Wales.

"Yes, he is. Kyle, can you pick up Jack's soother, please, and give it a rinse under the tap?"

But before he gets a chance to do so, there comes a jolly-sounding voice from inside the house. "Hello, it's only me!"

"Hurrah! Lily!"

The two boys jump down from the table and run inside. Seconds later, they come back out, dragging a bemused woman by both her arms. She's not, I see, unlike our own mother, same age, same hair – blonde, short, fluffy – but she's a great deal even more rotund which makes her seem more grandmotherly. And whereas my mother favours leisure suits in pinks and lavenders, Lily is dressed in more traditional grandmother attire: flat shoes, flowery skirt, pink blouse. She smiles when she sees me, her fat cheeks showing crater-like dimples.

"So you're the Auntie Rosie they're so keen for me to meet!" she says in a strong Aussie accent.

"Hi," I walk over to shake her hand but suddenly she

grabs me and gives me a hug which takes me back somewhat, as well as winding me. She lets me go, but then holds me by both hands and studies me. "Yes, I can see the similarity all right. Your colouring may be different but you have the same heart-shaped face, and the wide mouth and those wonderful, wonderful eyes." She's beaming at me now. "How lovely, absolutely lovely, to meet you."

I'm a little overwhelmed by her reaction but I like her already. She's kindliness personified. All children – and adults even – could do with having someone like her in their lives.

"It's so marvellous to meet you. It's wonderful you're here. It'll be great for Sarah to have some help."

"Lily –" Sarah goes to interrupt.

But Lily doesn't hear. "What with Rod being away for weeks on end I sometimes wonder just how she copes between her job, and the boys, and the new baby. Not that she complains. But, like I tell her, no one is Superwoman, we all need some back-up from time-to-time."

"Actually, Lily, Rosie's not staying long. She's flying back again tomorrow."

"Tomorrow?"

I nod.

"You're not staying around?" Lily looks puzzled.

"No." Suddenly I feel kind of ashamed. "I'm on a business trip."

"Business? But I thought –" She looks to Sarah.

"Oh my God! Look at the time!" says Sarah, now glancing at her watch. "I'd better head to work. Come on, Rosie. I can give you a lift to the tram."

On the tram back into town, I think over the time I spent with Sarah and the boys. I am glad I visited her but it's a pity it was so short and even more that she was so disappointed it was so short. I wish it had gone better. I wish we had had more time to talk, really talk. Her earlier mention of that trip to Bettystown reminds me of just how good she was to me when I was little. She was great for taking me places, for organising trips – even taking me out of school on an occasional sunny day, without Mum or Dad knowing, of course. We had some great adventures together. She always had the knack of turning the simplest thing – a game, a walk in the woods, a visit to an old ruin – into something wonderful. I guess now she does the same for Kyle and Lachlan, lucky little boys. She was always bringing me to town too, buying me stuff, and letting me tag along when she met her friends – she, and they, never seemed to mind a watchful little girl sitting quietly in their midst, sipping Coke, and listening to their teenage talk of boys and music and clothes, happy for a glimpse into their mysterious and exciting world. Some – most – of my best early memories are of times spent with Sarah.

I really missed her when she went away, and in the years since. I could have done with her nearby when I was in college, struggling with my course, or when our shop went belly-up. Though we talk on the phone the difference in our lives and the physical distance between us means we're just not as close as we could be, as we once were.

I think of Lily's assumption – that I'd flown here to help Sarah when it hadn't even occurred to me that she might need my help. Why didn't I know that? Why didn't she tell me? We really have grown too far apart. The first thing I'm going to do, I decide, when I get the money is book a flight back and spend some real time with them all. Or maybe I'll book a holiday to Ireland for all of them first. Or I could do both. But if Caroline and Dana really are intent on keeping our win a secret then I'd have to figure a way of doing these things without arousing suspicion. But my experience of lying to Sarah today makes me even less certain that we're doing the right thing. I think we all need to have another talk.

"£5 million lotto winner goes from millionaire to the dole in just three years." Newspaper headline.

Peter Kyle – £5 million – UK

That's what happens when you spend at the rate of £4,600 a day.

8

I look out the window and see Melbourne far, far below, a sprawling collection of streets, factories, shops, parks, swimming pools, hospitals, schools, offices and houses one of which is Sarah's. Somewhere in the middle of all this is Sarah and her family, getting on with their lives, putting down roots. For the first time ever, it strikes me that if, when, I have children they'll grow up hardly knowing Lachlan, Kyle and Jack.

Suddenly I feel a twinge of loneliness such as I haven't felt in years, not since Sarah first went away. Why did she have to fall for Rod? Why couldn't she have come home after her year out like most people? Why couldn't she have settled down around the corner with some boy with whom she went to school?

"Are you all right, Rosie?" Dana is peering at me with concern.

"Yeah, sure."

"You're looking very serious."

"I was just thinking about Sarah and how it's such a pity she lives so far away."

"At least now you can afford to go and see her whenever you want."

"True."

Dana's concern allayed, she now leans across me. Unfortunately, when boarding the plane, I drew the short straw and I'm stuck in the middle between her and Caroline.

"Caroline?" says Dana.

"Yes?" Caroline looks up from the in-flight magazine she's flicking through.

"Remember, before the lotto and all of this, you sent us an email from Oz telling us you had a great idea for a business?"

"Oh that!" Caroline laughs. "Yeah?"

"What was 'that'?"

"A detective agency."

"A detective agency! Were you having a laugh?"

"No, I wasn't," says Caroline miffed. "It's not such an outrageous idea."

"Whatever put that into your head?"

"Well, when we were staying with friends of Mick's up in Queensland, one of them happened to work in a detective agency and she told me all about it. She said that the private detective business has never been so big and that their workload comes from a bottomless well of clients – the unfaithful. Women, in her opinion, make the better detectives. They're naturally more curious and observant."

I smile. "What did Mick think of the idea?"

"Oh, you know Mick. Completely sceptical of course. But I'd expect that. Remember he was like that with our shop too, thought it would never work."

"But it didn't," I point out.

"But it *could* have. It *was* a good idea. We were unlucky. But you know, now that we have our own money – real money – behind us we could set it up again, if we wanted."

"*If* we wanted. But we don't." I look at her, suddenly concerned. "You don't, do you?"

"No, no, I don't," Caroline answers most definitely, as if she's already given the matter considerable thought.

"Anyway, we don't need a business now we have all this money," Dana chimes in.

"You think?" asks Caroline.

"Ah yeah?" She looks at Caroline, somewhat warily.

"I wouldn't say that."

"Dana," I say, "push back a little, will you? You're crowding me out."

"Sorry." She does sit back, but not for long. "What do you mean, Caroline – that you wouldn't say that?"

"It is true we do have a lot of money but unless we do something productive with it we could see it dwindle away. Remember, ninety per cent go through the lot in five years."

"I still find that hard to believe."

"I swear, Rosie, it's true!"

"So are you thinking of some other kind of business?" asks Dana.

Caroline shrugs.

"You are, aren't you?"

"Well, now that we have that all-important thing – capital – we can consider a lot more options. What attracted me to the idea of a detective agency was the fact it would be cheap to set up. But, then, the downside is, we'd have to work so hard to make it a profitable concern, like we had the shop. But everything's different now that we have so much money. We can afford to make *it* do the work for us instead."

"What are you thinking of, exactly?" asks Dana guardedly.

"Nothing exactly. I'm just thinking generally."

Dana looks worried. "Caroline, all I want from this win is to help out family and friends as best I can and without them knowing, to keep a roof over my head, to live a secure uncomplicated life, to finish off my counselling course and, then, to work as a counsellor. This money is going to make me financially secure. Nothing else will change in my life. I don't want it to. You can do what you want with your third but leave mine alone. Don't think for a moment I'm going to let you risk my share in some scheme of yours."

"Dana!" laughs Caroline. "Don't be such a worrier. As if I would!"

"Caroline, I know what you're like! You can be very persuasive."

It's like water off a duck's back. Caroline carries on regardless. "Look, as a matter of fact, what I was actually thinking we should do is just leave the bulk of the money in the bank for now. The one bit of advice we've come across again and again in those print-outs is to do nothing with the money to begin with. I was thinking that putting it in a deposit account, a joint deposit account, might be the most sensible option for the moment. It would act as a safeguard against any one of us going crazy. You see, to withdraw it, we'd have to give a certain period of notice before being able to do so *and* we'd have to have all three signatures. What do you think?"

"Maybe," says Dana.

I nod tentatively. "It's an idea."

Caroline goes on: "We could also set aside a sum in three

individual current accounts which we'd each have immediate access to. Not a huge sum. Just pin money if you like. Say, fifteen, twenty thousand?"

"You call twenty thousand pin money?" I laugh.

"In the overall context, yes."

"That's twenty thousand more than I have in the bank now."

"Twenty thousand more than I've ever had," adds Dana.

It's odd but eleven million is such a ridiculously large amount that it's kind of hard, impossible even, to get used to, to actually believe in – strange as that may seem. But a figure like twenty grand – well, now, that's easier to grasp and easier to begin thinking how to spend. It's much more real. Suddenly I remember a pair of shoes I tried on in an up-market shoe shop in Dublin last weekend. When I learned that they were priced at €255 I quickly took them off again, gave them back to the assistant, and told her I didn't like them that much after all. But she knew, she *knew* I couldn't afford them. Now, I could walk in and buy them, just like that.

In fact, I will. They're the first thing I'm going to buy.

Twenty-two weary hours later. Heathrow. Terminal One. Seating area for Gates 82-87. That little bit of England forever Ireland. Where the overriding accent is Irish. Where *The Irish Times* and *The Star* are read. Where travellers dream of soon having a decent pint of Murphy's or Guinness, or a nice cup of Barry's tea. Where the country's diaspora await to board the plane to take them on the final leg of their journey, back home again from wherever they were so recently far flung.

We too are waiting to board the plane that will take us

on the last leg of our journey. We've been here for hours now with hardly a bean between us. There is something incredibly bizarre about our contradictory state of being millionaires with barely enough readies to buy a packet of crisps from the vending machine.

"We should remember what this is like," says Dana, anxious as always to learn a life lesson from it.

In less than eighty-four hours we have traversed the world twice. I am exhausted. And hungry. And bored out of my mind. Idly I pick up a paper lying abandoned on the seat opposite and there it is, in big letters: '€ 11 million Lotto Win Still Unclaimed!' Suddenly, all boredom, all exhaustion has disappeared and I'm so excited again at the thought of what lies ahead.

I think of all the changes of the past few years. Going through college. Graduating with a science degree – even if it took longer than the prescribed time. Of the year I spent working in the boutique with Fay and Monica. Of setting up the shop with Caroline and Dana. Of that failing. Of finally finding work as a lab technician – a 'proper' job, as Mum says, and by that she means one in which I'm using finally my degree. But I will chuck it in.

So many changes gone past. And more to come – good ones. The lotto has blown my future wide open.

Suddenly I feel Dana nudging me.

"Come on. They've called our flight."

Soon we'll be home again. Soon we'll be collecting our money. And soon I'll be seeing Finn. I can't wait.

"Everybody wanted my money. Everybody had their hand out. I never learned one simple word in the English language – 'No'."

Evelyn Adams – $2.4m – US

A statistical freak

Evelyn Adams – $3m – US

Even second time around, she didn't learn her lesson. Today, all her money is gone – lost on the slots or given away to friends and relatives.

9

"Okay what's going on?" Shane asks, glancing around the breakfast table at each of us.

"What do you mean?" Caroline asks.

"I'm not sure," says Shane uncertainly, his eyes squinting in suspicion. "But there's something strange in the atmosphere. You all seem so – I don't know – giddy."

"Giddy?" laughs Dana.

"Yeah. And, anyway, why are you all up so early?"

"Probably still suffering from jet-lag," I say.

"Jet-lag? You don't get jet-lag flying back from London, Rosie."

Oops, I forgot my lie. "I was talking about Caroline."

"Hmmm." He goes back to his paper but, then, he looks up again.

"Rosie, you're humming."

"So?"

"In all the time I've known you, I don't believe I've ever heard you humming on a workday."

Ah yes – workday it may be, but I'm not going to work today. Tomorrow, yes, to hand in my notice and begin working it out, Caroline insists, lest any of my colleagues become suspicious. But today? Today as far as work is concerned, I'm still sick. Today we have other plans – like picking up a cheque for eleven million euros. *Not* that I say any of this to Shane.

"And you, Caroline," he goes on, "you definitely shouldn't be this chirpy. How come you're not suffering from post-holidays blues – they're traditional. Particularly when you had to cut it short." A question occurs to him. "Why did you have to cut it short, you never actually said."

"Pardon?"

"Why did you come home early?"

"Why did I come home early?"

"Yes?"

"Ahmm – my mother's sister," says Caroline vaguely.

'Right." Shane nods, but then thinks to ask: "What about her?"

"She's not well."

"What's the matter with her?"

"She's sick."

"I understood that when you said she's not well but what's wrong with her?"

"She has – ah – heart problems."

He waits for her to expand but she doesn't.

"Is it serious?"

"They're doing tests."

"What kind?"

"My mother didn't say exactly. The usual I expect."

"Is she old?"

"My mother?"

"No, your aunt."

"Late fifties."

"What hospital is she in?"

"Vincent's."

"Do you want me to get Loretta to look in on her?" Loretta is Shane's girlfriend. She works as a junior doctor, in Vincent's as (bad) luck would have it. Caroline should have thought to pick a different hospital.

"No, no, my aunt is the retiring type. She'd hate the attention."

'I guess you don't take after her so."

Now Dana interrupts. "Shane, shouldn't you be gone to work by now? I thought you young lawyers liked to be at your desks so early that your bosses got the impression you never went home."

Shane looks at his watch. "I guess I should be going. Does anyone want a lift?"

We all shake our heads.

He gets up, takes his jacket from the back of the chair, puts it on, goes to the hall, comes back with his coat, puts that on, then takes his time as he does up each button, still eyeing us all up charily. He looks around for his car keys, then his briefcase. He notices we're all watching him.

"Why do I get the impression you can't wait to be rid of me? You know, you people are acting seriously strange."

"If anyone is acting strange, it's you," counters Dana sounding like some kid in a playground.

"No, no. It's definitely you three."

The second the front door bangs, madness unfolds. Immediately I turn the radio that's been playing in the background up to full volume and the room fills with the fabulous sound of Frank Sinatra blasting out, "New York! New York!" I holler out the bits I know, as does Dana who has begun rapping out the tune with two cereal spoons on the table on top of which Caroline has now climbed and is acting out and bellowing out Frank's words with all the drama of a glittering diva on a Las Vegas stage before a glitzy audience of thousands. And not just us two in our dressing-gowns.

". . . *spreading the news* . . ."

". . . *leaving today* . . ."

". . . *wake up in* . . ."

"*Ne-ewww Yooorkkkkkkkkkkkkkkk!*"

Suddenly the radio goes silent.

I spin around.

"Shane! You're back!"

"I forgot my phone." He's looking at Caroline who's frozen in position on the table, feet wide apart, arms outstretched. Does she think that if she remains completely motionless he just might not notice her?

"I take it you and your aunt aren't terribly close then?"

"Not terribly, no."

"Okay. What's really going on?"

"Nothing."

"We're just glad to have Caroline back, that's all," says Dana.

Caroline climbs down from the table, then turns to Shane and asks:

"Before you go, you wouldn't have a loan of fifty euros?"

"Why can't you ask either of them?" he nods in our direction.

"I don't have a penny."

"Me neither," says Dana.

Shane sighs. "Honestly, you're hopeless." But he obliges and pulls out his wallet, takes out a fifty and hands it to Caroline. "I'll be wanting it back."

"Sure." Then she glances over at us and smirks. "When I win the lotto."

From the corner of my eye, I see Dana's jaw drop but Shane doesn't notice.

"I'll be waiting so. And don't even dare think of spending any of it on a ticket. All the lotto is, is a tax on –"

"– on bloody morons," finishes Caroline and she bursts out laughing

Shane shakes his head. Then, without another word, he leaves for a second time.

Dana turns on Caroline. "How could you have said that to him!"

"Oh come on, it was funny. He doesn't have a clue. Even if we came right out and told him we'd won the lotto he'd still think we were joking! Did you hear him, 'All the lotto is, is a tax on bloody morons!' If only he knew. But at least now we can afford to get a taxi. Come on you two, go and get dressed. We have a job to do."

An hour later the taxi arrives.

"Going in to do a bit of shopping are you, girls?" The driver asks as soon as we're settled, the other two in the back, me up front.

"That's right," answers Caroline "A browse around the shops, then coffee somewhere nice, somewhere new maybe."

"And why not? We all need to take time out every once in a while. Keeps the batteries charged."

A philosophical taxi-driver then.

"You know, I heard this fella on the radio the other day –"

Who listens to the radio.

"– and he was saying the prices we pay in Ireland for a lot of our everyday groceries and the like are about twenty per cent more than what they pay in Britain, even when you take into account the conversion rates."

Who has a keen interest in current affairs.

"I swear we're being ripped off by those bloody supermarkets and high street chains."

And strongly held views. What are the chances? In Dublin? Are people of a certain disposition attracted to the profession, or do they become like that with the years?

"It's the parents I blame. They're too indulgent these days what with buying . . ." he's moved on, unlike the traffic which is crawling along, inch by inch. It takes a long hour to reach the city centre by which time we're pretty well informed with regard to the taxi-driver's opinions on more or less everything.

"Where will I drop you?" he asks, turning into Abbey Street as per our directions.

"By the theatre," Caroline calls from the back

"Would you not be better off heading to Jervis Street or Grafton Street if you're in to do some shopping?"

"No, here's fine for now," Caroline tells him.

He pulls up and she pays him the fare.

"Enjoy your morning," he calls as we're getting out.

"Oh, we will," says Caroline. "We most certainly will. You never know what we might pick up!"

Caroline gets out and immediately begins walking ahead but Dana calls after her. "Hang on for us!" She hurries up to her. "You don't want the taxi-driver to see where we're going."

"What? He's not going to notice."

"Taxi-drivers notice everything. They're worse than the gardaí. And they're the eyes and ears of the press too – that fellow would have a dozen reporters down here, just like that, if he got an inkling. And why did you have to say that, about not knowing what we might pick up?"

Caroline looks at her. "Gee, Dana. Enough with the paranoia."

But we wait until the taxi is out of sight and only then do we begin walking down the street.

"Just look natural," hisses Dana.

Caroline gives her another look but doesn't say anything.

"Are you sure we shouldn't have phoned ahead first," I ask, "to let them know we were coming?"

"No, they'd only have the press waiting," answers Caroline.

"And you think they're going to hand over the money to us this morning, just like that?" I ask.

Caroline nods. "Of course it's ours. They'll give us a cheque, I expect."

"I hope it's not one of those big cardboard ones," Dana jokes. At least I think she's joking.

We come to a stop outside the National Lottery Headquarters. Suddenly I feel so nervous I think I'm going to throw up.

"Okay, this is it!" says Dana quietly. "This is it." She reaches out, takes my hand and squeezes it. I squeeze back.

Caroline doesn't appear to share our nerves. She goes in first and we follow after her. Then we stand for a moment, getting our bearings. I wonder if there's a toilet nearby – I really do feel nauseous. I notice a woman with sleek hair and a well-cut cream suit sitting behind the reception desk and see that Caroline's already on her way over to her.

"Excuse me," she says. "Where do we go to claim a prize?"

"Usually your local post office," the woman answers

politely but uninterestedly as she goes through some papers on the desk in front of her.

"What about the jackpot?"

The woman's head jerks up so suddenly I fear she'll have pulled a muscle.

"The eleven million euro jackpot," clarifies Caroline.

"Oh!" The woman picks up the phone. "Just hold on a moment." She presses some numbers, outlines the situation to someone she calls Mr Dunne, then puts the phone back down. Almost immediately, a gentleman — Mr Dunne I presume — emerges from the lift. He's in his mid-thirties I'd guess, and is dressed in a dark suit, crisp white shirt, and red tie. He's handsome enough to notice that he is handsome.

"Ladies!" he says coming towards us. His well-polished shoes sound loud on the marble floor. "I'm Mr Dunne. I hear you may have had some good luck recently?"

"Yes, we have." Caroline holds the ticket out to him.

He takes it, looks at it, turns it over and reads where we've written our three signatures. "Dana Vaughan, Rosie Kiely and Caroline Connolly." He looks up from the ticket and to us again. "I take it that's you three." He's smiling. He has very white teeth.

All of us nod.

"Congratulations."

I wonder if his smile is genuine. I wonder what it must be like for him, for all the people who work here to — week after week — meet people who are suddenly made rich beyond their wildest dreams. Are they jealous? Are their congratulations sincere? Do they buy a lotto ticket on the way home?

"And you have photo identification with you?" he asks.

"Yes," answers Caroline. At her behest, we've brought every piece of identification we could unearth.

And then the whirlwind starts. We're ushered into a lift, up to another floor, out of the lift and into a long, bright room. Some people start arriving in. We meet the chief executive and several others whose titles and names we don't catch. The room is filling up, men in dark suits with an intermittent splash of colour provided by a smattering of female executives. Champagne and glasses appear. Soon there's an odd party-like atmosphere in the room filled with us three and these strangers who seem genuinely pleased at our good fortune. Several times we're asked are we sure we don't want to go public. Each time we answer we're sure. Then we're taken into another room to receive financial advice from a very earnest-looking man who seems impressed when he learns we've already downloaded their information from their internet site.

"So, what are you young ladies going to do now?" he asks.

Caroline answers: "We've going to lodge the bulk of the cheque in a joint deposit account for the moment and smaller sums in three separate current accounts while we have a further think about how exactly we're going to use the money."

He nods and seems to approve.

When we go to leave, the lotto boss is insistent that he should accompany us to the bank which is just around the corner on O'Connell's Street but Caroline is having none of it. I'm guessing she's worried that we'll be spotted with him and our attempts at absolute secrecy will come to nothing. She does, however, agree to his suggestion that he ring ahead to the manager of the bank to tell her we're on our way but only after he assures us of her absolute discretion.

As soon as we set foot in the bank, the manager discreetly approaches; I guess she was on the lookout for us. She's a stout woman in her fifties with short dark hair, dressed in a black suit feminised by her surprisingly shapely legs which are shown off to good effect by the length of her skirt and her high-heel shoes.

"Congratulations," she says softly. "Please, come with me."

She leads us into an office which is disappointingly drab and cramped and impersonal. I think if I'd worked so hard to become manager of such a big branch, I'd expect something a little more plush.

She closes the door, then turns to us.

"Now we have a little privacy." She's beaming at us but I get the feeling she's sizing us up. "So, let me introduce myself. My name is Breda Hayes, I'm the branch manager and I'm also an investment consultant."

Caroline goes next. "I'm Caroline Connolly, lotto winner." She says this in a jokey manner and Breda Hayes smiles back but I get the feeling it's not a genuine smile, that she's just being professionally accommodating.

Then in turn, Dana and I give our names and Breda Hayes shakes hands with each of us as we do so.

"These are exciting times for you, aren't they? Well, first off, can I thank you for choosing our bank today. Now, please, take a seat – I'm sure all the excitement must be tiring."

We sit down on the three chairs set out in front of her desk and she sits on the bigger one behind.

"Would you like tea? Coffee?"

All of us answer in the negative.

"Champagne, perhaps?"

Caroline laughs. "I think the glass we had at the lotto offices is enough for now."

Now Caroline takes the cheque from the inside pocket of her jacket and hands it to the manager who studies it, then looks up.

"So have you any thoughts as to what you might do with it?"

Again, it's Caroline who answers. "For the moment we'd like to lodge the bulk of the money in a joint deposit account."

"Okay."

"Until we decide what we're going to do with it."

"Okay. You know a deposit account will require notice to make withdrawals and any such withdrawals will require all three signatures."

"That's what we want, as a safeguard, to prevent any of us running off with the whole amount," Caroline laughs.

Again, Breda Hayes smiles politely but doesn't laugh. I guess when you're in banking, money is a serious business.

"You've been friends for a long time?" she enquires.

"Yes, years and years. Dana and I went to school together, and we met Rosie when she moved in with us at the start of college."

Breda nods at this piece of information. Or should I call her Ms Hayes? I can't imagine anyone, not even her husband daring to call her Breda. 'My darling Ms Hayes, won't you come to bed?'

"And all three of you are agreed on a joint account?" She's looking at me.

"Sorry, what's that?"

"All three of you are agreed on a joint account?"

"Yes, I think it's a good idea."

Now she looks to Caroline. Caroline nods, then adds: "But we'd also like to set up individual current accounts too with – we were thinking – twenty grand in each, for the moment."

"Right." She looks thoughtful. "Can I ask where you're living at present?"

"We rent a house – together."

"Have any of you thought of buying? In some ways it's not a bad time to get on the property ladder, especially for cash buyers. There's huge choice right now and good value to be had too if you buy wisely."

"We may, but down the line."

"I take it that none of you is married?"

She's looking at Caroline but she doesn't seem to hear the question so I tell her we're not.

She laughs "It'll be the lucky man who'll get any of you wealthy young women."

"Well, we are all seeing someone," Dana tells her.

"I bet they were excited at the news."

There's a moment's pause, then Dana answers: "We've decided not to tell anyone."

"For now, at any rate," I add.

"Hmm." Ms Hayes considers this. "Perhaps you're wise. It's hard to know. Personally I don't know that I'd be able to keep it a secret." Then she shrugs. "But everyone is different. Okay, well, let's start setting up these accounts then."

And for the next hour, we're kept busy, filling in a myriad of forms.

With the cheque now safely lodged and our accounts finally set up, we come back out on to the street.

"I'm starving." says Dana. "Is it lunch-time yet?"

"Nearly," answers Caroline. "While you two were getting dressed this morning, I booked a table at Chapter One for twelve thirty. I thought it might be a nice way of celebrating."

"Good thinking," I say.

"Chapter One?" says Dana. "Isn't that very expensive?"

"It is. That's why I booked it."

"It's nearly twelve thirty now," notes Dana. "We should go straight there."

"Will we get a taxi?" I ask.

"Rosie!" Dana cries. "It's a five-minute walk!"

"Yeah, but we can afford to get a taxi."

"So? Just because you can afford to, does that mean you're never going to walk again?"

"Yep, from now on the only shoes I'm going to buy are taxi shoes," I joke. "Speaking of which, do you mind if I nip into *Schoos* first? It's just around the corner? There's a gorgeous pair there that I've had my eye on."

Caroline laughs. "Start as you mean to go on!"

I'm not the only one who's tempted by the expensive footwear, even Dana is, and each of us leaves *Schoos* with bags in hand and then, at Dana's insistence, we walk to the restaurant.

Now, we're sitting at our table in the subterranean, understated opulence of one of Dublin's finest restaurants – Chapter One – so called I presume because it's located in the basement of the building adjoining the Irish Writers' Centre on Parnell Square.

"I suppose you've been here before?" I ask Caroline.

"A couple of times."

Before we set up our shop, Caroline's job in marketing meant she regularly dined out with corporate clients.

"It *is* very expensive," says Dana, studying the menu. She and I have led rather less grand existences.

"Dana!" Caroline laughs. "It doesn't matter! Not today of all days!"

"They say Gerry Ryan from the radio eats here all the time." Dana looks around as if she expects to see him here at this very moment, tucking into quail or some such. "And U2."

This may be so but neither he, nor they, nor many other people famous or otherwise, are here today and, when I comment on just how quiet it is, Caroline's reply is that yes it is, surprisingly so, but that it suits us better this way. This way, she says, we can discuss matters without anyone eavesdropping.

"Matters?"

"Money matters."

"But I thought this was a celebratory lunch?"

"And it is, but no harm in discussing things as well."

"I thought we were going to wait for a while before doing anything."

"Yes, but we do need to start thinking about what we are going to do."

"You don't waste time, do you?"

And she doesn't. As soon as we've ordered our meal it's straight down to business.

"Okay then. First off, are we going to try to buy our house from my brother? I think we should. None of us are in any hurry to move out. We all get on very well."

"I'm in," says Dana. "I think it's a great idea."

Caroline looks to me.

I hesitate. I do think it's a good idea but . . .

"But what about Shane?" I ask.

"What about him?" asks Caroline.

"We'd be his landladies – wouldn't he have the right to know that? In fact, how could we go on charging him rent? It would be downright mean."

Caroline shakes her head. "Of course we'd have to keep on charging him rent. We don't want to arouse his suspicions. If we've decided to keep our win a secret then that's exactly what we have to do, keep it a secret."

I'm glad she's brought this up.

"Have we, though? Have we decided?" I ask her now.

"Okay," says Caroline, "we need to settle this once and for all. Are we, or are we not, keeping our win a secret?

I tell her how hard I found it to lie to Sarah.

"And you'll find it harder to say no to her when she phones to tell you her husband has always dreamed of owning some forty-foot yacht."

"Sarah wouldn't do that."

But Caroline goes on. "I vote that we do keep it a secret for all the reasons we discussed. My dad. Dana's mother. But most of all control – *we* can decide who we want to help and not be in a position where we have friends and family, and strangers too, coming to us with their hands out. "

"I second that," nods Dana emphatically.

Now both of them look to me. "Oh, I don't know."

"What are your brothers in America called?" Caroline suddenly asks.

Though puzzled by the question, I answer. "William and Con."

"Okay, so we tell everyone, right? Then William rings out of the blue and asks you for a couple of hundred grand for some business idea he has which sounds wacky to you though he claims it's rock solid. What do you do? Say yes, and risk losing your money? Say no, and risk losing your brother? Or Con rings you. It's his daughter, you see, she's a gifted musician, but she needs to go to this special school to fulfil her incredible potential. But the problem is, she needs a hundred thousand. How can you say no? People do not like hearing the word 'no'. You say no and that changes everything in a relationship."

By picking William and Con she's made her point better than she could imagine. They are the two people close to me who I could imagine demanding money and being infuriated if I dared refuse.

"Well?" Caroline is looking at me.

As is Dana.

I shrug. "I guess. We keep it secret."

"Okay then, that's settled." Caroline moves on swiftly. "Apart from buying the house, I think we really need to decide what we want this money to do for us, to decide how we're going to use it to get what we want in our lives. Let's start with you, Dana, what do you want from it?"

"Apart from buying No 40 together?"

"Yeah."

Dana thinks for a moment. "Well, I guess I might get a car. At some point. I suppose I should. But I'll have to learn to drive first."

We wait for her to go on but she doesn't.

"And?" prompts Caroline.

"And what?"

"And what else?"

Dana thinks for a moment.

"For now, nothing else. The big thing I want is security. The money itself, us buying No 40 together, will give me that. That's all I want really. Maybe down the line I'd like to move in with Doug but, for now, that's it. Like I told you, I'm happy to go on living the life I have. I like it. I'm just looking forward to working as a counsellor once I've finished studying – the money doesn't change that."

There's a moment's silence.

"That's it?" asks Caroline.

"Yes."

"Really?"

Dana shrugs. "For myself, for now, yes. But I would like to financially help others too. Doug, for one – though I haven't decided exactly how yet. My mum and dad too but I'm not sure what I can do for them. They've had their problems but money's never been one of them; they've paid off their mortgage years ago. I'm just happy they're back together again." She thinks for a moment. "I guess I would like to see my mum a little happier in herself, more fulfilled, but I don't see how money can achieve that."

Caroline is looking at Dana like she still expects more but, when she finally accepts that there really is no more coming, she turns her attention to me.

"Okay, what about you, Rosie?"

"I'd like to buy our own house too but, some time in the not-too-distant future, I'd like to buy a place where Finn and I would live. I was thinking of a penthouse in the city centre, overlooking the river, with a big, south-facing balcony. Maybe even a rooftop terrace too where we'd have these fabulous parties in the summertime." I smile as I picture the scene. Finn, me – late in the evening, after the last of our party guests have gone home. The pair of us snuggled up together on a lounger, his arms wrapped around me, as we lie there contently, looking out from our terrace over the city lights.

"But you're still planning to give up work?" I hear Caroline asking.

I nod. "You know I am."

"Don't you think you'll need something to fill your days?

Don't you think people will start to wonder how you're getting by? Where will Finn think the money came to buy your luxurious penthouse?"

"I'm not saying I'll never work again. But now I can afford to take time out, to consider my options."

"And what options are you considering?"

I shrug. I haven't really given it much thought.

But Caroline is persistent. "Have you any ideas at all of what you might like to do?"

"Not right now, no, but, like I say, I have time to think."

"And what else do you want from the money?"

"Well, like Dana I'd like to help out Finn and other friends and family too. For starters, I was thinking I could arrange to pay for Sarah and her family to come home on holiday but if we're not allowed to tell anyone –"

"Not allowed? You're a grown-up, Rosie. It's a joint decision. But if one of us opts not to keep our win a secret then none of us can. It just wouldn't work."

"Okay, okay. What I guess I mean then is, if we've made a decision not to tell anyone I just don't know how I can do this for Sarah – fly her and her family home – without her knowing it's me who's paying."

"Rosie, Rosie, Rosie." Caroline shakes her head. "That's just a small little detail. We can figure a way, there's always a way – don't worry. So, come on, anything else? Have you any other ideas?"

"Well, as it happens I do have one other idea that I've been playing around with."

"Go on."

I hesitate. It's something I've been thinking about a lot. It's something I do want to do. It's an odd idea in a way but one I can't get away from.

"Well, back in Melbourne, I read something in one of your print-outs that really struck me – about how you should spend some, save some and share some. Well, I want to share some with Seán."

"Seán?"

"Homeless Seán."

The girls nod. I see they know who I mean. Seán's a young homeless guy I'm friends with. Actually, I'm not sure if friends is the right word but he is someone I'm very fond of even if I haven't seen him in a while. I first met Seán over a year ago when he was seventeen, just a kid really, and got to know him when he was sleeping rough in a door opposite Elegance, the boutique I worked in before it closed and we opened our own shop in the same premises, as it happened. But I lost contact with him around that time until, a few months ago, he turned up again. Deciding the city was too dangerous, with so many other homeless people dependent on drink and drugs, he squatted for a while in an old youth hostel down by the sea, owned by Caroline's brother, Donald. Donald bought it with the intention of turning it into a luxury hotel. That's where our paths crossed for a second time. I don't know where Seán is now though I'm always expecting to run into him again around the place.

I go on. "You see, back in Melbourne, in that hostel, I thought about Seán a lot. I guess it was because of where we were staying. I kept comparing our good luck to Seán's bad luck and the bad luck of others like him and, now that I'm in a position to, I want to help him. I can't help everyone in the world who needs it but I might be able to help one – him."

How Seán came to be homeless really is a bad luck story.

Not long before I first met him, his girlfriend Hilda was beaten up so badly by a couple of mindless thugs that she'll be in care for the rest of her life. Without Hilda to help, Seán just couldn't manage everything. If he worked, he couldn't mind his two little daughters. If he minded his daughters, he couldn't work. Without any income coming in, he lost his home and, worse, he lost his kids. He told me they were being minded by Hilda's mum but later I heard they'd been taken into foster care. Seán went off the rails around that time. I guess he just found it all too hard to cope with – he didn't seem to have anyone, any family, to turn to. His girlfriend, his daughters – his own little family were his whole life.

"So what exactly do you want to do for Seán?" Caroline is asking.

"I was thinking that if he had his own place then, maybe, he could get his children back. You see, he's in a vicious circle. Without an address he can't get a job, without a job he can't get a home, without a home he'll never get his children back. But if he had a place of his own, he could get things back on track again."

Caroline looks thoughtful. "Your heart may be in the right place but I'm not sure your head is."

"Excuse me?"

"Well, so far you want to buy a share in our current home – a four-bedroom semi in a good suburb, a share of which will cost you roughly a third of a million, since almost a million is roughly what they're going for these days. You also want to buy the kind of penthouse that in Dublin won't see you getting much change out of a couple of million. And you want to buy – say – a three-bedroom semi for Seán and even the cheapest of those is going to cost you another couple of hundred thousand. So that doesn't exactly leave you a lot to live on for the rest of your life. And remember you don't – or won't soon – have a job and you have no immediate plans to get another."

"Hmmm, when you put it like that."

As I'm mulling this over, I hear Dana ask Caroline what it is she wants to do with her money.

"Simple." She relaxes back in her seat. "I want to use it to make a lot more money."

"*More*?"

"Three and a half million each may seem like a fortune to us now but the annals of lotto history are littered with people who've overestimated how far their winnings will take them. Despite the very best of intentions, it's easy to slip into a different mindset. To start travelling first-class instead of economy. To take taxis everywhere which, by the way, Rosie seems to have already succumbed to. To eat and to stay in only the very best. Then a few dodgy investments. Plus a few gifts to those nearest and dearest – twenty thousand here, ten thousand there. On top of that, a house, a holiday house, throw in a couple of expensive cars, some exotic holidays and, suddenly, there's not that much change out of eleven million, divided by three. There's not even enough to live on. Already Rosie has spent most of hers. She's made the mistake of spending the capital rather than using it to create any sustainable income. So yes, I want to make more money *but* I'm not adverse to helping people out as well, people like Seán." She looks to each of us in turn. "So, here's the thing, I have a plan –"

Both Dana and I groan. We've been here before.

" – I have a plan that could combine the two *but* it would involve all three of us. You see, I think we should merge the bulk of our money and go into business together."

"You're joking!" I cry. "Are you suffering from memory loss? Don't you remember your last plan? Don't you remember how that plan to go into business together ended in failure? Or perhaps you thought that was a good experience?"

"A learning experience would be more accurate. We were unlucky. It *was* a good idea. We *did* have the makings of a viable business."

She's right. It could have worked but, the fact is, it didn't. And its failure was traumatic enough for us not to want to go through anything like it a second time. Back then we had little to lose except face. But now the stakes are a lot higher, eleven million euros higher.

"Look, don't dismiss the idea out of hand. Will you just listen to what I have to say first? Please?"

Since this is Caroline, we've learned from experience that we're unlikely to have much option and both of us sit back with a resigned sigh.

She begins:

"It's a fact that the more money one has to start with, the easier it is to make more money still, and that's why ours is better staying together."

"For what purpose exactly? What kind of business are you talking about?" I ask.

"I want us to go into property investment."

"Property investment?"

"Yes.

"The reality is that, even with current prices, I can't put much of a property portfolio together with just my share. But eleven million is a different story and here's what I suggest. We combine our money to buy property."

"But is now a good time?" asks Dana.

"For us, yes – particularly if we take the long-term view.

There's never been so much availability, so many people wanting to sell – we'd just need to choose well. That we'd be using our own money is significant. There aren't too many cash buyers around right now. And because we have cash, we won't be taking any risks we can't afford. Nor are we ever going to be under pressure to sell so we can ride with the market – resell only when it suits."

She pauses for a moment.

"So we buy property. With no mortgages on these properties, all the rent we take in will be – aside from tax and upkeep costs – profit. This provides us with a steady income to live on and, over time, further capital to invest in other properties so we can keep adding judiciously to our portfolio over the years. Property prices may go up and down but, in the longer term, it's a sound investment. Now we may need to talk to the banks, get advice, it might make better sense, tax-wise and in other respects, to retain some mortgages on these properties . . ."

I'm getting the general idea but I don't see how she thinks Seán fits into all this.

". . . but with our own capital to begin with we're never going to be at risk of losing more than we can aff–"

"But what about Seán?" I interrupt. "How's this going to help him? You said you could combine making more money with helping him. So far, all I'm hearing is how you intend making money."

"Okay, well, my stay in Melbourne did open my eyes too and I'm not blind either to the fact that while we've had tremendous luck others are dealt a pretty rotten hand in life. I'm quite happy with the notion of using our money to do some good as well. Spend some, share some, save some, it's not a bad maxim. But still I don't know that you – we –

should just hand over a house to anyone, even Seán. I think a better way would be to let him and his family live in one of the houses we buy, at least until he's on his feet again. During that time we forgo any rent but we would still benefit from capital appreciation over the longer term."

"But –" I go to interrupt but Caroline ploughs on unheedingly.

"If you, Rosie, just hand over a house to Seán then that's quite a percentage of your original capital gone. Remember ninety per cent of people run through their money in five years."

"So you keep saying."

"Only because it's true. And that ninety per cent aren't much different to us – just ordinary people who've been given an extraordinary opportunity they've failed to realise. I hear what you're saying, Dana, that you just want to go on living your life, you don't want things to change but – I'm sorry – I think you're being short-sighted."

"Pardon?"

"To give you your due, you're probably one of the ten per cent who won't blow the lot but I don't think you fully grasp what a big opportunity you're being given. Sure, you can just go on living life as you do now with the benefit of financial security *but* that doesn't have to be all you do. You can do good as well, without jeopardising your security. Wouldn't that appeal to you?"

"It would. It does. But –"

"Look, I've never made any secret that I've always wanted to be rich. So, yes, I am rich now through chance but still I want to achieve something, something with this money, turn it into more. Call it a game if you like, whatever, but it's just something I want to do. So yes, I want to amass a fortune, an even bigger fortune, but I think I – we – can combine that with Rosie's idea. So we buy a house and let Seán live in it rent-free. But we don't have to stop just there. You, Rosie, like Dana, aren't seeing the bigger picture either. There are lots of Seáns in the world and I think we can go even further than helping just him. And the way we do that is by reserving a proportion of the properties we buy for people who are in need of accommodation while we rent out the rest at market rates. As our portfolio grows, so too does the number of charity homes – for want of a better word. So, instead of you, Rosie, just helping one person, all three of us are helping Seán and others like him *while* seeing our money grow." She pauses for a breath. "I know all this is a lot to take in, but how does it sound to you two? What's your initial reaction?"

Often in the past, Caroline has used her powers to persuade me against my better judgement but, right now, I can find no fault with this plan. If we can buy houses and make money over the longer term and, at the same time do some good in the world then, what is there to say no to?

I nod. "I like it, Caroline. I really do."

So too, it seems, does Dana. "Maybe I was thinking too narrowly about myself though I have to say I never thought you, Caroline, would be the one to point that out to me."

"Thanks a bundle."

"You know what I mean. But, yeah, it sounds like a good plan to me."

"Great!" Caroline is beaming. "Now I think we *really* do deserve some champagne."

New Year's Eve, and not everyone is celebrating. One 22-year-old deli clerk has the misfortune to be stuck with the late shift.

Waleed Alsaidi – $10 million – US

So what does he do to pass the time and raise his spirits? He takes his chances and sells himself a scratch card. Not so misfortunate now.

10

Ever since our return last night and all during our exciting morning, I'd put off ringing Finn or answering the many calls from him. It seems like ages since I've seen him or even spoken to him but I've been reluctant to get in contact, worried as I was that he'd sense something was up from the sound of my voice or that I'd leave something slip. But, when we arrive home after our very long lunch, I can't hold out any longer and I finally make the call.

"Hi, Finn!"

"Rosie, you're back from London!"

It is *so* good to hear his voice. "Sure am. Did you miss me?"

"Like crazy."

"But not as much as I missed you."

"I wouldn't bet on it. So, go on, tell me, had you a good time?"

"You know, so-so."

"Did you get to see any of the sights?"

"Not really."

"Did you go to any of the galleries?"

Finn is crazy about art and as well as being a singer/songwriter/drummer he's also a very accomplished artist. He does fabulously colourful abstract paintings on a huge scale, several of which hang in the living-room of his own home. He only paints as a hobby but he could be a professional artist he's so talented, and I don't think I'm being biased when I say that.

"No," I answer now. "I didn't have time. It was all go."

"What about any shows?"

"Ah, no."

"Any museums?"

"No, no museums."

"You really didn't do much, did you?"

I laugh. "I wasn't on holiday, I was working."

"Where did you stay?"

"Near – ah – Knightsbridge."

"What was it called?"

"The hotel?"

"Yeah."

"The Something Inn." What's with the twenty questions? Is he always so inquisitive but I just don't notice, not having anything to hide?

"Were you not bored being all on your own?" Finn is still going on.

"I would have preferred if you'd been there but no, I had –" I'm about to say I had Dana and Caroline with me but I stop myself in time – "I had plenty to do, work-wise. So, tell me, how did you get on in – where were you again – Donegal?"

"Yeah. We got on brilliantly. Full houses every night."

"Fantastic!"

"You know what else we did while you were away? We put some of the songs down on CD, including some of our new stuff. Mitch's cousin did it for us. He's not a professional or anything but it's good to be able to listen to it, hear what others hear."

"And are you pleased?"

"I think so."

"Can I hear it?"

"Sure. Why don't we meet up later and I'll bring it with me?"

"Sounds great. What do you feel like doing?"

"How about going for a pizza? My treat."

Despite having gone out for lunch, I think by evening time I'll probably be able to manage a pizza. "Perfect."

"Why don't we meet at Pizza Place? Say, eight o'clock?"

It's not quite in the same league as Chapter One but it's one of Finn's favourite places. We go there all the time.

"Okay, see you there then."

When I come downstairs I find Dana sitting cross-legged on the rug in the living-room with Cathy, her baby sister, or half-sister I should say, playing beside her with some little plastic figures.

"Hello there, fellow lotto winner!"

"Ssh! Doug will hear you. He's in the kitchen making coffee."

"Oops!" I kneel down beside Cathy. "I didn't know you were minding Cathy this afternoon."

"I wasn't supposed to be but her mother called and asked me to."

"Hi, Cathy," I say. "What are you playing?"

But Cathy doesn't look up. She's too busy lining up all the little plastic figures in a row. I like to think I've a way with kids but for some reason Cathy has never really taken to me.

"Ah look, isn't that clever, the way she's making the people into a little queue."

Dana laughs. "I think in a previous life she must have lived in Russia. She's always getting them to queue. It's her favourite game."

At first, Dana, out of loyalty to her mum and anger at her father, didn't want to have anything to do with Cathy but in the last couple of months she's begun to see a lot of her. Dana says it suits Cathy's mum as she doesn't have any family living in Dublin. It's handy for her to have someone nearby that she can call on sometimes to collect Cathy from the crèche if she gets held up and Dana is usually out early enough from college to do so.

Cathy's a pretty little thing though, with a sweet little face, lovely dark-brown eyes, and masses of thick chestnut-coloured hair that would be the envy of any grown-up woman.

"You know," I say, looking from Cathy to Dana, "I think she looks like you."

"Yeah?" Dana looks pleased. "Dad thinks the same." Then she laughs. "Doug says all babies look like me."

He may have a point. There is something baby-like – or more accurately perhaps, doll-like about Dana's appearance – the flawless skin, the round face, the delicate features and, most of all, the disproportionately big, beguiling eyes. Dana, however, usually wears glasses and, when not tied up which it usually is, her chestnut-brown hair reaches right down to her waist.

"What does your mum think?"

"She's never seen Cathy."

"Never?"

"God no! She can just about tolerate me and Dad having

anything to do with her but she certainly doesn't want to see her herself, or even hear about her."

"Oh, hi, Rosie."

I turn to see Doug at the doorway holding a cup in each hand.

Dana first met Doug when I dragged her along to a party being given by his mum, Monica. She used to own the boutique where I worked until she decided to retire and then, subsequently, she rented the premises out to us for our shop. Dana never really had a boyfriend before Doug, she was always too caught up in studying to be bothered but I'll never forget the first time she and Doug set eyes on one another at that party. It was the weirdest thing. They just stood there, staring at one another, like they couldn't believe what they were looking at. I don't think I really believed in love-at-first-sight before but I swear that's what I was looking at that night.

When he's not smiling, Doug can look a little intimidating with his strong features and his intense dark eyes. But his smile is gentle, shy – awkward even, and this reflects his character far more accurately; he is gentle, and a little awkward and shy too, and perhaps not as confident as he should be.

"Hi, Doug."

There are splatters of paint in his dark hair and on his tanned face. Doug works as a painter.

"Hi Rosie, want a coffee?" he asks.

"Yeah," I stand up, "but I'll go and make it myself."

When I come back in, Doug is on the couch beside Dana, with Cathy sitting contentedly on his lap. I sit down on the armchair opposite. I take a sip from my cup.

"She really likes you, doesn't she?"

Doug smiles. "I think it's more my buttons than me. She has a thing about them."

Dana may have fallen in love with Doug at first sight but, back when they first met, I couldn't figure out what she saw in him. He didn't know us then and didn't smile much and, like I say, I did find him quite intimidating and, if I'm honest, a little rude. But – in time – I came to realise he is just shy, *excruciatingly* shy, around people he doesn't know. And I've come to learn that, just because he doesn't say much, it doesn't mean there's not a lot going on. There is, it's just not all on the surface. In his own quiet way, he's one of the funniest, kindest, most genuine people I know. Now I think Dana is lucky to have him – they're a good couple.

But yes, he is quiet, one of those rare people who never feels the need to talk just for the sake of it. I, on the other hand, am not one of those people. Silence is all very well, as long as it doesn't go on too long, so now I ask: "How's the painting and decorating going?"

Doug has never quite managed to find his niche in life but has drifted from one job to another. Most recently he's been doing a bit of painting here and there.

He shrugs. "Okay."

"But it's not as busy as it was, sure it's not, Doug?" adds Dana. "There's just not that much work around."

Doug shrugs again. "Something always turns up."

Here's another thing I didn't get at the start. I couldn't understand how Dana, with her degree in Psychology behind her and all her ambition and focus centred on becoming a counsellor now, could be attracted to someone who seems so – I'm trying to think of a nice way of putting this but the most accurate is probably, well – directionless? And I say this cognizant of the fact that I've never been the most focused individual in the world.

"Rosie?"

"Sorry? What were you saying?"

"I was just telling Doug he really needs to think about doing a course and getting some formal qualifications." Dana's focus even extends beyond herself.

"Like what?" I ask Doug

Doug goes to answer but Dana gets there first.

"You know Doug's very good with his hands?"

Doug interrupts. "Dana, about this furniture course, to be honest –"

Suddenly Cathy leaves out a scream and I see her hair has got caught in one of Doug's buttons.

"Oh, God!" cries Dana.

"Hush, Dana, you'll frighten her!" Doug turns his attention to the little girl. "Now, Cathy," he coaxes gently, "hold still."

With one hand he keeps her head pressed against his chest though she's struggling to pull away and, with the other, he begins trying to untangle the strands of hair but he's getting nowhere, working with just one hand. "Hush now, Cathy, hush now," he soothes. "It'll be okay."

"You're okay, Cathy. You're okay," murmurs Dana. She looks to Doug. "It's a mess. We're just making it worse. Should I get a scissors? I could just snip off the pieces that are caught."

"No need to be that drastic. We'll manage, won't we, Cathy? Look, Dana, try and unwind that bit there."

It takes a full five minutes but finally all the hair is untangled.

"Now, honey, all done," says Doug.

Dana goes to take Cathy onto her lap but she clings to Doug instead.

Dana laughs, "Seems you're flavour of the month." She glances at her watch. "It's time I took her home to her mum. She'll be in from work by now. She hates when I'm late. Come on, Cathy, love, let me put on your cardie. Let's go home to Mummy."

Again she reaches out to pick Cathy up but Cathy is reluctant to let go of Doug and, in the end, it's Doug who dresses her and puts her in the buggy.

When they're gone I flitter away the hours doing nothing much. I'm not sure where Caroline is but I wouldn't put it past her to be down in some estate agent's already, checking out what's on the market. When I hear Shane come in from work at six, I go down to the kitchen and there I find him about to start making dinner for himself.

"Oh hi!" He looks surprised to see me. "I didn't realise there was anyone in. You're home early."

Where I work is on the other side of the city and since it takes me two buses I'm never home this early on a workday.

I shrug. "In the end, I decided not to go in. They didn't mind, seeing as how I was in London." Lies and more lies.

"So it was *you* in town then?"

"You saw me in town?"

"I didn't but I met Loretta in town at lunch-time and she thought she saw you and Caroline and Dana going into some posh shoe shop but, by the time I turned to look, I'd missed you."

"No, it was us all right."

"What were you all doing in town together?"

"Nothing much. Just catching up."

"Dana didn't have college?"

"She gave it a miss."

"That's not like her. So you were all free today?"

I nod.

"Has Caroline thought any more about what she's going to do now she's back from Australia? I can't see her staying idle for long."

"We didn't really get into it."

"Knowing her, she has something lined up."

"Probably."

"Do you want me to put some dinner on for you?"

"No thanks, I'm going out to meet Finn."

"So did you buy those today?"

"Pardon?"

"The shoes?"

I look down. "Yes, I did. I'm just wearing them now to break them in."

"I like them."

"Thanks. Me too."

I do. But they are, however, higher and considerably less comfortable than what I'm used to despite the price, maybe because of the price – I guess comfort and practicality isn't of foremost importance when it comes to designing shoes like these, for the kinds of people who usually buy them.

"I'm not sure they go with the rest of the outfit!" Shane now laughs.

"No, I guess not!" The rest of my 'outfit' is an old jogging pants and sweater. "I'd better go and get changed."

I leave Shane in the kitchen and go upstairs. It's hard to figure out what to wear with these shoes. Nothing I have is really good enough and, after changing clothes half-a-dozen times, I settle for the first outfit I tried on – my best jeans and a dressy green top that picks up the green in the shoes. I look at myself critically in the mirror. Finn may say he doesn't care what I wear, that he loves me regardless but, even so, I think maybe it's time I invested in some new clothes.

By the time I'm ready to go and meet Finn somehow it's already seven forty. I realise I'll be late if I take the bus and, anyway, in these shoes I don't fancy walking to the stop. Instead, I go out onto the street and flag down a taxi. As luck would have it, I manage to get one immediately and I arrive outside Pizza Place five minutes before time.

As I'm climbing out of the taxi, I notice Finn strolling up the street, hands in his pockets. Though he doesn't see me yet I can't help but smile at the sight of him. Oh, how I love this man. I can't hear over the city traffic but he looks like he's whistling. I bet he's whistling. Finn's always whistling. It's just one of many little endearing things about him. I see he's wearing his usual: black velvet jacket, crisp white shirt, faded denims. That's another thing I like, the way he dresses. He's found a style that suits him and he sticks to it though there has been the odd daring sartorial aberration along the way. A pair of checked plimsolls comes to mind but sense quickly returned when the malign influence of his one-time housemate Lola waned and they were chucked on fashion-disaster scrapheap – never to be spoken of again. Except when I want to tease him. His hair is a little longer than usual right now but he can carry it off. Caroline says he has hair too lovely for a man; and it is lovely – thick and curly, black and shiny.

He sees me, gives a big smile, waves, and speeds up. When he reaches me, he immediately wraps his arms around me and begins to kiss me before I even get a chance to say hello. Hmmm. Bliss. He has lovely lips – another of the things I like. He smells nice and fresh too, like he's not long out of the shower. Hmmm, again. Suddenly I feel happy. Contented. I'm back where I belong.

We pull apart. He smiles at me. "I missed you." Then he stands back to look at me. "You look lovely." And then he notices them. "Hey! I like your shoes."

"Thanks."

He thinks for a second. "Are they the shoes you were telling me about last week?"

"Yep, they're the ones."

"Didn't you decide not to get them because they were, to quote, 'so ridiculously expensive'?"

"They were, until they reduced them." And more lies.

"That was a stroke of luck."

"Wasn't it?"

Now he takes my hand. "I hope you're hungry."

I laugh. "Starving."

The restaurant is busy but we're lucky and a table by the window has just become free. The place is stereotypically Italian in that cheap and cheerful style more popular before than it is now: woven partitions, red and white chequered tablecloths, and, mid-centre each table, a candle in a wine bottle, dribbles of wax all down the sides. But it's not for the décor we come – they do the best pizzas in town. Despite the cost, lunch in Chapter One was a bit on the nouveau-cuisine side in terms of portion size and now I find I'm hungry again.

I look at the wine list first. Given the day it is, I decide to push the boat out. I notice a light, fresh, white and decide to go with that. It's way more expensive than I'd usually order but not *the* most expensive ... just the second. But what the hell!

"Will we order wine?" I ask.

"I'll think I'll stick with a beer."

"I'll get a bottle anyway."

Now to decide what I want with it. Usually when Finn and I come to Pizza Place we don't even look at the menu, just automatically order pizza but, tonight, I study all the options.

"I'm thinking of ordering oysters for starters –"

Finn looks up and raises an eyebrow in surprise.

"– and lobster as my main. What are you going to have?"

"I'm going to stick with my usual."

"Are you sure? You don't want to be more adventurous?"

"No, pizza is fine for me."

"Ah, come on, it can be my treat!"

He shakes his head. "No, I've been looking forward to this pizza all afternoon. Anyway, remember I said I was paying?"

Once the waiter has left, Finn reaches across the table and takes my hand.

"You know, it seems like you've been away for ages."

"Tell me about it!"

"I hate not having you around."

Suddenly I want to tell him all about the lotto. Why on earth am I keeping it a secret? What are we doing here in Pizza Place when we could be anywhere? I imagine his surprise if I told him. And his bewilderment. And his excitement too. We could do something crazy like, I don't know, head to the airport, get on the next flight to Paris, book ourselves into some posh hotel for the night. We could have the night of our lives, the time of our lives – who knows when we'd even come back! I look around. Instead we're here in this cheesy little pizza restaurant. Just who do I owe allegiance to? Caroline and Dana? Or Finn? Yes, Dana and Caroline are my best friends but Finn is my boyfriend. He's the one I want to share my whole future with. I shouldn't have secrets from him, and certainly not one as big as this. We should be enjoying the money together.

"Finn —"

"Rosie —"

We both say at the same time.

Finn laughs. "You go first."

"No, you," I say. "Go on."

"All right then." He sits back. "Well, on the way back from Donegal — God, it took us hours — I had to listen to Mitch and Ashley moaning about everything, how they couldn't find someone nice, how they're sick of the place they're renting, how the band is the only good thing they have in their lives right now and, you know, I couldn't help thinking how lucky I am by comparison. I really have everything I could possibly want."

"Do you mean that?"

"Of course I do."

"Wouldn't you like to have — I don't know — more money, for starters?"

He looks thoughtful. "In the future, maybe, but right now? Not really."

"But why? You could give up working for your dad and concentrate on the band."

"True." He thinks for a moment. "But if I were well-off and had all the time in the world, I'd worry it would make me too — I don't know — too lazy? Too complacent? I like being busy. I like all the components of my life — they're a good balance. I like working with Dad and the interaction with him, and with the builders and the public who come in and out of the store, especially the regulars. I like having you, being with you, doing simple things — like this — when we have the time. I like grabbing a couple of hours of quiet to write a song or finish a painting. I like going on stage at night. I like rushing from one thing to the other, being under pressure all the time, but a good kind of pressure, one that keeps the creative juices flowing. You know, I'm really happy right now."

"So you wouldn't change anything?"

He shakes his head. "No."

"I see. You wouldn't like to be able to just fly off to Paris tonight then?"

He laughs. "Paris? Tonight? Hmm." Then he's serious again. "In theory, maybe. In reality, no. I have too many things going on. And what does Paris have to offer that we don't already have? How would we know where to find a pizza as good as they serve here?"

"You really do mean it when you say you like things exactly the way they are?"

"Yes. Absolutely. The last year has been so rocky for me. I'm just happy to be back on an even keel again."

He takes his hand away, reaches into the pocket of his jacket and pulls out the CD. He hands it to me.

"Is this it?"

"Yep."

"It's a bit rough but I'd still like you to hear it."

Finn, and Finn's band *Dove*, have had a chequered past year. Mark, the band's original lead singer and Finn's best friend since childhood and my one-time boyfriend, died when his car crashed into a wall. Finn was devastated and the band fell apart. Several months later they regrouped but with a new lead, a girl called Lola and the less said about her, the better. The only good thing to say is that she didn't last long. After she left, Mitch and Ashley persuaded Finn to give it a go as lead singer and, reluctantly, he agreed but ever since he's been filling the role very successfully. With their original line-up, they were nearly signed up by a major record company but what with all the changes and all the drama the band were going through, the record company lost interest and it came to nothing. But, now, they're back on track again, so to speak.

I can understand Finn's reluctance to change. Maybe it would be better not to tell him. Why rock the boat now? He's happy with this calm period of his life. Things are finally going well for him again after one seriously tumultuous year for the band but in his personal life too.

"I can't wait to hear it." I take it from him. "We can listen to it afterwards, at my place." I look at him suggestively. "You know oysters are meant to be an aphrodisiac."

"Is that so?"

"So I hear."

"And?"

"*And* what I'm thinking is *maybe* we could go straight home from here."

His face falls. "Oh Rosie!"

"Oh Rosie, what?"

"Don't tease me. I'd love nothing better but I have a late gig tonight."

"Tonight? Oh!"

"I did tell you about it – remember?"

I now vaguely recollect him saying something about it last week but such a lot has been happening that it completely slipped my mind.

"You are coming?" he asks.

"Oh, Finn, I don't know. I'm exhausted after the flight and everything."

He laughs. "You're exhausted after a one-hour flight from London?"

"Not so much that but I didn't really get much sleep."

Which is true. I have lost twelve hours somewhere between here and Oz. "Look, I think I'll go home, have an early night, and listen to this. I am dying to hear it, to tell you what I think."

Suddenly he looks nervous. "I hope you like it."

"I know I will."

During the meal, Finn returns to the subject of London. He's still anxious to know exactly what I did there. Who could have known he was such a fan! Who could have known he knew London so well? I'm sure I never did. He says we should go there sometime together. I say, what about next weekend? He says, no, he was thinking in a few months' time, when he's less busy. I guide the subject away from London altogether and talk about other things, like his CD. Although he hasn't said as much and does seem nervous, underneath I think he's really quite proud of it.

When the waiter comes with the bill, he automatically hands it to Finn who glances at it. Then he whistles. "Boy!" He picks up the bottle which is still half full and looks at the label. "That wine was pricey."

I hold out my hand for the bill. "Here, let me pay. My meal was far more expensive than yours."

"You're not kidding!"

"Come on, just give me the bill!"

"I said it was my treat – remember!"

True, but my share of the bill really is too much to allow him pay. My oysters, my lobster and my expensive wine versus his bottle of beer and his pizza? I'd feel guilty. Especially now, what with my secret millions. Working in his dad's hardware business by day and gigging at night may make Finn happy but it doesn't make him awash with cash.

"Look Finn, just give me the bill and stop complaining!"

"No!" He shakes his head.

Suddenly we're distracted from our squabble by a sharp rat-a-tat on the window. We look up. Finn's dad and Fay, arms around one another's waists, are looking in at us, smiling. Mr Heelan is waving excitedly like he hasn't seen us in years. The similarity between him and his son is striking and I often feel when I see Mr Heelan that I'm looking at Finn as he will be in twenty-five years' time. As they stand at the window, grinning, the height difference between Fay and Mr Heelan is noticeable – she has a good few inches on him, as I have on his son. Yes, both Fay and I are tall, but not that tall – the fault, if you can call it that, lies on the men's side: shortness is a component of the Heelan DNA. Maybe if I could change one thing about Finn it would be his height but, given that the rest of the package is so perfect, it's worth overlooking – pun intended.

Mr Heelan is now mouthing something.

"What's he trying to say?" Finn asks.

"I think he's asking will they come in."

Now Finn nods. "Come in! Come in!" he shouts, too loudly, judging by the startled looks of those sitting nearest.

Soon Fay and Mr Heelan have joined us at our table and I call for two extra glasses and pour out the rest of the contentious wine. A year ago, before Dana, Caroline and I set up in business, our failed business, I worked with Fay in that city centre boutique. I still find it strange to think of my old colleague and Finn's dad as a couple; this is the first time I've seen them together.

Fay is reserved by nature so it's hard to gauge how she feels about Mr Heelan but she seems happy in his company, happy with his attentions. And he is very attentive. Passing her a napkin. Picking up her jacket when it slides off the back of her chair. Listening carefully when she speaks while stroking the back of her long, graceful neck where her white hair in an elfin-style cut leaves it bare.

I notice her smile over at him, then she gives the hand he's resting around her shoulder a squeeze with her own long, slim-fingered hand. Her neck, her short hair, her fingers, her finely boned face, her slender figure – everything about her really is quite lovely. She was wasted on Anthony Knowles.

I wonder if Mr Heelan knows what a big part Anthony Knowles has played in Fay's life. If he knows that he left his wife and the children when they were still little for Fay. Or that he and Fay went to England where she gave birth to a little baby girl who died, breaking Fay's heart, and her and Anthony's relationship apart. That, after leaving Fay he returned to his other family. That, twenty years later, Fay and he did meet again and did rekindle their relationship, but only briefly – his wife found out about it and, for a second time, he chose her and their life and family.

Poor Fay. All those years wasted when she could have spent them with someone else and, being as lovely as she is, even now in her fifties, I imagine her choice was wide. She wasted so much of her life on Anthony but at last it seems she's moved on and has met someone worth loving. Like his son, Mr Heelan is rather special: a kind, gentle, loving man – traits he's passed on to the son he reared so well all on his own.

Fay first met Mr Heelan, a widower for almost twenty years, at the opening of our ill-fated shop and she and he spent most of the evening chatting together. Some weeks later, Fay just 'happened' to be in the neighbourhood of one of Mr Heelan's hardware stores and popped in and, next thing, she was ensconced behind the counter, perched on an old stool, sipping tea from Mr Heelan's own cup. The rest, as they say, is history – recent history or what I really mean is the present and, hopefully, their future.

I really hope for both of their sakes that she's in love with Mr Heelan, as he is so evidently in love with her.

"So where are the pair of you off to then?" Finn is asking now, in an odd reversal of roles, like he's the father.

"To a late-night movie. Fay has tricked me into going to see some tear-jerker about a mother who spent years being held in captivity by guerrillas while her children grew up without her."

"You said you wanted to go!" laughs Fay.

"Only because I thought you said *gorillas*."

"What?" asks Finn, looking puzzled.

"You know, ape-like gorillas rather than gun-touting guerrillas," explains Mr Heelan. "I thought it was some Diane Fossett, wildlife kind of thing." Then he grins over at Fay. "You tricked me!"

"No, I didn't! How could it be about ape-like gorillas? Have you ever heard of them capturing someone and making them stay with them for twenty years? That's ridiculous." She laughs again. "Isn't it, Rosie?"

"Ridiculous!" I laugh.

"Hey, now, you're ganging up on me. That's what happens when you put two women together. Help me out here, Finn!"

"You're on your own, Dad. Kidnapping apes – come on!"

Mr Heelan takes the teasing well, he's even grinning himself.

Then Fay glances down at her watch. "We should go now if we're to be on time."

Mr Heelan drinks the last of his wine and they both stand up to go and we watch as he helps her with her coat.

"Have a good time," I call after them as they leave hand-in-hand.

"We will," Mr Heelan calls back.

"And don't be too late now, do you hear?" jokes Finn.

"We won't – *Dad*!"

Seconds later, they pass by the window, still hand-in-hand. They both give a wave and we wave back.

We watch them as they carry on down the street, until they turn the corner.

"It must be strange seeing your dad with someone after all these years."

Finn thinks for a second. "Strange, but good."

"You like Fay, don't you?"

"Of course I do. She's lovely. I can't remember Dad ever being so happy. I was too young to have any real memories of him and Mum together."

"Does it make you think of your mother when you see them together?"

"Funnily enough, no. But it does make me a little sad."

"Sad?"

"Yeah, for all those wasted years in Dad's life. All these years he's been on his own, no one to go with to something as simple as the movies. Probably the last time he was at the cinema – apart from children's matinees that is – was with my mother." He stands up. "Come on, we'd better go too."

"But what about the bill?"

"I paid it while you were busy talking."

"But I said I'd pay!"

"And I said I would."

When we come out, we find it's begun to rain.

"Where's your gig?" I ask.

"The Menagerie."

"So it's in my direction then. Why don't I drop you off on the way?"

I put out my hand to flag down an oncoming taxi.

"Hey, Rosie, what's wrong with getting a bus?"

"But it's so wet!"

The taxi flies by, without stopping. I notice Finn is looking at me.

"What?" I ask.

"How come you're so flush with cash all of a sudden?"

"Flush? Hardly."

"New shoes. *Expensive* new shoes. Taxi here, taxi home. Only last week you were complaining that your salary never lasts to the end of the month."

"Yes, well, I got expenses for my trip to London." The lie trips off my tongue and is readily accepted.

That night in bed when I listen to Finn's CD I am blown away by it. It is just fantastic. It's funny but in his own modest way, Finn has always been confident in his abilities as a songwriter and in those as a drummer too yet, oddly, he's not at all confident in his singing abilities when he has every right to be. His voice is very distinctive. It has tremendous depth and an unexpected but attractive roughness and – at times – a real goose-pimple, shivers-down-the-spine, hairs-standing-on-the-back-of-the-neck factor to it. When Mark sang some of these same songs, he made them sound kind of upbeat, preppy; Lola made them sound sexy; but with Finn singing them they're pure poetry with raw emotion – happiness, pain, love, lust, sadness, desperation – bursting through. I guess he's not just a mouthpiece for the songs like Mark and Lola and as he wrote them he always knew just how they should be sung.

A few of the songs are new to me but all my favourites are here. There's the song he wrote after he saw me for the first time at one of his gigs – 'Just a Glimpse of You'. There's the one he wrote when we split up for a little while a couple of months ago when I was mad at him for letting that predatory Lola move into his house when she 'needed' somewhere to stay. Finn thought I was being unreasonably jealous to begin but it was only a matter of time before he came to realise that Lola's intentions towards him were as dishonourable as I'd suspected all along. That's when he wrote, "I Don't Want To Be Your Linton" – Linton being Cathy's hapless husband in *Wuthering Heights* who so few remember since the central coupling in the book was Heathcliff and Cathy. Finn, so he tells me in that song, wants to be my Heathcliff, the person who'll matter most in the story of my life.

He won me back with that song. That plus the fact he'd asked Lola to leave his house and the band. Plus the fact that I was so desperately unhappy being apart from him. Having had so many short and ill-advised relationships before Finn, I knew I couldn't stand the thought of losing him.

One of the shortest, and definitely the most ill-advised of all was with Mark. I still get sad thinking about it, about him. I met both Mark and Finn for the first time on the same night, having been dragged along by Shane to see them play. It was easy to overlook Finn's interest in me that evening when Mark's interest was so much more obvious, which I learned later was born out of childish competition with Finn. And, despite everyone's warnings, I started going out with Mark only to discover that blond, handsome, charming Mark was also insecure, shallow and childish Mark. I quickly came to my senses but that's when Mark lost his – he developed something of an obsession and began stalking me. And here's the part I *really* hate thinking about most. The night he died he was following the taxi I was in when he lost control of the steering in his car.

So, yes, Finn and I have been through a lot together, survived a lot, we have history.

But back to the band. Lola's sudden departure also led to this other fortuitous happening – Finn taking over the role of singer, and the band in its pared down current line-up of three works better than either of its previous configurations. They sound better than ever before. They really deserve to make it. And they will. They have to. How could they not? They're just too brilliant not to be heard by more people, too brilliant not to make it. And if they sound this good on an amateurish recording they cobbled together without professional help, then how good would they sound if they did it properly, in a studio?

I try Finn's phone but I get no answer and figure he's probably on stage right now so I leave a gushing message telling him how great I think he is.

And so to sleep, to the sound of Finn's voice.

Decisions, decisions. How will he spend his very last pound? Be sensible and buy a meat pie?

John Roberts - £3 million - UK

Or take a chance and blow it on a lucky dip lottery ticket?

11

As the bus whizzes by without stopping, I catch a glimpse of its interior stuffed full of commuters. But these sardine-like beings are the lucky ones – at least they're on the move. Not like us hapless creatures left stranded on the pavement. Who knows when the next bus will be along, or if there will be room on it to pack in a few more. Now I feel a drop of rain. I look up. The heavy sky which has been threatening is finally coming good on its threat. And, foolishly, I have left the house without an umbrella. I see I am not the only one – half the queue is as ill-prepared as me and I have to think, truly, what a nation of optimists we are, that so many of us should leave home without factoring in the likelihood of rain.

Another drop and another. I sigh. I think of all the mornings, hail and shine (but in my memory mostly hail) I've risen early, made my way down to this bus stop, waited until a bus driver deigned to stop, crammed on, uncomfortably shared a seat with some complete and often very strange stranger, got out again, queued again, shuffled back on to a second bus – all to get to work.

Sod this! I hold out my hand to flag down an oncoming taxi.

The first thing I do when I reach work is look for Moira, my immediate boss. I find her in her office behind her desk. She smiles when she looks up and sees me there.

"Good morning, Rosie. Feeling better?"

"Much better, thanks."

"You still look a bit peaky. The flu can be a nasty thing – it can really knock you out. Are you sure you're fit enough to be back at work?"

"I'm fine – honest." I hold out an envelope. "Moira, can I give you this?"

"Oh! What is it?" she asks as she takes it from me but, not waiting for an answer, she opens it.

I stand there while she reads. She looks up.

"So, Rosie, you're moving on?"

I nod.

"We'll be sorry to lose you." As I'm wondering if this is her stock professional response in this particular situation, she goes on: "You were a great part of the team. It was a real pleasure to work with you. It really was. You'll be missed, you know."

I'm surprised enough to ask, "Really?"

"Of course. I think it's fair to say you found it hard to settle at first but in the last month your work has really come on. I was saying as much to the CEO just last week at Friday's meeting. You could have had a real future within the company."

I am surprised. Maybe I wasn't as hopeless as I thought after all.

Moira continues: "It's a young company. There are real

opportunities here for someone like you – for travel, for promotion, to diversify even, in time perhaps to move beyond the scientific side of things. Are you certain you want to leave?"

I nod. "Yes, I think it's time."

"Well, it will be our loss. Of course if you need a reference I'll be more than happy to give it to you."

"Thanks, Moira."

"Can I ask what are your plans for the future?"

I was hoping she wouldn't ask this but was expecting as much. The best lie is the truth cleverly told as someone once said and, bearing this in mind, I give my answer. I don't tell her the whole truth – just part of it.

"My friend Caroline is setting up a property management and development company. I'm going to work with her."

"Quite a change for you."

"I guess."

"And risky I should have thought in this present climate."

I shrug. "I think Caroline knows what she's doing."

"Well, if it doesn't work out, remember there's always a place for you here."

She's looking at me fondly and I'm surprised to suddenly find tears welling up. I guess I assumed they'd be as glad for me to be going as I am. For a moment, but only for a moment, I wonder if I'm doing the right thing. But I am, of course, I am. I've never been that happy working here – I guess I just managed to hide it a little better than I thought.

"Thanks," I manage. "That's good to know."

"Now there's the issue of working out your notice."

"Of course."

"Just a second."

She picks up the phone, makes a call to – from what I gather from her conversation – the personnel office. While she's talking, I get a text and I check it quickly and see it's from Mum. She wants to know if I'm still coming over this evening as promised. Had I? It's just as well she reminded me, I'd completely forgotten. I imagine what she'd say if she could see me now, handing in my notice. She'd have a heart attack. She was so thrilled when I finally got this job. I'll text her back later to tell her I'm coming.

Moira hangs up and, almost immediately, a young guy comes in carrying a file. Moira takes it from him, puts it on her desk and begins to flick through it. She looks up

"Under the terms of your contract, you need to give two weeks' notice."

I nod. "Of course. No problem."

"But . . ." Moira thinks for a moment. "I see that since you started you haven't taken any holiday leave and you've put in quite a lot of overtime. Hmm . . . things *are* quiet at the moment so . . . well . . . I can give you the option of either working out those two weeks and giving you the two weeks' holiday pay owing to you or . . . hmm . . . I guess you could simply finish up today. Like I say, it is fairly slow right now."

I don't answer immediately but let enough time pass to give the impression I'm weighing up these two options.

Moira is looking at me quizzically. "Well?" she prompts.

"I think I might finish up today."

"Are you sure? The holiday pay could come in handy?"

"No, I'll finish up today if that's okay."

All day as I tie up loose ends, people keep popping into the lab and saying things like:

"Rosie! I hear you're going!"

"Rosie, you're leaving us! I'm *so* going to miss you!"

"Is it true what I hear, Rosie? Are you really going?"

Hand-on-heart, I had *no* idea I was so popular. So popular in fact that goodbye drinks in the local pub after work seem unavoidable and I find I'm actually welcoming the prospect, so keyed up with good feelings am I for my colleagues.

So, for the last time, I leave my never-so-tidy bench, this shiny lab, these bright corridors, this glassy building, and then walk with my soon-to-be-no-longer colleagues to the pub around the corner.

I've never been a huge fan of after-work drinks. I don't know about other firms but, in ours, it seems that invariably conversations tend to be about what ties us all altogether – work and work colleagues, in particular those work colleagues who are absent. But this evening I find I'm enjoying the company, *even* Frank's company. Night after night, Finn, Dana, Shane – anyone who'd listen has heard me complaining about Frank who has the bench right beside mine. How he constantly sniffles but *never* has a handkerchief. How when I'm on the phone he stops whatever he's doing, all the better to listen in on my private conversations. How when he comes back after lunch, he always smells kind of onion-y.

And when Moira sits down after her speech in which she wishes me well for the future and Frank then stands up and gives his little speech telling me and the gathered crowd that I'll be missed, that I was like a ray of sunshine in the office, I feel a little guilty about all those times I bitched about him at home and I feel my eyes unexpectedly prick for the second time that day. When I say in response that I'll miss everyone too, I really mean it, at that moment at any rate.

Things end sooner than they might otherwise, for me at least – the others look like they're settling in for the night but I have promised Mum I'd call around. So, despite the others' protests, I get up to go. It's probably just as well as Frank is getting quite maudlin by now and his friendly arm around my shoulder is getting more and more proprietorial. After more hugs and kisses and good wishes from all for the future I make my exit. But, before I finally leave the pub, I have a bright idea and I stop off at the bar on my way out and order a half-a-dozen bottles of champagne for everyone to drink when I'm gone. I wonder what they'll make of that.

It's cold outside the pub and when I put my hands in my coat pockets I find the envelope Moira presented to me at the end of her speech and I take it out and open it. Inside I find a card signed with touching messages of good luck from everyone plus a cheque for €250 – the proceeds of a 'secret' whip-around Frank and some of the other were carrying out this afternoon and of which I had to feign total ignorance though, really, they couldn't have been more obvious between their furtive comings-and-goings and their snatched little exchanges. But €250! My God! I feel the tears rising up for the third time. €250! That's a record-breaking amount from this crowd. I'm really touched. I carefully put the cheque in my bag.

The end of another chapter in my life is closed. It's odd but I don't feel as ecstatic as I thought I would. If anything I feel oddly hollow. Suddenly, something I read in one of those print-outs Caroline gave us about lotto winners comes back to me. I remember reading that those who make hasty changes in their lives can suffer from social isolation and that it's wise to stay within one's comfort zone. But no, I've done the right thing. It'll just take a little getting used to. This feeling of deflation is temporary. It's onwards and upwards from here.

And anyway, it's not like I haven't been here before. Since leaving college I've had three different careers – boutique assistant at Monica's, entrepreneur with Caroline and Dana, and lab assistant at SciÉire and, now, I'm embarking on a fourth – in the property business. Really, I'm just following an established pattern. I glance down at my watch and see it's nearly seven. There's no time now to go home and change and I decide to go straight to my parents' house. I start walking, keeping an eye out for a taxi.

I turn the key, push in the door, and shout out: "Hello?"

No answer. The place is in darkness.

"Hello!" I shout again.

"We're in here!" I hear my mother's voice from the living-room at the end of the hall. Turning the lights on as I go, I make my way down.

I find my parents sitting side-by-side on the couch, watching some soap. My mum loves the soaps. My dad does too though he'd never admit it, not under pain of death. He says he watches them to keep her company but he's far too up-to-date on the various plot intricacies and frequent character changes for his interest to be merely casual. Despite my lack of interest, Mum often tries to fill me in on some current storyline, sometimes aided or even corrected by Dad. She, and Dad too, often neglect to mention at the beginning of their account that it is a soap they're telling me about so it's not always immediately apparent that Stacey or Ian aren't neighbours or friends who lead especially eventful lives and, sometimes, it's only when the stories get so outlandish that I realise she's talking about her fictional friends from Soapland.

By fortuitous chance, I've timed my entrance well and the familiar theme music now signals a break. At least I won't have to compete for attention with scripted dialogue – not for the next five minutes at any rate.

"Hi, folks. How come the rest of the house is in the dark?" I ask.

"Oh that's your dad!" Mum sighs. "He's gone all environmental on me. It's his latest fad."

"It's not a fad, Nora. Climate change is a real issue, something for which we all have to individually take more responsibility."

"And I do. Don't I recycle? Don't I walk whenever and wherever I can? But if you think I'm going to spend the rest of my days going around in mittens, bogged down in half-a-dozen cardigans and scarves, and stumbling over the furniture just because you're too tight to turn on the heating and the lights, well then you're very much mistaken."

"I'm thinking of my grandchildren, our grandchildren. Don't you want the world to be a place they can still live in long after you and I are pushing up the daisies?"

"We'll be pushing them up all the sooner if you keep going the way you are. Then what will your grandchildren think when they hear that their nana and gramps died in their beds from hypothermia?"

Someone unfamiliar with the pair of them might form the opinion that they're forever bickering, and I guess they are but, underneath it all, they're solid. Bickering is kind of like a hobby with them. Like the soaps it helps keep them busy.

I go over, put the box of cakes I bought on my way on top of the coffee table, then give them both a hug.

"You brought a present," remarks Mum.

"Just some cakes. I thought we might have them later with our cup of tea." Tea, taken on the couch in front of the TV, forms part of each evening at my parents'.

"What's the special occasion?" asks Dad.

"What do you mean?"

He nods towards the box. "Cakes from Sifton's, no less. Very fancy!"

I shrug. "I just thought you might like them. I noticed it was open late when I was passing."

"It's very thoughtful of you," says Mum, but she doesn't sound as pleased as she might. In fact I notice she's eying me up *very* coolly.

"What?" I ask. "Why are you looking at me like that?"

"Just wondering if you brought these to salve your conscience?"

"Pardon?"

"You *are* a dark horse. When were you going to tell us?"

"Tell you what?"

"Your big secret?"

"Pardon?"

"You told us you were going to London but then Sarah rings and tells us you turned up on her doorstep."

Oh *that* secret. I breathe a sigh of relief. There was no way she wasn't going to find out. There was never really any chance I was going to get away with my trip to Oz, or specifically my visit to Sarah, without her and Dad knowing. But I couldn't go to Australia and *not* see Sarah, despite the probability of the news of my visit reaching them.

"Oh that," I say, innocently. "There was a last-minute change."

"I'm very annoyed with you, Rosie, I really am. You should have told us. What if something had happened to you?"

"But it didn't and I'm back now."

"I could have given you some things to bring over, some presents for the boys, a little something for the baby, or some of the things Sarah's always saying she misses – Barry's tea, Taytos, Denny's rashers –" but then she remembers "– I'm really annoyed with you, Rosie!"

"Oh Mum, it all happened so fast!"

"Too fast to let us know?"

"I'm sorry. I should have told you."

"Yes, you should have."

There's another silence.

"Don't you want to hear what the baby's like?"

"I know what you're doing, Rosie, trying to soften me up."

There's another pause but then her curiosity gets the better of her.

"Go on then. Tell me about the baby."

"Oh Mum, he's just fantastic. A real little beauty. And as good – you wouldn't believe it."

"And how's Sarah?"

I think for a moment before answering. "Struggling a little maybe –"

"Struggling?" she worries.

"But she's fine."

"Oh, if I'd known you were going maybe I could have gone with you."

"I was only there for two days."

"You must be exhausted. Were you at work today?"

"Yes."

"They didn't give you a few days off to recover?"

161

"I didn't need them."

And anyway, I now have the rest of my life off! Imagine, I don't have to go to work ever again – it's hard to believe. I wonder how I'll spend my first day of freedom. I'll sleep in late for sure, and then maybe I'll –

"Rosie!"

"What?"

"I was saying, I still don't understand why you didn't tell me?"

"Tell you what?"

"About going to Australia, of course. Why, is there something else I should know?"

Well . . . I had intended to tell them about quitting work but I decide now to keep it quiet, until some more suitable moment. I don't want them to think there are too many sudden occurrences going on in my life. Suddenly flying off to Australia. Suddenly chucking my job in. I don't want to arouse their suspicions.

"You must have had to check in hours before your flight left – I really don't see how you couldn't have spared even a few moments just to phone us. Really, Rosie, if something had happened to –"

"So any news with you two?" High time for another quick change of subject. "Have you given any more thought to your anniversary?"

Mum looks momentarily torn. Sure, she'd like to keep talking about Australia but I can see she's keen too to talk about their anniversary. This was the major topic of conversation the last time I called. They were debating the merits of taking a trip versus having a party.

It's Dad who answers. "Well, as a matter of fact, we were just talking about it at dinner-time. We've decided to have a party. I think we've done enough travelling for one year."

He has a point. Dad was very sick last year with a perforated duodenal ulcer. He's back to full health again but it was something of a wake-up call for both of them and it gave them a new lease of life – they became the right jet-setters for a while, always planning a holiday, coming back from a holiday, or actually being on a holiday.

"Brilliant," I say. "Have you thought about where you might have it?"

"The Nutley," says Dad, referring to a local pub.

"The Nutley? How come you don't want to go somewhere – I don't know – a little more special?"

"The Nutley is perfect," protests Dad. "It's local. They know us there. They'll look after us well. And it's a place that would suit a lot of our friends and relatives."

"But you always go to the Nutley when you go out."

"Yes. Because we like it."

"So, don't you think it would be nicer to go somewhere more exciting?"

"The Nutley will be exciting enough. We don't usually go out with everyone we know and being surrounded by all those who matter to us on the night is what would really make it special."

I think of the depressing interior of the Nutley, of the grouchy staff all on the verge of retirement, of those dark patterned carpets which, last time I was dragged down there, still seemed to smell of cigarette smoke even though the smoking ban has been in place for years.

"Can't you push the boat out a little? I mean if you're expecting Con and William to go to the expense and trouble of travelling all the way back from America with their families, not to mind Sarah and hers coming from Australia, then maybe you should consider throwing something a little more glamorous."

"Rosie, I don't know that we do expect them to come back – it wouldn't be fair. We don't want to put pressure on them. Both William and Con were home only last year to see Dad after his operation. And Australia is such a long way to come for Sarah, especially with a new baby and, besides, it's not that long since we were there."

"But Mum, it's your fortieth! Of course they'll all want to come."

"Rosie, that's easy for you to say. They've young families. It's hard to travel with small children. Not to mind expensive."

"But it's your fortieth," I repeat. "And Con and William are minted. You're always going on about how well they're doing. Hasn't Con just bought a beach house? And hasn't William's wife been made partner? Of course they can afford to come."

"Rosie, you don't know what they can or cannot afford. Con and Evelyn have five children now. And William and Eithne lead very busy lives – they work so hard the pair of them. And they can't just take the twins out of school at the drop of a hat, for any old reason."

"Your fortieth wedding anniversary is hardly any old reason."

"Look, a low-key night out down in the Nutley is exactly what we want. We don't want a big fuss and we don't want to put pressure on your brothers or your sister to come home."

I think for a second. "Is it exactly what you want, or is it just what you're settling for?"

"It's what we want. Now, look, *Coronation Street* is back on."

I get up. "I'll go and make the tea."

I sip my cup of tea and gaze at the television screen though I have no idea what on earth's going on. Some woman is shouting at some man to, "Get out! Get out!" and trying to shove him back out her front door but he's resisting and is snarling back at her in a threatening way, telling her, "You'll be sorry. You'll be begging me to come back."

I look over at my parents. They're sitting side by side, both staring intently at the screen. But now Dad reaches forward, takes the pot of tea from the tray and pours another drop into Mum's cup, then hands it to her and, she takes it without even having to look. It's like they communicate by telepathy.

"Well," says Mum, between bites of her cake – her third if I'm not mistaken, "at last she's seen sense. She should have thrown him out a long time ago."

"I bet you any money she'll take him back again."

"You think?"

Dad nods.

They go on staring at the screen, enthralled.

"Mum?"

"What?"

"If you had enough money in the world to do anything you like, what's the first thing you'd do?"

There's a pause. "I don't know if there is anything. I'm happy with what I have."

"What about you, Dad?"

"What about what?"

"If you had enough money in the world to do anything, what's the first thing you'd do?"

"I have enough money. I'm not saying we're loaded but there's nothing I want to do that I can't."

"So you're completely happy with your life?"

"I'd have to say, yes. After that fright I got last year, I'm lucky to be alive. I appreciate what I have. I know the value of it."

"There's nothing you'd like to buy?"

"No."

"A fancy new car?"

"What would I want that for? I'd only be lying awake at night, worrying that some lout might steal it."

"Wouldn't you like to move to a new house?"

"Why? We're happy here," says Dad.

"Where else would you get neighbours like ours?" adds Mum. "Your dad's right. We have everything." She reaches over and gives his hand a squeeze. "Now hush, Rosie, and let us watch our programme."

"It was a hell of a good ride for three or four years, but now he lives more simply."

Ken Proxmire - $1 million - US.

"There's no more talk of owning a helicopter or riding in limos. We're just everyday folk. Dad's now back to work as a machinist." Rick Proxmire speaking of his father.

12

The next day, I do sleep in late. When I finally wake, I head into town, have a leisurely breakfast, spend some time shopping, and then go to meet Caroline and Dana in a coffee shop in town as arranged. When I arrive I find they're both already there, ensconced in a booth in the corner.

"You're obviously adjusting well to the lack of a nine-to-five regime," observes Dana, when I make my way over to where they're sitting.

"What do you mean?"

"Well, I see you've found something to fill your time." She nods towards the shopping bags I'm carrying.

I put them down – my arms are nearly coming out of their sockets. I sit in beside her.

"Is that a new coat?" asks Caroline.

I glance down, then shrug. "This old thing?"

"Yes, that old thing. But it's not an old thing, is it?"

"Ah – no."

"You bought it today, didn't you?"

I nod.

"It looks expensive."

"I guess that would be because it was."

"By whose standards?" asks Dana. "Caroline's or mine?"

"Ah – Caroline's."

"Oh dear!" says Dana. "So how much?"

"That's not a question any polite person should ask."

Whatever about Caroline, Dana would be horrified if she heard the price. She hangs onto the same old clothes year-in, year-out, although that may change now . . . but I wouldn't hold my breath.

"You mean you're too embarrassed to say."

Actually I am. I can't quite believe what I did spend on it. It was a moment of madness. I gave in to temptation. In fact, the coat was one of several moments of madness, one of several temptations I gave into this morning – all the others are contained in these bulging bags of mine. I've never been a great fan of shopping. I guess I've never really had the money to indulge. But now I'm finding out what so many women before me already know, that shopping *is* like a drug. The rush of blood to my head when I hand over my credit card to have obscene amounts taken out really is quite addictive. Not that I'm actually addicted or anything. It's understandable that I would get carried away at the start. The novelty will soon wear off. It's not like I'm going to go on spending like this forever.

I notice Dana is looking over at me.

"What? What?" I demand. "Look, I had to get something to go with those shoes I bought."

"Rosie, I didn't say anything!"

"You didn't have to. Your look says it all. So I went a little crazy? I think that's allowed in the circumstances."

"People *are* going to wonder where you're getting the money. Especially since you've just given up work."

"Nobody I know could possibly have any idea how much I spent on this coat or, for that matter, on any of this stuff – apart from Caroline maybe. Anyway, everyone still thinks I'm working out in SciÉire."

"What? You haven't told them you've left?"

"It was only yesterday – give me a chance."

"So you've not told Finn?" asks Dana.

"Not yet. I haven't seen him since."

"But you spoke to him on the phone. So why didn't you tell him then?"

"I just couldn't think of the right words."

"Ah –'Finn, I've given up work' – would probably do."

"That's the easy part. It's what comes after is difficult. I don't know how I'd answer all the questions that would follow."

"Didn't I warn you about that?" demands Caroline.

"Look, I'll tell him in my own good time."

"Well, just make sure that whatever you say is plausible. You don't want him getting suspicious."

"You called out to your parents last night," says Dana "Didn't you tell them?"

"In light of my recent surprise trip to Australia which they know all about courtesy of Sarah, I thought it better not to tell them about my recent surprise decision to give up work. Too many surprises and they just might begin to wonder. Now, I'm going to go up for coffee. Does anyone else want one?"

Both of them shake their heads.

The place isn't terribly busy but the service is excruciatingly slow. Eventually, I do get my coffee and I come back, set my cup down on the table, and begin to take off my coat.

"You may as well leave that on," says Caroline. "No point in getting too comfortable."

"Pardon?"

"While you were so busy shopping, we were sitting here waiting for you. Now we want to get going."

"Where?"

"To see the office Caroline found for us," answers Dana. "That's the reason I took time off college."

"You found an office for us already?" I turn to Caroline.

"Yes, so drink up and we can go and see it."

Leaving on my coat, I take the first sip from my coffee to find it tepid and far too strong. I put the cup back down again. "Let's go then. What are you waiting for?"

When we leave the coffee shop, Caroline takes the lead and we follow her down the street, then around the corner, until we come to a glass-fronted building. She turns, goes in, and we go in after her, me still with all my bags. Past the receptionist whose huge desk positively dwarfs her we go, and then on over to the elevator. Caroline presses the button. Doors open. We step in. Doors close. Up we go. 2,3,4 . . . 7,8, . . .11,12. Doors open again. Out we come and now trail down a long hall after Caroline, past many doors. She comes to a stop outside one, inserts a key in the keyhole, pushes the door open, in she goes, in we go.

"Da-da!" she announces proudly.

There's a moment's stunned silence. Then:

"Oh my God!" cries Dana looking around her in amazement.

I'm looking around in amazement too because this place *is* absolutely amazing. It's like some glitzy office one would see on TV with huge windows looking out over the city.

"Welcome to the offices of CKV Properties," announces Caroline.

"Pardon?"

"CKV – Connolly, Kiely, Vaughan."

"I like it!" I laugh.

"Very catchy," agrees Dana. She walks towards the big window. "Would you look at the view!"

I go and stand beside her. "It's incredible!"

"I take it you like our new offices then?" asks Caroline, joining us.

"Like it? What's not to like?"

Dana now turns around. She cranes her neck up. "God these ceilings are high!" She looks down. She notices the highly polished floor. "And look at this!" Immediately she throws off her shoes to reveal two mismatching socks and, before we can even ask what on earth she's doing, she goes sliding across the floor.

"Weeeeeeee!"

When she comes to a halt, she spies the large desk. "Bags that!" she cries and goes sliding off again, this time over to the desk, and, on reaching it, she plonks herself down in the chair behind it. She props her mismatching feet up on the desk, leans back in the chair, and stretches her arms out behind her head. "You know," she says, "being a property tycoon isn't half bad!" Then she looks to me and suddenly barks. "You, yes you, bring me my cheque book!" Then at Caroline. "Just tell me how much! Show me where I sign!"

"All right! Enough!" laughs Caroline. She pulls up a chair on the other side of the desk. "Come on, let's get down to business. Dana, take your legs down. Rosie, get yourself a chair." As I do, Caroline keeps talking. "I want you both to look at these." She opens her bag, takes out a bunch of estate agents' brochures and lays them across that part of the desk not occupied by Dana's legs. "Dana, can you move it!" She looks up and notices that Dana isn't paying any attention. Instead she appears to be – well – puffing happily on what I can only construe is an imaginary cigar.

My own bemusement is only exceeded by Caroline's. "Dana, what on earth are you doing?"

Dana takes no notice but goes on puffing. But then, suddenly: "Have one," she orders Caroline in a deep male voice, or at least her attempt at one.

"One what?"

"A Cuban. I had a whole box of them imported," she booms. "The very best. Go on."

"Dana –"

"Take one!"

"Dana, we have –"

"Take one!"

"All right!" Caroline surrenders with an exasperated sigh. "Give me one then!"

Dana begins another mime – thoughtfully selecting a cigar from the box, taking it out, carefully cutting the tip off, and then holding it out to Caroline.

"Here."

Caroline takes it from her and looking somewhat self-conscious, clearly feeling somewhat foolish, she brings it to her mouth.

"Let me light that for you," booms Dana, leaning across with an imaginary lighter. "Rosie? Will you join us?"

"Ah, sure," I say.

Dana repeats her mime and I take my 'cigar'

"But mind," warns Dana, "you don't inhale when you smoke these babies. Hey!" she suddenly cries between puffs. "Would you guys like a little tipple to go with that? What do you say to a drop of bourbon or a shot of whiskey – I have them all." She gives a fling of her arm to indicate an imaginary drinks cabinet somewhere off to her right.

Caroline's patience for this make-believe has come to an end. I'm surprised it went on this long.

"Dana! Seriously! Enough! We need to take a look at these brochures I printed off from some estate agencies."

Dana throws a cursory glance down at them, then in a flamboyant gesture sweeps her arm across the desk. "Buy the whole damn lot of them!"

"Dana! Come on, be serious!"

"All right, all right!" She takes her legs down from the desk, sits up straight, stumps her imaginary cigar out in an imaginary ashtray, and then leans forward attentively. "So, what have you got?"

"Okay, let's look at this one first." Caroline picks up one colour print-out. "It's a fine-sized apartment in a very good development in the southside built just four years ago. It's the only unit to have come up for resale and it's been on the market for months now. The vendor is pretty desperate to sell and the price has dropped by €400,000."

"Dropped by €400,000! How much was it to begin with?" I ask.

"€1.3 million."

Dana gives a long whistle.

Caroline goes on. "It is a particularly attractive apartment. South-facing. Great view of the mountains. Two balconies. Three double bedrooms – all ensuite. Great living area too and a state-of-the-art kitchen. It even has two parking spaces. Now all the units in this development sold out immediately when it was first built but, like everywhere, the resale market has bottomed out. However, the long-term rental market is still very strong in this area. As well, given its location, there's the option of renting it out by the night or by the week to the corporate sector which would be a lot more lucrative, even if it would be more hassle." She looks at me, then Dana. "What do you say? Is it worth taking a look at?"

I take the brochure from her and scan through the details.

"Yeah, I think it's worth considering."

"Dana?"

"Sounds good."

"And how about these? They're a pair of . . ."

Over the next couple of hours we go through all the brochures, setting aside the ones we agree are worth taking a look at, until finally, we've got through them all. Caroline checks her mobile for the time.

"It's nearly two o'clock. Tomorrow, I'll start ringing to make some appointments to view these places. We should go to see as many as we can, as soon as we can. So let's go and eat. There's a good sandwich bar round the corner."

While we're waiting for our sandwiches to arrive, I go to the ladies' and, when I come back, both of them are tucking in and Dana is talking about Doug.

"He's really finding it tough going – the work just isn't out there any more. I think he'd be better off doing a course, getting a proper qualification – he really doesn't have any. He just fell into painting and decorating. So, there's this course I was thinking might suit. It's in Galway. It's in furniture-making and it's meant to be brilliant – there's a big emphasis on good design and it's really well-known, very respected. People come from all over to do it. It's the best one of its kind in the country – maybe even in Europe. A

175

qualification from this place would really set him up. The thing is, it's expensive. The fees alone are five thousand and he'd have to move temporarily to the west so he'd need money to cover his accommodation costs there, for his travel costs up and down at the weekends, for his living expenses, for materials for his course, et cetera, et cetera, et cetera. I'd say we're talking about a minimum of twenty thousand."

Caroline looks thoughtful. "But Dana, are you sure this is something Doug would want?"

"How do you mean?"

"Well, where did the idea of him doing this come from? Has he ever said he was interested?"

"No, but you know Doug. He's quite happy to drift along. But I know he'd enjoy it. Something like this would really suit him to a tee."

"Why do you think that?"

"He's very quiet; he likes his own company; he's good with his hands. He's a real perfectionist and that's what you really need for this kind of work."

"Hmm." Caroline doesn't look completely convinced yet she goes on: "Have you thought how you're going to give him the money without him knowing where it's coming from?"

"I've been thinking about it a lot and I've come up with what I think is a good idea."

"Go on."

"Doug was never a great fan of school but just last month one of his teachers died, a Mrs Clancy – the only one I ever heard him saying anything good about. Doug says she was always on at him to study. Maybe we could pretend that she left him the money, to give him this second chance."

"Hmm," thinks Caroline. "It's an idea."

"But how would we arrange it?" I ask.

"I haven't quite worked out the details," admits Dana.

We fall silent as we think. It's Caroline who speaks first.

"How about this? We draft up a letter for Doug to say that this Mrs Clancy has left a bequest for him. We give the draft to a solicitor. We then ask the solicitor to have it typed up and sent to Doug on his headed notepaper. Doug then rings the solicitor and together they arrange the transfer of the money from the deceased Mrs Clancy's estate into Doug's bank account.

"What if Doug wants to contact the family? Say, to thank them?"

"No problem. He can send a letter care of the solicitor who, of course, keeps it."

"But a solicitor wouldn't do all this, knowing the money wasn't really from Mrs Clancy," notes Dana.

Caroline doesn't answer immediately but then: "You're right. A reputable solicitor might not but . . ."

"But?"

". . . but a disreputable solicitor, now that's another matter entirely."

"Pardon?"

"Particularly if we pay them enough." Caroline goes on. "Okay, do either of you remember Tom Redmond – he was in college at the same time as us?"

Dana looks blank but the name sounds familiar to me.

"It rings a bell but I can't place him."

"Tall, skinny guy with a mop of orange hair and very pale skin. His nickname was Red – not surprisingly."

I nod. "Yeah – I know who you mean. He was in Shane's class. He was kind of notorious, wasn't he?"

Caroline nods: "He rarely went to lectures, spent his

time propping up the bar, was always getting into scrapes – he was even arrested at least once for being drunk and disorderly but the charge was dropped. Rumour had it that his daddy, a big solicitor down in Co Kilkenny, sorted it out for him. Anyway, he managed to scrape through his degree much to everyone's surprise, then qualified as a solicitor, and went to work with Daddy. He took over when the old man died but he's not exactly making a tremendous success of the practice. He's been up before the Solicitors Disciplinary Tribunal for all sorts. He was censured for not paying fees to a barrister, and for not carrying out a client's instructions, and for non-compliance with tax matters."

"How do you know all this?" I ask.

"Mostly from Clodagh Flynn. Remember her? I was quite friendly with her in college. She lives down in Kilkenny now but I bumped into her in the airport in Bangkok of all places when I was on my way to Australia and she was coming back from holiday. Anyway the day I met her, we got talking about college and about some of the people we knew back then and she happened to mention that she runs into Tom Redmond occasionally, usually in some pub late at night – he's based down in Kilkenny too. The part about the tribunal I read in the 'Law Society Gazette'."

"Why were you reading the 'Law Society Gazette'?"

"I remembered the conversation with Clodagh and I decided to check Tom out."

"But why?"

"Because I had a feeling we might be in need of a solicitor who isn't going to enquire too deeply when we ask him to do something. We will need someone like that. And Tom Redmond is perfect. He's based outside of Dublin.

He's probably hungry for money – his practice isn't exactly booming according to Clodagh. If we're clever there's no reason why he should suspect where our money has come from; he's not the brightest. We can spin him some story. And if we put him on a good retainer I'm sure he'll do what we ask without too many questions."

"But would we be able to trust him?" I ask doubtfully.

"We'd never put ourselves in a position where we'd have to – we'd keep him on a very tight rein, have him working for us on a need-to-know basis."

But I'm uneasy. "I don't like the idea of using a dead woman like this, or getting involved with someone like this Redmond guy."

"But don't you see, we're going to need someone to act as an intermediary from time to time. Like now. Doug can't know the money is coming from Dana."

"Hmm, still, I'm not sure."

"Well, I think it sounds good," says Dana. "And anyway, if Mrs Clancy was as nice as Doug says she was, I'm sure she'd understand why we're doing what we're doing, and using her name to do it."

"My sentiments exactly!" says Caroline. "The end justifies the means."

Later that evening, I'm putting some pasta on to cook when Dana comes in.

"Hi! I thought you were babysitting Cathy?"

"I was but her mum came home early."

"Where's Doug? Wasn't he with you?"

"Yeah, but he's gone home."

"Will I make you some too?"

"What?" She seems distracted.

"Pasta?"

"No, thanks."

As I grate some cheese, she stands there, staring absent-mindedly into space, deep in thought.

"Is everything okay?" I ask.

"Sure, sure," she answers distractedly. But then. "Rosie, you've seen Cathy. You've seen how she reacts – do you think there's something, well, something a little different about her?"

"Like what?"

"Well, have you noticed anything unusual in the way she behaves compared to other kids?"

"Dana, I'm not the one to ask. I don't know anything about children. All my nieces and nephews are thousands of miles away. Why do you ask?"

"Just something Doug said. He thinks her responses are a little slow."

"In what way?"

"He thinks she doesn't react to stimuli the way she should."

"What do you think?"

She shrugs. "Child psychology was one of my subjects back in the first year of my degree course so I have studied it but it's hard to know – theory is one thing, real life is another. And it's hard to be objective. I guess she *is* slow to smile, in fact she rarely smiles, and I know when I call her name she hardly ever reacts. She's never been the most interactive of children but I've been inclined to think that's just her personality."

"Maybe, but still it might be no harm to suggest to Cathy's mother that she take her to see her GP."

"Easier said than done. Like how would I even broach something like that with her? Ann is quite reserved. Even with Cathy, she's reserved. We're just not that close. All we have in common is Cathy. Sometimes I think the only reason Ann lets me spend time with her daughter is because it suits her. Besides, I'm not sure if Doug is right. What if he isn't and I just end up upsetting Ann? She can be quite prickly especially if she suspects her skills as a mother are being questioned. She tends to find slights where none are intended. I bought Cathy a hat the other day when we were out walking because it got so cold and Ann took it as a criticism of herself."

"Could the fact that Ann is reserved be part of the problem?"

"Doug and I talked about that. She probably doesn't spend as much time engaging with Cathy as she might, not least because she works such long hours. But he – I – both of us feel it could be more than that."

"Have the crèche noticed anything?"

"If they have, Ann hasn't said. Besides I could see her dismissing any advice from them that she finds unpalatable. She's very strong-willed and set in her opinions."

"What about your dad? Has he noticed anything?"

"No, but then I wouldn't really expect him to."

"Even so, couldn't you get him to talk to her?"

"Maybe." She sounds doubtful. "But he'd be even more nervous about upsetting Ann. They're not on the best of terms and if he upsets her she could stop him seeing Cathy."

I'm about to sit down at the table to eat my bowl of pasta when Dana suddenly looks at it like she's noticed it for the first time.

"Is there any left?"

I sigh. "Here, have this. I'll make some more."

"Thanks."

Broke and charged with murder within two years.

Willie Hurt - $3.1 million - US

Hurt's lawyers say he spent his fortune on a divorce and crack cocaine.

13

Two days later Caroline hires a car and, following the agenda she's planned, we first set off down the country, to a town that's just outside the commuter belt of Dublin.

I do listen to the radio. I do read the newspapers. I did know the economy was bad but, until this morning, I don't think I fully grasped just how bad. The abundance of 'For Sale' signs outside houses in some of the towns we pass through along the way or – more particularly – on the housing estates on their outskirts is really quite scary and very stark evidence of the downturn in the economy.

At around ten, we pull into our first destination, one of these estates on the outskirts of one of these small towns. We look around. On one side of the street there's an entire row of houses for sale. Caroline tells us that ever since they were built they've lain empty and are still owned by the developer. On the other side are identical houses but these were part of an earlier phase and are being resold by individual owners whose circumstances and fortunes have changed since they bought them at the height of the boom for top prices. Out of a block of six of these second-hand homes, four are now for sale. At the sound of our car pulling up, a smart-suited, pretty-ish young woman appears at the door of one of these second-hand houses.

"That must be the estate agent," says Caroline and hops out of the car and goes over to her.

They're greeting one another as Dana and I follow over. Now Caroline introduces us.

"Mandy, these are my colleagues, Rosie Kiely and Dana Vaughan. Dana, Rosie, this is Mandy Fennell."

"Pleased to meet you," says Mandy. She smiles but it seems a weary kind of smile in someone this young.

We shake hands or, rather, she limply holds hers out and allows me to shake it. Maybe in her real life she's a lovely person, maybe she's just drained by her challenging task – trying to off-load houses in these recessionary times while her older, more experienced colleagues remain back in the office.

The first house Mandy takes us into is the one she came out of, one of the second-hand ones, but it's in such pristine condition it doesn't even feel lived in. I say as much.

"You're right," says Mandy. "No one is living here at the moment."

"Where are the owners?"

She thinks for a moment, like she's considering how much she wants to say but then goes on. "The house has in fact been repossessed by the bank."

"Really?"

"Did I read in the papers that a big factory near here closed down recently?" asks Caroline.

Again Mandy hesitates for a second. "Yes. That's right."

"Wasn't it the main employer in the town?"

Mandy nods her head.

"So I guess unemployment has shot up?"

"Yes, it has."

"And a lot of people have had to default on their mortgage?"

"Yes."

Suddenly I feel uneasy. Here we are hoping to buy cheap property but it's at the expense of others.

But Mandy goes on. "The local enterprise board and local politicians are trying to get another company to take over the factory."

"And have they had any luck?" asks Caroline.

"I can't say I know."

"But right now there's a huge number of houses available in the town but no demand," observes Caroline. "So I guess anybody who buys these houses does so with the expectation that – in the longer term – the fortunes of the town and the whole economic climate will turn around and demand and prices will pick up."

"Shall we move on to the next?" suggests Mandy.

Next door is spotlessly tidy too.

"I guess there's nobody living here either," I remark.

"Actually there is but the older children are in school and the parents have taken the younger ones off in the car to facilitate this viewing."

I go from one neat-as-a-pin, comfortable, tastefully decorated room to another and think of the mother and father and the little ones hanging around somewhere, maybe in a café, or just sitting in their car, waiting until we're gone – their hopes pinned on us buying the house they poured such effort and hope into. What is this family going to do now? Where are they going to live? It isn't right. They created this lovely family home and now they have to just let it all go. I feel like a vulture. But if we don't buy it, who will?

"Come on," calls Caroline. "We're going across the road."

I follow after the others, into one brand-new house after another, all built at the tail-end of the building boom and never occupied. Each of them is identical and it doesn't take us long to go through them. Eventually we thank Mandy and take our leave.

As we drive back to Dublin, we talk about what we've seen.

"If," I say, thinking aloud, "we were considering buying any of those houses, then I think we should start with the house owned by the young family – they're the ones who could do with the money most of all. I'm guessing that neither of the parents are working if they're both free in the middle of the week."

"Developers have families too, you know," observes Caroline. "And they're more realistic when it comes to setting their prices."

"So are you saying it's the new houses we should be thinking of?"

Caroline shakes her head. "No, I think we shouldn't buy any of them. I guess I really wanted to see these houses just to get a feel for the market right across the board. Given the climate, we need to think very carefully about what and where we buy. If we bought one of those houses who knows when we'd be able to sell it on, especially for any kind of profit. It would be years and years, if ever. And there would be no demand for a rental property in a town like that, where there's no employment opportunities to attract people in. No, we'd be wise to stay away."

"I see."

I hear what Caroline is saying and agree with her. But I can't helping worrying about that family, and other people in similar positions who never imagined that their dreams, their plans, would end like this; that they would end up saddled with mortgages bigger than the value of their homes and would be forced to sell at a loss, or worse – have their homes repossessed.

We stop off several times on the way back to the city to look at properties within commuting distance. As we draw nearer the city we look at properties in the suburbs. We check out some new apartments including that one in the first brochure Caroline showed us the day before back in the office, the one with the three ensuite bedrooms and two balconies. We look at smaller units too, ones at the other end of the scale. And we look at town houses, some well-built, some not; some attractive, some not; some new, some old. We look at so many properties that it's difficult to remember them all.

The last properties we go to see are two turn-of-the-century redbrick cottages which are next-door to one another in the middle of a terrace of six, in an old part of the city, within walking distance of the centre. They're small and rundown but – as Caroline points out – have many advantages: for their urban location they've got unusually large and south-facing back gardens, they're in a quiet cul-de-sac, their interiors are well laid out and roomier than the exterior suggest. Standing in the garden of one, it strikes me that it would be just perfect for Seán and his family. I can see them now: Seán pushing both girls on the side-by-side swings he'd erect, laughing along with their excited screams. Or watching over them as they splash about in a little paddling pool, in colourful little swimsuits.

"So what do you think?" asks Caroline when we get

back into the car for the last time. "Should we take things further with any we saw today?"

"How about you? What's your feeling?" asks Dana. "It's hard to remember all the different places."

"Most I wouldn't be interested in but I think we should consider that very large apartment we saw. The location is excellent and it would be a very good corporate-rental property. The only other ones that really interest me are those two adjoining terraced houses we just saw. They each have three fine bedrooms which would be a plus when it comes to renting and, because they're so close to town, there'd always be a demand for them."

"Yeah," I agree. "I liked them too."

"What's more," Caroline goes on, "having two properties side-by-side is always a plus. It would be worth keeping an eye out to see if any of the other houses in the terrace come up for sale, or even approaching their owners at some point in the future, to see if they're interested in selling. One already looks unoccupied and the others don't look especially well-maintained. They're nice houses but they're not listed. In time, we could try and buy up the rest of the terrace and then, when the market picks up, knock the whole lot down and redevelop the entire site."

"What?" I turn to her in surprise. "You'd like to knock that sweet little terrace down?"

Caroline shrugs. "They're amongst the few single-storey buildings in the area. If we were to knock them and then build on the footprint of the terrace but go upwards as well we'd fit in an awful lot of units. Fifteen – twenty apartments, maybe even a lot more – depending on how many storeys we'd get planning permission to build. We could stand to make real money down the line."

Now I see Seán and his kids running from their little house as the wrecking ball goes in for the first hit.

It occurs to me how different Caroline and I are. I don't see any further than Seán and his family living happily-ever-after in that sweet little terrace whereas Caroline sees a big shining apartment block in its stead, and even more money in the bank for us. I think of saying as much to her but I don't. She might take it as a criticism which it isn't. Part of me admires her vision.

"I was doing a bit of a spring-clean when I noticed the ticket in a pile of rubbish on the front seat."

Anonymous – $386,848 – US

"I'm going to buy a small place so I won't have to pay huge rent any more, and will treat myself to all the things people do who have money."

14

I pick up the photo frame that's been standing on the desk in my bedroom these past months and wipe away the light film of dust that covers it. The frame with its large studio portrait is more suited to sitting on a mantelpiece but it's a long time since it has done so. Before my desk, its previous home was Seán's backpack during the day and, at night, a sleeping bag. Seán liked to keep it close by him.

It's a posed shot set against a plain white background: a family of four – two children, two parents – a child for each parents' lap. No matter how often I look at this photo, I can't help but think how ridiculously young Seán and Hilda are. Hilda looks like she's barely outgrown dressing her baby dolls but for this photo she's dressed her real-life dolls, her daughters Julia and Queenie, in matching pink party-style dresses, white lace-trimmed ankle socks, and black patent shoes – such well-cared-for children, so healthy and happy. Both Hilda and Seán are dressed in suits that make them look oddly old-fashioned and, again, only serve to emphasise their extreme youth; they themselves could be kids dressing up – dressing up in the way they *think* parents should for such an occasion. And in a way I guess they were.

When Seán first told me he had two daughters I remember thinking he was just a kid himself. When he told me he'd been fourteen when Julia was born I kept repeating in shock, "Fourteen! Fourteen!" until finally Seán was annoyed enough to say something like, "Yes, fourteen, you know, comes after thirteen! Can't you count?"

I study the smiling faces. First, the two children – Queenie, the blonde; Julia, the dark one. When Seán showed me this photo, he remarked that Queenie was the spitting image of her mum and she is, a pretty little miniature of the very pretty original – same blue eyes, same curly fair hair, same gentle expression. Julia, on the other hand, is more like her dad. She has his wide mouth, his whiter than white teeth with the very same gap in the middle. Her hair is dark like his, her eyes too and, again, like his, they hint at mischief. I imagine she's just like him in temperament. Cheeky. Chatty. Optimistic. Brave. Proud. Independent.

When Seán showed me the photo he neglected to tell me that, by then, Hilda was in hospital and would be for the rest of her life. Actually, not so much neglected to tell me as told me a different version. He did say Hilda had been beaten up by some thugs on her way to her cleaning job early one Saturday morning. He did say she had been in hospital for several months. But that's as far as he went with the truth. When he told me she was recuperating at her mum's and the girls were there too, that was just pure fantasy – Hilda was still in hospital, the girls were in foster care. Neither did he tell me about his mental health problems, problems – it turns out – that were so severe he too spent periods in hospital. I learnt all of this when I went looking for him a while back not having seen him around for some time. Then I met two other homeless guys who knew him and filled me in. Seán never knew I knew any of this.

I slide the photograph – thick frame included – into my bag. I run a brush quickly through my hair and then, looking around to see if there is anything else I need, I pick up a scarf and wind it around my neck. I gather up my bag and hurry down the stairs. Figuring I can get something to eat later in town, I quietly leave the house and the others sleeping. It's not yet seven.

I have a reason for this early start. I have this idea I might find Seán in some doorway, still bedded down for the night in his sleeping bag. Seán told me once he avoided staying in hostels because he didn't want to be tempted by drugs and drinks as so many of the guys who stay in hostels are, who come to rely upon them as a means of coping with their situation if – that is – it wasn't drink or drugs that put them in the situation in the first place.

I decide to take the bus this morning. I think I'll see more from the top of a bus than from the back of a taxi. As luck would have it, my arrival at my stop coincides with the arrival of a bus. I hop on, pay my fare, and make my way past somnolent commuters most of whom look as if they could have done with a couple of extra hours in the comfort of their own beds. Up the stairs I go and take my place at the very front.

I first encountered Seán asleep in a shop doorway opposite what was then Monica's Elegance boutique, latterly our Love Potions shop and, currently – as I noticed when passing recently – a mobile phone outlet. That morning, when we first met, I was early for work for once and, as I waited for Fay or Monica to arrive with a key, I passed the time leaning against the shop window, sipping from one of the three takeaway coffees I always bought on the way to work to kick-start us all into our working day, and nibbling on one of the doughnuts I'd bought for an even bigger kick. But I couldn't enjoy either the doughnut or the coffee that morning, not with Seán staring over at me with – what seemed to me – greedy eyes – and, finally, I went over to him and offered him one of the coffees. I guess I expected him to be really thankful but instead his first words were to ask was there sugar in the coffee which I thought was a bit cheeky at the time, and maybe it was, but I liked him for it. Still, I was wary of talking to a down-and-out. In fact, as I recollect, he did most of the talking that morning – he's quite the talker as I soon learned. It turned out he'd noticed me hurrying to work on many mornings before. In fact, he'd noticed quite a lot of things from his vantage point as I was to find out. The homeless may be invisible to the rest of us as we hurry here and there, wrapped up in our busy lives but they, with less to occupy them, have ample opportunity to notice us – at least that was the case with Seán.

Now all the way into town on the bus I scan the streets, the doorways, the benches, but I see no one who could be Seán. When we reach the centre of town I get off at the stop that was once my usual and walk that last couple of hundred metres. I round the last corner and then I come to an involuntary stop. There *is* a figure buried deep in a sleeping bag and curled up in Seán's old spot, his back to the world. Seán?

"Seán?"

I hurry over. I kneel down beside the prone figure and call Seán's name again, but even as I'm doing so, I'm realising already it's not him. This guy is bulkier. And he smells – a pungent mixture of odours the origins of which I'd prefer not to think about. Despite the fact that he was homeless, Seán always managed to keep himself clean. Now I notice the scattering of beer cans around the sleeping bag. No, it's not Seán – he didn't drink. At least he didn't when last I met him.

No, it's not Seán, I'm sure of that. I get up quickly but not quickly enough to get away unnoticed. The figure turns. I see the face of a man in his fifties, with few teeth and a grubby, battered, weather-reddened look about him, staring up at me. He's sizing me up and deciding, perhaps, that I'm not desperate or mean enough to try to rob one of life's unfortunates, he mumbles:

"You wouldn't have change for a cup of tea on you, would you?"

"Ah – sure." Not wanting to take my purse out in front of him, I search my coat pocket and find a couple of euros and I place them in his out stretched hand.

"Ta very much."

I get up to go but then I think again. I take the frame from my bag. "Do you know this guy?" I point at Seán.

The man considers the picture so keenly I begin to think there could be a chance he does know Seán. I wait for his answer. Then he goes on looking and I begin to wonder if his lifestyle has dulled his responses so much he's doesn't understand the question. Or maybe he's already forgotten it. I repeat it.

"Have you seen this guy around?"

The man finally answers. He shakes his head.

I walk away but before I get far, I think: what was I doing giving him a couple of miserly euros? Given how much money I have, how mean is that? I take out my purse and see that I have four fifties. I take them out. But then, I think again – what if he uses them to go on a serious bender? Chances are, that is how he'll use any money I give him. So? Is that any of my business? But what if there are consequences? What if he gets so drunk he falls out in front of a car? Or he gets into a fight with another drunk over the drink or drugs he's bought with my money? Or he assaults some innocent when out of his head? I change my mind. I put the notes back in my purse. I walk on.

For the next couple of hours I wander the sidestreets, but I don't find Seán or anyone who knows him or anything about him. I guess I'm not surprised. To think I'd track down Seán this easily would be overly optimistic. I stop off at a busy little café to get some breakfast and to have a think. There's a free high stool facing the counter running along the front window and, after I've ordered a croissant and a strong coffee, I sit up.

Maybe I should have started with the last place I saw Seán rather than the first – in that disused youth hostel down in Wicklow which Caroline's brother bought to redevelop as a hotel and where we found Seán squatting last summer. But Donald had the place boarded up immediately after that. He was worried about arson. It's still boarded up. Caroline says that Donald's plans to develop it have been put on hold. Maybe I should go down and have a look, to double-check.

But now I think over all the conversations I remember having with Seán, tying to recollect some detail that might give me a lead but only come to realise how, really, I know next to nothing about him. For all his talk, I don't remember him ever telling me his surname or remember him saying a single thing about his parents. Nor did he ever mention brothers or sisters. I don't know what school he went to though I do know he left before doing any exams. I don't recall him ever telling me where he was from but I know by his accent it was Dublin, inner city Dublin I'm pretty sure, but that doesn't exactly narrow it down enough to be able to trace him.

I search in my bag for a pen and then I take a napkin from the holder and list out the facts that I do know.

From: Dublin. Probably inner city?

Aged: eighteen/nineteen.

Daughters: Julia now aged 5, Queenie now aged 4.

Girlfriend: Hilda – in long-term care.

I stare at these scant facts, considering if any of them offer a promising lead. Queenie is an unusual name yet without a surname how can I track her down? She and Julia are probably school-going by now but even if I rang up every school in Dublin and found the right one, would they confirm that two girls whose surname I don't even know are on their roll?

I consider Hilda. If she's still in care, which I presume she is, would it be possible to track her down without knowing her surname? And would the relevant authorities give out information about her to me – a complete stranger? Would they divulge her next of kin? And would Seán even be considered her next of kin? Possibly not. They weren't married. Would there be accounts of her assault in the papers? Highly likely, I think – maybe I should do a search on the internet, see what I can find. Or I could visit the library and go back through old editions of newspapers from around that time. I think I could work out roughly when it happened to within a few months, sometime between the photo being taken and when I first met Seán. There might even be an account of a court case if they ever found who was responsible.

I finish up my coffee and decide to head to our new offices to log on there to see what I can find. But then, two doors down from the coffee shop, I notice an internet café and decide to use one of their computers instead.

I go in. The contrast with outside is marked – there's little by the way of natural daylight and insufficient artificial light. From front-to-back, the place is long and extremely narrow and, right at the back, sits a guy on a high stool leaning over a desk. He has lank, Goth-black hair with a fringe that falls across one eye. I make my way towards him finding there's just room enough to pass between the backs of customers logged on to computers on the benches that run along each side. When I reach him, I ask if I can use a computer and he replies by pointing one black nail-varnished finger in the direction of a free computer smack bang in the middle of the row to my right.

"Thanks," I say, and go and take my place on a rickety old office chair. I log on.

Thinking back, trying to recollect the details as told to me by Seán, I type in some search terms: *Hilda – early morning assault – vicious – critical condition.*

Seconds later, a list of matches come up. I open the first.

'In a shocking weekend of crime, a young woman was assaulted in a vicious attack in the early hours of Saturday morning in Dublin city centre. The woman was attacked by two youths just yards from the office block where she worked as a cleaner and where she was on her way to start her pre-dawn shift. The eighteen-year-old woman has been identified as Hilda Cosgrave of Hart's Road. She was taken to St James's Hospital and is said to be in a critical

condition. Gardaí are asking members of the public to come forward with any information.

Elsewhere in the city . . .'

The newspaper piece goes on to detail several other equally nasty incidents which took place that same weekend but I quickly scan over these. Now is not the time to fall into a depression through dwelling on the evils of the world. I take out my pen and the same napkin I used in the café and jot down Hilda's full name and this partial address. The address is probably not much use. For one, it is only partial – there is no house or apartment number. For another it's probably where Hilda and Seán were renting and any trace of them ever having lived there is likely to be long gone. If I don't come up with anything better, I will follow it up and call out to Hart's Road to see what I can see. There could be a chance some old neighbour might remember them.

I scan through the other matches on the screen but find they're just more of the same. I wondered if the two men were charged with the assault. I type in a new search.

Two men charged – assault – Hilda Cosgrave.

Again the internet comes good and, within seconds, I find what I'm looking for. In fact – sadly – more than what I was looking for

"Two men have been charged with the manslaughter of Hilda Cosgrave who was attacked in October of last year in Dublin city centre. Anthony Power of Menloe Place and Philip McManus of Frankwell Road were arrested and charged with assault within days of the incident but the charge has now been changed to that of manslaughter as Ms Cosgrave has since died after spending several months in a coma.

Ms Cosgrave was on her way to work in the early hours of Saturday morning when she was set upon by the two in what gardaí

described as a vicious and unprovoked assault. Ms Cosgrave of Hart's Road was the mother of two young daughters, Queenie and Julia. She is also survived by her parents Dolores and Hugh Cosgrave and brothers and sisters."

Hilda is dead. I guess part of me was hoping for much better news, a miraculous recovery perhaps. Certainly not this. Poor Hilda. Poor Seán. And those two poor little girls. I read the article again. I don't know. Is Hilda better off? Lying in a permanent coma wasn't a life but I guess as long as she was alive there was always hope. I wonder how Seán coped with her death. And then it occurs to me. There is no mention of the fact that Seán was her partner, no mention that he is the father of her two daughters, no mention of him – full stop. I feel annoyed for him at this omission – she, they, were his life.

Suddenly I feel the tears rising but tell myself how ridiculous I'm being – I never even met Hilda. But so? I never met her but I do feel I knew her through Seán. And objectively all this is so sad – a young life cut short by the actions of mindless thugs, two young girls left motherless. Why couldn't they have just beaten each other up and put each other in comas instead of turning their nastiness on a young mother? Poor Hilda.

Her sad death only increases my resolve to find Seán and help him and the girls. And now I do have some other concrete information – the full names of Hilda's parents. Surely the grandparents will know where the girls are, maybe even where Seán is.

I type in – *Irish telephone numbers* – and get the Éircom webpage. I type in – *Dolores and Hugh Cosgrave, Dublin* – but here I draw a blank. There are no matches. I log off. I go to pay for the time used on the computer and, since technology has failed, I decide to go down the old-fashioned route and I ask the disaffected Goth for a phone book. Without a word, he hands it to me. I search through it and find three Hugh Cosgraves in the inner city. I jot down their numbers and addresses, pay for the time I was logged on. (Me: "So how much do I owe you?" Him: "Three." Me: "Three euros?" Him: "Yeah." Me: "Here you go, thanks very much. Bye now." Him: Nothing.) Does he think there's a world word shortage going on, or that a tax has been introduced on smiling? God, I feel cross – with him, with everything! I leave him and the dull interior behind and step back out into the light.

Later at home, when I sit down at the kitchen table to ring these numbers, it occurs to me it really isn't as simple as that. I can't just ring all these Cosgraves out of the blue and ask are they Hilda's parents. This is too delicate to do over the phone. I should call out instead. I study the addresses. One, Copley Gardens, is not far from Hart's Road where Seán and Hilda were living. It's likely, I think, that Hilda would rent near where she grew up. I decide Copley Gardens is the most promising and to start with there, first thing tomorrow.

"Hi!"

I look up. "Oh, hi, Dana. Did you just come in?"

She nods. Then she sits down opposite me. "Well, I did it."

"Did what?"

"I tried speaking to Ann after I dropped Cathy home today."

"And?"

"Oh, Rosie, it was awful. She got the wrong end of the stick totally. She got so angry. She thought I was implying that she wasn't bringing Cathy up properly, that I was saying she was neglecting her. She was so defensive."

"Yes, but she must know you were only acting out of Cathy's best interests?"

"I'm not sure she does or, even if she does, whether she appreciates my interference. I'd say I wasn't gone ten minutes when I got a text from her telling me that there was no need for me to collect Cathy from the crèche tomorrow. I hope she isn't cutting me out completely."

"Oh come on – you're probably reading too much into it."

"I'm not sure I am. When I text back to tell her I'd be free to collect Cathy most days next week if she needed, she immediately got back to say she'd be okay, that she wouldn't."

"She'll change her mind as soon as she's stuck."

"You think?"

I nod. "Sure. Anyway, how come you decided to talk to her? I thought you'd decided not to do so."

"I felt I had to." She thinks for a minute. "It's strange but ever since Doug mentioned his concerns I keep noticing all these things about Cathy that were there all along but I'd never paid any attention to them. Like, before she settles down to sleep she lines up the same toys in a row every time. Before I used to think it cute and quite clever even – that she should remember the exact order she always puts them in but now I think maybe it's a form of ritualistic behaviour that could indicate some underlying psychological disorder. And there's lots of other things too. Like she never asks for something. In fact she hardly ever talks at all and, when she does, it's usually to repeat whatever has just been said to her."

"So you think there may be something wrong with her?"

She nods. "Yes, I do."

"What are you going to do now? What about your dad, are you going to talk to him about it?"

"Well, after I got the text from Ann, I rang him and told him more or less what I've told you and he was quite put out. He thinks I'm being alarmist and told me to stop interfering. He said that Ann would surely know her own daughter better than anyone and that, if there really was a problem, she'd have spotted it. He was really annoyed that I'd said anything to Ann. But I really think Cathy should be seen by her GP."

"Why don't you take her so?"

"I can't, not without her mother's consent." She shrugs. "Anyway, I'd only have that opportunity if I was minding her. I think I'll go into college early tomorrow and spend some time doing some research on child development, see if there really is any cause for concern. Maybe I'm worrying unnecessarily."

Finally his luck comes in

Carl Atwood - $57,000 - US

But very quickly it runs out again. Atwood was knocked down by a truck and killed within hours of the lottery game show he appeared on being taped.

The winning cheque was still in his pocket.

15

The following day I take a taxi to Copley Gardens and find a depressing little part of the city that is badly misnamed. Copley Gardens turns out to be a collection of high-rise blocks. I don't know who Copley was but I don't imagine he would be too proud to have these dreary buildings named after him. And whoever tagged on Gardens was either deluded or having a sadistic laugh. Copley Gardens? Copley Balconies more like, tiny little balconies suspended in midair, with room enough for a clothes horse, a rubbish bin and little else.

So Copley Gardens as an address isn't very specific. It doesn't exactly narrow things down. In all, there are four blocks around an area of patchy grass (the Gardens?) with, say, two hundred flats in each. I glance from one block to another and see that, on closer inspection, the two opposite don't just look abandoned but actually are and most of the units in them are boarded up. That still leaves two blocks.

Across the patchy grass, where strewn litter provides the colour one might expect from flowers, I notice a bunch of kids. My first instinct is to go over and ask if they know where Dolores and Hugh Cosgrave live. Quickly, however, I revisit this instinct when I notice they're looking over at me from beneath their hoodies with what feels like hostile interest. I pull my bag closer and decide I need to look less like a sitting duck. I need to look purposeful and, before my inactivity prompts the bunch of youths to approach with menace, I quickly begin walking to the nearest block.

I start on the bottom floor. At the first door I ring the doorbell but there's no answer. The second, the same, even though I can hear voices coming from within. It could be the telly left on but I can't really say. I move on to the next door. I press the bell. I hear the sound of someone coming. I wait. They're certainly not in too much of a hurry. But then, I hear a bolt being shoved back. I hear a key turning. Slowly the door opens a fraction, just the width of a thick security chain. I look downward and see an eye looking up at me, a watery-blue eye, slightly bloodshot: the eye of an elderly person I think, though male or female I can't tell in the absence of any other information; the rest of the body is hidden behind the door. All I know, from the relative position of this eye fixed upon me is that, whoever it is, he or she is small, very small.

"Hello," I say in my most friendly, non-threatening voice, "I'm looking for Dolores and Hugh Cosgrave, do you know where they live?"

The eye studies me. I guess I pass. The chain is undone. The door is opened fully. A very elderly woman who barely comes up to my elbow stands before me. She's so thin that if I sneezed I fear I'd knock her over.

"Dolores and Hugh Cosgrave?" she asks in a raspy voice that tells of a lifetime of smokes.

"Yes."

"Course I do." Then a spasm of coughing overtakes her.

"Are you okay?" I ask

"I'm grand, love, grand," she says when she recovers. "Just a bit of a cough. Ah yes, Poor Hilda. Terrible business that. Such a lovely girl too. A lot better than most around here. Always had a smile on her face and a 'hello' for me. 'Hello, Mrs Williams', she'd call out whenever she'd see me. 'Do you want anything in the supermarket, Mrs Williams?' she'd ask. And pretty too, pretty as a picture."

She begins coughing again.

"Do you need to get a glass of water?" I ask.

She shakes her head but it takes a while before she's able to continue. "Awful. Just awful it was. You know, I saw her with her daughters the week before she was attacked and I remember thinking how clean and mannerly and how well brought up they were, the children that is, and I remembering thinking to myself at the time, how could a girl like Hilda who was dragged up herself turn out to be such a great little mammy? And then, after she died, I remember how I'd thought all that when I'd seen her that last time. As I said to my friend, Mary Nicholas, at the time, 'Mary,' I said, 'isn't life a terrible thing when such awful things happen to good ones like poor Hilda Cosgrave yet no harm ever seems to come to thugs who go around raping and stealing and killing and whatnot?' I'm telling you, no one's safe these days. Of course, Mary's as deaf as a –"

"So they're living around here?"

"What?"

"Dolores and Hugh Cosgrave?"

"Ah, sure, they've lived here for years. Hugh was born and bred here."

"Can you tell me which flat?"

She steps out of the doorway. "It's right there, at the end of the hall."

"That's great, thanks so much for your help."

But Mrs Williams isn't ready to say goodbye to me just yet.

"Were you friends with young Hilda then?"

I think for a moment. It's really too complicated to get into. "Yes."

"And did you know her a long time?" she fishes.

"No, not very long. Look, thanks for your help."

"Any time. And if there's anything else you need to know, make sure to call again. I'm here most of the time. Except Fridays when I go to collect my pension but I like to go early and I'm usually back by eleven even if I stop off at the shop to pick up a few things. But of course this Friday is my birthday, I'll be eighty – would you believe, so I'll be going to Bren's Grill with my friend Mary Nicholas. They do a nice lunch there. Frank, that's my husband, God-rest-his-soul, well he used to take me every year and, of course, it's not the same going with Mary Nicholas but it's something. And then Wednesday nights myself and Mary Nicholas go to –"

Despite Mrs Williams' reluctance to let me go, I need to move on.

"Thanks again for your help, Mrs Williams."

I walk down the hall and when I come to the last door, I ring the bell. As I'm waiting, I glance back. Mrs Williams is watching from her doorway. I give a wave and, not in the slightest bit embarrassed to have been found so interested in her neighbours' affairs, she waves back and shamelessly stays *in situ*.

The door opens. I guess I was expecting Mrs Dolores

Cosgrave to be an older woman. After all, she is grandmother to at least two children but the woman standing before me now looks like she's not yet hit forty.

"Mrs Cosgrave?"

"Yeah?" She looks me up-and-down warily.

Is she like her daughter? Yes and no. Yes, she has Hilda's regular features. Yes, she has her light blue eyes. But the woman standing before me now has none of Hilda's appeal. For one, her expression is off-putting: there's a dull look in her eyes, a firm, defensive set to her jaw. For another, her greasy hair – part dark roots, part an unflattering unnatural yellow shade of blonde – is scraped back in a tight ponytail. I wouldn't say she's particularly fat but what fat she does have is all on show. Her tight T-shirt hugs every bulge, apart from the ample cleavage sitting high in the low V-neck, apart from her stomach erupting out over the top of her skinny jeans strained over her not-very-skinny legs. She has an amateurishly tattooed scorpion on the rise of her left breast. On her feet, she wears outsized, fluffy, deep pink slippers.

"Hi, I'm Rosie Kiely. I'm . . ." I hesitate as I try to think what I should say. Keep it simple I decide. "I'm trying to track down your daughter Hilda's boyfriend, Seán?"

"Seán?" She laughs. It's not a pleasant laugh. Sour. "Why?"

"I need to pass on some information to him."

"What information?"

"It's – ah – private."

She looks me up-and-down again, slowly. I see her taking in every detail: my expensive new coat, my expensive new shoes. What was I thinking wearing these?

"So, how do you know Seán then?" she finally asks.

"Just from around," I say vaguely.

"From around?"

"Yes. Around the city."

A little girl, thin and wan, in a grubby nightie comes padding up the hall in bare feet. I stare at her. She's about the right age. And she has the same colouring. She doesn't look anyway near as healthy or happy as the little girl in the photo but . . .

"Is that Queenie?" Maybe she and Julia aren't in care after all.

"No, that's my youngest. Do you know Queenie and Julia?"

"Not exactly. But I've seen a photo."

"Mum, I'm hungry. Can I have my breakfast?"

"Jesus, Aileen! Can't you see I'm talking!"

"But, Mum, I haven't had –"

"Aileen! Back inside! Now!" The little girl hurries away. "Christ! I swear she does my head in sometimes. A right little whiner."

"Queenie and Julia don't live with you here, do they?" I ask.

"God, no! They did for a short while but there's no room for them in this hole! I have seven of my own and all of them bar Hilda, God rest her, are still living with me. Her death was a terrible loss to me. And what am I left with? A pack of bloody wasters, the lot of them. Hilda was the only one with any get-up-and-go. You know, if she hadn't got pregnant like she did, there's no knowing what she could have done with her life. A real bright spark she was. After she passed away one of her teachers said to me that she had a real way with words and that she had – what was it again – 'tremendous recall'."

"Dolores!" A man shouts from inside. "Close the door, would you! You're leaving all the heat out!"

"Would you *shut* up! I'm talking to someone!"

"Who?"

"Nobody. Just someone asking about Hilda's young ones and her fella."

"Is it the Social?"

She looks at me. I shake my head.

"She says she's not!"

"Ask her for ID!"

"Didn't I tell you, she's not! Would you ever just shut up and feed the bloody child her breakfast!" She turns back to me, and throws her eyes to heaven. "Jesus! Men! Now what were you saying?"

"What I'm really trying to find out is where I might locate Seán."

"Ha?" For a second she looks like she's totally forgotten who he is. Then: "Oh, yeah. Seán." She gives another one of those sour laughs. "In the loony bin I expect. That's where he was last I heard of him. He went fucking loopers soon after Hilda was attacked. I mean, we all could have gone that way, couldn't we? It was terrible for all of us. Like, she was my daughter, you know? But if you ask me, he was always going to end up like that. I mean, you only have to look at his parents. When I first found out Hilda was going out with him, I swear I —"

Finally something tangible. "You know Seán's parents?"

"Course."

"So Seán grew up around here?"

"Yeah, of course, he did. I thought you said you knew him." She looks at me again. "You're not a reporter, are you?"

"A reporter?"

"Yeah, there was a few of them sniffing around at the time of the court case."

211

"No, no, I'm not a reporter."

"So why are you looking for him then?"

"Like I said, I have a message to pass on to him."

"What kind of message?"

"I can't really say. But it would be – ah – to his benefit."

She's looking at me suspiciously. I can't blame her, even to myself I sound suspicious.

"Are you a solicitor?"

I can see where she's coming from. To his benefit! But how else am I to phrase it? I'm hardly going to tell her I'm a lotto winner going around like some fairy godmother, dispensing houses as I go.

"No, I'm not a solicitor – just a friend."

I see her still looking at me, taking in every detail of my dress. Maybe I'm wronging her but I get the feeling she's trying to figure out what possibly could be in this for her.

"So Julia and Queenie are in foster care?" I ask.

"Yeah, like I said."

"Do you ever see them?"

She sighs. "I have enough on my plate looking after my own children."

"But they're your grandchildren."

She stares at me blankly as if she doesn't quite follow.

"Do you know who's minding them?"

She's still looking at me blankly as if her own thought process has never gone in this direction before. It seems she no longer feels any responsibility towards them, if she ever did. That she's never wondered where they are. Or how they're doing. I do not like this woman.

"They're in care, that's all I know."

I change tactic. "Are Seán's parents still around?"

"Nah."

"Do you know where they are now?"

Dolores shrugs. "The da's probably in the Joy – as likely as not. He could count the days he's spent on the outside. And, as for the mother, there's no knowing where that piece of junkie trash is. Everyone around here turned a blind eye when she was turning tricks from the house but when she started dealing, *and* to kids too, from around *here*, people thought, 'enough is enough' and took matters into their own hands. She hasn't been around since – wouldn't dare show her face."

Okay, I'd already figured that Seán probably didn't grow up in the bosom of a loving and happy family but, still, it takes a moment for this horror to sink in.

"What's their surname?"

"Ha?"

"What's Seán's surname?"

"Blake, of course."

"Dolores!" comes a cry from inside.

"What?"

"Look, thanks for your help," I quickly say. "I won't take up any more of your time."

"Dolores!"

"Jesus! Keep what hair you've left on your baldy head! I'm coming!"

The door slams closed. I walk away.

Mrs Williams is still there when I reach her door.

"Bye now," she says.

"Bye. It was nice to meet you and thanks again for your help." But then I think to ask. "You wouldn't know Seán Blake, would you? He's from around here."

"Seán Blake? Seán Blake?" she thinks aloud.

"He was going out with Hilda Cosgrave."

"Yes, yes, I know who you mean now. I saw them

213

together a couple of times – out walking with that big double buggy with the two little ones all wrapped up nice and cosy inside. I'd say he was the father. Far too young to be a father, of course, but a nice-looking fellow. A nice little family. He used to be the one pushing the buggy. In my day, a man would die before they'd dream of doing that – and around here some still would, even the young fellas. But he pushed it, and proud out too he was of his little family." She pauses for a moment. "Yes, nice-looking fellow. Nice smile. I remember he had a gap there in the front."

"He's from around here, isn't he?"

"He is? I don't know about that. What did you say his name was?"

"Seán Blake."

"Blake? The only Blakes around here are gone. The father's been in jail for years and she's a –" she leans into me and whispers, "– prostitute." She nods her head conspiratorially. "Drugs too. The last time I saw her, and this was a while ago now, she was all skin and bones, pitiful." Then she thinks for a moment. "But, you know, you're right, they *did* have a son, I remember when he was little he used to be always sitting on the step outside Morgan's Pub. God love him. At ten o'clock at night, he'd be there in the dark and the cold with not even a coat on him. And the father was an awful bully – just as well for the boy's sake he spent most of the time locked up." Now she looks puzzled. "Are you saying they're one and the same, that that little boy was the chap who was going out with Hilda Cosgrave?"

"Yes, it seems so."

She shakes her head in wonder. "Who'd have thought? You just never know how people are going to turn out." She thinks for a moment. "One day – " Then she breaks off suddenly. "What am I like, rambling like this? Wouldn't you know I'm living on my own?"

"Mrs Williams, I'd like to hear."

"Are you sure you're not just humouring a foolish old woman?"

"No, I am interested."

"Okay, well, a couple of years ago now, my shopping bag burst open and all my stuff went tumbling out and you know what he did? He took one of his little girls out of the buggy, put her on his shoulders, put all my shopping in her seat and wheeled it all the way back here for me. I thought it was very kind of him – very thoughtful, like." She thinks for a second. "He must have been broken-hearted after poor Hilda. Him who'd already put up with so much in life. That father was a nasty piece of work, and the mother wasn't much better. She should have stood up for the boy more. Tell me, where is he now?"

I hesitate for a moment and think how much I want to tell her. "That's just it – I'm trying to track him down."

"If you find him, tell him Mrs Williams was asking after him, will you? Course, I don't suppose he'll remember me."

"It's time I got going. Look, thanks again for all your help."

"You're more than welcome." She gives my arm a little pat. "And if there's anything else you need to know, just give a ring on the bell."

"I will."

"I'm here most of the time except Fridays because of the pension and this Friday it's my birthday too so I'll be out until the afternoon. Me and my friend Mary Nic –"

Oh dear, I think she's already forgotten she's told me. "I'd better go. Thanks again for your help, Mrs Williams."

"My pleasure."

As I walk off in the direction of the main road where I'm planning to flag down a taxi, I just know that if I glance back I'll see Mrs Williams still standing there, looking after me.

While I'm waiting for a taxi to come along, I think back over our exchange. I'm glad now I have a picture of Seán when he was at his happiest, strolling along with Hilda with the kids in the double-buggy. It's a pity that's not all I have and I try not to think of Seán as a skinny little boy, shivering on a pub doorstep in the dark when he should have been tucked up in his bed.

A taxi pulls up and I hop in and I'm about to give the driver my own address but then I change my mind and give him my parents' instead.

When we reach their house, I'm pleased to see the car is there. I didn't phone ahead but counted on them being here, foolishly perhaps because they're always busy during the day. But my luck is in and they're at home. I don't have my key with me but I don't ring the front door bell, I just go around to the side door. Glancing in the kitchen window as I pass by, I see Dad sitting at the table, the newspaper spread out before him and Mum busy with a pile of ironing. Neither of them notice me. The radio is on, I can hear it, but they're not listening to it. They're chatting. What decent, normal, contented people my parents are. And how fortunate I am.

"Hi," I walk in.

"Why, hello, Rosie!" says Mum. "This is a surprise! We don't usually see you at this time of the day. How come you're not at work?"

"I just thought I'd drop in." I ignore her question.

I go over to Mum first and give her a big hug and a smacker of a kiss.

"Rosie!" She's a little taken aback by my over-exuberance but then I turn to Dad, bend down, and do the same to him.

"What's all this about?" he laughs as he sets his glasses to rights again.

But then I see them exchange concerned glances.

"Is something the matter, Rosie?" asks Dad.

"No, course not! Why?"

"Well, you don't usually pop in like this, unannounced and out-of-the-blue. And what's with all the hugging and kissing?"

"Can't a daughter show her parents some affection when she feels like it?"

"Yes, of course, but —"

"I was in the area. I just felt like dropping in, to tell you how much I love you and to say what great parents you've always been. I don't say it enough. Not everyone is quite so lucky."

If I thought this would put their minds at rest, it doesn't, it has the opposite effect. Now they're looking seriously worried.

"Are you sure there's nothing the matter?" asks Mum.

"Yes! God! You're a suspicious pair. Nothing's the matter!"

"You're sure?"

"I'm sure."

"It *is* good to see you." Mum relaxes. "I was about to make a cup of tea. Will you have one?"

"Okay, I'll stick the kettle on."

While my mum puts away her ironing, I make a pot of tea, then take out some cups and put them on the table. On the way here, I got the taxi man to stop outside Sifton's again and I bought another box of their cakes. I lay them out on a plate.

"Oh my! More delicious cakes!" says Mum, coming back in. She joins us at the table. "Don't you know I'm supposed to be on a diet, Rosie!"

"One cake won't make much of a difference."

"One mightn't. But it's just hard to stop at one – they're so tempting." She eyes them, deciding which one – ones – to have. "Anyway, how come you're not at work?"

Again, I ignore her question. "So any thoughts about your anniversary celebrations?" I ask instead as I begin to pour.

"It's all arranged," says Dad. "The Nutley is going to do food for eighty on the night."

"You're still set on the Nutley then?"

"Yes."

"Have you given any thought as to what you might like me to buy you for a present?"

"Oh, Rosie," says Mum, "you don't have to buy us anything, you know that. We have everything we need."

"And you know just as well that I will be getting something. So, what's it to be?"

"Really, Rosie, there's no need."

"Mum, I'm going to buy you *something* so you might as well tell me what you'd like."

"I'll let you know if I can think of anything."

I take a sip of tea. I'm going to have to tell them sometime. Maybe I should just get it over with.

"Mum, Dad, the reason I'm not in work today is because I've given up my job."

"I knew it!" cries Mum! "I knew something was up. Why else would you call like this so unexpectedly?"

There's no point in explaining that my encounters with

Hilda Cosgrave and Mrs Williams and finding out all about Seán's background was what really prompted me to call, that I just wanted to take comfort in their normalness. Besides, it would be too complicated to explain. It would lead to so many other questions.

"So, come on, tell us, what did you do?" asks Mum.

"What do you mean, what did I do?"

"Why did they fire you?"

"Thanks a lot! What makes you think I was fired?"

"So you weren't?"

"No, I resigned."

"Ah, Rosie, it was such a good job. You were lucky to have it. You only have to glance through the papers to see that. It's scary just how many people are being laid off these days."

"Don't worry, Mum. I've already found something else."

"Something else? What is it?"

I've thought a lot about how I'm going to put this. I've decided to fudge the truth a little, for their peace of mind. It's better if they believe Caroline's the one taking what I know they will perceive as such a risk. Besides, it sounds more plausible, they'd believe it more readily of Caroline. So I tell them what I told Moira at work. "Caroline is setting up a property management and development company. I'll be working for her."

"Oh sweetest hour! Tell me you're joking!" cries Mum.

I shake my head.

"I knew it, I just knew it was too good to last. For the first time in your life you were well set up and now you've gone and thrown it all away. Why do you do these things, Rosie?"

"Mum, you don't have to worry! Look –"

219

"Of course, I'm going to worry! Rosie, what are you thinking? What does Caroline know about property? And now is hardly the time to get into it with the way things are going."

"Mum, Caroline knows what she's doing."

"Like the last time? Oh Rosie, I can't believe it. I really can't."

"Mum! I —"

"You asked me if there was anything I wanted for my anniversary, well there is."

"What?"

"You to go straight into SciÉire and ask them for your job back."

"Mum, that's not going to happen. I'm sorry but —"

"I don't want to hear you're sorry, I want to hear you telling me that you've made a stupid mistake but you're going to sort it out."

"Mum, I haven't made a mistake!"

"Don't you ever think about the future?"

"Mum —" But what's the point? I *knew* she'd react like this. I swear I should just tell them about the lotto and be done with it. At least then she wouldn't have to worry about me.

"Nora, Rosie is a grown woman. It's up to her to make her own decisions."

"Even if they're stupid ones like this?"

"Yes."

"So you think it's stupid too, Dad?"

"What else can I think, Rosie? Your last venture with Caroline wasn't exactly a success."

"Look, Mum, Dad, I promise you I know what I'm doing. You don't have to worry about me or my future. I'll be fine."

"Of course we're going to worry."

After that, everything is strained. Dad hardly says a word and Mum is so upset she doesn't even touch the cakes. I soon take my leave.

Okay, so my surprise visit went badly but at least I've told them I'm not working at SciÉire any longer. That's a small load off my chest, one secret less I have to worry about keeping. While I'm at it, I decide I might as well tell Finn too so I ring him and we arrange to meet at Pizza Place that evening.

While we're waiting to order, I'm about to tell Finn about chucking in my job but before I get a chance he launches into a story from the previous night.

"So, as we're about to leave the club after the gig, Mitch asks Ashley to take a look outside first, so he does and, when he comes back in, he tells Mitch that the coast is clear but at the same time gives me this wink so I know he's lying. Then when poor unsuspecting Mitch steps outside he walks smack back into her. That's the fourth night in a row she's been hanging around waiting for him. He calls her Big Bertha. You should hear him going on and on about how unfair it is that the one groupie stalking him is twice his weight and has even more facial hair than him." Suddenly he breaks off. "Rosie?"

"What?"

"Are you even listening? Don't you think it's funny?"

But I'm not in the mood to find much funny this evening. What I found out about poor Seán and Hilda is still on my mind but, also, I need to get what I have to say off my chest. I decide to come straight out with it. "Finn, I've given up my job."

The smile immediately drops from his face. "What?"

"I've given up my job. I'm going to go and work for Caroline."

"You *are* joking?"

"No, I'm not."

"I don't believe it! What crazy scheme is it this time?"

"It's not a crazy scheme. Nor – by the way – was the last."

He ignores this comment. "So, go on, what is it then?"

"Caroline is setting up a property company."

"A property company?"

"Yes."

"You mean like – what – managing other people's properties?"

"Yes. And, in time, property investment too."

"With what? Fresh air?"

"No, Caroline hopes to make money from the management side of things."

"Oh Rosie! Are you ever going to learn?"

"Pardon!"

"Okay, I admit the shop could have worked, you were unlucky but – come on, property? And at this point in time? You're chucking in a sensible secure job to hook up with someone who knows nothing about property at a time when the property market is in complete turmoil. While the rats are abandoning the sinking ship, Caroline is stepping over them to get on. You're leaving your well-paying job for this!"

"I have already left. And it wasn't that well-paying, by the way."

"But it was secure."

"*This* from the person who wants to make his living as a singer!"

"True. But I take heed of the 'don't give up the day job' maxim. I do work for my dad too, you know."

"And now I work with – for – Caroline. Why are you getting so worked up?"

"Because I care about you. I have to say what I think – what kind of boyfriend would I be if I didn't?" Then he gives this half-smile and reaches across for my hand. "I worry about you, you know."

"There's no need. Can't you just have faith in me?"

"But this all sounds so crazy to me."

I guess it does but then Finn isn't in command of the full facts.

I sigh. "Can we just order?"

"Rosie, pl– "

But I'm busy now looking around. I spot the waiter and make a beckoning gesture. He comes straight over.

"So are you folks ready?"

"Yes."

But I find I'm not and, as Finn orders pizza, I look at the menu again. The lobster was delicious the last time and I decide to go with that.

"I've have the lobster."

Finn raises one eyebrow. "Lobster?"

"Yes. Lobster." I look up at the waiter. "And a glass of the Chilean white." I close the menu and hand it back. "That'll be all for me, thanks."

Finn is still looking at me.

"Jesus, Finn! It's what I wanted. Why do you have to make such an issue out of it?"

"All I said was, 'lobster?'"

"Yes, but it was the *way* you said it. And that disapproving eyebrow of yours does plenty of talking for you. What

223

business is it of yours what I order? It's not like I'm asking you to pay."

"That's not the point."

"What is the point?"

He sighs. "Rosie, don't you remember how gutted you were when you had to close the shop? Do you really want to go through all that again? I mean you seemed happy enough working in SciÉire. You had a steady wage and –"

"Happy *enough* – you've hit the nail on the head. Look, can we just drop the whole subject?" I sigh. "Can't we just enjoy our meal?"

And Finn does let the subject drop but I can't say we enjoy our meal. He's no longer in the mood to tell amusing stories from his life and there's little I can tell him about what's going on in mine since so much of it is bound up with the taboo subject of our lotto win. My lobster tastes nowhere near as good as it did the last time.

"I think if you have something, there's always someone else that wants it. I wish I'd torn that ticket up."

Jack Whittaker - $93 million - US

Within four years he'd lost the lot, plus his wife and his daughter.

He also had 460 legal actions against him.

16

That Thursday, I spend most of the morning in Marks & Spencer's, shopping. In the ladies' department I buy a couple of warm nightdresses, a velvet dressing-gown, some woollen cardigans and jumpers, a couple of pairs of slacks, a few skirts and blouses, plus an overcoat – all in size eight. The items I select may not be the cutting edge of fashion but, then, that's not what I'm after, but they're all warm, comfortable and serviceable. Next, in the cosmetic section, I find a nice little basket with some fancy bath oils, moisturising lotions and soaps. In their plants section, I select a beautiful white orchid. Then I go to the food hall and there I pick out a selection of their gourmet ready-meals, a posh box of chocolates and a tin of their most expensive biscuits. Then, since I can't carry everything, I enlist the help of one of the shop assistants and together we bring all my purchases out to the street, as far as the nearest taxi rank where we load everything into the boot of a taxi.

En route, I ask the taxi-driver who's a chatty, obliging sort of fellow to stop off at Bren's Grill where I meet with the manageress. I tell her that two women – a Mrs Williams and a Mrs Nicholas – will be coming tomorrow for lunch and I want to pay for both lunches and want them to know it's been paid for so they feel free to splurge. Also, I order a birthday cake with candles and a bottle of champagne. I give the helpful manageress my credit card details plus a description of Mrs Williams so she'll be able to identify her when she comes in.

And then back in the taxi once again and on to Copley Gardens. The taxi-driver helps me carry everything out. Once we get to Mrs William's door, I'm not sure what to do. I can't just leave the stuff here, someone might steal it. I wouldn't trust Dolores Cosgrave to walk past it without pilfering whatever she wanted. But, I like the idea of Mrs Williams not knowing who sent her all this stuff. I imagine her discussing it with Mary Nicholas, over and over (maybe at their lunch tomorrow, when the champagne is going to their head), wondering where it could possibly have come from? In the end I ask the taxi-driver to wait until Mrs Williams answers the door but to not say a word about who brought all this stuff. I go and wait in the taxi.

Five minutes later, the taxi-driver comes back.

"Well, you certainly made someone's day," he tells me. "Is she your nan?"

"No, just someone nice who I thought could do with a treat."

"Well, you've given her one, that's for sure. So, where to next?"

"Back into town, please."

When we pull up at the end of Grafton Street, I'm still thinking of Mrs Williams. I still have that nice feeling inside. What I'd give to be a fly on the wall in Bren's Café tomorrow at lunch-time!

I spot Caroline and Dana standing in the doorway of Brown Thomas where we'd arranged to meet.

"Hiya."

"Hi, Rosie!" says Dana in her usual cheery way.

"Hi," says Caroline but without her usual bounce.

"Everything okay?" I ask her.

She shrugs. She does seem subdued. But then I remember what I was going to ask her. I've been thinking a lot about Hilda's parents and Seán's too, but also about my own, and of my good fortune to have such normal ones. It's made me more determined than ever to do something for them.

"I'm going to need some money," I announce. "A lot."

"For?"

"Well, you know my parents are planning a knees-up down in their local to celebrate their anniversary?"

"You mentioned it."

"The thing is, it *is* their fortieth. I think they deserve something better. Something, you know, more once-in-a-lifetime."

"Like?"

"I was thinking of holding a big dinner in some five-star hotel for all their friends and relatives. I was thinking of the Bayview Hotel. I was thinking of maybe even hiring out the whole place for the entire weekend so that everyone could stay. I could fly my brothers and Sarah and their families home. I could hire a band. Maybe even the band that played at their wedding – *if* I can track them down, *if* they're still alive – it is forty years after all."

"Yeah, that all sounds good," says Caroline.

But Dana looks thoughtful. "Are you sure they'd like that? Your parents aren't exactly short of cash. They could do it themselves if they wanted."

"The dinner, maybe. But, I think part of the reason why they're not doing something on a bigger scale is because they don't want my brothers and Sarah to feel they have to come home – the flights are so expensive. And paying everyone's airfare would be a huge cost to Mum and Dad, as well as accommodation. They may be well-off but they're not *that* well-off."

"But how would you explain all this to your parents?"

"Okay, well, I was thinking I could tell them I won it on a radio phone-in."

"A radio phone-in?"

"Yeah. I could say there was a competition on the radio, asking for a romantic story about parents, maybe about the moment they fell in love – something like that, and the prize could be an anniversary party in the hotel, plus accommodation, plus flights for their closest relatives and friends living abroad."

"Hmm," says Caroline. "Could work, I suppose." Maybe not the most enthusiastic response, but then she's not in the most enthusiastic of moods and at least she hasn't dismissed it out of hand. She goes on. "As long as you plan it properly."

"Of course."

"It's all in the detail, isn't it?"

"What do you mean?"

"For one, you've got to pick some radio station your parents don't listen to so they won't wonder why they didn't hear it. And you definitely will have to know what your winning story is. Your parents are going to want to know. Everyone is."

"I'll think of something," I say but I probably sound more confident than I feel. Romantic isn't exactly the first characteristic to spring to mind when I think of my parents' relationship.

"D'you know, they really get on my nerves!" Caroline suddenly snaps.

"Who?" I look around. The street is jam-packed with people.

"People like that."

I haven't the foggiest who she's talking about. "Caroline, who? Can you be more specific?"

She points in the direction of a person dressed from top-to-toe in grey: his shoes, suit, shirt, top hat, even the flower on his lapel all look like they've been spray-painted grey, and his face too is covered in matching grey make-up. He's standing on a grey plinth, pretending to be a statue – remaining completely still until someone throws a coin.

"Like, what is the point?" demands Caroline crossly.

"Caroline, he's just making a bit of cash."

"But it's just such a stupid thing. Like where's the skill? Anyone could do it."

"I couldn't," says Dana. "Nor would I want to – stand there while people gather around gaping."

"It's just so pointless," grumbles Caroline.

"Caroline, it's kind of harmless."

She shrugs grumpily.

"What on earth has you in such a bad mood anyway?" I ask.

"Nothing." She gives a weary sigh. And then another. "Well, all right then, my dad." She looks at her watch. "Come on. Let's go for coffee and I'll tell you all about it."

Five minutes later we're seated around a table in a nearby café. Caroline takes a sip from her mug, puts it down, then flops back in her seat.

"So, I got a phone call from him," she announces.

"Your dad?" I ask.

"Yep. Out of the blue. I haven't heard from him in ages. As you know we're not exactly close."

"So this phone call is a good thing, then?"

She shrugs. "The only reason he rung is because, no doubt, he's gearing up to come looking for money."

"He doesn't know about the lotto, does he?"

"Of course not! Are you mad? He's one of the main reasons I wanted to keep it quiet. If he knew about it, he'd never let up. He'd be on our doorstep, morning to night, tapping me for money."

"But if he doesn't know about the lotto, how come you think he's looking for money now?"

"Because I can't think of any other reason he'd ring."

Caroline rarely talks about her Dad so now I make full use of this opportunity to learn more.

"So what *is* it he does exactly?"

"Chases women half his age."

"No, I mean for money. What does he work at?"

"You know."

"That's the thing. I don't."

"Oh, like, a little bit of this, a little bit of that," she says in a cockney accent.

"Like?"

"Like, a little bit of this, a little bit of that."

"Caroline! That's the kind of thing you always say. You're always so vague. You know, you never actually answer any questions about him."

"Sure I do. I told you he was involved in racehorses though I think he's given that up. And I told you he was an inventor, didn't I?"

"You've mentioned it but you've never said what it is he's invented. Has he actually invented anything?"

"Sure. All sorts. He's quite talented in his way. Let me see. A teabag with a difference – with tea plus dried milk plus sugar already in it. A shoe with a stiletto heel which converts to a flat shoe in an instant. A golf ball that –"

"That's clever," I interrupt.

"Pardon?"

"The stiletto. How does it work?"

"That's the trouble. It never really did. The stiletto heel is supposed to fold up into the sole but he hasn't got the mechanics quite right."

"And has he made any money from these inventions?"

"Are you kidding! He keeps finding out that all his inventions that actually work have already been invented." She laughs. "You could say, his original ones aren't very good and his good ones aren't very original." She shakes her head. "Nah, his inventions cost him money! He's spent an absolute fortune on them over the years on patents alone, not to mind all the time he's put into them, and all the time he spent touting them around to trade shows and whatnot. And then there's the cost of all his equipment, of course, and all the materials he uses."

"So what does he do to earn a living then?"

"As little as possible. Nowadays just odd jobs here and there. He was working in a multi-storey carpark last I heard. Plus he sponges off people and, when that doesn't work, he scams them."

A vague recollection comes back to me. "Did you once say he was into property?"

"I could have. He has dabbled."

"It's quite the family business then, isn't it? Him, your brother and soon you."

"There is one big difference. Donald actually owns the properties he develops and those he rents out. As I intend to. Such legalities have never bothered my father much."

"What do you mean?"

"Jeez, Rosie! What's with the twenty questions?"

"Because it's all so interesting. My dad is just so boring, so normal in comparison."

"Give me normal any day." She looks at me speculatively. "Did I ever tell you he was inside for three months when Donald and I were little?"

If she's trying to shock me, then she's succeeded. "Inside? Inside prison?"

She nods.

"You're joking! You *never* told me that!"

"Are you sure?"

"You know you haven't! I think we'd have remembered, wouldn't we, Dana?"

"You're right, she never told us –"

"See!"

"– but," Dana goes on, "I remember hearing my mum talking about it to my dad when I was little. I remember because I found it all so excitingly shocking at the time. I was secretly thrilled because I'd never known anyone 'bad' before. I think I'd just started primary school. Maybe it was when I came home and told them that you were my new best friend. I guess they were worried. My parents didn't know I was listening of course."

"And you never mentioned you knew in all these years?" asks Caroline.

"And you never mentioned it – at all."

"But why didn't you?" asks Caroline.

"Well, even though I was little I understood that going

to prison was a very bad thing. Then, as we got older, I figured you'd be embarrassed if you knew I knew. More to the point, why didn't you tell me?"

"I used to find the idea mortifying. I lived in dread of anyone finding out." She shrugs. "I'm not quite so sensitive any more. I guess I've grown up."

I interrupt. "So, is anyone going to tell me why the man was in prison?"

Caroline turns to me. "Oh, for this scam he used to run. He'd put down a deposit and a month's rent on some swanky place, immediately re-advertise it as his own and, then, re-let it out to as many people as he could. Then, after they'd paid him in turn a month's rent plus their deposit, he'd give them a key except, when these poor trusting fools arrived to move in, they'd find the key didn't work and that they'd been duped. And Dad, of course, had absconded with all their money. Once he rented out the same apartment to twenty different people – that was his record. In fact, I think that was the time he was caught. He'd probably have got away with it except he didn't notice one of the potential renters taking photos of the flat's interior when he came to view it – this was in the days before camera phones and digital cameras. But as I recall, the guy's girlfriend was living abroad and he wanted to send her some images. Anyway, he caught Dad in one photo, in the background. They used that to identify him."

"Gosh!"

Caroline shrugs. "It was a long time ago. Just part of my dubious family history. He's a reformed character now." She laughs. "So he says." She takes another sip of her coffee. "I guess now that I'm older I can be more objective about it. I don't feel it's, like, a personal refection on me like I used to when I was younger."

"So, will we get to meet him?" I ask.

"Not if I can help it."

Later that evening I ring the Bayview only to find they're booked solid for the next year. I start ringing other five-star hotels but, at such short notice, I learn that one after another is booked up on the night of the anniversary. Finally I do get lucky – the Bloomsbury Court has had a wedding cancellation and the woman on the line tells me its function room is available on the night in question and most of the bedrooms are free too. It's probably *the* most expensive hotel in the city but I book it immediately.

No sooner have I put down the phone when Finn rings.

"Hi, Rosie."

"Hi, Finn."

I'm glad to hear from him. It's the first time I have since our disastrous meal.

"We're going on stage soon but I just wanted to say goodnight."

"I'm glad you rang."

"So you're not still mad at me?"

"Of course not. Are you mad with me?"

"God no!" He pauses. "Rosie, I'm sorry if you thought I was being so negative."

"Don't worry about it. I understand why you're concerned." And the thing is, I do. It is understandable. No wonder he is. Me going to work for Caroline must seem crazy to him. He doesn't know the full story. That she – we – have the finance. "So we're okay?"

"Of course."

"Good. By the way, can you keep the night of Friday, the twenty-eight, free?"

235

"I think I already have. Isn't that the night of your parents' anniversary do in the Nutley?"

"Yes, and no. Yes, it is the night of their anniversary do, but it's no longer in the Nutley Arms."

"I thought your parents were set on having it there. How come they've changed?"

"They didn't. They don't even know yet. Instead of the Nutley, it's now going to be held at the Bloomsbury Court."

Finn leaves out a whistle. "The Bloomsbury Court – wow!"

"Pretty impressive, don't you think?"

"Ah – yeah. It'll cost them a fortune."

"They're not paying for it."

"So who is?"

"Me."

"What? You're kidding!"

"I had a bit of good luck."

"What? You won the lotto?"

If only you knew, I think, but I laugh and say: "I wish! But I did win a prize. Remember, before I went to London there was this competition on the *Gerry Ryan Show*?"

"No."

"Well, there was. And I found out I won today. To be honest I'd more or less forgotten I'd entered. Who ever imagines they're going to win something like this? Anyway, the prize is an all-expenses anniversary party at the Bloomsbury – a sit-down meal, with music afterwards, plus flights and accommodation for all immediate family. I was about to give you a call to tell you when you rang."

"But that's just brilliant, Rosie! What did you have to do?"

"What do you mean?"

"To win the prize?"

"I had to submit a romantic little anecdote about my parents."

"What was it?"

"The anecdote?"

"Yes."

Oh dear! I haven't thought that far yet. "Well, I told them about the time . . . Look, Finn, I have to go – can I tell you another time?"

"Why? What's up?"

I try to think of an excuse. "It's just that Caroline wants to talk. She's pretty upset. Her dad rang her out of the blue today and wants to meet up with her. I'll tell you another time, okay?"

"Sure, but –"

"Okay, then, talk to you tomorrow. Love you."

On the day of his win, his wife filed the paperwork for a
divorce

Juan Rodriguez - $149 million - US

. . . and the paperwork for her share of the winnings.

17

The very last time I bumped into Seán was when he was squatting in the old youth hostel belonging to Caroline's brother, Donald. After Donald bought it, and while he was waiting for planning permission, he let Dana use it for a weekend when she was carrying out some research for college and needed a place to bring a group of students. Caroline, Doug and I went with her to help her supervise the students but even our help wasn't enough. Although there were gale force winds blowing that weekend, two of them stupidly decided to take a walk along the cliff edge by the property and were swept into sea. They'd have drowned too but for the fact that, while the rest of us stood around gaping, Doug and Seán (who we'd discovered squatting the day before but who we couldn't even think of turning out in such inclement weather regardless of what Donald might say) dived in after them. And, yes, quiet, gentle Doug and thin, malnourished Seán – the two unlikely heroes – saved the lives of those foolish students. Afterwards, a coastal rescue helicopter airlifted everyone to hospital.

But before Seán dived into the water, he left his

belongings on a heap on the beach and I brought them with me to the hospital only to find he'd already discharged himself. Not knowing what to do with his things I kept them, thinking I was bound to bump into him again. But as time passed, I got rid of most of it. It was just replaceable stuff, clothes mainly. But I did hold on to his precious photo.

Having got Donald's number from Caroline, I leave her in the kitchen and go into the quiet of the living-room to phone him.

"Donald, hi! This is Rosie Kiely, Caroline's friend."

"Rosie, long time no hear! How're things?"

"Good. How are you?"

"So-so. I'd like to say business was never better but I'd be lying. Anyway, you don't want to hear my woes, what can I do for you?"

"Donald, you still have the youth hostel down in Wicklow, don't you?"

"Unfortunately yes."

"You haven't gone ahead with your plans to redevelop it?"

"No. Why? Are you interested in buying it?" he says jokingly.

"Afraid not."

"I didn't think so. Anyway, why do you want to know?"

"Well, remember the homeless guy who was squatting there last summer?"

"That madman who jumped in with Dana's boyfriend and saved those crazy kids?"

"Yeah. He didn't ever come back again after that, did he?"

"No. Or even if he did there's no way he or anyone else

240

could get in – that place is like Fort Knox now. I had it all boarded up."

"Caroline told me as much but I figured there was no harm in double-checking."

Now Dana comes in. I mouth, "Hi!" to her as she flops down on the couch beside me.

"Oh well," I say to Donald, "it was worth a shot."

"Why are you looking for him?" Donald asks.

"It's a long story. Listen, would it be okay if I went down there anyway? Just to take a look around."

"Sure, though it'll be a wasted journey. A security firm keeps an eye on the place for me – they'd have noticed anything untoward."

"I might just pay a visit, if that's okay."

"It's fine by me."

"Thanks Donald."

"Rosie?"

"Yes?"

"You'd better warn Caroline that our dad rang me yesterday."

"He rang her too. He wanted to meet her."

"Well, if she does meet him tell her to be wary. No doubt he's looking for money. Whenever else do we hear from him?"

"She suspects as much. Thanks again, Donald."

"No problem, see you, Rosie."

I hang up.

I look over at Dana. She has her eyes shut.

"What's up with you? You look wrecked."

"What a day!" groans Dana.

"Why, what happened?"

She sits up. "Where will I start?" She thinks for a second.

"Okay, well, Cathy's mum rang me out of the blue this afternoon to ask if I'd collect Cathy from the crèche and mind her for a couple of hours because something had come up at work and she was going to be delayed."

"But I thought she didn't want you minding Cathy any more?"

"She never quite said that but she had stopped asking me. I guess she must have been badly stuck today and there was no one else she could turn to. Anyway, I did collect Cathy but, since I'd already arranged to meet my own mum in town for something to eat, I decided to bring Cathy with me."

"But your mum doesn't want to have anything to do with Cathy?"

"She doesn't. Or didn't."

"So why did you meet her when you had Cathy with you?"

"I wanted Mum to see Cathy and to tell me what she thought. I felt I needed another opinion from someone . . . well . . . someone whose judgement I'd trust."

I'm a little surprised to hear this. Mrs Vaughan is the last person I thought Dana would turn to. She's spent so much time worrying about her this past year.

"Well, actually it was Doug's idea to involve her," she concedes. "He was with me when Ann rang."

"So, what did she think?"

"Well, she spent some time engaging with Cathy in the restaurant and then, afterwards, Doug and I showed her some of my psychology textbooks, parts we'd picked out that we thought were important and, as it turns out, she too thinks Cathy may be autistic."

"Autistic. Oh dear! Poor Cathy."

"I know but it's what I've been thinking myself. And

Doug too. So anyway, Mum insisted on coming with me when I went to drop Cathy home. I swear, Ann nearly died when she opened the door and I introduced them. They've never met, you know. I think Ann thought maybe Mum was drinking again and had come to cause trouble. She must have thought her worst nightmare was coming true!" Dana manages a laugh. "But you should have seen my mum, Rosie – she was so collected, so together. It's the first time she's come face-to-face with the 'other woman'."

"That must have been hard for her."

"I imagine, but you'd never have known by her. Very calmly, she asked Ann could she come in, that she wanted to have a few words about Cathy and, I swear, Ann was so taken aback she just let her in. So Ann took us into the living-room and then Mum outlined clearly her concerns regarding Cathy, very calmly, point-by-point. She didn't mention autism *per se* but suggested in the gentlest way that Ann should take Cathy to see her GP. Mum didn't really say any more than what I'd already said but, this time, Ann actually listened and agreed she would.

"That's amazing."

"Isn't it? I think Ann was so dumbstruck by the whole situation she'd have agreed to anything. Then, when we were getting up to go, Ann was the one who brought up the past. She started telling Mum how she never meant to get involved with Dad but Mum just gave her this look, and said something like, 'Let's just leave that in the past, shall we, and concern ourselves with what's important now, with Cathy.' And then she just walked out regally. I had to hurry to keep up with her." Dana smiles. "You know, I have never been so proud of her in my life. I know she's done some difficult things, like take Dad back for one, and give up drinking completely for another but, today, she really was just fantastic! I think I, and Dad too, have forgotten what she can be like. We're so nervous of upsetting her, we've tended to treat her with kid gloves this past year."

"Well, that's understandable. She has been through a rough time."

"Yes, but we tend to forget what she was like before the whole business with Dad and Ann, and Cathy of course, and her drinking too. And, even more so that, years ago, she was this capable, driven, high-flying manager with dozens of staff under her."

"I didn't know that."

"She was. She only gave up work when she had me. Dad's job was so all-consuming and hers too that she felt they couldn't both keep working at that level. That's when she decided to gave it all up to stay at home and mind me. But, really, isn't it incredible what she did today?"

"It is."

"What's more – and you won't believe this – she even told Ann that she understood how difficult it must be trying to work and to bring up a child with so little family support but that if Ann wanted her to go with her to the GP then she would. After all, as she said, Cathy was her own daughter's – my – half-sister and her husband's daughter and that made her family, no matter that either of them might like to think otherwise."

Who says you have to be good to be lucky?

Iorworth Hoare - €7 million - UK

What do prisoners do when out on day release? Purchase a lottery ticket?

18

The doorbell rings. It's probably Caroline's dad. Despite
what she said, somehow he has managed to persuade her to
meet him and he's calling this evening. She told us there was
no need to hang around. In fact, I think she'd have preferred
if we all went out but I'm staying put, there's no way I'm
going to miss the chance of meeting him.

The doorbell rings again.

"Caroline! The door!" I listen for a moment but I don't
hear any movement from her room upstairs. "Caroline!" She
probably can't hear over the music. I pull myself up from the
couch and go to answer it myself.

The first thing I notice about the man standing on our
doorstep is his hair and, suddenly, the term 'bouffant' leaps
into my mind though I've never had call to use it before and
I'm not even sure what it means. But I think I'm looking at
it now. I think this man's white, wavy, luxuriant hair is it.
Next I notice his tan and his teeth – at the same time really,
they kind of go hand-in-hand: his deep mahogany leathery
tan emphasising his brilliant white, prominent teeth; his
brilliant white, prominent teeth emphasising his deep

mahogany leathery tan. The other details are less remarkable. He's dressed conventionally enough in a neat, well-cut dark grey suit; black, highly polished shoes; and a pink shirt, open at the neck. I'm guessing he's in his late fifties, early sixties. For some reason I expected him to be taller but this guy is a dapper little fellow, a little over five-and-a-half foot, and his hair contributes quite a few inches.

"Hi there!" His smile is so broad and so white I almost expect to be blinded by a cartoon dazzle, but it's a charismatic smile and I find I'm automatically smiling back at him. I like his eyes too. They're very smiley. Roguish.

"Hello. Mr Connolly?"

"Right first time. And don't tell me, you must be . . .?" He begins, like my name is on the very tip of his tongue.

"Rosie," I tell him.

"Rosie, of course, of course." His voice is low, throaty, smooth. I catch a glimpse of diamond cufflink sparkling at his wrist where his pink cuff peeps out as he takes my hand in his and brings it to his lips. "A perfect name for a perfect creature," he says as he kisses it.

"Oh!" Of course I can see how corny all this is, he is, but still I find I'm practically simpering.

"Eddie!" I hear a shout,

Over his shoulder, I now see a peroxide blonde clattering up our path in small steps restricted by her tight skirt, her stiletto heels, her full-length leopard-patterned coat and her outsized handbag. Everything about her – apart from her slim, shapely legs – is big: big hair, big eyes, big lips, big boobs. She is, I see, younger than I thought at first glance, younger that her clothes suggest, and far younger than Mr Connolly. I'm guessing mid-twenties.

"Pay the taxi-man, honey. I don't have a red cent."

"Sure, sure, my sweet." Eddie gently drops my hand, gives me a wink, then turns and goes back down the path. He's got a jaunty walk. He's like a little bantam hen. Despite Caroline's warnings, despite his shady past, I think I'm going to like him.

"Hi there!" says the blonde and then, before I know what's happening, I find the woman is hugging me. "Caroline! I'm so pleased to finally meet you."

I try to pull away but she has a surprisingly firm hold. "Ah, I'm not Caroline, I'm her friend, Rosie."

She lets go. "Oh." She looks me up and down, and up again. "I did wonder how my little Eddie could have such an Amazon as a daughter. "Well, hello, Rosie. Nice to meet you. I'm Mrs Connolly."

"Mrs Connolly?"

"That's right."

To me, Mrs Connolly is Caroline's mum. I didn't know there was another Mrs Connolly. A *new* Mrs Connolly? Nor – as far as I know – does Caroline. Oh! My! God! *What* is Caroline going to say?

Unaware of my astonishment, Mrs Connolly No 2 goes on. "Course, you can call me Vivienne, or Viv for short."

"Ahmm so, you and Mr Connolly are – ah – married?"

"Yeah! Sure are. Me and Eddie tied the knot in Vegas."

"Ah – congratulations!"

"Thanks! Want to see my ring? It all happened so fast it's a combined engagement and wedding ring." She holds out her hand.

I know nothing about diamonds but this one is enormous. "Wow, it's amazing!"

"Glad you think so." She leans in and whispers conspiratorially. "It cost Eddie a fortune!"

Out of idle curiosity, I'm tempted to ask how much. Seriously, like how much are we talking here? I have no idea. I do refrain from asking. Instead:

"So you got married in Vegas?"

"Yep. What a hoot! We had the Elvis package."

"Pardon?"

"The Elvis package," she repeats like everyone – like I – should know exactly what this means.

"What's that?"

"Elvis married us. Not the real one, of course, but an impersonator. I'm telling you it was just amazing! He walked me up the aisle. He sang at the ceremony: 'Love me Tender', 'Blue Moon', and 'Be my Teddy Bear' – though he changed the words for us to, 'Be my Eddie Bear'. Eddie Bear? Get it? And afterwards he gave us gifts of special Elvis glasses!"

"Elvis glasses? So you could toast your wedding?"

"No, no, to wear! You know, silver ones with pink lenses – just like the ones Elvis wore. There's a great photo of me with them on, in my wedding dress. What a laugh! Ah, it was just the best! Such a day! Course, the Elvis was a real minister. I mean, trust me, it was a legit wedding, all properly legal." Suddenly she squeals. Eddie, who has come back up the path has surprised her by giving her a pat on the bum. "Eddie! You're terrible!"

"But ya gotta love me!"

"Sure do, with all my heart!"

Now he gives her a full-on kiss.

As I'm standing there, wondering whether they're kind of (a) cute or (b) nauseating, they break off and Mr Connolly turns to me.

"So, Rosie, is Caroline in?"

"Sure, come in, I'll tell her you're here." Oh, this is going to be good!

Mr Connolly takes his wife's hand and I go in first and they follow in after me. "You go ahead into the living-room," I tell them. "It's there on the right and I'll go upstairs and get Caroline."

I climb the stairs, knock on Caroline's door loudly and call out her name.

"Caroline?"

The music goes dead. "Yes?"

I go in. She's sitting cross-legged on her bed. Spread out before her are brochures from estate agents and sheets of her writing, pages of notes and calculations.

"Your dad's here."

"Oh! I didn't hear the bell." She throws her legs over the side of the bed, then stands up. "I'd better go down to him."

"Ah – there's one thing."

"What?"

"He's with someone."

"Oh! Who?"

"Well – ahmm – his wife."

She looks puzzled. "What? *Mum's* here? With *him*?"

"No, I mean his, well, his *new* wife. It appears he's just got married in Vegas."

"Rosie, that is *not* funny! How could you say such a thing?"

"Caroline, I'm not kidding. I'm telling you the truth." Suddenly, aware of the bombshell I'm dropping, I feel sorry for her. I'm no longer amused by the situation.

"I don't believe this!"

"Caroline!" I call after her but she's already gone storming out.

Seconds later, I hear her barging into the living-room. I hear her father's happy cry of "Hello there!" I hear Vivienne say something too. Then I hear Caroline – rat-tat-tat-tat-tat – like she's shooting off questions. Then I hear everyone talking at once. I hear Caroline's voice raised above the others. I hear her father's plaintive tones. I hear the living-room door opening again. I hear them all out in the hall. I hear the front door opening now and the sounds of cars passing outside. "Caroline, come on! You're being childish!" I hear her dad protest. I hear no response from her. "Right, then we will go," I hear him say. I hear the front door being slammed shut. Then a moment's silence. And then, I hear Caroline bounding back up the stairs to where I'm still standing on the landing.

She is – I see – furious.

"Can you believe it! Of all the ridiculous things! Married! Vegas! Elvis! Pink glasses!" She can hardly spit the words out fast enough. "I mean, seriously! He's an old man for crying out loud! What's he doing heading off to Vegas at his age to get married? And, like, what age is she anyway? Twenty-eight? Twenty-nine? Where on earth did he find her? The internet? Bloody Lisdoonvarna? Soho? And did you see her outfit! Come on! Leopard skin! Jeez! I swear there's no fool like an old fool. He's old enough to be her father! And just how thick is he? Can't he see she's only after him for his money? I mean –"

"But you said he doesn't have money," I interrupt.

"And he doesn't." She gives a bitter laugh. "But *she* clearly doesn't know that! Did you see her flashing around that diamond like it's real?"

"Isn't it?"

"Of course it isn't! When he picked it out of the catalogue, he probably got change out of his tenner!"

Caroline is my friend so I know that my role at this moment is to just listen to her. It is not my place to say that I thought they were kind of cute together – over-the-top but cute. Or say, that – in an odd way – they looked really suited. Or that – hey – they might actually be in love. And, unless I want to be permanently estranged from her, I will not say at this delicate point in time that I don't really see what the problem is. That, after all, he and Caroline's mum have been divorced for years.

The other thing I will not say to Caroline is that she was wrong about this whole evening. She assumed he was calling around to get something from her, to scrounge off her, whereas, it seems to me, all he wanted to do was show off his new wife and to share their happiness with his daughter.

"I wonder if he's told Mum or Donald yet? I'm going to give them a call."

"If this can help even a little those who have met with unhappiness and disaster, I would be very happy."

Anonymous - 200 million yen - Japan

So wrote the anonymous benefactor in a letter accompanying his winning lottery ticket sent to help disaster victims of landslides and floods which had caused some 9,141 people to flee their homes.

19

In light of the disclosure of Mr Connolly's hasty marriage yesterday, the events of today seem even *more* extraordinary than they might otherwise though they are extraordinary, quite extraordinary, in their own right.

There I am, walking down Grafton Street doing a bit of shopping, when I notice this guy coming in the opposite direction. As in love as I am with Finn, I admit to casting sneaky glances at this absolute Adonis strolling so casually amongst us when it occurs to me that he looks oddly familiar. I think maybe I know him from the movies, or TV. I swear, he's that good-looking.

"Rosie!" Suddenly he comes to a halt before me.

I'm tempted to look around, to see if there's another Rosie standing behind me but, no, he's looking straight at me and then, in a flash, recognition dawns. It's Mick – yes, Caroline's Mick.

"Oh my God, Mick!"

"Good to see you, Rosie. How's it going?"

I'm stunned. I can't stop staring at him. I swear I've never seen anyone undergo such a dramatic transformation. Yes,

Mick-the-farmer-cum-actor has undergone the most extraordinary metamorphosis and has turned into Mick-the-actor-cum-Adonis! Since Caroline first brought Mick into our lives I've always liked him. What's not to like in someone with such a big heart, such a big personality? But – hand on my own heart – *never* in all the time I've known him have I ever considered him particularly attractive. Until now, that is. In the several months since I've seen him, his hair has grown much longer, to shoulder-length, and while it used to be an unruly bush now it's a sexily wavy head of locks. It's a different shade too. Before it was more straw-coloured – as perhaps befits his rural background, now it's a surfer-blond – courtesy, I presume, of the Oz sun. And his skin is less Irishman-ruddy and more cosmopolitan-tanned. And his clothes are different too – far more fashionable than they used to be, which isn't saying much and what I guess I mean is that they are actually fashionable now but before they weren't – at all. And whereas Dana and I once used to tease Caroline about the fact that Mick is ten years older than her, now he seems to have lost several of those years since I saw him last. And sure, Mick was always comfortable in his own skin but the way he carries himself now is different, there's a self-confidence about him that I just don't remember. Maybe that's the biggest difference of all.

Anyway, after further exclamations of surprise and delight, and a big rib-compressing bear hug from him – Mick was always a little over-exuberant – he suggests we go for coffee.

So there I am, sitting at one of the tables at a little kiosk on that boardwalk running along by the Liffey, waiting for Mick, marvelling at the difference in him as he stands in line for our coffees. In due time, he gets served, then comes back carrying a cup in each hand. He sits down opposite me.

"Thanks, Mick."

"My pleasure," he says and smiles. He always had a great smile. That hasn't changed. His accent, I notice, hasn't changed either. It's still the same – pure Cork.

"So when did you get back?"

"Just a couple of days ago. I had to cut short my trip – my agent wanted me to go to London to audition for a part."

"Is it a big part?"

"Not very big, no, but it's a good one – one I'd love to get. It would be a chance to work on a big budget movie. Edward Norton has already been cast in the lead. The part I'm up for is that of his brother."

"That's amazing!"

"Steady on! I haven't got it yet."

"When will you hear if you have?"

"Well, I'm flying over to London again tonight. I have a call back tomorrow."

"That sounds promising."

"It could be."

"When is *Fate Farm* coming out?" Mick's role as the main character in that movie was his big break in acting. He'd just finished filming it when he left for Australia with Caroline. In fact, the fee he got for his role paid for their entire trip.

"The premiere is coming up. You should come."

"I'd love to."

"Great! I'll make sure you get an invitation."

As Mick takes a sip of his coffee, I can't help thinking how much things have changed for him and, again, how much he's changed. Okay, in all the important ways he's still the same old Mick but, listening as all these terms – agents, call-backs, auditions – come tripping of his tongue so easily, it's like he's been at this game forever. Yet, it's less than a year since he got his big break which he might never have got but for Caroline's persistence. When she learned that the director Kevin North was a patient in the hospital where Shane's girlfriend, Loretta, worked Caroline managed to persuade Loretta to ask North to let Mick read for the part in *Fate Farm*.

There has, I realise now, been no mention of Caroline yet. I tear open another sachet of sugar and pour it into my coffee as I think what I'm going to say. "You know, this really is such a surprise. Caroline never said you were back."

"Well, she wouldn't, would she? She doesn't know."

"She told me about your big fight."

"Yeah?"

"Yeah." Then I hesitate. I think what I'm going to say next. I like Mick, always have. I certainly don't want to fall out with him but I see no point in beating around the bush. I'm just going to come straight out with it. "Look, I know Caroline can be impossible sometimes but, to be honest, I was surprised you left her on her own in Melbourne like that."

Mick looks puzzled. "Pardon?"

"Especially when you knew she hadn't any money."

Mick sits back in his seat. "Ah, what did she tell you happened – exactly?"

"Well, that you were both heading up to Queensland and had got as far as the bus station but then you had a stupid fight over you giving money to some beggar and that you just got on the bus and left her behind in Melbourne."

"I see." He doesn't say anything immediately but takes another sip from his cup. He seems to be mulling over what

I've just said. Finally he responds. "Okay, well, we did have a big fight — that much is true. But not much else."

"Oh?"

"First off, she wasn't penniless. She had a card and a pin number for my bank account. Second, it is true we were going up to Queensland but what Caroline seems to have omitted to tell you is that we were going on . . ." he pauses for a moment — I notice he's looking at me keenly, ". . . our honeymoon."

"Pardon?" I just about manage not to splutter coffee all over him.

"I take it she neglected to tell you we got married?"

"Married! You've got to be joking!"

He shakes his head.

"She never said a word!"

"That's probably because she regretted it right from the start. I think she was looking for an excuse not to come to Queensland. I think she was just looking for something — anything — to fight about."

"You and Caroline married? You're serious?"

"Deadly serious."

"But how? When? And why?"

"Okay." He sighs. "Do you remember when Caroline and I first met?"

"Sure, on the train from Cork."

He nods. "I was moving to Dublin, she was returning from some business meeting. We sat beside each other for over two and a half hours and I don't think we stopped talking once. It was weird really but there was so much I wanted to tell her and I just wanted to know every little thing about her too. Then, when we arrived in Dublin, she offered to put me up. I guess I knew she was being kind, that she just felt sorry for me, but I said yes anyway though I already had somewhere else to stay."

I laugh. "We were so amazed when she walked in the door with you. It was so unlike Caroline to be the Good Samaritan to a complete stranger."

Mick smiles. "I remember lying on your couch that night, when you'd all gone to bed, and I just couldn't get to sleep for thinking about her. I kept going back over our conversation on the train, I kept thinking over every little detail of her appearance, and all the other little things too: how good she smelled, how she threw her head back when she laughed that great big laugh of hers. I think I was a little in love with her right from that very first day."

I smile. "I think we all kind of guessed that."

"But Caroline wasn't in love with me –"

I'm about to protest because that's simply not true. I think she was in love with him too from the word go but she just refused to admit it to herself. But Mick doesn't give me a chance.

"– she just wanted us to be friends. If it was up to her that's what we'd have remained. You know, I worry sometimes that I – like – well – I – that because I loved her so much I practically convinced her she was in love with me. The same with the wedding. It wouldn't have occurred to Caroline that we should get married but once I got the idea into my head, I got carried away. On hindsight, I guess I should have told her about my plans but maybe – deep down – I was afraid of her reaction."

"So, what are you saying? You arranged it all without her knowing?"

"Yeah."

"She knew nothing?"

He shakes his head. "Nothing. I filed a notice of intended marriage a month before the wedding as required. Then, a few days before the big day, we were out shopping when she spotted a dress she really liked but it was very expensive so I went back later that day and got it for her. On the morning of the wedding, I gave her the dress, persuaded her to put it on, then we took a tram out to St Kilda's where Jan and Rick, two friends we made when we were travelling, were waiting on the beach with the celebrant. It was only then she realised what was going on. I know she was very surprised but she seemed okay with everything. But, looking back, I think she just didn't know how to get out of it."

I shake my head. "You're wrong, Mick. Caroline wouldn't have gone through with it unless she wanted to. And you didn't persuade her she was in love with you either. I know she was, maybe even right from the beginning. She just didn't want to admit it because you were so far from the kind of fellow she imagined loving. No offence but you weren't exactly the hotshot young corporate type she imagined ending up with. But she was – is – definitely in love with you."

Mick doesn't look convinced. "Well, how do you explain the next day then? There we were, off on honeymoon. We were going to spend a week surfing up in Cairns and then a second week in the Daintree where I'd booked this amazing little romantic tree-house in the middle of the rainforest – all wooden decks and hammocks and views out over the trees. It cost a fortune! Everything was okay, or so I thought, until we got to the bus station. And then she started this ridiculous fight. She was *looking* for a reason not to go."

"I think you're wrong, Mick."

He shrugs. "You know what her last words to me were? That I was a control freak and that she should never have married me." He's silent for a moment. "I did wonder why she never used my bank card. I presume she changed her flight and flew straight home."

"She's home now but she stayed on in Melbourne for a while."

"But how did she survive? She didn't have a work permit or anywhere to stay or any cash either."

"She was working in a hostel for the homeless."

He stares. "Am I hearing things or did you just say she was working in a hostel for the homeless?"

"I did."

"I don't understand."

I get my thoughts together. "Caroline did tell me your fight started off over some homeless girl *but* she also told me that you said she was heartless with no compassion for anyone."

Mick looks a little shamefaced. "I might have."

"Well, it seems something of that sank in."

"You think she was working in this hostel because of what I said?"

"Yes. But also it was a means for her to stay on in Melbourne without your help."

He gives a loud laugh. "The silly fool!" But he has a fond look on his face.

"Are you going to ring her?"

He nods his head. "You have no idea how miserable I've been without her. She drives me crazy but I love her."

It's early evening when I get home and I find Caroline in front of the TV. She has the remote control in one hand and is idly flicking from channel to channel. She has this annoying habit of half-looking at several programmes at once.

She glances up. "Hi there." Then, before I get a chance to say anything, she goes on, "I hope you're free tomorrow. Tom Redmond, that solicitor, finally rang this morning. He's back at work after his holidays and happens to be travelling up to Dublin tomorrow. He has some business in the High Court in the afternoon but he can meet us in the morning. I suggested the Shelbourne Hotel and he was happy with that."

"Fine."

"What's up? You look very solemn."

I go to the screen and turn it off.

"Hey! I was watching that!"

"Did you get a phone call?"

"Yes, from Tom Redmond. Didn't I just tell you?"

"I mean any others."

"I don't know. My phone's upstairs now."

"You'll never guess who I met in town."

"No, I probably wouldn't so why don't you just tell me."

"Surprise marriages seem to run in your family. I met your *husband*!"

"Oh!"

"Oh! Is that all you have to say? Why the hell didn't you tell us about you and Mick?"

"Why?"

"Yes, why? Caroline, don't just sit there, looking at me. Why didn't you tell me about Mick? About you getting married?"

She throws her hands up in the air. "Because I wish it had never happened. Because it was the stupidest mistake of my life. Because . . . because . . . he'll soon be my ex-husband."

"You're going to divorce him?"

"I am divorcing him but it'll take bloody ages. Because we married in Australia we have to be legally separated for twelve months."

"First I hear you got married. And now I hear you're getting divorced! For God's sake! Don't you think you could try to make it work?"

"It would never work! It should never have happened in the first place. It was a stupid mistake!"

"But you were happy together before, weren't you?"

She shrugs.

"You were, Caroline. You know you were! Admit it!"

"All right! All right! Maybe we were."

"So then, what changed?"

"Being married – of course. It changed *everything*."

"Caroline! How can you be so ridiculous! You were married what – a day?"

"And that was enough for me to know!"

"I've never heard anything so absurd! Who gives up on a marriage that soon?"

"Britney Spears – for one."

"Ah well, that's okay so. And tell me, what next? Are you going to shave off all your hair too? Caroline, I really don't get any of this. What went wrong?"

"Our relationship was never right to begin with!"

"Caroline, that's just not tru –"

"Well, maybe at the start. But when we got to Australia he was insufferable. Flashing his money all over the place. Making sure we both knew who was paying for everything."

"I don't believe that. That's not Mick! You were probably

just too sensitive. When you met, he was the one who was struggling in his career and you were doing so well. You probably couldn't get used to it when it became the other way around."

"Yes, well, all I know is he spent the whole time when we were away rubbing my nose into just how well he got paid for his role in *Fate Farm*. He really delighted in paying for everything."

"Come on! He paid because you had no money to pay. You'd lost everything in our shop. He took you with him to help you get over that disappointment. But you knew that before you went away. His money was what allowed you to go in the first place."

Caroline shrugs. I can see she's not listening to me. "You know he even paid for my bloody wedding dress."

"Oh, for crying out loud, Caroline! Others might look upon that as incredibly romantic."

"Incredibly romantic? Incredibly controlling, you mean. And who organises a wedding without telling the other person?"

"Someone who is incredibly romantic?"

"Or someone who is incredibly controlling."

"Oh, come on, Caroline! This is Mick we're talking about. You're being ridiculous. And, anyway, why did you go through with the wedding if you felt like this?"

She shrugs. "I was taken so completely off-guard. I had no idea what he was planning. Not when he persuaded me to put on the dress he bought for me. Not when we were on that tram out to St Kilda's. Not even when I saw our friends, Jan and Rick, on the beach. I only realised what was going on when he introduced me to the celebrant. And, yes, I should have called a halt to things then but I was carried away by the moment. And it all happened so quickly. There was hardly time to think. It was all so unreal. Mick – everybody else – was just so excited, even the crowd of strangers who had gathered around to watch and take photos. It wasn't until later, after we'd had this fabulous meal and had gone back to the swanky honeymoon suite Mick had booked for the night that I began to panic. It occurred to me that Mick was the one planning everything now – my dress, the wedding, the expensive meal afterwards, the honeymoon suite, and then the exotic two-week trip. Suddenly he was the one making all the decisions, he was the one controlling everything. All my life, I'd made my own choices but here was Mick taking over. I began thinking what it would be like when we got home to Ireland. I'd be Mrs Mick Boylan, the wife of an up-and-coming actor, with no job, no role of my own. That was what the fight at the train station was really about. I knew I had made a terrible mistake."

I guess I can understand all this, even if I do think she overreacted. Caroline has worked hard all her life. Until the failure of our shop, she had always been very successful, independent and in control. But Mick isn't an unreasonable person. If Caroline had talked to him about her fears, he'd have listened. I think they could have worked things out.

Now something occurs to me.

"You know when Dana and I turned up in Melbourne?"

"Yeah?"

"And you told us you'd no money?"

"I hadn't."

"But Mick told me you had a bank card with access to his account."

"I did, but I threw it away when I started working in the hostel. I'd had enough of him and his money."

"But you gave us the impression Mick left you stranded without a penny."

Caroline shrugs.

Then another thought occurs to me. "Caroline, since you and Mick are married then isn't he entitled to a share of your lotto win?"

"Excuse me?"

Something in her response tells me this notion isn't a new one to her.

"Is that the reason you wanted to keep the win a secret?"

"No!"

"But it occurred to you?"

"If you remember it was your and Dana's idea to keep it quiet in the first place."

"To keep it quiet *only* until we met you. You were the one who persuaded both of us to keep on doing so."

"But you were only too happy to go along with it."

"That's not strictly true. I still wonder if we did the right thing but let's not go there. Tell me the truth, when you persuaded us to keep it a secret, was it because of Mick?"

"No," she answers vehemently.

"Really?"

"I swear I hadn't even thought of it at that stage. That only dawned on me later." Then suddenly she explodes. "Rosie, we were married for just one day! Why should I hand over more than one-and-a-half million euros because of a stupid mistake that lasted a day? Why should I hand over so much as a single penny? And anyway, what difference would it make to Mick? He has more money than he knows what to do with and that's aside from being the only offspring of farmers who own a house the size of a palace, plus half the land in County Cork. Look, Mick neither wants nor needs this money. But I do. Maybe legally speaking he is entitled to a share, but not morally. I'm sure I could get an annulment if I wanted. We split up after a day, *one* day, *and* it had nothing to do with the lotto – I didn't even know about that then. It hadn't even happened yet."

She's obviously given considerable thought to all this already. She goes on.

"Rosie, this money is a chance for me to really make something of myself. If I just hand over half to Mick do you think he'd ever let me invest it in the way we're doing? He'd never take that chance. He's much too cautious."

"Unlike us?"

"Pardon?"

"You persuaded Dana and me to let you use *our* money. Because of us, you have eleven million at your disposal to invest. Actually . . ." A thought occurs to me. Given that Caroline hadn't paid any money into the syndicate in the months before our win and, given that she didn't even consider herself still part of it then, it could be argued that Dana and I weren't morally obliged, or legally, to give her anything, not a cent.

"Actually, what?" Caroline is demanding.

But I hold my tongue. If I say all this, I can't easily take it back. Besides, I'm okay with Caroline having her share. From the start I've always thought of it as hers.

"Actually what?" repeats Caroline.

I need to think this through. Before I blurt out something I'll regret.

"Rosie?"

"Nothing. Forget it."

"Are you going to tell Dana about me and Mick?" Caroline demands.

"Why shouldn't I?"

"Because you know what she'll be like. She'll probably try to practise some of the theory she's learning in college on me and Mick, try to get us back together."

"And would that be such a bad thing?"

"Rosie, I don't want to get back together. I don't ever even want to see Mick again. And I don't want to talk about him either. All right!"

"You don't want to talk about who?" Dana is standing in the doorway.

"Nobody!" snaps Caroline.

"Mick!" I snap.

"What about Mick?"

"He and Caroline got married in Australia."

Dana looks confused. "You're winding me up?"

"But it didn't last long. Caroline walked out on him the very next day!"

"So what if I did! It's nobody else's business." And with that, she storms out of the room.

"What *are* you talking about?" asks Dana looking baffled.

And so I explain as best I can and Dana listens, her eyes growing bigger and bigger with every detail. There is one detail I leave out however. That Mick could be entitled to a share of Caroline's win doesn't occur to Dana and I don't point it out. I really need time to think that one through.

"I can't believe she's divorcing him!" says Dana when I'm finished. "Is she mad? They're perfect for each other. I can't believe how stupid she's being!"

"Me neither." But then I think. "Dana, let's keep all this to ourselves for the moment."

"But why?"

"Mick's back in the country now. I know he's keen to

get in touch with her. Maybe they can work things out. It's not going to help matters if everyone is gossiping about them."

"I guess."

Later that night I go to one of Finn's gigs and despite the day's events I enjoy myself. The band are really on form and the crowd are very receptive. Afterwards I even get to see Big Bertha. I can understand why Mitch doesn't reciprocate her feelings. She looks like she could eat him for breakfast, and then some. And, yes, there's definitely a hint of a moustache above her upper lip. Ashley tries to persuade me to pretend I'm Mitch's girlfriend just to see what would happen but I decline – Big Bertha is one lady I wouldn't like to mess with. Poor Mitch! Then, when Finn suggests I go back to his house, that as well as Mitch and Ashley, some others are coming too, I tell him I want to go home on my own, that I'm tired. But that's a lie. Yet another one. I can see Finn's disappointed and I would really like to go but I can't talk to him about Caroline and Mick and what I do need is some time and space to think it through on my own.

For ages I lie there in my bed thinking about Caroline and Mick. The trouble with the pair of them is that they come from two such different places as regards money. What it means to each of them is so opposite. Mick's ambition in life is to be a success as an actor. To achieve this, he left the comfortable existence he had down in County Cork helping in the running of his parents' farm. Mick has no interest in money *per se* – probably because he's always had it. He grew up with doting parents, in a huge house, with the innate knowledge that, one day, he would stand to inherit it and the acres upon acres of surrounding land. Making money has never been his ambition. It's never had to be. Conversely, Caroline's overriding ambition is to make money. This I can understand too. Even when her parents were together, Caroline's young life must have been pretty fraught with her dad chasing after – and failing in – one-get-rich-quick scheme after another. When he finally left them, Caroline's mother struggled financially and I know she instilled in both Caroline and Donald a deep conviction that they needed to be successful in their own right, not to rely on others. And in Caroline's mind – success means money, but money she's made herself, and lots of it.

Caroline is one of my closest friends but Mick is a very good friend too. Even if they were married for just one day before splitting, shouldn't she tell him about her winnings? I don't even know if he is entitled to a share but if he is then shouldn't she give it to him? How would I feel if someone other than Caroline, some stranger, was keeping what was his? I'd be annoyed. And I am annoyed with her too – for how she's dealing with all of this.

But what's really important here? That Mick and Caroline get back together – yes, I would like to see that happen, but has the lotto win now make this less likely? Maybe. I don't know. I wish I could talk to Finn about it. I seem to be accumulating more and more secrets. I wish I didn't have any secrets. I wish I didn't have to think about any of this. That I didn't have to do anything about Mick and Caroline.

And then I realise maybe, just maybe, that is what I should do for now – nothing.

I have faith in Caroline's abilities to turn our money into more. With all three of us pooling our winnings as we are now, she will be able to achieve a lot. Maybe the key is to let that happen. If, when, Caroline begins to feel she is achieving something in her life, maybe she won't be so prickly about Mick. Like Dana said, they're perfect for each other. Despite everything, I do believe Caroline does love him and I know he loves her. It was the timing of their wedding that was wrong. I can see how it must have been for her in Australia – this young woman who never took a penny from anyone being completely dependent on someone else, someone who had no real concept of how hard that would be for her. And Mick surprising her with a wedding would have been the fatal twist of the blade in her self-respect.

So maybe, just maybe, I should leave things as they are for now. Mick isn't in need of the money. Maybe I should allow Caroline the time to make money out of our capital. When she's achieved that, maybe she'll be able to look at her and Mick's relationship differently – maybe she'll start seeing herself as a success again, and as Mick's equal. Maybe then she'll be ready to see that there could be a future for them together and, if there is a future for them then, Mick and whatever family they might have together, will automatically benefit from whatever Caroline owns. So, maybe the solution is not to interfere, to say nothing.

For now at any rate. While I wait and see what happens.

Unlucky or lucky? He survived a derailed train, a door-less plane, a bus crash, a car in flames, and another two car accidents.

Frane Selak – $1 million – Croatia

But when he bought his first lottery ticket in over 40 years luck was definitely on his side.

20

"Why did you pick here to meet?" Dana asks Caroline as we climb out of the taxi when it pulls up outside the Shelbourne Hotel.

"Same reason as the suits we're wearing," answers Caroline. "To impress Tom Redmond."

"But why do we need to impress him? We're the ones who are going to be employing him."

"I told you. I want him to buy us as successful business people without even thinking about it. Not for a second do I want him to doubt that, or to have any cause to wonder where our money is coming from."

It's odd to be dressed like this. I don't feel like myself; I never even wore a suit to work. And Dana doesn't even look like herself – I'd hardly recognise her. I haven't ever seen her in a suit before either, much less the severe dark one Caroline picked out for her. And her hair is scraped so tightly back in a bun that her eyebrows look as if they might take flight at any moment.

This is my first time coming to the Shelbourne. To be honest, I've always been a little intimidated by its grand façade and the city's well-heeled that confidently parade in and out. Caroline has been here before, of course, many times, but then where hasn't she been? Places like this were her old stomping ground when she worked in marketing. Maybe that's why she wasn't as overawed with our lotto win as Dana and I were. She's had more dealing with the wealthy; she was able to keep our newfound fortune in perspective. It's no surprise then that on our way in she meets some old business acquaintance of hers and, while she stops to have a word with him, Dana and I go on ahead. When Caroline does catch up with us, she finds us standing in the middle of the lobby, just staring around us.

"Try not to look so in awe," she tells us, which is reasonable but the newly renovated, old-world opulence is pretty impressive. "You know, maybe I shouldn't have agreed to here, maybe we should have arranged to go somewhere more discreet. Oh – well – too late. He's on his way over." She gives a wave.

I look around. I see a tall, gangly man taking long strides towards us. I didn't know Tom Redmond well in college but I don't remember him being quite so tall or gangly back then. The red hair I do remember and it's still there but less of it. It's no longer a wild stock but is shorn close to his head which I can't say is flattering. He was no oil painting in college but he's even less of one now and this new tight hair really emphasises the impossibly bony features of his face – a pavement caricaturist would have no need to exaggerate. But he is very well turned out in a dark suit, and a shirt and tie, the uniform of his profession. He's smiling over at us. So why then am I reminded of a predatory hyena? With sudden clarity, I remember how little I liked him even if I didn't know him particularly well.

He comes to a stop before us.

"Caroline!" He shakes her hand.

"And, if memory serves me, Dana?" He shakes her hand.

"And, of course Rosie – how could I forget!" When he shakes my hand I'm struck by how bony and corpse-like cold his is. "Ah, yes, Rosie." He gives me another smile. It's definitely a hyena that he calls to mind. "Well, I have to say you ladies are looking as lovely as ever." Unexpectedly, he gives a sort of whooping laugh but then, abruptly, he stops. "So, shall we go and find a quiet spot?" he asks, somehow managing to make it sound disconcertingly suggestive.

"Sure, you lead the way," says Caroline. "The Lord Mayor's Lounge would suit."

"Perfect! Nice and secluded." And then I swear he gives me a wink. But it's so quick and unexpected I immediately wonder if I imagined it. I look at the others but they don't seem to have noticed. "So onward then."

He strides on ahead of us and we follow after him. When we come to a set of doors, he makes a huge fuss of opening them and allowing each of us through before him but then, I notice, let's them swing shut on the pair of old ladies who are following behind us. When we reach what I presume is the Lord Mayor's Lounge we find a quiet corner and settle ourselves around a low round table in four deep red high-backed armchairs.

This is nice, I think, looking around, really nice: the gold wallpaper, the ridiculously high but very impressive ceilings, the heavy chandeliers, the floor-to-ceiling windows with their elegant drapes. I get the smell of fresh flowers before I see them but then I notice the huge arrangements throughout the room. I see a grand piano in one corner. Yes, very nice indeed.

But what is not very nice, not very nice at all, is what else I now see. Relaxing back into his armchair, Tom has crossed his long legs which has caused one of his trouser legs to rise up to reveal a stripy sock and several inches of thin, white, hairless shin.

"So," he says, "what can I do you for?" Once again he laughs as if he's made a hilarious joke.

"Well," begins Caroline, "we need a solicitor."

"Then you've come to the right man!" He gives yet another of his ridiculous laughs.

Is he though? Is he really the right man? I know we want someone who won't think to ask too many questions and will be happy to do what we want of him, again without too many questions. But, do we really want to saddle ourselves with a complete moron? Caroline, however, doesn't seem to have such reservations. Ignoring his skittish manner, she goes on in her most professional one:

"You see, Tom, in addition to our independent concerns which have been very successful for us as you're quite possibly aware –"

"Ah yes, sure."

What a liar! We have no independent concerns. All he could possibly have heard about us, and even that's unlikely, was our Love Potions shop and if he knows anything about it at all he'll know it ended in failure. I tune back in.

"So anyway, Tom," Caroline goes on, "all three of us are interested in exploring some financial opportunities together. Now we do each have our own solicitors – of course – but we need someone impartial to act for us collectively. You see, we feel it would be better to keep our own affairs separate from our joint affairs."

"Sure, sure. Very wise"

The waitress comes down. "Sir, ladies, may I offer you menus?"

Tom is about to respond but it's Caroline who gets there first.

"No, we've already decided," she says authoritatively, without consulting Tom or us. "We'll have afternoon tea for four, please."

"Certainly. I'll bring it down immediately."

"Thank you." Caroline waits until the waitress is out of earshot. "Anyway, as I was about to say, our main interest is property. Collectively we have the funds to accumulate a very substantial portfolio and we'll need someone – you hopefully – to look after the legal side of that."

"Sure, sure."

"Also, we do want to use a percentage of our shared capital to fund some philanthropic projects."

"Philanthropic projects?"

"Yes. For a start, we want to dedicate a proportion of the property we purchase for the use of those who, for whatever reason, we feel are deserving of rent-free accommodation and who – again for whatever reasons – aren't being helped by the agencies already in existence but have fallen through the cracks. We'll need you to consider all the legal implications of this too for us and to either advise us or seek advice on our behalf of the tax implications."

"Sure, sure."

"Also we want to anonymously donate money in other ways too to individuals who come to our attention and who we feel are worthy of our financial assistance say – for example – for furthering their education."

Tom looks a little bemused by all this but, before he can voice any questions, the waitress returns along with a colleague. As they lay out the dainty little china delft, the little plates of scones and sandwiches, the pot of tea, and all the accompanying bits and pieces, we watch in silence. Then, as soon as they're gone, Caroline asks:

"I guess you have some questions?"

"Sure, sure." There's a moment's pause as we wait to hear what they are.

"Perhaps," prompts Caroline, "you're wondering why young successful businesswomen like us are taking such a charitable direction?"

"Yes, I am, I have to admit," he nods his head but, then, adds unconvincingly, "though of course it's to be admired."

Caroline shrugs. "I don't know about that but I think there comes a point in time for many successful people when simply making money isn't everything, that profit is no longer sufficient motivation in itself. Think Bill Gates. Think Richard Branson. No doubt you've heard of his initiatives in South Africa?"

"Ah yes, sure, sure."

"You'll know then he set up the Branson School of Entrepreneurship to promote business skills and entrepreneurial flair among students in the belief that developing successful companies is the way to spread prosperity within South Africa."

"Sure. I think I remember reading something about that."

"Of course we're not in Branson's league but, like him, we want to give something back – in our own small way. So, tell me, Tom, would you be interested in representing our joint interests?"

"Yes, very much so."

"Great!" Suddenly she looks at her cup of tea. "What are we doing with this? This will never do! We need something stronger to celebrate the start of what I hope is our very successful professional relationship." She looks around for the waitress. "I wonder if they're still stocking that Hine Antique XO I had here the last time? Tell me, Tom, are you a brandy man?"

"Sure. I sure am."

A few brandies later, Tom takes his leave and cautiously makes his way across the lounge to the exit.

"I think that went well," says Caroline.

"What will his next appointment think when they see him?" wonders Dana as she watches him go. "Did you have to ply him with quite so much brandy, Caroline?"

"Excuse me? I didn't ply him. He was the one who did all the pouring – and nearly all of it into his own glass too."

"Yes, but you're the one who told the waitress to leave the bottle on the table." Dana brings her own untouched glass up to her mouth. She smells it. "I don't know how he can drink this stuff." She takes the tiniest of sips. "Ugh! Is it expensive?"

"Very – that little taste you had just now probably cost five euro."

"Really?"

"Really."

"Why did we waste it on Redmond so?"

"It wasn't a waste. He'll know how expensive it is. It'll give the right impression. I want him to be suitably awed."

Just then Caroline's phone rings. She picks it up from where she's left it on the table, checks to see who's calling, but doesn't answer.

"Who's that?" asks Dana.

"No one," Caroline tells her.

"Is it Mick?" Dana eyes her with curiosity.

Caroline shrugs but otherwise doesn't respond.

"Caroline, will you answer it!"

"No, not with the two of you sitting there."

"You can take the call outside."

But the ringing stops. "Anyway, it's too late," says Caroline.

"Are you going to ring him back?" asks Dana.

Caroline doesn't answer.

"Caroline, you're being ridiculous! You can't just ignore him."

But it seems Caroline feels she can, and can ignore Dana too. Now she changes the subject. "Anyway, what do you think of Redmond?" she looks to me.

I'm surprised she's asking me. Things are still chilly between us.

"Well," I begin, "he's not the sharpest knife in the drawer that's for sure."

"But we don't want the sharpest, do we? We're not going to give him anything too complicated to handle, just the straightforward stuff – the conveyancing and that. And of course we'll use him when we need to retain our anonymity – like when we're buying the house from Donald, or sending that bequest to Doug."

"Yeah, I need to sort that out," says Dana. "Doug will have to get his application for the furniture-making course in soon – the closing date is coming up."

"Sending that letter from Mrs Clancy can be the first thing we ask Redmond to do," answers Caroline. Then she looks to me. "What's wrong, Rosie? You don't look very happy."

I shrug. "It's just, well, I can't say I like Tom Redmond very much."

"You don't have to like him."

"Are you sure we can trust him?"

"No, not entirely, but we need someone like him. We'll need a solicitor from time to time who's happy to do what we need. But you can be sure I'll keep a very close eye on him."

"But aren't you worried he might talk? We don't want him going around discussing our affairs."

"I'll ring him later and reiterate again how we need him to be the soul of discretion. He stands to get a lot of business from us and make a lot of money. I'm sure he appreciates that but I'll remind him in any case." Suddenly, she's distracted by a shriek of laughter. "What the hell is that?" She looks towards the door. "Oh dear God! What on *earth* are they doing here?"

I look to where she's looking and see that her father and his new wife have just arrived into the room, arm in arm, in big overcoats though it's a mild day. Both have huge grins on their faces, like they're enjoying each other's company enormously.

"Quick! Turn around! I don't want them to see us." Caroline slides down in her seat.

"Too late," I tell her. "You've been spotted!"

"Great!" Caroline sits reluctantly back up again.

If Mr Connolly noticed anything he doesn't show it but the pair of them are now making directly for our table. If possible, their grins are even bigger now.

"Caroline!" Mr Connolly booms when he reaches us. "Well now, isn't this a surprise! Fancy meeting you here! And so soon after our last meeting. And Rosie, lovely to meet you again! And – well, well, well – if it isn't little Dana, if I'm not mistaken! Why, Dana, the last time I saw you, you were in school uniform. And now look at you – all grown-up!"

"Well, she would be, that was years ago," grumbles Caroline.

"True! True! Doesn't time fly? So can we join you?" he asks and, without waiting for an answer, he pulls over an armchair for Vivienne, and then, once she's seated, settles into Tom Redmond's vacated chair.

"Dana, let me introduce you to my wife, the lovely Vivienne."

"Hello, Dana!"

"Hello, Vivienne!"

Vivienne stretches her hand out and, as Dana takes it, I see she notices the diamond ring and that Vivienne notices her noticing it too – Dana does look a little gobsmacked.

Vivienne laughs. "It is a bit of a whopper, isn't it? But I have to say I love it!"

"I bet!" Dana gives her a big smile. "Congratulations on your wedding, Caroline told me all about it. It sounded really exciting."

At this, Caroline throws her a look but Dana is only being polite. What does she want Dana to do? Ignore her? Be rude to her? Probably.

"Oh, it was," says Vivienne. "It was a dream come true!"

"There's been quite a few weddings lately," I remark, looking straight at Caroline but she just pretends she doesn't hear me and the remark goes right over the heads of the new arrivals.

As it so happens, Mr Connolly's attention is elsewhere. He's just noticed the bottle of brandy on the table.

"Well, you ladies are certainly living the high life! Hine Antique – no less! Mind if we join you in a glass? You see, we're celebrating – that's why we're here in such august surroundings – it's not our usual haunt but we've had some very good news today"

Again, he doesn't wait for an answer but looks around, then calls to the waitress who happens to be passing near our table and asks her for two more glasses. As she goes to get them, he turns his attentions back to us.

"But isn't this a happy coincidence? Just when I thought my day couldn't get any better!" he says looking at Caroline but she pretends not to hear him. Undeterred, he turns his attention to Dana. "So how are your folks, Dana? Still living in the same place?"

"Yep, still there."

"Give them my regards."

"I will."

Caroline snorts, causing Mr Connolly to look to her.

"Like they'd remember you! You've been gone for years."

"Maybe they won't. But I always liked them. I used to see your mum in the park a lot with you, Dana, when you were very little."

"Really?"

"Yes, when I used to take Caroline there as a toddler."

"You used to take me to the park?"

"Of course. But you're too small to remember." He turns again to Dana. "I really only knew your mum to say hello to back then – little did I know you two would end up being such life-long friends. But I do remember your mum always looked so contented being with you, watching you play." A question occurs to him. "Tell me, do you have younger brothers and sisters?"

"No." But then she hesitates. "Well, yes, a little half-sister, Cathy – but she's my dad's daughter. She'll be two next month."

A look of curiosity crosses Mr Connolly face but he doesn't ask any questions. "Isn't that nice for him? Two is a lovely age."

And although he doesn't ask any questions, maybe *because* he doesn't, Dana goes on, "My parents went though a rocky patch but they're back together again."

"That is good to hear. They seemed like a close couple."

"They were, until Cathy was born but Mum's coming to terms with it. They're doing okay now."

"Good."

"Mum couldn't have any more children after me. I think it was a disappointment to her."

Caroline throws her a look, like she's wondering why on *earth* Dana's telling him all this, but I can understand why she would. He looks so interested, so genuinely sympathetic.

Now he nods. "Yes, I imagine it might have been. She struck me as being very maternal."

Dana looks thoughtful. "Yes, I guess she was – is."

The waitress arrives back with the glasses and, after thanking her, Mr Connolly tops up ours first, then pours out a substantial measure for Vivienne and for himself. Then he picks up his glass, sits back in his seat, closes his eyes, and takes a sip. There's a moment's silence as he savours the taste, and then:

"Ahh – perfection! As wise old Dr Johnson once said, 'Claret is the liquor for boys; port, for men; but he who aspires to be a hero must drink brandy!'" He takes another sip. "Delicious! Truly, what more could a man ask for?" He gives a contented sigh. "Here I am, sitting in these beautiful surroundings, sipping this extraordinary creation, with the sweet love of my life at my side, enjoying the company of my one and only daughter and her two delightful friends.

Life *is* good. *This* is a moment to savour! Who was it that said, 'There is no happiness. There are only moments of happiness.'?" He gives another long and deep sigh of satisfaction. "Such as this."

Caroline doesn't appear to share his sentiments. She's looking at him as if she'd like to remove him bodily from the room.

Now he puts the glass down.

"So tell me, Caroline, what are you up to these days? What's going on in your life?"

"You know, this and that."

Mr Connolly is not deterred by his daughter's less-than-forthcoming answer. He turns to Vivienne. "Viv, one thing you should know about my daughter is that she's one smart cookie. Both of my children are. But Caroline, well, she's something special. She's got it up here." He taps the side of his head.

"She must take after you then," says Vivienne and reaches over and gives him a kiss on the lips.

Caroline throws her eyes to heaven.

"No, no, Caroline's got real brains," says Mr Connolly. "Me? I never passed an exam in my life!"

"What does a man like you need with exams," Vivienne says and I can't help noticing the genuine admiration in her voice.

Mr Connolly shrugs but doesn't disagree. Instead, he goes on. "Do you know, when Caroline started school she used to bring home these little books to read. Well, we – her mother and I – *thought* they were for her to read because that's what she did but, as a matter of fact, we were meant to read them to her but – get this – she'd already taught herself while all the other little kids were still struggling with their ABCs."

"I don't remember that," says Caroline.

"Well, you wouldn't, would you? You were only four!" He throws his eyes to heaven causing us all, but Caroline, to laugh which in turn causes Caroline to throw Dana and myself a whose-side-are-you-on-anyway look.

Despite everything she's said about him, despite knowing all the reasons I shouldn't, I can't help liking Mr Connolly. He is just very likable.

Perhaps sensing my – and I think Dana's too – waning allegiance, Caroline quickly points out: "Anyway, weren't you in prison the year I started school?"

If Caroline hopes this will embarrass him, or will be news to Vivienne, she fails on both accounts. Vivienne doesn't look in the slightest bit surprised and Mr Connolly just goes on to calmly inform Caroline:

"Not for the whole year – just a few months." Then he looks to me. "I'm afraid. Rosie, my past isn't as squeaky clean as I might like. I have done things of which I'm not proud. But we all make mistakes and unless we're fools we learn from those mistakes. I like to think I have. Now where were we again? Oh yes, on the topic of my dearest daughter." He laughs as he thinks of what he is about to say. "You won't remember this one either, Caroline, but, once, when you were no more than five, you arrived home from school one morning around eleven. I was on my own, sitting in the kitchen, when you just strode in all kitted out in your little uniform, with your hair in pigtails, wearing those white little ankle socks – you were such a cute little thing. Anyway, you didn't say a word to me, didn't even look at me. You just went straight for a chair, pushed it over to the counter, climbed up, picked up your lunchbox which was still sitting there, then climbed back down, turned to me and said, 'Mummy forgot to give me my lunch. Does she want me to starve, or what?' Just then your mum came in. The minute she saw you she went ballistic. I remember her screaming, 'How did you get here?'"

"What? I walked all the way home from school?"

"You sure did."

"On my own? But we lived half a mile away."

"Over half a mile. So you can see why your mum was so upset! I guess when you found your lunchbox was missing, you slipped out of the classroom, out of the school, then down the road, across at the zebra crossing and on again until you'd reached home."

"Oh that's so cute!" says Vivienne.

Caroline gives her a withering look by way of response. But she looks puzzled. "That's funny," she says. "I don't remember that either."

"You were always an independent little thing. Still are. Making your own way. Needing help from no one."

"Who says I didn't need any help? If I did, you weren't exactly around to give it."

"True, true – I can't argue with that."

"I was five, right?"

Mr Connolly nods. "And what a cute little five-year-old you were!"

"Not cute enough to tempt you to stay at home where you belonged. That would have been around the time you ran out on us to go live with – what was her name again – that horrible woman with the bulging eyes who stank of some awful perfume?"

"Ah, yes, poor Mrs Power. Our short-lived relationship was doomed from the start. Fortunately Mr Power took her back."

"At least Mum had the sense not to do the same with you."

"Indeed she had." Mr Connolly looks serious for the first time.

"You know," says Vivienne, "we must have been in school around the same time, Caroline. What year did you start?"

She says this in a friendly way but Caroline just gives her another withering look, then turns back to her dad. "Anyway, you said you were celebrating today. What exactly are you celebrating?" she demands.

Eddie and Vivienne look at each other. He winks at her, she smiles, and then he answers.

"It's too early to say just yet. But just watch this space! Anyway, I guess it's time we were going, loath as I am to leave you, but business calls." He gets up. "It was really lovely bumping into you like this – it's made a very good day even more perfect. Perhaps we could go out to dinner sometime, all of us. What do you think, Caroline?"

Caroline shrugs. "We're pretty busy."

"Well, maybe I'll give you a ring and we can arrange it when things are quieter for you?"

Caroline shrugs non-committally.

We watch them as they go. I understand Caroline's issues with him but it's so hard not to like him.

"So what do think they're celebrating?" asks Dana.

"It's obvious, isn't it?" says Caroline.

"Is it?"

"Clearly she's pregnant."

"What? You think?"

"Yes, why on earth would he be harping on about my childhood otherwise? He's just trying to make out in front of her that he was this really loving father."

"It kind of sounds like he was," I say. "At least when he was around."

"I got the impression he was saying all that stuff for your benefit, not hers," Dana dares to add.

"Oh for God's sake, Dana, don't say you were taken in by his charm! Loving fathers do not walk out on their children for some floozy! And, by the way, did you see the make-up! I don't know how she could even keep her eyelids open with the weight of her mascara."

"Vivienne isn't the reason he walked out," I point out.

"I wasn't talking about her. She's just the latest in a long line of many. And they're all the same − identikit busty blondes, all half his age but with the gap ever-widening as he hurtles into his senior years. And did you hear her, 'Oh Caroline, we probably were in school around the same time!' Like I want to have *that* conversation!"

"She was just trying to be friendly."

"I have enough friends. I certainly don't need to look to my father's girlfriend −"

"Wife."

"− Wife! Jeez! I'm practically as old as my stepmother. Talk about head-wrecking."

"He never married any of the others though, did he?" I point out. "That must mean something?"

"Of course it does!" says Caroline triumphantly. "It means, a) she *thinks* he's got money; or b) she's got money; or −"

I interrupt. "Not everyone's relationships are solely determined by money, you know," I say pointedly.

But Caroline ignores me. "− *or* c) she's pregnant."

"She'd hardly be drinking brandy if she were pregnant," remarks Dana.

Caroline shrugs. "What's all that stuff about my

childhood then? It's not like he was even there for most of it – you know that, Dana, better than anyone. And did you see how he helped himself to our brandy but didn't even offer to pay for it though he knew damn well how expensive it is. And – excuse me – what do you mean, not everyone is motivated by money? Is that some little dig at me, Rosie?"

I shrug. "If the shoe fits . . ."

"What do you mean, Rosie?" asks Dana.

"Caroline knows what I mean."

"Do I?"

"Yes."

"Oh come on, you two, leave it go," entreats Dana.

"Fine, I will leave it go!" Caroline stands up. She puts on her coat.

We're still sitting there. "Oh, so we're going, are we?" I ask.

"Yes! I'm going up to pay."

By the time we reach her, there seems to be some confusion between her and the waitress.

"Yes," the waitress is saying, "I'm quite sure. The gentleman who just left with the blonde woman did already take care of the bill."

"Just what the hell is he playing at?" Caroline mutters.

"But I thought you said he doesn't have any money," I remark.

"And he doesn't. Not least because when he does have it, he flitters it away."

At 18, a visa to America, followed by years of scraping a living as a security guard and a cab driver.

Ihsan Khan - $55 million - US

At 38, back in his native Pakistan and Mayor of his home-town, using his wealth to help the survivors of that town when a earthquake hits and kills 3,000.

21

I've arranged to meet Mum at the National Museum for lunch and, afterwards, we're going to go shopping for an outfit for her to wear on her anniversary. Normally I avoid shopping with Mum. It is not the most enjoyable of experiences – she has a habit of trying on dozens upon dozens of outfits but ultimately coming home dejected and empty-handed. She just never seems to find anything she likes. But, today, I've agreed to go, for two reasons. She's shopping with the Nutley in mind but I need to steer her a lot more upmarket than that. All her guests will be dressing for the Bloomsbury; I can't have her being outshone on the night. Plus I need to get her talking. I need a romantic story about her and Dad falling in love, one that will be a worthy prize-winner.

Everything else has been arranged – the party itself, plus the accommodation and the flights for immediate family as per the 'prize'. All friends and relatives have been informed of the change in venue and warned to keep quiet. When I rang my brothers in America both of them were full of excuses from the outset – they didn't want to take the kids out of school, it would be hard to get the time off work –

but when I finally got the opportunity to interrupt and to tell them that all their expenses would be paid for, all these complications faded away.

Surprisingly, Sarah was still reluctant even after I told her that. "Oh, I don't know if I can, Rosie. Things are crazy here right now. And flying with the kids on my own would be a nightmare."

"But there's a ticket for Rod too. The prize covers all close family. Oh, please come, Sarah – Mum and Dad haven't even seen baby Jack yet."

"Well, I'll try and work something out."

To be honest, I felt annoyed. Here she was, being offered free tickets home and the opportunity to stay in a five-star hotel for the duration of her visit and she has to think about it! Hello!

As arranged, I find Mum in the museum's restaurant but she's not on her own. She's joined two old school-friends she bumped into on her way in so we end up having lunch with them at their table which means I get no opportunity to grill her, and instead I have to listen to, 'Do you remember so-and-so?' conversations.

After lunch, as we leave the restaurant, she puts a hand on my arm.

"Rosie, before we go shopping there's an exhibition I'd like to pop in to see."

"Oh, okay. What is it?"

"It's called The Exhibition of Artistic Luxury. I read about it in the Sunday papers and I've been dying to see it."

"Great," I say. Not – I think. But she's keen and we do have the whole afternoon so I follow after her as she proceeds with purpose. At the entrance to the exhibition room there's a brief description of what the show is about.

Mum reads it aloud:

"'*Artistic Luxury displays the work of the three greatest jewellery and decorative arts designers at the turn of the 20th century: Peter Carl Fabergé, Louis Comfort Tiffany, and René Lalique. Their rivalry found its stage at the 1900 World's Fair in Paris – the only exposition where all three showed their work simultaneously. Looking critically at the development, design, and marketing of each, this exhibition explores how these designers responded to the demand for luxury goods in the years leading up to World War I.*'"

Oh dear God! What fresh hell is this! I trail in after her.

"Rosie, come over here, I'm going to take a look at the Lalique Crystal first."

I follow after her as she wanders from one piece to the other, full of "Ooohs" and "Ahhhs" and "Oh mys!". She really seems to love this stuff. I can't say I get it – it's all a bit fussy and old-fashioned for my taste.

"Mum?"

"Yes? Come on, let's move on to the Fabergé collection."

"Mum, do you remember when you and Dad started going out together?"

"Yes – oh look!" She comes to such a sudden stop I nearly go colliding into her. "Look!"

"What?"

She points to a little blue egg displayed in a big glass case. "Oh my!" she gasps and then goes right up to it. I follow behind. Again I listen, or don't, as she reads aloud the details mounted on the plinth beside it.

"'*The Blue Serpent Clock Egg is a jewelled Easter egg made under the supervision of the Russian jeweller Peter Carl Fabergé in 1887, for the then Czar of Russia, Alexander III, who presented the egg to his wife, the Czarina Maria Feodorovna. It now belongs to the Princess Grace of Monaco's Collection, currently owned by*"

Prince Albert II.' You know it was one of Princess Grace's most treasured possessions," Mum tells me.

"Really? So anyway, what I wanted to ask you was —"

"See the way the serpent winds around the pedestal of the egg and acts as the clock's hand with its tongue pointing to the hour, and see how the whole upper half of the egg with the hours of the day marked out on it acts as a rotating clock."

"Oh yeah, that is cool." Which it is. And very clever. But, still, I've had enough. I'd like to move on from here. I think I've seen more than I want to see.

"Did you know this egg is similar to the 'Duchess of Marlborough Egg' which is interesting because Fabergé had a rule of not repeating a design."

"How do you know all that?"

"Why shouldn't I? You might think I spend all my evenings watching *Corrie* but I am a woman of many interests. Remember last year before Dad got sick I took that course on decorative arts?"

"Oh yeah, I remember now."

She stands back, "Oh, have you ever seen anything more beautiful!"

"It is pretty."

"Pretty? It's just magnificent."

She stands there for what seems like an age just staring at it until I finally interrupt.

"Mum, we are in town to get you an outfit. We should move on."

"I know, I know. But not before we see the Tiffany exhibits."

We *finally* leave the museum, but only after Mum's examined every single exhibit and read every description.

I swear it feels like the longest day in my life. And we haven't even hit the shops yet.

"Well, that was fun," Mum says as we emerge back onto the street.

"As much fun as lying on a bed of nails."

"Rosie, don't be such a philistine! I'm so glad I got to see it."

But Mum's good humour soon evaporates and mine doesn't improve much either. In shop after shop I wait outside changing-room after changing-room while she tries on outfit after outfit. Most of the time Mum doesn't even come out to show me what she's put on but emerges – finally – back in her own clothes, having decided against every outfit. There is no question of trying to get a romantic little anecdote out of her right now. She's just too hassled.

"Mum, can't you at least show me the outfits when you try them on?"

"I would – if I liked any of them. You know, I don't know why everyone insists on designing for skinny ones like you. Don't they know that most of the population carries a bit of weight and that we're not all young things either."

In the next shop we enlist the help of a shop assistant. The dresses she selects all look very mumsy to me but, still, Mum optimistically decides to try a couple anyway, hoping they might look better on.

While I'm waiting I wander off. And then I spot it, this beautiful green velvet dress that I think would look fabulous on her. I check the size, take it off the rail and rush back to her.

"Mum?" I call from the other side of the curtain. "I found one I think might suit you."

She sticks her head out. "Oh I don't know. It's a bit much. It is very low-cut."

"Just give it a try. And this time, come out and show it to me!"

While she's in the dressing-room, I make another attempt.

"Mum, do you remember when it was that you realised Dad might be the one for you?"

But her response from behind the curtain is annoyed. "Rosie, for crying out loud! Just let me concentrate on what I'm doing."

Time passes and still there's no sign of her.

"Mum, are you nearly done?"

"Nearly."

More time passes. She's been in there for over five minutes now.

"Mum?"

"One moment."

"Mum, if you're not coming out, I'm coming in."

She pulls back the curtain. Okay, she doesn't have the make-up for it and she's in her stocking-feet but this is the one – she'll look fantastic in it on the night.

"That's it. That's the one!"

She looks at her reflection doubtfully. "Oh, I don't know. It's very glamorous!"

"Exactly! It's perfect!"

"I'd feel very self-conscious arriving into the Nutley in this."

"But, Mum, it's your anniversary!"

The helpful assistant now comes back with a pair of shoes. Mum puts them on. She turns this way and that, considering her image in the mirror.

"It *is* nice."

"It's fabulous."

"But it's very low-cut. Don't you think it's a little revealing?"

"Yes, but in a very flattering way."

"Oh I don't know. I'm just not sure I'd be able to carry it off."

"Sure you will."

"Do you think it's slimming?"

"Very. And it makes you look younger."

"You think?"

"Yes!"

"Hmmm. It *is* very expensive."

"Yes, but you're not going to get anything nicer."

"I'm not sure I can justify spending so much."

"Mum, it's for your anniversary!"

"I know but . . ." She's still studying herself in the mirror.

"Okay, if you're not going to buy it, then I am. It can be a present – for your anniversary."

"Are you out of your mind! You couldn't afford this!"

"Mum, please just let –"

"Rosie, it's very kind of you to offer, really, but it's out of the question."

"Mum, look –"

"Now hush, not another word. But you know what? I *will* get it."

Shopping bag in hand, we go back downstairs. I direct her towards the main jewellery section.

"What are we doing here?" she asks.

"If you won't let me buy the dress, I can buy you a piece of jewellery to go with it."

"Rosie, listen to me now. I don't want you spending your money on me. God knows what's going to happen to you now you've left SciÉire."

"Mum, I have another job."

"Yes, but who knows how long that will last?"

"Look, I am going to buy you something."

"Well, not jewellery. Anyway, I already know what I'm going to wear with it. Your dad has bought me a necklace. He doesn't know I know. I found it by accident."

In the end, I never get the chance to ask her.

When I finally get home, I find Doug and Dana in the kitchen. They're sitting at the table, opposite one another.

"Hi, guys. How are things?" I ask, as I breeze past on my way to the fridge.

"Fine," snaps Dana.

"Fine," snaps Doug.

They don't sound fine to me. I stop. I turn. I look. I see they're both wearing thunderous faces. I'm surprised. Doug and Dana are an unusually, loved-up couple – almost annoyingly so. They never quarrel. Something serious must be going on to have them sitting here like this, glaring at each other so grimly. Hmm. I'm sure they won't want me around. I'm not sure I want to *be* around. This is uncharted territory.

"Good, good," I say with false jollity – like I'm oblivious to the atmosphere. "Okay, then, well, I'll just get a yoghurt and – ah – I'll be on my way."

Quickly I gather up the yoghurt from the fridge, grab a spoon from the drawer, and hurry to the door but, just as I'm within a hair's breadth of getting away, Dana calls out:

"Rosie?"

Oh God, no, I think. I don't want to be dragged into whatever's going on. "Ah yes?" I answer.

"Doug got a gift of €25,000 today."

"What! You're kidding?"

"No, seriously Rosie, I did! Well, I didn't get the money

yet but I rang the solicitor who contacted me about it and he's arranging to have the money lodged to my account."

"Oh my God, Doug, that's fantastic!" And then I think to ask the obvious question though I already know the answer of course. "Who from?"

"Well, one of my old teachers died a short while ago and then today I got this letter out of the blue from her solicitor, this guy down in Kilkenny, saying that she'd left the money to me on the proviso that I spend it on furthering my education."

"That's just brilliant, Doug!"

"Yeah, it is, isn't it?" His countenance has changed completely from when I first came into the kitchen – he's beaming now.

"Twenty-five thousand!" I whistle. "That's a lot of money."

"Isn't it?"

I see the letter lying on the table. From where I'm standing I can read Tom Redmond's letterhead in big bold writing. "Is that the letter?"

"Yeah." As he picks it up and hands it to me, he goes on. "I know it might sound corny but in a way the fact she remembered me like this means almost as much to me as the money."

"Sure, that's great but have you –"

"That she had such faith in me."

"Of course, but have you thought about –"

"I've never got such a surprise in all my life! Sure, she was one of the nicest teachers I ever had but to get such a gift from her, to know she thought so much of me is just amazing." In all the time I've known Doug, I don't believe I've ever seen him so animated. I feel really happy for him. "You see, the letter explains it all, how she wanted to make a change in the lives of a couple of students who she didn't feel benefited as much as they could have from the educational system."

"So I'm reading."

"I know she was a really nice woman and she was one of those teachers who seemed to actually care about the students in our school but, to be honest, I never imagined she thought so much of me. I was always kind of quiet."

I can well believe that. Yes, I can picture Doug, quiet and unassuming, sitting at the back of the classroom unnoticed, overlooked, year in, year out – no bother to anyone. Now he's shaking his head at the wonder of it all. Now he gives a buoyant shrug. "But I guess she must have noticed me, seen something in me."

"Have you decided what you're going to do with it?" I ask.

Dana goes to answer but Doug gets there first.

"Dana has this bizarre idea I should use it to enrol in a furniture-making course up the country." He laughs. "God only knows why! I have no interest whatsoever in furniture-making."

"But why not Doug? What's so bizarre about my idea? You know you're really good with your hands," insists Dana.

"Good with my hands? Yeah, right! That's what people say when they think someone isn't too bright, you know," he taps the side of his head, "up here."

"That's not true! I'm saying it because you *are* good with your hands."

"In what way?"

"What?"

"In what way am I good with my hands – exactly?"

"Well, you're a painter, aren't you? And a very good one."

"Dana, I'm a painter by chance. I fell into it. It wasn't something I ever set out to be."

"Yes, but you li –"

I interrupt. "So the letter didn't specify what course you should do?" I ask, scanning through it to see.

"No."

"So this – ah – teacher left it open, left it up to you to decide?"

"Yes."

"So if you don't want to do this furniture course, what do you want to do?"

"Well –"

Dana interrupts. "He wants to train as a relationship counsellor."

Well, knock me down with a feather! Now here's an interesting development. I look from one to the other, then ask Dana, "What? You mean just like you?"

"Yes."

"Seriously?" I ask Doug

Doug sighs. "I didn't actually say relationship counsellor but, yes, definitely something in the psychology field. And, yes, I would like to train in an area where I would be helping people in their relationships."

"So a relationship counsellor?" demands Dana.

"Is it? I don't know. I'm not the expert. I don't know the terms but I'd have thought that was more specific, that it referred to couples. There are other kinds of relationships. Look, the whole idea is new to me. I've only just got this letter. I really need to get advice, to talk to someone, to *you* – at least that's what I would have hoped."

He's looking over at Dana but she doesn't react.

"What *is* your problem, Dana? What is so strange about

what I'm saying? Why are you fixated on me doing that bloody furniture course? When Mrs Clancy chose me – chose *me* – out of so many students who passed through her class I'm sure she wasn't thinking I should use the money to do something with my hands."

"But why do you want to do the same thing as me?"

"I didn't say the same thing, just something in the same field. And why? Because I happen to think psychology is fascinating. I've learned that from you. I've listened to you talking after your classes. I've flicked through the textbooks you leave around. It interests me, just as it interests you. I don't want to study it *because* you're studying it, I want to *despite* that."

Dana sighs. "You know, I've worked really hard to get where I am. I already spent years in college and if you think you can ju –"

"Dana, I get that," says Doug. "I admire how hard you've worked, how hard you *do* work. And I would – will – too."

"Yes, but –"

"I know you already have a degree behind you but that isn't mandatory to do the counselling course you're doing, is it?"

"No, but –"

"Didn't you tell me about some woman, some mature student, in your class who never went to college before and how she's now one of the best in your class?"

"But she's exceptional. And the exception. Everyone else in the class does have a degree already."

"Yeah, well –"

"Yeah, well, what?"

"I could be an exception. Or I could start by doing a degree first. Or maybe there's some introductory course I could enrol in. I don't know. That's why I'll need your advice."

Dana sighs, "Oh Doug!"

"'Oh Doug!' What? Why do you suddenly sound like you feel sorry for me? Look, Dana, Mrs Clancy saw something. Just because I didn't do so well in school it doesn't mean I'm thick."

"I didn't say that."

"It's what you think."

"Of course it isn't."

"Whatever. No matter. Mrs Clancy didn't. That's what this money is about."

But Dana is just looking at him – she's not saying anything now.

"Why," Doug asks eventually, "have you such a big problem? Did you like it when you were the brainy one in the relationship, the educated one?"

"Doug, you haven't even enrolled yet so please spare me the psychology." Dana sighs now, pushes her chair back and stands up. "I'm sure you'll do whatever you want."

"I will. It isn't your money, Dana."

Dana glances over at me and, for a second, I get the feeling she's *that* close to telling him the truth but the moment passes.

"Okay, I'm going now."

When she leaves there's silence as we both stare after her. Then Doug looks over to me.

"Why is she reacting like this? Of all people I thought she would be supportive."

"And I'm sure she will, given time. I guess she just has to get used to the idea."

Now Doug picks up his jacket from where it's hanging

on the back of his chair. "Will you tell her that I've gone home."

"Sure."

"See you, Rosie."

"See you, Doug." But then I call out after him. "Doug?"

"What?"

"I'm really glad for you."

"Thanks. I just wish Dana was."

No sooner have I gone up to my own room when I hear a knock on the door and, not waiting for an answer, Dana comes right in.

"Well, what do you think?"

"About Doug?"

"Yeah." She throws her eyes to heaven. "Doug has told me what he was like at school and there's no way any teacher of his would want to fund him on a university course. I should have made sure that it was specified in the letter Tom Redmond sent what sort of course the money was intended to cover."

"Well, I think it's great Doug will be able to study what he wants."

"Rosie, I don't really think he *knows* what he wants. He only wants to study psychology because of me."

"Don't you think you're being patronising?" Suddenly I feel really annoyed with her. "Jeez, Dana, the lotto people didn't stipulate how you should go about spending your money and I don't see how you think you should have any control over how Doug spends his."

"But I gave it to him for a specific reason."

"Yes, so that he could get some qualifications, improve himself, improve his prospects for the future. It's his money now. It's up to him to use it how he sees fit. Maybe Doug is right – that you do feel threatened by the prospect of him studying in the same area as you."

"Oh please! That's not it at all. Aren't you forgetting something? Mrs Clancy didn't leave him the money. She didn't mark him out as some genius who lacked in opportunity. I don't want to see him being disappointed."

"And that's all you're worried about?"

"Of course it is! I love Doug. I don't want him setting himself up for a fall."

"And maybe he won't fall. Maybe he'll surprise you."

"And maybe he won't. And then it'll be all my fault."

Later that night, when I'm just about to fall asleep, it suddenly comes to me – my prize-winning anecdote. I don't know why I didn't think of it before. Why was I trying to inveigle it out of Mum when she'd already told me?

She told me the story last year, during one of the worst nights of our lives, when she and I were waiting anxiously outside the operating theatre in the middle of the night. You see, Dad had been brought by ambulance to hospital earlier after he'd collapsed at home and, because he had a perforated duodenal ulcer and there was a lot of internal bleeding, the doctors had to carry out this emergency high-risk operation – we really didn't know if he was going to live or die.

Anyway, the story she told me while we were waiting was this. She and Dad hadn't been going out together very long when, one day, he arrived at her parents' house with a present for her: a pair of sexy high heels. Mum was completely taken aback. This was such an unlikely gift from this shy but handsome boy who she was only just beginning to get to know. Her own mother was scandalised when she saw them – she was a strict woman and thought it very forward of him and, for the times, it probably was. But I can still picture Mum, her face white with worry as we waited so anxiously for news, as she remembered back. How – ignoring the glares from her own mother – Dad knelt in front of Mum and put the shoes on her feet. She said she felt like Cinderella albeit a racy one, with red high-heels in lieu of a glass slipper. But it was, so she told me, that night she just knew he was the man for her. This man who saw past her weight and the loose clothes she wore to camouflage it, and thought of her as a red stiletto kind of girl.

That was the moment she fell in love with him, all those years ago. And that was the night, as we sat waiting for news that would determine their future. As I listened to the story that had got them to this point, I understood just how much he meant to her. I almost wish now there was a radio competition so I might send it in and win.

A share in a £2,395,710 jackpot split between five winners.

Derek Ladner – £479,142 – UK

A week later, and – "Hang on a minute, did I buy one or two tickets?"

Derek Ladner – £479,142 – UK

Another share in that same £2,395,710. Sometimes it pays to be forgetful.

22

My search for Seán on the streets of the city has come to nothing. So too did the trip I took to Wicklow, to the old youth hostel. Donald was right – the place is like Fort Knox, all boarded up – there was no sign of Seán there. Hilda's parents have thrown up no leads either and I can't locate his own parents.

He could, I guess, be anywhere in the country but my feeling is he wouldn't have ventured too far away from Dublin. So, one morning I sit down at nine and begin ringing around the various agencies who provide accommodation for the homeless. I know Seán said he preferred sleeping on the streets but maybe there's only so much of that a body can take and the comfort of a bed has lured him inside on harsh nights. But each time I give all the details I have of Seán and a description, I draw a blank.

Most of the people I talk to on the phone are courteous and helpful but, though they don't say it, I get the feeling they think I'm looking for a needle in a haystack. One particularly helpful woman does suggest I make out a poster with Seán's details and a photo and circulate this as widely as possible. It's a sensible piece of advice and I take it. Later that same day I scan that family photo into my computer, crop Seán's face, enlarge it, then paste it into a separate document. Then I type in his name and a brief description of his height, weight and so forth, together with my contact details. The next day I visit every refuge and every temporary hostel where, after unsuccessfully enquiring after Seán again, I ask them to hang up my poster.

After each place I visit, I come away feeling more and more deflated. The world I'm encountering is like some depressing parallel one, full of people who lead such desperate, chaotic lives, people that largely go unnoticed by the rest of us.

The poster yields no results; it prompts no response.

But another helpful woman I meet suggests I visit the drop-in centres and the food centres. She tells me that people who are reluctant to take a bed will often take a meal or will use these places just to break up their day. She gives me a list of names and addresses and I call to one after another. Once again it proves fruitless. But, again, I leave a copy of my poster in each.

I even find myself volunteering to help out at a nightly soup kitchen after one man tells me that a lot of homeless turn up to avail of it each evening. So, for several evenings, I spend hours doling out soup to one unfortunate after another. But not to the one unfortunate I'm looking for.

I do meet people who know Seán, or think maybe they know him, but nobody who can say they have definitely seen him in the last few months. It occurs to me that I keep encountering the same people over and over again. I think if Seán's still out there, living rough, I'd surely have found him by now, or heard word of his current whereabouts from someone. But if he's not living rough, then where could he be?

I set aside another day to make another round of phone calls. If the worst-case scenario is the case, if he's back in a mental hospital again, I want to know but it's what I dread most finding out – that fear has always been lurking in the back of my mind.

So I spend more time on the phone. But it's hopeless. Each time I get an answer, I give my name and explain how I'm looking for Seán Blake who I believe may have been a patient at one time, and maybe even is one currently. Each time I get the same reply: that they can't give out details of former or current patients. I can understand this.

I decide I might have better luck in person. I write down a list of the names and addresses of each of the hospitals I've rung. Then, next day, I leave the house early and go from one hospital to another. At the reception of each, I give the same white lie, that I'm here to see my brother, Seán Blake, but again and again I'm told they've no patient of that name and, on hearing this, my reaction is the same mixed one: relief that he isn't in one of these institutions, tempered by a slight disappointment that I still haven't located him.

"I know you think a mental hospital is the worst-case scenario but there are others as bad," Caroline observes when I come back home after my long and fruitless day, feeling completely wrecked and utterly deflated.

"What do you mean?" I ask.

"Well, have you thought about the fact that he could be in prison?"

"Oh come on! This is Seán we're talking about! Kind, decent Seán. He's as unlikely to end up in prison as you or I."

"Seán may be kind and decent but it has to be difficult if not impossible to stay out of trouble when you've been leading the kind of life he has."

"Yes, but Seán made a point of avoiding people and situations that might lead to trouble. He didn't want to get involved in drugs and drink, or with people who were. That's why he didn't stay in hostels."

"But you have checked the hostels, haven't you?"

"I did, just in case, but, like I say, he tried to avoid them. That's why he was squatting in Wicklow. That's why he slept on the streets."

"Squatting in Wicklow, sleeping on the streets – just listen to what you're saying, Rosie. How long do you think anyone, even the most peace-loving individual in the world, can keep out of trouble on the streets?"

I don't want to hear this, or what she has to say next.

"Rosie, I think you've got to face the possibility that you're not going to find him."

"What do you mean?"

"I don't *mean* anything but it seems to me that if you were going to find him you would have by now."

"But he has to *be* somewhere? He can't have just disappeared."

"People do, you know," says Caroline.

"How? How can someone just disappear?"

"Maybe you should check to see if anyone's reported him officially missing."

Reluctant as I am to admit that 'missing' with all its scary connotations is a possibility, it's increasingly becoming a probability and I take her advice. I log on to my computer and input several search terms – *Missing persons – Dublin – how to find*. Immediately dozens of matches come up. I scan through them and choose the Garda Síochána website first – the official police site seems like a good place to start. I press their dedicated 'missing persons' menu and, suddenly, the screen fills with photos. There are dozens – men, women, young, old. I begin scanning through them, all these faces, all these strangers, with nothing in common but that they're missing. Nearly all of them are smiling which seems incongruous but, then, most of these photos were taken at a moment in life worth recording – at a party, at a wedding, at a grads (surprisingly and rather poignantly, several of the men are in tux). I guess as they smiled for the camera, they could never have imagined that this particular photo would be put to such a use, the one chosen by family or friends.

Some of these people have been missing a long time and several of the photos – grainy ones, black and white ones – date back to the seventies and show young women with old-fashioned perms and men with equally old-fashioned moustaches and hair so out-of-date it's back in again. To think that someone is still looking for them, still hoping, believing even, their loved one is still out there, nearly forty years on.

The details accompanying all of the photos are pared-down and factual – a written description plus the time and date and the circumstance in which they went missing. But there is no photo of Seán.

I phone the number given on the website to ask how I can report him missing but learn I'm not in position to do so since, as the garda on the phone tells me, I'm not family and I hadn't been in regular contact with him prior to his 'disappearance'. But helpfully she suggests that, if he's not there already, then I could list him on one of the websites that are dedicated to helping people track down those they've lost contact with.

When she hangs up, I log onto the site she recommends and, again, am faced with the same photos I found on the official Garda site as well as many more too. The details here are more fleshed out. I read of people who left their house as if they were to return at any moment. I read accounts of when people were last seen: on the ferry to Holyhead, waiting for a bus at eleven in the evening, on the way home from a party at two in the morning. Time and time again, their loved ones seem to assume that they're alive and well somewhere, that they will come back someday, despite all indications to the contrary.

Again, there is no photo of Seán but I upload the one I have of him and give a contact email. I can't imagine why Seán would be reading such a site but, taking my cue from other posters, I put a direct appeal to him, asking him to get in touch if he sees my message.

One night it occurs to me that maybe the fact that I can't find him is a positive, not a negative. Seán is young, and smart too – despite his lack of formal education. Yes, he was in a mental hospital once but maybe he got the help he needed to deal with all that had happened to him: losing his girlfriend, his home, his children, even help to deal with his crappy childhood. I've learned that there is a lot of support out there for people like Seán. He could have done a course, found a job, found a home for himself and maybe even got his children back. Maybe he has managed to turn his life around. Maybe he doesn't even need my help.

But maybe he does.

Tom Redmond is already negotiating the purchase of the pair of houses in that old inner-city terrace, one of which I always think of as Seán's, even if I am no nearer to finding him. I haven't lost hope yet. I just wish I could channel that hope into something practical but I really don't know how.

But every day I check if there's a response from him or about him on the lost contact website. There never is. I just don't know what else I can do.

Throw in the job. Splash out on the obligatory lavish holiday, plus a wedding and a brand-new home. And then what?

Luke Pittard – £1.3 million – UK

Hmmm . . . Bored, so back to work at MacDonald's.

23

"What's this? More shopping?" asks Caroline when she sees me putting the bags down on the table.

I throw her a look but don't answer.

"Don't you ever get bored? Don't you ever feel you want to do something more productive with your time?"

"It's not *all* I do."

"Isn't it? What else do you do?"

"Planning my parents' party took up a lot of time and looking for Seán is —"

"Haven't you a private detective searching for him now?"

"Yes." At Caroline's prompting I do though I doubt he'll be able to turn up anything extra. "But I like to keep an eye on the websites and —"

"How long does that take you? Five minutes? Why don't you come into the office more often?"

"I do come in when I need to."

"You could come in more."

"You're so efficient, what's the point? Between you, you and Tom Redmond have everything under control."

"It would give you something to do besides shopping."

"Caroline, that's not *all* I do."

But I guess these days it is how I spend a lot of my time. I wouldn't say I enjoyed my search for Seán but it did give me a focus. Same with my parents' party but that's all sorted now – down to the present I bought to give them on the night.

For the first time in a while, I think of my old colleagues in SciÉire and wonder how they're getting along. I got the occasional text from them when I first left, asking me if I wanted to join them for Friday after-work drinks but I never went. Sitting on the sidelines listening as they all talked about work didn't sound too enticing. I wonder now if I should have gone along to meet them but it's too late; the texts have stopped coming. I guess they've forgotten about me at this stage. But I probably wouldn't have enjoyed it anyway.

Finn, Dana, Caroline, Shane – everyone else just seems so annoyingly busy. Maybe I could plan a holiday but who would go with me? I could go on my own. People do. They go off travelling for months on end. But I know I won't. I'd hate that.

I realise Caroline is looking at me, questioningly.

"What?" I ask.

"I'm waiting for you to tell me what else you do with your time?"

"Oh, for God's sake!" To turn the conversation quickly around to something less disagreeable for me, if not for Caroline, I ask, "So, have you talked to Mick yet?"

"Hmm?"

"Caroline, don't act like you can hardly recall who I mean. I know he's been ringing you. So, have you returned any of his calls?"

"Calls? There haven't been that many."

"Have you returned the ones you got?"

"No, not yet."

"Are you going to?"

She shrugs.

"Caroline, you have to meet him. You can't just leave things the way they are."

She just shrugs again. She can be so infuriating at times.

"You do know the premiere of *Fate Farm* is coming up?"

"Oh, is it?" she asks managing to look and sound completely uninterested.

"Has Mick texted you or phoned you about it?"

"Hmm?"

"I'll take that as a yes. You know the rest of us will be going?"

"Yes, I guess you will. It should be an enjoyable night."

"It should. So are you going?"

Though I can probably guess what her answer would have been, I don't get a chance to hear it because, just then, Dana walks in.

"Guess what?" she immediately asks.

"What?" both of us want to know.

"Doug is starting his course – tomorrow."

"He moves fast," says Caroline.

"Tell me about it!"

"How did that come about so quickly?" I ask.

"Well, he asked me to arrange a meeting with one of my lecturers, to talk over what possibilities are open to him so I did and Mr Dunne agreed to see him this morning. When they met up, Mr Dunne told him about this ten-week full-time introductory course in psychology that's just starting and, as it turns out, because one of the people who'd already enrolled had to drop out at the last moment, there's one free place and Mr Dunne offered it to Doug. Honestly, that guy is just so lucky. From all accounts it's a fantastic course and, as Mr Dunne said to Doug, it'll give him a taste for the subject and, also, it would be a definite plus if he were to make an application for the degree course next year."

"Is that what he's planning?"

"I think he's considering it."

"Are you happier about all this now?" asks Caroline. "You seem to be."

Dana hesitates. "I guess. I was just taken aback at first. But this full-time course will be a good introduction. Only . . ."

"Only?"

"I hope Doug will be able to manage. I looked through his timetable and it's pretty intensive. Right now he's buoyed up by the notice he thinks Mrs Clancy took of him but, the truth is, he just wasn't all that good in school – he's told me that himself. At least with a ten-week course he'll find out soon if he's cut out for it. He'll soon know if he's up to embarking on a degree, or if he isn't. Anyway, I have some of the books on his prescribed reading list so I'm going to drop them over to him."

"That's helpful of you," I say.

"Well, that's exactly what I plan to be. I've made up my mind I'm going to do what I can for him, to give him all the help possible. I don't want him to fail. Besides, it'll be fun." She looks at her watch. "I'd better go. I want Doug to have a look through these books before he starts. I don't want him to be completely at sea."

"There's no shops in the cemetery, is there? I can't spend any of the money there."

Stephen Smith – £19 million – UK

When you suffer from life-threatening ill-health, it tends to put things in perspective.

24

The whole morning is spent going to and from the airport. Without telling him why I needed it, I've borrowed my dad's car. First I collect my elder brother William, his Irish-born wife Eithne, and their twin ten-year-old daughters Kay-Leigh and Tara-Anne, who all arrive in at ten in the morning on a flight from Boston. Our journey to the hotel in Portmarnock is uneventful but certainly not quiet. I drive as they talk and talk – about getting to the airport, about their flight, about the food they were served, about the movies they saw, about their hassles at the luggage carousel – all talking, all at the same time, all in very loud voices, punctuated by loud hollers of laughter. It's true to say that William and Eithne have embraced their host country and have become – to enlist a cliché – more American than the Americans themselves.

At twelve thirty I return to the airport to collect my other brother, Con, and his American (but of Chinese extraction) wife, Evelyn, and their five kids; boys, Cooper (6), Logan (4), Chase (3), Wyatt (2), and daughter Nevaeh (6 months). Nevaeh is Heaven spelt backwards, but then, as my father has pointed out (on many more than one occasion) since Cooper is a profession, Chase is a verb, Logan is an airport, and Wyatt a question, it was unlikely they were ever going to name her Mary or Anne. (Yes, I know Wyatt is pronounced Wait, not What, but I don't think Dad is ever going to get it right, not now.)

My two brothers have become outrageously fat. William's wife, Eithne, is every bit as substantial as her husband (and the twins look like they're on the same trajectory) but they're a happy, jolly family who enjoy one another's company and really do find each other's jokes hilarious. Con's wife Evelyn, on the other hand, is whippet-thin and not nearly as jolly, giving credence to the stereotype. Their offspring take after her, even baby Nevaeh considers me with a solemn, knowing look – no baby chuckles here.

After dropping this second family off at the hotel, I turn around and head straight back to the airport but the traffic is heavier now and it takes me longer than I'd anticipated and, by the time I arrive, I see on the arrivals board that the flight from Melbourne (via Singapore) arrived half an hour ago.

Damn it! Of all people, of all circumstances – I especially didn't want to be late for Sarah and her family after a journey that took them the guts of twenty-four hours. I scan the jam-packed arrivals hall and, at first, I see no sign of them amongst the hordes milling but then I catch a glimpse of Sarah through a momentary gap, seated and asleep in the middle of a row of people. I make my way through the crowd towards her. She's sound to the world. The baby too is sleeping, in a sling across her chest, and the two boys are stretched out on top of an extremely laden-down trolley – both sound to the world, not a care in the world. I look at Sarah for a second and consider her like I would a stranger.

Her head is flung right back and her mouth is open but even in this particularly inelegant pose, even after her long journey, she's still lovely. Sure, she looks like she could do with a good night's (or week's) sleep, a long soak in a bath, a change of clothes, but she still has it. No wonder I thought she was just gorgeous growing up – she was. Is.

At that exact moment, as if she feels my stare, she suddenly sits up and looks directly at me but there's a second's delay before she recognises me.

"Rosie!"

"Hi, Sarah!"

She stands up and we hug.

"Welcome home!"

"Thanks." Then she laughs. "Mind Jack!"

I look down to see the baby squashed between us.

"Gosh, he's got so big. How is he?"

"Fine." Then she laughs. "At least he is *now*. He's worn himself out with all his crying. I pity the other people on the flight."

I nod in the direction of the trolley. "Are you planning on staying forever?"

She shrugs. "Oh, you know me. Couldn't decide what to bring so I just chucked everything in. Easier than having to make a decision."

"All that luggage must have cost you a fortune."

"More than I could ever have imagined. But – hey! – thanks to your good luck the flights were free. I still can't believe you won them on a radio phone-in."

"But I did, and now you're here. So, shall we go?"

"Sure."

"What are the chances of getting as far as the car without waking these two?" She asks as she catches hold of the trolley.

"Here, let me." I say. "You've already got the baby." Then I remember. I look around. "Hang on, what about Rod? Where is he?"

"He couldn't make it."

"Oh!"

"He had to pull out at the last moment. Work is hectic."

"You flew all this way on your own with two small children and a baby. It must have been hell!"

"That's one way of putting it." She laughs. "Like I say, as much for the other passengers as myself."

Suddenly I'm in awe. She must really be wrecked. My flight from Australia seemed hellish and never-ending and I was with Caroline and Dana. But Sarah flew with three small kids, on her own, and yet she's not complaining. I would, if I were in her shoes.

"Let's get you to your hotel." I start pushing carefully but the movement causes Lachlan to wake.

"Auntie Rosie!"

He jumps down and gives me a bear hug.

Kyle, now awake too, follows suit. "Auntie Rosie!"

I suddenly feel quite emotional. They're such cool kids. I wouldn't mind ones like these, some day.

Unlike Con's four boys who were like little studious professors, so quiet and eerily grown-up, Kyle and Lachlan chatter non-stop in the car on the way to the hotel.

". . . Koala, Kangaroo, Platypus, Wombat . . ." Now Lachlan is listing out the animals of Australia. ". . . Dingo, Tasmanian Devil . . ."

I didn't ask him to, it's just something he seems to think I should know. I guess his childhood logic is that if he's interested then I'll be interested.

". . . Emu," contributes Kyle.

". . . Emu," repeats Lachlan. "Shark, Crocodile . . ."

"Who'd have thought there could be so many!" I look over at Sarah.

She laughs. "The second confusing thing about Australia, as Douglas Adams once said, are the animals and that they can be divided into three categories: poisonous, odd, and sheep."

". . . Camels, Blue-tongued Skink . . ."

"Are there camels in Australia?" I ask.

"Of course!" Lachlan responds with more than a hint of disdain at my ignorance. ". . . Blue-tongued Skink, Kangaroo . . ."

"What's the first thing?" I ask Sarah.

"Pardon?"

"That Douglas Adams found confusing?"

Sarah laughs. "You know, I don't know."

"Auntie Rosie, did you know that the nine most poisonous arachnids in the world all live in Australia?"

"No, Kyle, I did not! You'd better not tell Nana or she'll not be visiting again."

"I did tell her the last time she came to stay and she said she was going to wear elastic bands at the end of her pants to stop them crawling up."

I laugh.

But then disappointedly, he adds: "But I think she was kidding because she never did."

As we're pulling up at the hotel I realise Sarah and I hadn't much of a chance to talk. When I say as much to her as we're getting out of the car, she shrugs.

"It's like that when you have kids. I can't remember the last time I had a nice, normal, adult conversation."

"Not even with Rod?"

"Not even with Rod." She has the baby in her arms and the older boys are standing by the car, looking up at the hotel, counting out all the windows on the front.

"Boys, do you want to go and play for ten minutes?" Sarah nods towards the hotel's little playground just metres from where we've parked. The boys don't even answer. They just go tearing off, shouting in wild delight.

Now Sarah turns to me.

"Rosie?"

"Yes?"

"If I tell you something will you promise not to say anything to Mum and Dad, just for now?"

Another secret? Oh dear. Don't I have enough of my own I think but then I answer: "Sure." I'm too distracted by everything, by all the coming-and-going of the morning to be as concerned as perhaps I should.

But then she drops her bombshell.

"I lied about Rod. It's not work that kept him from coming. The fact is, he and I have split up."

"Ah, Sarah, no! You're kidding me!"

She sighs, but doesn't say anything.

"Why didn't you tell me when I was over there?"

"There was no reason. This is all new. I'd no idea it was coming. It's Rod's idea. I didn't want it. He just came home one day and out-of-the-blue announced that he was leaving me. It was a total shock."

"You never saw it coming?"

She shakes her head. "During the last couple of years he's been away a lot, travelling with work. We never seemed to get the chance to talk but we didn't have any fights or arguments either. I mean I knew he wasn't happy. When he was at home he was so distant and uninvolved. But I

327

thought things were okay – not great – far from it. But I felt we'd be able to get through them and that our life, our relationship, would improve again. When the children got older. When things started going better for Rod at work. When I'd finally be able to cut down on the hours I put in at the hospital. I guess I thought that, sometime in the future, we'd get back to the way we were. After all I still loved him. *Do* love him – despite what's happened."

I dare to ask the obvious. "Do you think there's someone else?"

"No, he says there's not."

"And you believe him?"

"Yes. I know he travels a lot and I can't swear he's never been unfaithful but I don't think he has. I'm as sure as I can be that he didn't leave me for someone. Maybe it would be easier if that was the case." She shrugs.

"So why did he leave you?"

"He says he does still love me but he's no longer in love with me." She sighs. "He says he feels trapped with the children, the house, the domesticity of it all."

"You'd kind of think he'd have thought of all that sooner?"

"I guess I knew he was feeling like that but I'd convinced myself it was a phase, just a reaction after the baby was born. He really didn't want a third. But it's not. It's for real. He's not coming back."

"Oh Sarah!"

"I haven't told the boys yet. Rod's always been away so much that they haven't noticed anything different. I want them – us – to have a good time on this trip."

But she looks so unhappy as she says this. I can't bear to see her looking so dejected. I go to give her a hug and she yields readily, coming in close to me as I wrap my arms around her. It's strange. She was always the big one, the one minding me. But now, for the first time in my life, I don't feel like the 'baby' sister.

"You know I'll do anything I can to help you."

She nods. "I know." She stays where she is for a long while. I like that she does. It feels good. I missed my sister.

She pulls away finally. "Rosie, I will tell Mum and Dad in my own time but I'm not ready yet. It's all still so raw. I couldn't bear their disappointment. I don't want them worrying. I don't want them feeling sorry for me. You won't say anything, will you?"

I shake my head. "Of course not."

"Besides, I'm meant to be home for a happy occasion, their anniversary." Despite everything, she manages a laugh now. "Have they really no idea that all of us – me, William, Con, their wives, and all the grandchildren are here?"

"No, not a clue."

"I can't wait to see their faces!"

"Sarah –"

"It's going to be great!"

"Sarah –"

"Rosie, just leave it for now. I want to park my problems and just enjoy myself as best I can. I can't wait to see William and Con. It's years since all four of us have been together." She laughs. "I hope the shock of seeing all of us won't cause Dad to drop down dead with a heart attack!"

"Sarah! You're terrible!"

She laughs again. "Come on," she grabs my hand. "I need to freshen up. Boys! Come on! Let's go and see your room!"

So what's the largest jackpot to have gone unclaimed?

Unknown – $51 million – US

$51 million! Just lying there . . .

25

"Come on, Mum. We'll be late," I call from the bottom of the stairs.

I hear her moving about in her bedroom. I hear her grumbling though what about I can't make out.

"Mum!"

I hear her coming out onto the landing, still grumbling.

"I really don't know why we have to go for a meal first with your Uncle Dave and Auntie Margaret. Won't we be seeing them later on? Hmm." There's a pause. "I'm still not sure about this dress." I imagine she's standing in front of the mirror on the landing, looking at herself critically as she says this. "Anyway, don't Dave and Margaret know there will be food at the Nutley? Oh dear, it really is very low-cut."

"Just come on, Mum, please," I call up to her.

She comes to the top of the stairs and I swear my jaw drops. She looks amazing.

"Well, would you look!" says Dad, who's come up behind me. He gives a wolf whistle.

"Oh, stop it now!"

We both stare as – very carefully – she makes her way down the stairs on high heels. Mum's wardrobe consists of leisure suits and more leisure suits. She rarely wears anything else and, now, to see her in this fabulous green velvet, low-cut (for her), fitted frock is something of a revelation. I have never seen her looking so good. I feel like one of those people who barely recognise their own mother/daughter/lover/wife/whatever after they've undergone some extreme make-over on television.

"Stop staring, the pair of you!" Mum now protests crossly. "You're making me feel self-conscious!"

"But we can't help it," says Dad. "I swear, Nora, you look even more lovely than you did on the day I married you."

"Oh stop it, Will!"

"Twice as lovely."

"Twice as big you mean."

"Come here," Dad orders in an uncharacteristically commanding voice.

"Will! Stop now!"

"Come here!"

"Will!"

But she yields and he takes her in his arms and gives her a kiss on the lips – an uncommon public display of affection from a generally very private man.

"Oh, Will!" gasps my mother sounding embarrassingly coquettish.

"Oh please!" I say. "Not in front of your daughter!"

The pair of them ignore me.

But before we leave for their surprise party there is one thing I have to do first. I delve into my handbag, find what I'm looking for, and take out a black leather box.

"Mum, Dad, happy anniversary," I say and hold it out to them.

The party and bringing everyone home for it is my real present to them but I wanted to give them something else to mark the occasion, something they would know was from me. I racked my brains trying to think of something really special for the pair of them but I genuinely don't believe there's anything left in the world Dad wants, or needs. Every Christmas and every birthday when asked, he always gives the stock reply of, 'Socks', so I figured that as long as Mum is happy with what I give them, he'll be happy too, whichis why I went for the one thing I knew she'd really appreciate.

"What is it?" asks Mum, looking at the box.

"Open it and you'll find out."

She lifts off the lid. "Oh my!"

"What is it?" asks Dad.

"Oh, Rosie!"

"Nora, what is it?"

There are tears in her eyes. "A Fabergé egg!"

"It's The Great Peter," I tell her.

"Rosie, you really shouldn't have."

"Course I should. You deserve it," I tell them, then quickly add, "It's not the original, of course." Just in case there's any chance she might think it could be.

"Of course not – I know that."

"Czar Nicholas, the second, presented the original to his wife, the Empress Alexandra Fedorovna in 1903."

"Is that so?" asks Mum.

I nod. I've learned a lot about Fabergé eggs since the exhibition. When I first got the idea to buy Mum one I figured I'd – well – I'd get a real one having really no idea just how expensive or rare they are. I didn't know then that only sixty-one of them have survived to the present and most of these are now in museums. One that did come up for sale in 2007 made a price of something like eighteen-and-half million dollars so, although our lotto win may have made Dana, Caroline and me rich by most people's standards, we're not exactly in the Fabergé-egg-buying league. I guess it's all relative.

Now Mum lifts the egg out of the box and opens it up to reveal a little man on horseback.

"Oh, how lovely!"

"It's a miniature of the statue that still stands on the banks of the Neva River in Russia."

"Just look at the detail. It's so perfect." She drags her eyes away from it. "But, Rosie, this must have set you back hundreds."

Thousands actually but I don't tell her that. It may not be the original but it's the finest copy I could find. It's decorated with six hundred and seventy-five Swarovski crystals representing the same number of hand-set Austrian crystals in the original.

"Rosie, it's very generous of you, too generous," says Dad. "You shouldn't be spending your money on us like this."

"Come here!" says Mum. "Let me give you a hug." But even as she does, she carries on talking. "You know, it's the nicest present I've – we've – ever received, isn't it, Will? The question now is where shall we put it? Aren't you just the best daughter, ever! Honestly, I'll treasure it always." She finally lets me go. "Ah, look at what you're making me do now, Rosie." She wipes a tear from her eye. "My make-up will be ruined."

"You look perfect," I say. "Now come on. We'd better go."

"Rosie's right," says Dad. "Dave will throw a fit if we keep him and Margaret waiting."

Mum puts the egg back in the box and then the box in her bag.

"Are you bringing it with you?' I ask in alarm.

"Of course I am. I want to show it to everyone."

I'm worried she'll lose it. I want to tell her to leave it at home. But I guess half the pleasure will be in showing it off.

As Dad looks for a parking space, I send a quick text to Sarah to let everyone know the eagles have landed. When he does eventually find a space, it's so far away from the front door of the hotel that Mum complains we'd have been as well off leaving the car at home. We climb out.

"Come on," says Dad ushering us along.

When we reach the front door, I turn left to go to the function room.

"Where are you going, Rosie?" asks Mum, "The sign says the restaurant is the other way. Margaret and Dave will be waiting."

"I – ah – I was just thinking I'd like to take a look at the function room now that we're here."

"Whatever for? What possible reason –" And then she lets out a gasp. "Oh Rosie, don't tell me you and Finn are thinking of setting a date?"

"A date?"

"You know . . ." She gives me this knowing look and begins humming "Here Comes the Bride".

I have to wonder sometimes about Mum and what goes on in her head. I have to wonder how she reaches the conclusions she does. I say function room. She thinks wedding!

But since I need to get her into the function room, I give an ambiguous, you-never-know shrug. If that's what it takes to get her in there, then so be it. What Finn doesn't know won't hurt him and, anyway, Mum will know the real reason soon enough.

Mum now gives this mischievous giggle. "Come on so. Let's take a quick look."

All three of us walk down the corridor together but then, as we near the double doors, I stoop and pretend to fix the strap of my shoe. "You go ahead. I'll follow."

And off they go together, Dad guiding Mum by the arm – out of affection or to hurry her along, I can't say. I stand up and wait. Dad opens the door and is ushering Mum in when I hear cries of:

"Surprise!"

When I reach them, they're surrounded by everyone.

"Will! Sarah! Con! You're all here! Oh, Eithne, so lovely to see you!" Dad is kissing this one. Mum is hugging that one. "And Chase? Or Logan, is it? My, how you've grown! Tara-Anne, my own darling!"

Looking on, seeing them surrounded by all their family, seeing them so joyful, I really don't think it's possible to be any happier than I am at this moment.

"Rosie, which radio show was running the competition?"

It's Auntie Margaret who's asking now but I've lost count the number of times I've had to answer this same question in the course of the night.

"*The Gerry Ryan Show.*"

"But I always listen to him and I never heard about it."

I shrug. The less said the better. It's not like she can prove I didn't – not unless she rings the show and I don't think even she would do that.

"How could I not have heard about it?"

"It *was* a couple of months ago."

"I suppose I must have missed it somehow. Maybe it was on around the time we were in Crete. Tell me exactly when they were ru—"

"Oh, look. There's Dad," I say, looking for an escape, "I need to tell him something."

I hurry away and go over to where Dad is talking to Evelyn.

"*So you're staying for the week?*" Dad always speaks very loudly, very slowly and very distinctly, when he's talking to this particular daughter-in-law. Evelyn may have been born in America, she may have grown up there speaking English all the way through preschool, school and college but, influenced by her obvious Asian appearance, my dad always talks to her as if she's a recent immigrant.

I leave them at it. I wander in the direction of the bar. I see Con and William standing there and, spotting me, Con beckons me over.

"So, Rosie, set up any more businesses lately?" he asks.

"Ah, no." I don't tell him about my true involvement in CKV Property.

"I mean, come on, Rosie. What were you thinking? A shop selling love potions you concocted yourself!"

"How was that ever going to work?" William now joins in. "You must have seen the writing on the wall from the word go."

"Where did you think the market was going to be?" asks Con.

"It could have worked," I protest. "It *was* working. We'd started to make a profit."

"Yeah?" Con glances over at William and smirks. "How come you're not still in business so?"

"There were other issues. We never applied for planning for the kitchen for one and there was a problem with one of our investors which —"

Neither is listening. I can see they've no interest in what I have to say. They've decided upon the version they like best – with me, their kid sister, centre-rolling as hapless fool. They're not interested in hearing any other. If they had lost their jobs or had some other misfortune in their lives, I wouldn't be laughing at them. Yet they think it's okay to laugh at me and at what they perceive as my failure. The way the pair of them casually dismiss what Caroline, Dana and I worked so hard to achieve, and dismiss our ambition and our disappointment is nasty but I try telling myself that, perhaps, they just don't understand; that maybe they simply don't have an inkling of how we put our heart, soul, blood, sweat and tears into that business.

But they move on.

"In any case, you must be getting well paid with that new crowd you're working for," says William. "What are they called again?"

"CKV."

"What does that stand for?"

I pretend I don't hear him.

"Mum was saying a friend of yours set it up," Con now joins in.

"That's right."

"Well, tell her I think she's paying you too much."

"What do you mean?"

"I mean the Fabergé egg you bought Mum. That was pretty pricey."

"That's not the real thing, just a reproduction."

"Yes, but there are reproductions and reproductions."

"I guess. I don't know much about them really. I just bought it online."

"Well, Evelyn does know about these things. Her parents have a jewellery store and she tells me the egg is an excellent reproduction, that there must be almost a thousand Swarovski crystals on it."

"Swarovski? I don't think so."

"That's not what Evelyn says."

"Well, *maybe* Evelyn is wrong."

"No." He shakes his head with conviction. Clearly this is beyond possibility in Con's world.

"Well, then I guess she has to be right so. In which case I bagged myself a bargain."

"Hmmm."

He's looking at me now, but it's far more than just a casual look. It's like he's trying to figure something out – me, I guess, and the egg, and the truth about it. I begin to grow uncomfortable but, then, William nudges him.

"What?"

William nods in the direction of the dance floor, towards Sarah who is smack-bang in the middle, swinging Kyle around and around by his arms – he's stretched out to the full, like a chairoplane, with everyone else keeping a safe distance.

"So what do you make of Sarah coming home on her own then?" he asks Con.

"What? Are you thinking what I'm thinking?" responds William. "Trouble in Paradise?"

I look from one to the other. At their rotund, sweaty, laughing faces and at their equally rotund bellies on which they could rest their pints if they took the notion. What gives this satisfied pair, this Twiddledum and Twiddledee, the right to be so bloody negative about others? First me and now

Sarah? What gives them the right to relish the misfortunes of others while enjoying their own good fortune in life?

"Hmm, maybe so," agrees Con. "She's not looking the Mae West, is she?"

"I've seen her looking better," concurs William.

"Hey!" I butt in. "Come on! She's just had a baby. And she's travelled all the way from Australia, on her own."

"Evelyn's just had a baby too, Rosie."

Con nods his head. "Too many women use that as an excuse to let themselves go."

"Sarah has not let herself go!" I protest.

"She could have made more of an effort given the occasion. You and Mum both look fantastic. But, like Evelyn –"

"Evelyn?"

"Like Evelyn said, that dress Sarah's wearing is very casual and she hasn't bothered with make-up. I think she could –"

"She doesn't *need* make-up," I say defensively. "She's naturally beautiful."

"Maybe so, but she is pushing on."

I stare from one to the other. Why do they have to be so negative?

Now Con changes the subject. "So, Rosie, this fellow of yours, Flynn –"

"Finn."

"He tells me he's a musician?"

"Yes, he is."

"Like we all were at one stage?" Con laughs. Then he looks to William. "Remember *The Someits?*"

"How could I forget?"

"I wonder where Fergus O'Rourke is now? He was devastated when we broke up. He thought he was going to be the next Bono? I guess your Flynn –"

"Finn."

"— Finn thinks that too, eh, Rosie?"

"No, he's happy being Finn Heelan."

I just don't get them. They're doing so well for themselves: good careers, fine houses, big cars, lovely families and wives who appear to love them. So why do they have to be so negative and cynical about everyone else? For a split second I imagine telling them about my lotto win just to whip the self-satisfied grins off their faces but the price for my short-term satisfaction would be too high. Apart from everything else I'd be faced with their jealousy and their schemes to get their hands on my share of the win. Not to mention Dana and Caroline's wrath.

They hardly notice when I walk away.

Later, I stand at the side, looking on at everyone out on the dance floor. I couldn't get the original band from my parents' wedding – half of them are dead and the surviving half are now resident in Florida. But the band I did get are sufficiently old-fashioned and non-threatening to bring the older people onto the dance floor in their droves, and sufficiently talented not to drive the younger crowd off. Now the dance floor is packed with couples dancing with varying degrees of ability and intimacy to 'Love me Tender'. Darting between these couples, some of the younger kids are playing a game of tag. I see Sarah is on the dance floor again, this time bouncing baby Jack up and down in her arms in time to the music. I spot the twins, Tara-Anne and Kay-Leigh, dancing in a little circle with Mum who seems to be enjoying it even more than they – her grin is so wide it makes her look like she's a little bit simple, or drunk. Or just very, very happy. A contented sigh suddenly escapes me. Yes, tonight I did a good thing.

I feel someone gently kiss the back of my neck and I turn to find Finn standing there.

"Oh, thank God it's you!" I laugh.

He smirks. "Who else did you think it could be?"

"That lecherous old friend of my dad's? Charlie What's-his-name. He's been giving me the eye all evening."

"Do you want me to take him outside?" Finn deadpans. "Rough him up a little?"

I laugh at the image of Finn doing something so uncharacteristic as giving an old man a thumping.

"Anyway," Finn goes on, "sorry to disappoint you but I don't think you're the only one old Charlie has his eye on. He's over at the bar now, chatting someone else up."

"The Casanova! And I really thought I was on to something there."

"At least he's keeping it in the family. I think it's your Auntie Margaret."

I laugh again. "Oh dear! I hope Uncle Dave doesn't spot him."

Finn smiles at me now. "You're really enjoying this evening, aren't you?"

"I sure am."

It's true. I am enjoying tonight. Yes, at this moment I feel utterly contented with my lot. Yes, life *is* good.

Finn puts his arms around me.

"So, Rosie Kiely, would you like to dance?"

Life is *very* good.

Time is running out but he feels lucky and despite the store manager's warning he insists on buying a Super 7 lottery ticket.

Joel Ifergan - $0 million - Canada

Yes! All seven winning numbers come up.
Yes! He has the winning ticket in his hand!
Yes! It's for a whopping $27 million.
But, oh no!

He's seven seconds - seven seconds - past the 9pm cut-off.

26

Although it was a very late night, I wake early in our hotel room and stretch across the bed only to find Finn is already gone – 'to work but love you loads', as the note he leaves tells me. Reluctantly I climb out of the bed and, after a long leisurely shower, I head down for breakfast.

All the family stayed in the hotel and I find Mum and Dad are already in the dining-room when I get there, midway through a fry-up.

"You're up early," I say as I join them at their table.

"Your dad insisted on coming down for breakfast even though he knows fatty food isn't good for him."

"Nora, a fry every now and then isn't going to do me any harm."

"Oh right, that's what your doctor says, is it?"

"So you enjoyed last night?" I ask as I reach for their basket of toast in the centre of the table.

"You're an awful girl, Rosie," says Mum.

"What do you mean?"

"Leading us on like that!"

I laugh. "But you enjoyed yourselves, didn't you?"

Mum laughs. "Of course! I still can't quite believe it! It was wonderful. It was the best night of my life."

"Is anybody else up?"

My mother nods. "Con and William are, and their families. We met them in the foyer. They were on their way out when we were coming down for breakfast. They said they were heading into town to have a look around."

"What about Sarah and the boys?"

"No sign yet."

A young, slim waitress in a black and white uniform comes and offers me tea or coffee. I ask for coffee. Then add that I'll have the fry – the full works bar mushrooms, plus a fresh basket of toast. It'll save her coming back and I am starving.

"It's a pity Rod couldn't come with Sarah," says Mum when the waitress has gone.

I nod. "True."

"Rosie, tell me, do you think everything is okay between them?"

"Why do you ask?"

Mum shrugs. "Oh, I don't know. I just have this feeling."

"Come on now, Nora," says Dad. "Don't start on that again."

"Will, I can't help if I worry. No matter how old they get, I'm still going to be anxious about them – that's just the way I am." She sighs. "Oh, maybe you're right and everything is fine."

"I'm sure it is," Dad tells her and pats her arm.

"I *hope* it is." She turns to me. "Oh yes, before I forget, are you and Finn free tomorrow evening?"

"I am but I'll have to check with Finn."

"It would be lovely if you could come around. The boys

and their families are going to stay on here in the hotel but Sarah and her crowd have decided to stay with us so I thought I might do a nice little supper for everyone. Make the most of having everyone home. Who knows when the next time will be."

"Sounds good."

"I was thinking around about seven."

When he finishes work, Finn calls around to our house. Shane lets him in and he finds me in the kitchen where I'm cooking some pasta.

"Hi!"

"Oh hi, Finn."

He comes over and gives me a kiss.

"You look tired," I say, when we pull apart.

He takes a seat at the table. "Well, it was a late night and I had an early start this morning. So tell me, did your parents enjoy last night?"

"They'd a great time, everyone had. Wasn't it the best night ever?"

He nods. "It was. Really great!"

"Do you want some pasta?" I ask

"Okay. If there's enough."

"Before I forget, Mum wants us all to come around tomorrow evening at seven, will you be free?"

"Sure, but I might be a little late. Can I meet you there?"

"Whatever suits you." I drain the pasta and then add some sauce.

"So you didn't have work today?" Finn asks.

"No, it's Saturday."

He nods. "Of course." Then he thinks for a moment. "But you don't seem to go to work all that much."

"Sure I do."

"Mitch said he saw you walking down O'Connell Street the other day when he was on the bus."

"I'm not in the office all the time. It's the nature of the job."

"You were laden down with shopping bags."

"I was probably on my lunch break."

"At eleven in the morning?"

I feign a laugh. "Ah well, now you know he's lying. Since when has Mitch ever been out of bed at that time of the day?"

Finn is silent for a moment. "Rosie, can I ask you something?"

"Yeah, fire ahead."

"Where are you getting all the money from?"

"What do you mean?"

"Well, Con's wife said the present you bought your parents must have cost a fortune."

"She said that to you?"

He nodÛ.

"That it must have cost thousands?"

What business is it of hers? She seems to have spent the entire night going around discussing my present. "She doesn't know what she's talking about. Her parents, not her, are the ones with the jewellery shop. I mean, okay, it was expensive but not *that* expensive!"

"And that outfit you'd on last night . . ."

"What about it?"

"It was lovely. You were lovely. But . . ."

"Good, I'm glad you thought so."

"That was expensive."

"And how would you know?"

"I don't but I heard some of your mother's friends talking. One of them was saying she reckoned you couldn't have got much change out of a couple of grand."

"Jeez, Finn. It was my parents' anniversary – of course I was going to wear something special. You've heard of credit, haven't you? Anyway, for your information, it was nowhere near as much as that."

"Rosie, maybe you should be more careful. I'd hate to see you getting too far into debt. Caroline could be out of business tomorrow."

"Oh Finn, you worry too much." I give him a kiss. "It's nice that you worry about me but, really, there's no need."

"I can't help it!"

Just then, Shane comes back.

"Okay, where did it come from?"

"What?"

"That platinum TV in the living-room? It's enormous! I didn't even know they made them that big!"

"Oh that! Caroline had it delivered this afternoon. It's fantastic, isn't it?"

"It must have cost a fortune. Where did Caroline get the money for it?"

From the corner of my eye, I can see Finn looking on and listening with interest. I wish Shane would shut up.

"For someone who's just set up in business she's being very free with her cash. And here's another thing. Yesterday, I left a file at home so I had to pop back and I discovered this woman, a stranger, here in our kitchen and when I asked her who she was, she said she was the cleaner."

"Oh – yeah, Yvonne. Was yesterday the first time you met her?"

"The first time I even *knew* we had a cleaner."

"Really?"

"Yes, though I had noticed the place was much tidier. But can I ask why we need a cleaner? We're four adults – surely we can look after ourselves?"

I'm inclined to agree with him but it was Caroline's idea. I shrug. "Like you say the place is tidier."

"Yes, but how much is she costing? And how come no one asked me to pay any money towards her?"

I shrug. "I'm sure Caroline will. She probably forgot. She has been very busy lately."

"Doing what? Buying platinum TVs?"

"No, with her business of course."

"Hmm." Shane doesn't look convinced but doesn't press the matter. Instead he reverts to the topic of our new cleaner. "Look, I pay rent too. I'd appreciate it if, from now on, I was consulted more about what went on around here. I don't think that's asking too much."

"Course not." And it's not. But if he only knew there were far bigger changes afoot, changes he knows nothing about. Like the fact that Tom Redmond has approached Caroline's brother with an offer for this house.

"Good! I didn't think so." Now Shane turns to Finn. "So are you coming, Finn?"

"Where?" Finn asks.

"The rugby match is about to start. I was going to go to the pub to watch it but I think I'll stay in now."

I laugh. "But you weren't consulted about the TV. Don't you want to boycott it on a point of principle?"

"Both it and I are big enough to make an exception this once."

He takes a beer from the fridge and heads off.

Finn looks over to me. He has this puzzled look on his face. I get the feeling he has more questions for me.

I go to the fridge, pick out a beer and hold it and the bowl of pasta out to him. "Go on. You don't want to miss the start."

"Are you coming, Finn?" Shane calls from the living-room.

Finn stands there for a moment, just looking at me, then sighs and, taking the beer and pasta from me, follows after Shane.

"I think God heard us. God put that ticket in his hands."

Anonymous - $3 million - US

Pastor Bertrand Crabbe speaking after a generous and anonymous parishioner donated his winning ticket to his church.

27

It isn't long before Mum finds out that her suspicions regarding Sarah aren't without foundation. The next evening, in fact.

When I call out to Mum and Dad's at seven as arranged I find I don't have a key and it's Dad who opens the door and lets me in. It strikes me immediately that the house seems very quiet so I ask Dad where everyone is.

"Sarah is upstairs giving the boys a bath and the others should be here soon."

"Where's Mum?"

She's in the living-room." I go to walk in but Dad holds me back. "Rosie, she's very upset."

"Oh?"

"Sarah's just told her that she and Rod have split up."

"Oh dear!"

Mum is sitting in the middle of the couch. She looks up. "Rosie!" Her eyes are red from crying and she's clutching a ball of paper tissue in her fist. "Did your dad tell you about Sarah and Rod?"

I nod.

"Can you believe it!"

I sit down beside her and put my arm around her shoulder.

"Come on, Mum. Try not to be so upset."

"How can I be anything but upset! Poor Sarah. And the poor boys. Oh God, I hate to think of it. To think of them. How could Rod do this, walk out on them like that? And what is Sarah going to do now? Does she have any idea how expensive Ireland has become?"

"What's that got to do with anything?"

"Didn't Dad tell you?"

"Tell me what?"

"Sarah says she's going to live here. She's not going back to Australia."

I admit part of me is pleased, not about the break-up, of course, but about this new development. "But Mum, isn't it good that she's decided to stay here?"

"For us, maybe, but it's not good for Sarah or the children. If she and Rod were in the same country they might have some chance of getting back together again. But what chance will they have now, if she's over here and he's over there."

"I hadn't thought of that."

"And it's not right to take the children so far away from him. They'll grow up not knowing him and everyone has the right to know their father."

"I guess." What Mum's saying is true. I am being selfish.

"No matter what a scumbag lowlife worthless piece of trash he is."

"Mum!"

"What? Don't look surprised. I'm just telling the truth."

"I've never heard you say a bad word about him before."

"That's because he never left my daughter and my

grandchildren before. As long as he made Sarah happy, I liked him well enough, or told myself I did. But he was always too good to be true, with his 'Mum this' and his 'Mum that' like I was the one who'd given birth to him!" She shakes her head. "No, I never really liked him. I can say that now. All kind words and gushing compliments but with no real feeling behind them. And I never completely trusted him either and I know your dad felt the same. But, from the moment she set eyes on him, there was no one else for Sarah. He could do no wrong in her eyes. What choice did I have but to put my own feelings aside and try to see what it was Sarah saw?" She gives a loud sigh and, calmer now after her outburst, she goes on, "But I really don't think Sarah's thought all this through. Is she going to be able to work and mind the children? Does she know how expensive childcare is here? How is she going to be able to afford somewhere to live?" And then a thought strikes Mum. "Is she going to want to move in here with us?"

"I don't know, Mum."

"I mean your dad and I are used to having our own space. I love the kids, I do, but having them here would change everything." She thinks for a second. "But I suppose we'd manage. It wouldn't be the worst thing in the world."

Sarah comes in. She looks to Mum, then me. "I take it you've heard the news?"

I nod. "I'm sure you've made the right decision."

Mum snorts. "Well, I'm not so sure. I don't think you know what you're doing, Sarah."

"Mum, I do. Look, I wasn't the one who broke up our marriage. Rod did. *He* was the one who decided he wanted out."

"But what about the children? It's not fair to take them so far away from him."

"Mum, the children were part of the reason he left. I'm not saying he doesn't love them, just not enough to want to be the father he should."

"But how are you going to manage on your own?"

"Mum, since they were been born I've been the one minding them and –"

"Yes, but you had Rod helping, working to provide for you all."

Sarah sighs. "For a salesman he wasn't all that good at selling. On the other hand, he was good at spending – spending money on himself and spending time on the golf course. You could say his job interfered with his golf."

"But what about all the travelling he had to do? He worked so hard. He seemed to be doing so well."

"Not that well. He was just good at giving that impression but it was always someone else's fault when he missed another promotion. I had to work all the hours I could get to help make ends meet."

"Even so, do you really think you're going to be able to manage on your own?"

"I'll manage. I'll have to."

"I wish I had your confidence."

"Look, Mum, I already know what it's like trying to bring the boys up on my own, Rod was hardly ever there – like you said, he was always away travelling. And I already know how lonesome it is to be in the house on my own, night after night, but at least I always knew Rod would be home again in a week or two. But that's no longer the case. He no longer wants to live with us – I would be totally on my own if I went back to Australia. But at least here I will have you, Dad, and Rosie around."

"But –"

"I've made my decision. I'm not going back."

"So because he's going through some ridiculous midlife crisis you all have to suffer?"

"Mum, this isn't how I wanted things to work out either."

"I know, but —"

"Mum, I'm staying."

"We were happy before all this and we're certainly happy now."

Ray and Barbara Wragg – £7 million – UK

"I'd say we're the happiest couple ever to win the lotto."

28

Dana knocks on the bedroom door. "Caroline?"

"What?" comes the abrupt response.

"We're leaving now. The taxi is outside the door. It's a minibus. Doug, Finn, Loretta and Shane are already in it. There's room for you too so are you coming?"

There's no answer.

Dana looks over at me. She sighs.

"Caroline, please come," I call out.

No answer.

"Well, all right then," says Dana. "We're going now."

"See you later," I call.

We go down the stairs and out to the taxi but, just when we've climbed in and I'm about to close the car, Caroline emerges from the house. She looks amazing. She's wearing a red three-quarter-length dress, matching high heels and has her blonde hair tied up in a high, sophisticated bun.

"Wow! Don't you look classy!" I tell her as she climbs in beside me.

"Thanks," she mutters. "Push in."

"I'm glad you decided to come."

She doesn't answer.

"Mick will be glad too."

Again she doesn't answer.

For the entire journey, as we all chat excitedly about the evening ahead, she doesn't say a word but just sits there mutely in our midst.

When we pull up outside the cinema we find a huge crowd outside. There's even a red carpet. But tonight we're not part of the hoi polloi, no, no. *We* have invitations for the Irish premiere of *Fate Farm*. We show our invitations to a doorman and, once inside, we make our way to the foyer, where there's a reception in full swing. The place is packed.

"This is incredible!" Dana looks around. "Can you believe the crowd? Look at the style. I bet there's some pretty famous people here. Look, look, there's one of them now – the star of the evening – Mick!"

All of us turn to where she's looking and see Mick, looking incredibly suave in his black tux, white bow tie and white dress shirt.

"Wow!" says Loretta. "I've never seen him looking so good. Is that Audrey Turner with him?"

I nod. "Isn't she stunning!"

We've met Mick's famous American co-star once before when we visited the set but she was in character for most of that day, her character being that of the downtrodden wife of a bully who's in love with the bully's brother – as played by Mick. But, tonight, she looks every inch the film star. At that moment, Mick spots us, excuses himself from Audrey and the rest of the group he's with, and comes over.

"Hi, everyone, thanks for coming!"

He looks to Caroline. She looks back at him. They don't

say anything, just stare at one another for what seems like ages. Until, finally:

"You look beautiful, Caroline."

"Thanks. You're not looking too bad either."

"I'm glad you're here."

She shrugs. "I couldn't miss your big night."

"Which I owe all to you. If you hadn't dragged me off to see Kevin North, none of this would have happened."

"You'd have got there in the end."

"I'm not too sure about that. Anyway, you're here now. That's good. It just wouldn't have been the same without you." Then he notices that we're all standing there, watching on. He gives us this meaningful look.

"Right," says Shane, taking the cue. "We're just going to the bar. "Caroline? Mick? Do you want anything?" Neither of them reply. "Right, I'll take that as a no then."

We slip away, but not so far away that we can't see them.

"They seem to be getting on well," notes Loretta from our vantage point.

And they do. Mick looks a little nervous perhaps, but he's talking animatedly. Caroline looks a little solemn maybe, but she is listening intently.

"It is nice to see them together again," observes Dana.

Suddenly Caroline throws her head back and laughs. And then Mick – after a moment's surprise – joins in with her laughter.

I give a sigh of relief. "Look, they're actually laughing together," I say. "This *is* good."

"I knew if they could just meet up everything would be fine," says Dana.

But, then, they're joined by someone else, a young,

pretty woman in stilettos that are inches high and a very tiny dress that covers little of her very tiny body.

"Who is *that*?" asks Dana.

"Who knows? But I wish she'd clear off."

But she doesn't. She stands close to Mick, talking excitedly to him, and then she stretches up and gives him a hug. He hugs her back. Then we see him introducing her to Caroline. We see Caroline smile at the woman and hold out her hand but the young woman doesn't appear to notice it. She just gives Caroline a perfunctory nod and immediately turns back to Mick and again talks enthusiastically to him. Even from here, I can see her bare back is ever-so-slightly turned from Caroline, subtle enough so that Mick probably doesn't even notice but there's no doubt from the expression on her face that Caroline feels put out.

"Can't she just leave them on their own," mutters Dana.

Finally, the woman does take her leave – but not before she gives Mick another hug and offers her cheek for a parting kiss which he obligingly gives.

"Good riddance," says Dana.

Mick turns his attention back to Caroline. He says something to her which – after a moment's hesitation – causes her to smile. He smiles back at her. But then – almost immediately – they're joined again by others.

"Damn!" mutters Dana. "Can't people leave them alone!"

This time it's a couple in their thirties – a very handsome, successful-looking man with a suitably stylish and beautiful woman. Again, Mick introduces them to Caroline and they smile in her direction but immediately turn their interest back to Mick and vie for his attention. Both are talking to him at the same time, neither giving Mick a chance to say anything in response. It doesn't look like they've any interest in anything Caroline might want to add to the conversation – not that she looks like she's inclined to contribute. She's just staring tensely at them. Now the woman lays her hand on Mick's arm, perhaps to emphasise a point she's making, or perhaps to get even closer to the man-of-the-moment. The hand stays there for what seems like a very long time to me.

Caroline is beginning to look royally browned off.

"Oh, this is not good," mutters Dana.

Just then an usher comes over to us and tells us the movie is about to commence and that we need to start moving inside.

"Should we wait for them?" asks Dana.

"No," says Shane. "Let's just leave them."

We move with the crowd, leaving Caroline and Mick behind.

We take our seats and wait for the movie to begin. But, before that, the director, Kevin North, takes to the stage. After a round of applause, we all settle into silence as he begins his speech. First, he welcomes us all. Then he begins to recount the first time he ever read the book on which the film is based and tells us all how he was blown away by it. "Literally, blown away," he says which gets a laugh from the audience who seem to be familiar with the story and get the joke; there is quite a lot of people being blown away in the story, most notably Mick's character who meets a very bloody end. North goes on. He tells of how, from the start, he knew that Audrey Turner, though an American actress, would be perfect for the female lead, and then he pauses.

"But who was I going to cast opposite Audrey – that was my conundrum. I had every name in the business read for that part but no one seemed quite right. But then, one day, a certain woman I chanced to meet tried to convince me that her boyfriend would be absolutely perfect. Would I have heard of him, I asked. Sure, she assured me. What would I have seen him in, I enquired. Well, lots of things, she told me. Like, I then wanted to know. *Fair City*, she answered. So what's the name of his character, was my next question. And, to this day, I remember her response: 'Well, I don't know that he had a name as such. He was more in the background – but he was brilliant!'" Again the crowd laugh. When they stop, North goes on, "At that point I was about to walk away but this young lady was terribly persuasive and when she subsequently turned up on my door with Mick Boylan, I took one look at him and knew I had found the right man." He pauses again. "The right man – as long as he could act!" Again everyone laughs. "And boy! Could he act! Mick Boylan has brought something to the role, something much more than what was on the page, much more than I saw in it. Mick has made the character his own."

"Can you see them anywhere?" Dana leans over and whispers to me.

"No, I guess they're somewhere up the front."

Finally, the movie begins. We sit there in the dark watching. And Kevin North is right in everything he says about Mick. I've read the book, I know Mick's character but Mick has brought him to life in the most extraordinary way. I forget it's Mick. I can't imagine anyone else playing the part. He is the part. I laugh with him when he jokes with his brother's wife. I worry when it's clear they're falling in love. I fear for him when his brother begins to suspect their growing feelings for one another. I share his lover's interest when he strips off and showers in the yard of her farmhouse, having shown up while on the run. And I hold my breath when his own father points a shotgun at him and shoots him at point-blank range. And then the credits roll.

I sit there without moving, still stunned. I can't remember the last time I was so affected by a movie. And I am not alone. There's complete silence in the auditorium. And then the clapping starts. And it grows and grows until it's thunderous. And it keeps on going for what seems like an age. Everyone is on their feet.

As the lights go on, I quickly wipe away the tears and notice that both Loretta and Dana are doing the same. The males amongst us aren't entirely unmoved either. Either Doug has something in his eye or he's furiously blinking back his own tears.

From the front row, Audrey Turner stands up, turns and takes a bow. A couple of seats over from her, Mick does the same. He looks overwhelmed by the audience's reaction and all this attention. But happy too. Very happy.

"Can you see Caroline?" Dana calls to me.

"Not from here, no. There are too many people in the way."

We come back out and, after a while, Mick finally manages to make his way over to us. We all crowd around him.

"Mick, you were outstanding!" Shane tells him.

"Come here and give us a hug," laughs Dana.

"Here, don't hog him!" I push my way in and give him a kiss when I get the chance.

"Is Caroline not with you?" asks Mick when he finally gets the opportunity.

"We thought she was with you."

He shakes his head. "No, she said she was going to the ladies' just before we went in but she never came back. I thought she must have met you lot."

"She has to be somewhere around," says Dana. "Try her on her mobile."

I do. But I get no answer.

Kevin North is gesturing to Mick to come over. "I'd better mingle." But he looks reluctant to go.

"Don't worry. I'll have a look around for Caroline," Shane tells him.

"When you find her, will you tell her where I am?"

"Sure."

"You are all coming to the party afterwards?" Mick asks before he goes.

"Of course!"

"You'd think we'd miss that!"

Mick makes his way over to Kevin North and Shane disappears in search of Caroline but, ten minutes later, he comes back without her.

"No sign."

"Maybe she's already gone on to the party," speculates Dana.

"Maybe," I say. But it seems an odd thing to do. "Why would she go on ahead of us?"

At two o'clock when the party is still in full swing, Finn and I are the first of our crowd to leave – apart from Caroline, who never showed up. When the taxi drops us home, Finn goes straight upstairs but I hear the sound of the TV in the living-room so I go in to check first. I find Caroline lying on the couch, asleep. She stirs.

"Oh, I must have dozed off," she says, sitting up.

"When did you get home?" I ask.

"Oh, a while ago," she answers vaguely.

"You didn't go to the party?"

She shakes her head. "I just wasn't feeling up to it."

"So what did you think of the movie?"

"Yeah – great!"

"Where were you sitting? We lost you on the way in."

"In the middle."

I look at her. Something isn't quite right. Something prompts me to ask: "Did you even go into the movie?"

"Hmm?"

"You didn't, did you?"

She shakes her head.

"Why not?"

"I had this . . . ahmm . . . awful headache."

"You should have told us. I could have come home with you."

"No, I didn't want that."

"It's a pity you missed it. Mick was brilliant. Honestly, Caroline, you would have been so proud of him. I was expecting him to be good but he just blew me away. There was this one scene, right, where . . ."

I go on and on and, as I do, Caroline hangs on my every word but, then, I notice her eyes beginning to fill up.

"Caroline! What's the matter?"

"Nothing." She stands up and abruptly announces, "You know, I should go to bed. I still have that headache."

"Oh, right," I say, taken aback. "Well, okay, goodnight then."

"Night."

The next day over a late breakfast, we're still talking about Mick's triumph when Caroline comes down. She doesn't join in, just pours out some cereal. Looking somewhat subdued, she's about to head back out again with her bowl when Shane turns his attention to her.

"So you and Mick seemed to be getting along well last night?"

"Pardon?"

"He couldn't keep his eyes off you – at least when you were around. By the way, where did you get to?"

"Look, Shane, there is no me and Mick, not any more, and there never will be, all right!"

With that she walks out of the kitchen.

I go after her, in time to have the living-room door shut in my face. I open it and follow her in. She's already sitting on the couch, the bowl of cereal on her lap. Ignoring me, she picks up the remote and flicks on the TV.

"Caroline, what's the matter?"

"Nothing."

"Oh come on, Caroline. Talk to me."

She sighs.

I wait.

"Well?"

No answer.

"Caroline, what's the matter? Really?"

She sighs again. "Did you see that girl who came over to Mick?"

"Which one?"

"Good question. There were so many. But I mean the skinny little one with the skimpy dress and the high heels. The one at the start of the evening."

"When just you and he were talking?"

"Yes."

"Okay, I know who you mean."

"You know, I used to be her boss and last night she acted like she didn't even know me! She acted like I was nobody." She sighs again. "I guess I'm jealous."

"Of . . . her?"

"No, of Mick, of course! And I hate myself for even feeling this way, really I do. If I could stop I would but I can't. There's a mean jealous sliver inside me and I can't make it go away."

"But why?"

"What have I achieved in my life? Nothing. I left my job, set up our shop and it failed. And look at Mick, he's such a success, with all these people clamouring for his attention. He's doing so well."

"So now he's exactly the kind of person you wanted before you fell for him?"

"Yes, the kind of man I wanted when *I* was successful. But now I'm not. I'm just another hanger-on!"

"But you have all this money, don't you?"

"It's not the same. And I haven't done anything with it yet."

"But you're in the process. You will. Oh, Caroline! Can't you be happy for him?"

"I am, really I am. I am happy for him. I'm just not happy for ..." But she lets it go. She manages a smile. "So he really was as good as you're all saying?"

"He was brilliant."

She nods. "Of course. I knew he would be. I'm glad."

"Come on out and finish your breakfast with the rest of us."

She shrugs. "I suppose I could."

Just as we're going back into the kitchen, there's a ring on the doorbell.

"You go on ahead," I say. "I'll get it."

I answer it to find Mick standing there.

"Hello there, movie star! Come on in, we're all having breakfast."

There's a loud cheer the minute he steps into the kitchen.

"Now, now," laughs Shane. "Form an orderly queue if you want autographs."

Mick looks around, at all the smiling faces, then he laughs. "Thank you, thank you, everyone. I'm just so happy to be here today. I want to thank my mum and my dad, my old drama teacher, the man in the corner shop, my barber, my make-up artist, the . . . what are you doing?" he asks when he sees Shane coming towards him with a measuring tape he must have found lying around.

"I want to check just how big your head has got."

"Give over," laughs Mick.

"Mick, I'm making coffee," says Dana. "Do you want a cup?"

"Yes, please. I haven't been home yet." He turns to Caroline. "So where did you get to last night?"

"I had this headache."

"But did you see any of the movie?"

"No, like I said. I had this headache."

"It must have been pretty bad."

"It was."

"I tried ringing you."

"I know."

There's an awkward silence. "It's a pity you missed it," says Mick after a while. "I'd really have liked you to have been there with me last night."

Caroline mumbles something. I don't catch it but Mick does.

"Pardon? What do you mean it didn't seem like that to you? Of course I did. You know I did."

"Okay."

"Why would you say such a thing?"

"Look Mick, I'm so glad last night went so well and –"

But Mick interrupts. "I'm sorry, Caroline. You just can't say something like that and then not explain what you mean."

"Look, Mick, forget it. I didn't mean anything."

"Yes, you did," he persists.

"Mick, I didn't."

"Come on. I want to hear."

"Mick –"

"Just tell me what you meant?"

"Please, I didn't –"

"Caroline! Just spit it out!"

"Please, can't you just let it go?"

"No! I want to hear what you have to say!"

Caroline takes a deep breath. "Okay then. I'd like to know why you ignored me?"

"Ignored you? Hardly."

"Yes, you did. You talked to everyone but me!"

He stares at her. "Oh, for crying out loud! How selfish can you get!"

"Selfish – I came last night to support you, didn't I?"

"And I was happy you did."

"It didn't seem like that to me."

Mick begins nodding his head, like everything is clear to him now. "Oh, so that's why you went home. You didn't have a headache at all, did you? You stormed off in a fit of pique."

"Mick, I –"

But she doesn't go on and he's just staring at her in disgust now. The rest of us are rooted to the spot, not daring to breathe.

"Really, Caroline, just how did you think the evening

was going to pan out? That, on the biggest night of my life, when for the first time ever *I* was the focus of attention, I was going to devote all my time to you, just you, because *you* suddenly decide to stop ignoring me. Caroline, *you* were the one who walked out on me in Australia yet how many times have I rung you since I got back and not once have you picked up! You know, I'm only beginning to see what a selfish person you are. If there's anything I can do to speed up our divorce, will you please let me know."

With that, he storms out.

"Caroline, did he just say divorce?" demands Shane, looking totally bewildered.

But she doesn't answer. As soon as she hears the front door bang shut, she hurries out and goes pounding up the stairs. Leaving me to explain everything.

Some people have all the luck.

Anonymous - £26.5million - UK

"It's incredible that a millionaire should scoop the jackpot but he's desperate to keep it secret." - Newspaper article.

29

It's a buyer's market right now as Caroline keeps saying, and she's determined to get the very best prices possible. Negotiations are ongoing on that first executive apartment we visited and another two similar to it. Caroline's also made an offer on our own house. Tom Redmond says Donald was surprised when he approached him but indicated he could be prepared to sell, at the right price. And that's where the problem lies: just what is the right price? Donald is reluctant to reduce his asking price but Caroline is as unwilling to revise her offer upward. It seems one sibling is as hardheaded as the other.

But we have just closed the deal on our first two properties, that pair of old terraced houses within walking distance of the city centre – 3 and 4 Church View. Number 3 is in such a poor state that we're going to have to carry out renovations on it before we can even think of renting it out. Number 4 is set aside for Seán. If I find him. *When* I find him.

But, in the meantime, I'm taking Sarah to see it. I figure it would suit her in the short-term. Until she gets herself sorted. Until I find Seán.

"Explain again how I come to be getting this place to live in for free," she asks as we sit in the back of a taxi in slow-moving traffic on our way there.

"I told you. The company was set up and is run in such a way that a percentage of the properties on the books are given up for the use of people who are in need of accommodation. The rent from the other properties and their expected long-term capital accumulation in effect subsidise them."

"So the company own a lot of properties then?"

"Yes," I lie. But it's only a small lie. We will soon. This is just the start.

"But I'm not in need of accommodation – not really. I'll sort something out myself soon and I can go on living with Mum and Dad until I do."

"Would you really like that?"

Sarah laughs. "No, it's like being a teenager again."

I laugh.

"Although there are plusses. Mum puts on my electric blanket every night and Dad brings up a cup of tea to me each morning."

"You're kidding! They never did that for me when I was living at home."

Sarah is serious again. "But there must be people far more in need of this house than me."

"I'm sure there are but they're not my sister and, like I already told you, down the line the house is earmarked for a young father with two small children."

"Why isn't he moving in now then?"

I hesitate. "There are complications. So, until we get them sorted out, you can live there. It's so near where you'll be working." Sarah has already managed to line up a three-month contract. "That's why I thought it might suit you so well until you do find a place. You could walk to the hospital from it."

"And Caroline doesn't mind?"

"No."

"So where did she get all the money to start the company?"

I shrug. "She's a clever businesswoman."

"So why is Mum so worried then? She says she doesn't know which will end sooner – your position, or the company itself."

"I know. She's told me too, but she needn't worry."

"How can you be so sure?"

"Sarah, both my job and the company are secure, believe me."

"How did she make all this money to start the business?" persists Sarah.

"Come on," I say with some relief as the taxi is now pulling up outside the house. "We're here."

"So what do you think?" I ask Sarah once I've shown her around.

"It's nice."

"The kitchen is a little old-fashioned but it's well-laid out, isn't it?"

"It is."

"What do you think of the garden?"

"Lovely."

"Can you imagine fine evenings, sitting out with the kids? And you're so near all the shops."

"It does seem convenient."

"It is, very. Did you notice the little local shop opposite? That will be handy when you run out of milk. And the primary school is just two streets away. You'll probably need to make an appointment with the principal to see how soon the boys can start."

"True."

It occurs to me that Sarah isn't quite as excited as I imagined she would be. I seem to be more excited than she is.

"You do like it, don't you?"

"Of course I do."

"Good."

"And you like the area?"

"Sure. This terrace is a little run-down but the house is great, as is the general area. I've always liked this part of town. It is very convenient like you said. I could imagine staying around here long term. But . . ." she trails off.

"But what?"

"But?"

"But I wonder if I'm doing the right thing. Maybe coming back to Ireland is stupid. I was well settled in Melbourne. So were the boys. Starting all over again is going to be so hard."

"I know."

She shakes her head. "No, you don't, Rosie, not really. The children and Rod – that was my whole life. That's what I really want again. I wish none of this had happened. I just want to fly home, back to our old house, back to our old life, back to Rod."

"But, Sarah, that's not going to happen."

She sighs. "I know. I know. Everything's changed. But I keep thinking that he's just going through some midlife crisis, that he'll see sense. Despite all he's done, I still love him. I sometimes think I didn't make things easy for him. He'd come back after a week away and I'd be so stressed by having had to juggle everything while he was away that I never had time for him, for us."

"Sarah, come on, don't blame yourself. You're the one who had the most to deal with. Maybe he should have been more of a help when he came back."

"Yes, but he was always so tired and —"

"From what? Playing golf?"

"No, he did work too, you know —"

"Are you forgetting already what he was like?"

But she's not listening to me.

"— and as soon as he'd set foot in the door, I'd start asking him to do this, or that. I'd have a list of jobs lined up for him." She sighs. "But I guess you're right. He doesn't want us any more. I need to move on. And being here, with you, with Mum and Dad close by, will be better in the long run. I just wish I felt happier about it."

When we leave the house, I drop back out to Mum's with Sarah for a while and then, afterwards, I carry on into town. I had planned to help Sarah move her stuff this afternoon but now she's going to wait until tomorrow, to prepare the boys. She doesn't have a lot — just what she came with. Her neighbour, Lily, is arranging for the rest to be shipped over. In the taxi into town, I make a few phone calls to try to persuade someone — anyone — to come in and meet me but everyone's too busy — Finn is in work, Dana's in college and Caroline's at our office. In the end, I just spend a few hours on my own wandering around the shops.

When I do get home it's late in the afternoon but I find Dana is already there, sitting at the kitchen table.

"Hi, Dana. Wait until you see what I bought!"

"Not now, Rosie."

"Okay, I know you're not usually that interested but you have to see this top, it's fabulous."

"I said, not now."

It's only then I notice how upset she is.

"Whatever's the matter, Dana?"

"Cathy's mum and my mum took her to see the GP."

"And? How did it go?"

"Not great. They arranged for her to have a hearing test."

"A hearing test? Why?"

"To establish whether hearing, or poor hearing rather, is the cause of her communication problems."

"And?"

"Her hearing is fine which leads the GP to think the same way we're thinking, that she may have autism."

"Oh, poor little Cathy. That's terrible news."

"It is."

"So what does this mean? What happens now?"

"Well, there's no medical test that can diagnose autism. It's based purely on observing a child's communicative, behavioural and developmental levels. The GP is going to refer Cathy to a developmental paediatrician who, in turn, will involve a multi-disciplinary team – a clinical psychologist, an educational psychologist, a speech and language therapist and an occupational therapist. The whole process – from being referred to this team to getting a diagnosis – can take eighteen months to two years."

"But that's ages. What's going to happen in the meantime?"

"Not much – that's the big problem. The earlier the intervention, the better it is for the child. I'm going to look into seeing if we can get things done faster. Money isn't an issue. I can pay for the very best."

I hear someone at the front door. Seconds later, Doug comes in.

"Hi!"

"Oh, hi, Doug."

"Doug, I was telling Rosie that –"

But Doug doesn't hear her – he's too excited with news of his own. "*Wait* until you see this!" He proudly holds a stapled bunch of A4 sheets out to Dana

"What is it?"

"Only one of the most insightful and original essays my lecturer ever had the pleasure of marking. And those are not my words – they came out of the mouth of one Mr Frank McHale."

"Frank McHale said that?" Dana looks dubious.

"And see there, in the corner, that would be an A you're looking at."

"He gave you an A? He *never* gives out A's – everyone knows that."

"Well, he does now." Doug is beaming down at Dana but then he notices her expression. "You don't look too happy."

"I am. Of course. But I've just been on the phone to my Mum. She had some bad news."

"Oh?"

"She and Ann, they took Cathy to see the GP and it seems likely she does have autism but it could be at least eighteen months before she's diagnosed. The GP is sending her to a development psychologist who, in turn, will have her assessed by a whole assortment of therapist and psychologists."

"I see."

"I'm going to see if we can speed things up by going privately."

"But that would cost a fortune!"

"Doug, how can you think of money at a time like this?"

"I'm only being practical. How would Ann pay for that?"

She looks to me. "We'll figure something out. Anyway, Ann has a good job and –"

"You don't think she's going to keep working, do you? She's Cathy's primary carer although . . ."

"I'm not sure she is considering quitting. Mum never said."

". . . although," repeats Doug following his own train of thought, "maybe she shouldn't give up work. Think about it. Is Ann really the best person to mind Cathy all day, all night, every day, every night?"

"But she is her mother."

"Even so. Look, I like Cathy's mum – well, I like her enough but she's not exactly the most patient person in the world, is she? I think she'd just get frustrated. You've seen her with Cathy. She has no patience with her. And I don't think a diagnosis will change that. It might even make matters worse."

"Yes, well. But what then are you suggesting?

"You've also seen your mother with Cathy – you must have noticed the difference in the way they both interact with her."

"Yes, of course but . . ."

"I think your mother should get involved in looking after her when Ann is at work. It would be of huge benefit to Cathy, and to Ann too because she –"

"My mum?"

"Yes. Of course Cathy will benefit from professional sessions hugely when she does get them but what's going to be as important is who's looking after her on a day-to-day basis. If your mum were to mind Cathy during the day, Ann could keep working, and keep bringing in money which is a very important consideration, and it would take a lot of the burden off Ann. Plus Cathy would have someone additional in her life who's better suited to the task of caring for her. Your mum would be a good mentor to Ann too. She'd help her let go of her expectations, to stop comparing Cathy to other children, to focus on the child she has got and on giving that child the attention and care she needs to reach her potential."

"It's a lot to ask of my mum."

"Yes, but maybe that's a good thing. You've said your mum's not happy in herself and I think that's a lot to do with the fact that she's lost her main role in life now that you've grown up. Didn't you say she was thinking of looking for a job —"

"Sure, she says that but I'm not sure she really means it."

"— *not* because she needs to work again but because she wants to. Maybe this could be exactly what she needs."

"Oh, I don't know."

"Think about it. Talk to her."

Aged sixteen, a foster child, living on a council estate.

Callie Rogers – £1.9 million – UK

A dream come true for young Callie? Not quite.
"Ever since, I haven't had a happy moment."

30

A few days later on my way out from town I decide, on a whim, to call to Finn. It's past six so I figure he should be home from work by now. When I knock it's Mitch who opens the door. He and Ashley have just moved in. The place they were renting was pretty basic and quite far out of town so, when their lease came up for renewal, they decided to leave and move in here instead. It works well for Finn too as their rent contributes to the mortgage. Finn's nearly always had someone living with him and, as chance would have it, a band member. First Mark, then Lola, and now Ashley and Mitch. I hope things work out better than they did with either of the previous two.

"Oh, hiya, Rosie."

"Hi, Mitch. Is Finn in?"

"He's upstairs."

"So how are things?"

Mitch shrugs. "So-so."

"Only so-so?"

"Afraid so." Mitch really isn't his usual chirpy self.

"What's up?" I ask.

He sighs. "Oh, you know." He rubs the tip of his index finger and his thumb together.

"Money?"

"Yeah, money."

"But you're doing well."

"To a point."

"Your gigs are always packed."

"Yeah, but we're not exactly talking Wembley Arena, are we? Just grotty little pubs and basement clubs tucked away in back streets."

"I suppose."

"No supposing about it, Rosie, and that's what the future holds in store for us too, until we're so old and infirm we can't get our wheelchairs down those basement steps."

I smirk at the image he conjures up.

"It's no laughing matter, Rosie."

"In a wheelchair you'll be a sitting target for Big Bertha."

Mitch groans. "Honestly it's getting worse."

"But aren't you overstating things?"

"She has my mobile number now. He swears he didn't but I think Ashley gave it to her."

"No, I don't mean Big Bertha. I mean your future."

He sighs. "Am I, Rosie, am I? That is our future unless we can step things up, take them to a new level. Yeah, sure, our gigs are packed out but that's through word of mouth – we're not getting any attention from the media, and even less from the industry professionals. Now, if we had money, then we could promote ourselves properly. We could record some songs independently, with professional help, and then spend the time and the money necessary to make sure we reach the ears that count in this business. Do you hear what I'm saying?"

I nod my head. "But what about the whole YouTube thing? You don't need money for that. When I was in Australia there was huge hype about some band that had been discovered through the internet. An indie band. From Sydney."

"You mean *Fallow*?"

I nod my head. "So you've heard of them?"

"Sure, and you're right. There have been some success stories. But YouTube successes aren't always quite what they seem. You've heard of Marianne Dillon?"

"Yeah. Of course. There you go – another YouTube sensation!"

"You mean that's what people were led to believe."

"Isn't it true?"

He shakes his head. "No. Even though she was presented as this undiscovered amateur strumming away in her bedroom, the reality is she'd already been signed by a major company. Instead of putting money into radio time and TV appearances and such, they choose to promote her as an unsigned artist via the internet."

"Really?"

"Really."

"That's kind of sneaky. But, still, it doesn't take from the fact that there have been some genuine discoveries."

"True. But we're not likely to be one of them. We have already put videos of ourselves playing live on YouTube, as have some of our fans though, in the main, they're so amateurish you can hardly hear us over the background noise of the crowd. So, yeah, we're already there –"

"That's a start."

"– amongst the one hundred million videos viewed daily."

"One hundred million?"

"Around that. So you see, it's not quite as easy as you might think. Sure, some music mogul might just chance upon us one evening when he's surfing the net and decide we're exactly what he's been looking for but we'd be foolish to sit back and wait for that to happen. Which leads us right back to the more traditional methods and for those we need money."

"I see."

"Anyway, I'd better go. I'm off into town."

"Okay, see you, Mitch."

As I walk up the stairs to Finn's room, I mull over what Mitch has said. Their problem is money, or the lack of it. But I have money, lots of it. They need it. I have it. But how would I go about giving it to them? Another mysterious bequest? Another prize? But there's been a run of these fortunate events lately in our immediate circle. Would yet another be just too much of a coincidence?

Finn's door is ajar and I catch sight of him sitting in the armchair at the foot of his bed, in jeans and T-shirt, hair tousled, bare feet propped up on the window ledge, guitar resting on his lap. Suddenly my heart fills up. I'm taken off guard. It's stupid but I feel tears well up. Sometimes I wonder if Finn has any idea just how much I love him – really, really, really love him.

But now there's this anxious knot in my stomach. What's causing that? Why – out of nowhere – has it suddenly struck me how awful it would be to lose him? Why should I think such a thing? What's put that ridiculous thought in my head? I love him. He loves me. We're okay. But are we? I might try to ignore the fact but things really aren't as easy between us of late. We don't see as much of each other as we might because he's so busy. But that's not it. That's not the problem. He's always been busy. What is it then? Where's this distance coming from? Is it because I can't talk to him like I used to? That I can't talk to him about all the things that concern me, that preoccupy me ever since I won the lotto? I've never told him about my search for Seán. Or what it was like meeting Hilda's parents and learning of her background and Seán's too. I didn't, couldn't, tell him of the nice things that have happened either – like buying all that stuff for old Mrs Williams in Marks & Spencer's. Or the satisfaction of being able to give Sarah a home until she's sorted. Since our lottery win, there are just so many things he knows nothing about. And when he worries about me, about my future, about how much I'm spending, he doesn't hear when I reassure him there's no need because he's so sure there is.

Perhaps sensing me, he looks around. His face breaks into a broad grin. "Hey! What are you doing creeping around?"

"Excuse me! I wasn't creeping around! Mitch let me in."

"Why the worried look?"

"What worried look?" I smile now.

I go to kiss him. It's more than a 'hi' kiss. I want to show him how I feel, and to feel reassured.

"Wow!" he laughs when we pull apart. "Someone certainly loves me!"

"You'd better believe it." I hand him the shopping bag I'm carrying.

"What's this?"

"Open it."

He does and takes out a black velvet jacket. He holds it up.

"This is nice, very nice. But . . ." he hesitates.

"But?"

"Well, it's exactly the same as the one I have."

"Believe me, it isn't," I say. It probably cost, like, ten times more than the one he wears day-in, day-out.

"It looks the same to me."

"But this one is new and your old one is on its last legs."

"Excuse me! I've just finally managed to wear it in! But thanks, you shouldn't have."

He puts the jacket back in the bag and then tosses it onto the bed. I look to where he's thrown it. I spent hours searching for it. I thought he'd be thrilled. He wouldn't do that if he knew how expensive it was.

I notice he's looking at me.

"What?"

"You look really good."

"Why, thank you."

"You are looking really well these days. And your hair, it's nice – really shiny."

"Ah – thanks."

I guess money does make a difference. After I bought Finn's new jacket, I went to this trendy new hairdresser's, one Caroline recommended. When it came to paying, I thought I'd misheard it was so expensive. But they must have done something right if Finn notices.

Now I run my fingers through his mop. "On the subject of hair, has this lot even seen a comb today?"

Finn grins. "Maybe not."

I go to sit down on the bed but first I have to remove a few things – the bag with his new jacket, some CDs, a sketch book, his old jacket.

"So how are things?" I ask.

"Fine."

Finn has the main bedroom in the house. It's a lovely,

spacious, light-filled, south-facing room – white-walled and wooden-floored. For its size it's sparsely furnished – his bed, a chest of drawers, a hanging rail for his not-very-extensive wardrobe, and the armchair he's sitting in. But most of the space is taken up with all his other stuff: his drum kit, his music system, his easel, plus numerous and assorted stacks: stacks of books, stacks of newspapers, stacks of CDs, stacks of paint tubs. And, propped up against the wall are dozens of his canvases – Finn has long since run out of room downstairs to hang his finished paintings and is content to let them accumulate up here.

"I thought Mitch was going out," says Finn.

"He has. He was on his way when I met him. He said he was heading into town."

"Good. He's been moping about all day. He's become obsessed with 'where-the-band-is-going'."

"I gathered. And what about you?"

"What?"

"Does it worry you?"

"Nope. We're alive. We're playing to full houses. We're having a good time."

He sounds like he means it but . . .

"But once you were that close to being signed up. Think how different things might be now if that had happened."

"Rosie, there's no point in thinking about that, any of that."

By any of that, I guess he means he and Mark falling out, Mark dying in the car crash, the band subsequently disbanding. Apart from the inevitable sense of loss, I think there was a myriad of other feelings too for Finn, not least that of survivor's guilt and it took him a long time to recover enough to become interested in music again. But he did. In time. And the band was reformed, with a new lead singer – Lola.

Ah yes – Lola. Quirky, blonde Lola, with the looks and voice of an angel and the heart of a – well – let's just say it wasn't quite so angelic. That Finn had a girlfriend – me – was of no concern to Lola. Right from the word go, it was obvious she was crazy about him. I could see that. Anyone who spent more than a few seconds in their company could see that. But Finn didn't. Until Lola finally came right out and told him and when Finn told her in response that – ah – actually he didn't feel the same, she flung her pink guitar over her shoulder (oh, how I hated that red shaggy jacket of hers), and in her green little cutesy diamanté shoes walked out of the band and out of Finn's life forever. Or more accurately, she walked as far as her yellow Volkswagen parked proprietorially in his driveway and then drove furiously out of his life, her outsized furry dice swinging madly from side-to-side mirroring her feelings. I wasn't actually there for that particular scene but I like to picture it. All I can say is good riddance to bad rubbish. I never liked her. But we survived her. And we'll survive this . . . this . . . patch we're going through now too.

It was after Lola left that Finn took over as lead singer and now Ashley, Mitch and he make a rock-solid team. They've never sounded better. Their fans think so as well. They always play to packed houses – albeit small, and not Albert Hall – and their MySpace page is full of praise from their dedicated fans. But the record company's interest wasn't so steadfast through those tumultuous times.

"But things might have been different." I persist now. "It must bother you."

Finn shrugs. "Look – it could – if I let it. That's why I don't think about it."

"Wouldn't you like to be more successful?"

He shrugs. "I guess." But he seems uncertain. "I don't know. I understand that I should be more ambitious. More like Mitch. I was once. But now every time we play it's to a full house. After all we've been through, I'm grateful for that. I like my life now. I enjoy it. I'd be happier working less hours for my dad but only because it would give me more time to write music and to paint. But I've come to the realisation that it's the creative side of things I enjoy most. If we were more successful maybe life would be too complicated."

"I see."

"Success – big success would be good in that it would be a validation but it's not like my overriding ambition – not any more. If it's to happen, it'll happen."

Does he really mean what he says or is it his way of protecting himself? There was, as he says himself, a time when he was far more ambitious.

"Anyway," he says, "enough about me. What did you get up to today?"

I shrug. "Nothing much." Then I lie, as has become my habit. "Work mainly."

I spot a new painting, one I haven't seen before. I get up from where I'm sitting and I go over, pick it up, prop it up on part of the window-sill and stand back.

"I really like this."

I never used to 'get' abstract art. I always harboured a suspicion it was what people who couldn't draw did but Finn can draw, very well. And abstract or not, there's something genuinely appealing about his paintings: the colours he uses, the way he combines those colours, the vibrancy, the overall effect, the impact. They don't feature people or places and in that respect they're not 'of' anything. Finn says they represent emotions. He doesn't like talking about his art but when I press him he will tell me what he was feeling when he was creating a particular painting and, certainly, a sense of that comes out on the canvas. True, I may not know a lot about art but I like what he does.

I notice a few other new ones and I examine each in turn.

"You've been busy."

"Yeah, I have."

"Do you feel the same about painting?"

"Pardon?"

"Are you happy just to keep doing it? To let your work mount up? Wouldn't you like if others could see how talented you are?"

He shrugs. "I'm not sure I am that talented."

"Come on! Who are you kidding? Your problem is that you're so gifted in so many ways. You don't appreciate just how lucky you are."

"Stop! You'll give me a big head."

"But it's true!"

Now he's grinning at me.

"What? Why are you looking at me like that?"

"You know the one thing I'd really like to think I'm talented at?"

"What?"

He looks towards the bed – suggestively.

"Finn! I came here to ask if you wanted to go out!"

"Haven't you heard? Staying in is the new going out? So what do you say, Rosie Kiely?"

"Finn!"

"They said it was a winner. I said, 'OK'. I don't get excited about a hell of a lot. Something like that takes a long while to settle in."

Jim Hall - $65 million - US

"Now I ain't any sadder. Let's put it that way."

31

I keep thinking about Finn and the band. I have always believed in them. Maybe I'm biased but, the fact is, people who know more about these things have believed in them too, not least the music company who nearly signed them up. I know Finn says he's happy with where they are now but maybe he's just convinced himself of that. If he tells himself he doesn't want anything more then he can't be disappointed. But Mitch and Ashley do want more. And I think Finn does too, even if he won't admit it, not even to himself.

Maybe they will be discovered a second time. But when, if ever? There are so many talented bands out there, the competition is immense. Maybe, like Mitch says, they need to make a really professional demo of their songs. But they'd need money for that – which they don't have. But I do. I could finance it. But how would I do so without them knowing? And if I could manage it, wouldn't I be adding yet another layer to the already complicated layers of lies I've already woven?

And then I have a brainwave. Maybe I don't have to

think of some secret way of financing them. After all, Finn is one of those fortunates who's just bursting with creativity. Maybe my money isn't needed, not when Finn could have an exhibition and a sale of his paintings. I wouldn't need to lie to him then. But would there be a market for his paintings? His fans are likely to be interested. By advertising on the band's MySpace page we'd reach all those people who're well-disposed towards him. Plus, an exhibition by someone like him, a lead singer in an established band, might be worthy of some media publicity. I wonder if it's a runner. I need to talk to Caroline, hear what she thinks and, with her marketing background, she'd be a great help – if we decided it was worth pursuing. If Finn can be convinced.

All this sorted in my mind, I turn my attention to making myself some dinner. As I'm doing so, Caroline comes into the kitchen. I see she has her coat on.

"I didn't know you were going out?"

"Just for a while."

"Where?"

"Nowhere special."

I don't press it. "Can I ask you for some advice?"

"Sure." She glances at the clock on the wall.

"Are you in a hurry?"

"Just go on, I'm listening."

"Okay, well –"

"But it's not going to take too long, is it?"

"If you're in a hurry I can al –"

"Rosie, go on, tell me, what is it you want to ask?"

"You've seen some of Finn's paintings. What do you think of them?"

"They're brilliant."

"Would you buy one?"

"Sure, if he were selling them. Is he selling them?"

"Well, not yet, but do you think it would be a good idea if he had an exhibition?"

"What's put that idea in his head?"

"Well, it's not exactly in his head – yet – but I was thinking of suggesting it to him."

"But why?"

"I was thinking it would be a good way of raising money."

"For?" She looks at the clock again.

"For promoting the band. They need money to professionally record some of their tracks. I was trying to think of some way of secretly giving them my money but, then, I came up with this idea instead."

"But making a professional recording would be very expensive, wouldn't it?"

"It would. But you've no idea how many paintings he has, stacks of them."

She looks dubious. "I don't know. He *is* an unknown artist . . ."

"Yes, but he has a reputation as a singer, albeit limited. If he were just depending on his fans to make up a crowd, just a small proportion of them, he'd still have a respectable number of people."

"Hmm, true."

"So, what do you think?'

"I'm not sure you'd raise all the money you need but, yeah, I think it's a good idea. It would be exciting. Imagine, Finn's first exhibition. If . . ." she trails off.

"If what?"

"If you can persuade Finn to go through with it."

"And if I can, will you tell me how to go about organising it."

"Yeah, sure."

"Brilliant!"

"Okay, I'd better go."

"Where did you say you were going again?"

"Out."

"But where?"

"I should be back before ten."

And, with that, she's gone without, I realise, answering my question.

Just when I'm finished eating dinner, Dana comes storming in. She takes off her coat and slings it across a chair, pulls out the chair opposite me and slumps down on it. Then she begins theatrically banging her head on the table.

"Ah, is something the matter, Dana?"

She sits back up.

"I swear Doug is doing my head in!"

"Oh?"

"Have you noticed anything about him lately?"

"I can't say I have. Come to think of it, he's not around here as much as he used to be."

"Of course not. How could he be? He's just so busy. Studying at home, or hurrying off to the library, or dashing to a lecture, or sitting around the canteen or bar in college talking about his studies with his intense, unshaven, studenty buddies. Have you noticed that he's stopped shaving?"

"Now that you mention it. What's that about?"

"God only knows."

"But it's good he's so busy, right?"

"Is it?"

"Is it not?"

"No! When we started going out, Doug had his world and I had mine. Doug went off to work each morning. I went off to college. At the end of the day we met up and talked about our respective worlds. I talked about what I was learning in college and he talked about what he was doing at work. But now! Now when we meet he just goes on and on about some book he's reading or about some point one of his lecturers made in class. He finds it all so bloody fascinating. I swear it's doing my head in!"

"But I'd have thought it would be good to have so much in common?"

But Dana's not even listening. "You know we share some of the same lecturers?"

"You do?"

"Yes. And there's this one visiting lecturer, right, from Columbia, a guy called Gordon Smith, and –"

"Gordon Smith?" I think even I've heard of him. "Did he write that book – what was it again? Something like, *Psychology for the Common Man*?"

"You mean, *Psychology for the Uncommon Man*. Yes he did. Anyway –"

"Finn bought it for his dad for his birthday. He said it's really –"

"– *anyway* he's written dozens of other books too that are less populist and more academic, some of which are on my reading list this year and on Doug's too. So this guy Smith is over for the year teaching, which was a major coup for the college. In the psychology world this guy is a deity! His lectures are always packed out. Anyway, the other day, I go into the canteen and I spot Gordon Smith sitting at a table in the corner, deep in conversation with someone who I automatically assume is one of the other lecturers but, then, that 'someone' happens to glance up and – guess what – it's Doug. Doug! So Doug sees me and he calls me over and introduces me. Now I've never missed a lecture of Smith's but the guy doesn't recognise me from Adam. Yet Doug and him are carrying on like they're best friends. They're in the middle of discussing some study Smith was involved in back in the '70s and even though I've read all about it and probably know as much as Doug does, more even, Smith has no interest in what I have to say. He's already forgotten my name, or that I'm even there. *But* no matter what Doug says, Smith leans back in his chair and says, 'Interesting point, Doug.' Like, I don't get it! I came first in my class as an undergrad. Okay, my Master's went awry and I have changed direction by switching to this counselling course but there's no way Doug knows more than me. It's not long since he was working as a painter and now he's going about like some prodigy, some leading light of college." She flops back in her chair. "It's just so ridiculous!"

I know I'm probably going to regret what I'm about to say but I decide to anyway.

"You said that before you had your own separate worlds – Doug had his work, you had your studies?"

"Yes – that's the way it was."

"And you used to meet up and talk about them to each other?"

"Yeah."

"What did Doug say?"

"Pardon?"

"Dana, Doug used to work on his own. He spent his days painting some empty premises – alone. I don't think he really had all that much to talk about. I know I wasn't party to your every conversation but it seemed to me that you used to do most of the talking and he used to do the listening."

"That's not so!"

"Isn't it? I hate to say this but you sound a little jealous."

"Excuse me!"

"Doug has come into your world. He's enthused by it. It sounds like he's doing really well in it. Maybe you're jealous by how well he is doing and I can understand that —"

"That's not so!"

"Okay, maybe I'm wrong but —"

"You are! But you know, maybe you should share your half-baked theories with Doug — I'm sure he'd be interested in them."

With that she storms out of the room.

Dana doesn't come back down again that evening but stays sulking in her room and, since there's no one else at home, I watch some TV on my own until about ten when I hear someone putting their key in the front door.

"Hello!" I shout out.

"Hi," Caroline calls back.

Moments later, she comes into the room and sits down beside me without taking off her coat.

"Where were you?" I ask.

"I went to the cinema."

"With?"

"On my own."

"I could have gone with you if you'd asked."

"You've already seen the movie. Anyway I wanted to go on my own. I went to see *Fate Farm*."

"And? What did you think?" I look at her properly now for the first time and notice her face is red and puffy. "Caroline, don't tell me you were crying! You never cry at movies!"

"Of course I was crying! I'd want to be made of stone not to cry. Oh, Rosie, wasn't it just fabulous! I can't believe Mick was so good. I swear when he got shot at the end I thought I'd never stop bawling. The guy cleaning up the cinema must have thought I was a nutcase, sitting there long after everyone else had left, snivelling into my hankie. The poor fellow just carried on cleaning up around me, too embarrassed for me to ask me to leave."

"So did you ring Mick and tell him what you thought?"

She nods. "As soon as I'd collected myself together enough to leave the auditorium."

"And? What did he say?"

"He didn't answer."

"Well, try him again."

"I did, several times, but he's just not answering."

Are you happier since you've won the money?

Brad Duke - $85 million - US

"Absolutely. When it comes down to it, I get to do the things professionally that I've always wanted to do. I get to invent a piece of equipment that I've always been thinking about doing. I get to give back to some people that have given to me over the years."

32

It's Saturday and Finn and I are having breakfast at his house before he goes to work. He's engrossed in the newspaper and I'm thinking. I went to his gig last night and, afterwards, when we went for a drink, I had to listen again to Mitch and Ashley grumbling about the band's finances. Now I'm thinking it's definitely time to try out my idea on Finn. So here goes.

"Finn, I think you should have an exhibition."

He looks up from his paper. "Excuse me?"

"I think you should have an exhibition. It seems such a pity to have all these paintings and never do anything with them and —"

"But why should I want to do anything with them?"

"Wouldn't you like to think of them hanging on people's walls?"

"Maybe. I guess but —"

"The other day I went around a lot of galleries and you know paintings nowhere near as good as yours sell for thousands."

Just then Mitch walks in. "What sell for thousands?"

"Painting in galleries that are nowhere near as good as Finn's."

"Really?"

"I'm trying to convince him to have an exhibition."

"Good idea!"

But Finn is doubtful. "Ah, Rosie, I don't know. I don't really think so."

"Think of the money you could make."

"What do I need the money for?"

"Well –"

But Mitch cuts in. "Like, hello? Money, or lack of it, is what's holding us back. If we had money we could hire out a studio, some professionals, everything we need to make a really top-class recording."

"That's exactly what I was going to say," I tell him.

Mitch gives a laugh. "Geniuses think alike."

"I think you mean genii," Finn corrects him.

Mitch turns to me. "So what kind of money are we talking about here, Rosie?"

"How many paintings do you have?" I ask Finn.

"Fifty, sixty that I'm pleased with, maybe more – there are others over in my dad's. But come on, Rosie. Be realistic. Who's going to buy my paintings?"

"People who buy other people's paintings."

"And you think they'd pay thousands?"

Before I get a chance to answer, Mitch is already doing the maths. "Fifty paintings at a couple of grand each, that's – that's – a hundred thousand euros!" He whistles. "Come on, Finn, it's a no-brainer, man!"

Suddenly Finn is looking interested. "A hundred thousand euros?"

"A hundred thousand smackers," reiterates Mitch. "Think what we could do with that!"

"Do you seriously think I could make that kind of money, Rosie?"

"Sure you could," answers Mitch. "You deserve to. Think of all the hours you put in. No point in underselling yourself, Finn. Aim high."

I decide to temper things a little. "Even if you made a fraction, that could still be a lot of money."

"How would Finn go about it?" Mitch asks.

"Okay, well, I was talking to Caroline about this already."

Finn cocks an eyebrow. "You were?"

I didn't mean to let that slip. "Well, yes," I admit and move on quickly. "So, we rent out a premises somewhere, she suggested some big old warehouse down the docks – it doesn't have to be pretty, just big, given the scale of your paintings and the number. So we hang all your paintings there. We send out invitations. We advertise it as widely as possible. We lay on some drinks on the opening night." I pause. "And there's not much more to it than that. It wouldn't be too difficult."

The two are considering all this.

"But what if no one shows up?" asks Finn. "What if no one buys them? I mean it's not like I'm a professional. I've never even been to art college."

"So – not all great artists go to art college," Mitch reassures him. "Like . . . like . . ." But he fails to come up with anyone. I guess art isn't exactly his area of expertise.

But Finn isn't paying him much attention, he looks deep in thought.

Mitch goes on. "Here's an idea, Finn. You could get that

friend of yours – the one in the movie everyone's talking about – to open the exhibition. It would get people talking."

"I think Mick might be too busy right now." Finn pushes his newspaper across to me. "I was just about to show you this before we got talking. Take a look."

I take the paper from him. I do take a look. I see Mick smiling out at me. "Oh my lord, it's Mick!"

Mitch whistles. "And who is that honey with him?"

The 'honey' in question is a stunning redhead who's leaning in very close to Mick. Both of them are smiling and holding up glasses of champagne. I read the caption. "'*Amongst the glitterati at the opening of Foxy's Nightclub were actor Mick Boylan, star of* Fate Farm *and top model Tammy Winters*'."

"Well, he's certainly losing no time in making the most of the opportunities his new-found fame is offering him," says Mitch. "Wow! She is a stunner! Lucky devil!"

"I just hope Caroline doesn't see this," I fret.

"But I thought they'd split up?"

"It's not as clear-cut as that. Anyway, what do you think?"

"I think," says Mitch, "that Caroline is a really lovely girl but if it were me, and I were suddenly sought after by cute little Tammy here and her model friends, I'd kind of go with the flow."

"No! About the exhibition, and I was asking Finn!"

Mitch answers for him. "He thinks it's a great idea."

I look at Finn.

"Yeah, all right. What have I to lose but my pride?"

"So you'll do it?"

"I guess."

Soon after, Mitch wanders back upstairs and Finn goes to

work. As I tidy up after breakfast, I plan out my day. I would like to talk to Caroline some more about the exhibition but I know she has a meeting with Tom Redmond. I do need to go into town – the other day I bought a pair of jeans in a dark navy and they're such a good fit that I want to buy a couple more in other shades. But maybe I should leave that for later and call into Sarah first. I haven't seen her all week. It's been a hectic time for her – she's started work, the two older boys have started in their new school, and Jack has started at the childminder's. I give her a ring and, since it's Saturday and she's at home with the boys, I suggest I call in for coffee. Her response isn't as enthusiastic as it could be but she says okay, that she'll see me at around eleven. I tell her I'll bring the cakes.

When I get there, it's Kyle who opens the door.

"Hi, Auntie Rosie!"

"Hi, Kyle."

He turns on his heel and runs off, calling out, "Mum! Mum! Auntie Rosie's here!" while I follow more sedately after him, down the hall and on into the kitchen. There I find Sarah sitting at the table.

"Hiya!"

She looks up. She barely manages a smile.

"Hi," she says in a flat voice.

Oh, dear! I sit down opposite her.

"Did you see this?" she asks pointing at the same picture Finn showed me earlier. "Your friend Mick is in the paper."

"I know. I've seen it. So – ah – how are things?" I ask.

She doesn't answer – she's still looking at the photo. "He's very handsome, isn't he?"

"I guess he is. So, tell me, how did your first week go?"

"Have you seen the movie?"

"Yes. Remember I went to the premiere?"

"Oh, yes, I forgot."

"So, Sarah, tell me –"

"Was it good?"

"Yeah, brilliant."

But we've had this conversation already so I don't expand. Her eyes are still on the picture. I'm beginning to get the feeling she's avoiding my questions so I ask again, "So, how was your first week?"

I wait. She finally looks up. She sighs. "Amm – crap?"

"Oh! I see. So, do you want to talk about it?"

She shrugs and doesn't say anything immediately, but then: "Where would I start? Well, work is a nightmare! I swear I'll never get used to how that place is run – it's like being back in the bloody Dark Ages. Like, where did all the money from the Celtic Tiger go? Not into the wards – that's for sure! And then there's the kids – if they don't stop talking about how much they miss home, I swear I'll go crazy. It's non-stop. How they miss their friends, their school, the weather, the beach, their father, Lily from next-door, even the possums in the garden. But, you know, I don't blame them. It's a big change for them, for all of us. And the thing is, all of that is to be expected. It's bound to take time. I'm sure work will get easier. I'm sure the boys will settle. But –"

I wait for her to go on but she doesn't.

"Sarah, what is it?"

"Oh, I can't even bring myself to talk about it."

"About what? Come on, Sarah, what is it? It can't be that bad?"

"It is."

Again I wait but she doesn't say anything.

"Sarah, come on. Please tell me."

She takes a deep breath. "Okay. Where do I start?"

I wait, but still nothing. "Come on, Sarah, what is it?"

I see her brace herself. "Right. There's this mix-up in the rota yesterday and when I arrive in to start my shift I find I'm not scheduled to work. But no surprise there, given the way that place is run. So, instead, I take the opportunity to head into town to sort out a few things. Then, when I finish, I decide to pick Jack up from the childminder – it's earlier than usual but I don't see any point in leaving him there when I'm free. So, I take the bus straight out from town to Mrs Twohig's – that's the childminder – and when I get there I knock on the door several times, but there's no answer. Then I notice the door isn't locked – which is a little careless I think to myself – but I go right in. Anyway, I call out but still no answer. So then, I hear crying coming from the sitting-room and I go in and – oh God – there they are, in a row, five babies all sitting in their baby seats, all still in their coats and hats – which maybe is just as well as the room is freezing. And the smell! Who knows how many of them have dirty nappies, or for how long. And nearly all of them are whimpering. And my Jack's in the middle of them – the poor little mite with his little face all wet from crying and snot running down his nose."

"Oh, Sarah – that's awful."

"It was. Just awful! I don't think I've ever been so upset."

"What did you do?"

"Straightaway, I pick Jack up and go into the kitchen but there's no sign of Mrs Twohig or the daughter who helps her but, do you know where I eventually find Mrs Twohig? Lying sprawled out on her bed, asleep, snoring her stupid head off and there's no sign of Eloise anywhere."

"God!"

"I swear I was so mad I was afraid of what I'd do to her so I just got the hell out of there. That monster of a woman probably hasn't even noticed he's missing yet!"

"How could she do that?"

"She really had me fooled. You know, I thought she was kindness personified. I think I convinced myself I'd found another Lily. How could I have been so stupid! And I might never have found out. Months could have gone by with Jack sitting strapped in, day after day after day. Up to now I've collected Jack at the same time every evening and, every evening, he had his coat on but I assumed Mrs Twohig had him ready because she knew when to expect me. To think now she was saving herself trouble, and saving on heating bills, by never taking it off! And she probably only changed his nappy right before I called. You know I'm just so mad at myself. I feel so bloody guilty!"

"Guilty? But it's not your fault!"

"I shouldn't have let it happen!"

"But how could you have known?"

"I'm his mother – I should have known. But Mrs Twohig and Eloise seemed so nice. Her house was so clean. I thought it was one of the better places. I was paying her a fortune. Not that money's important but I gave her a month up front plus a month's deposit – I won't see any of that again. And why isn't childcare subsidised in this country? And does anybody even check these places out?"

I shrug. "I don't know."

"You know, when I got back here I felt so bad about having left all those other children there that I rang the Health Service Executive to report Mrs Twohig but their bloody offices are closed until after the weekend. But believe me, I'll be on to them first thing on Monday!"

"Good. I hope they shut her down!"

"So do I. In the meantime I have no idea what I'm going to do with Jack."

"What about Mum?"

"I don't know. The traffic is so bad in the mornings. Between going to work and dropping the other two to school, I don't think I'd have time to bring Jack out to her. Besides, I don't even have a car yet."

"She could come here?"

"It wouldn't be fair to ask her to commute in and out everyday. She has her own life to lead."

"You could ask her, see what she says."

"No, she'd only feel obliged to say yes. I know she worries about how I'm coping." She sighs. "Having this house for free is a real bonus but I know it's only temporary. I have to work but I just don't know what to do about Jack. Honestly I didn't know how lucky I was having Lily next-door in Melbourne. Maybe I should just go back. Maybe this was a crazy idea after all – uprooting everyone and trying to start over."

"Don't say that, Sarah!"

"But what am I going to do? Maybe I was wrong to take the boys away from their dad. I never envisioned him reacting so badly but he's ringing every night, ranting and raving down the phone. And whatever chance I stood of getting money from him if we were still in Australia, I've no chance here. And everything is so expensive. Do you know I got a letter from Kyle and Lachlan's school yesterday, from the Parents' Association. They're fund-raising for electronic whiteboards. Electronic whiteboards! The school doesn't have any – can you believe that! They want to raise enough money for two, just two. In the boys' old school there was one in every classroom and I don't remember parents ever being asked to give a penny towards them. I don't get it! We kept hearing how well everyone was doing in Ireland – what a great economic miracle the country was. I know it's over now but where did all the money go? Seriously, where did it all go?"

Suddenly, she flops her head on the table. "Oh what have I done? I should never have come home."

"Sarah – look, things will work out."

"How? I have to be in work for nine on Monday. What am I supposed to do with Jack?"

"I guess I could mind him sometimes."

"Yeah, but you have your own job to go to."

"True but –" I do go along to all the viewings of potential properties and, when Caroline is going into the office, I go with her sometimes but she's so efficient there's not a lot for me to do. I do seem to have a lot of time on my hands. "I could manage a couple of mornings or afternoons."

"Thanks, but that really wouldn't be enough."

"Well, maybe I could manage more than that." With Finn so busy with his work and his music and everything and Dana so busy with college I do seem to spend a lot of time on my own. "Sarah, my job is fairly flexible and –"

"Thanks, Rosie, but –"

"Really, Sarah, I wouldn't mind – at least until you get something better sorted." Maybe it would be nice to have Jack's company now and then. I wouldn't say I'm bored exactly but there's really just no one to meet up with during the day.

But she's shaking her head. "I don't think it would work. Jack needs continuity."

"I guess." I don't think I'd be up for minding him all day, every day – and, anyway, how could I even offer when I am supposed to have a job.

"Oh, what am I going to do?" sighs Sarah.

"Couldn't you get someone to come and mind him here while you're in work? Someone properly qualified, you know, like a nanny? She could collect the boys too so they wouldn't have to go to after-school care."

"Wouldn't I love it! But, Rosie, I couldn't afford that!"

"I suppose."

We both fall silent. I really wish I could help Sarah. I hate to see her looking so troubled. But what can I do? And then, suddenly, I find myself telling her: "I can."

"You can what?"

"I can afford a full-time nanny for you."

"Rosie! Be serious."

"I *am* being serious."

"This isn't a joking matter."

"I know that. Look –" I can't let her go back to Australia. I have to help her. "Sarah, I have something to tell you." I think for a second, about Dana and Caroline, and what they'll say if they find out. But Sarah won't tell them, or anyone. She's my sister. I can trust her. I want to tell her. I want to help her. "The thing is . . . is . . . the thing is, Caroline and Dana and I, well, we won the lotto a while back."

There, I've said it.

Her response is as to be expected – complete incredulity.

"Oh, come on!"

"I swear it's true. We won eleven million euros between us."

"Rosie, really I think –"

"We won eleven million euros. Part of that paid for this

house. It's what paid for Mum and Dad's anniversary bash – there was no competition on the *Gerry Ryan Show*."

"No way!"

"Yes way."

She's staring at me. I don't think she quite knows what to make of what I'm saying. It's clear she doesn't believe me. It's possible she thinks I'm mad.

"Nobody knows, Sarah. Well, except you now."

"What? Not even Finn?"

"Not even Finn."

"What about Mum and Dad?"

I shake my head.

"Did you really win the lotto?"

"Yes."

"But you didn't tell anyone?"

"No."

"But why didn't you tell anyone?"

I sigh. "I ask myself that same question. It would probably have been easier."

"So why didn't you?"

"For all sorts of reasons."

"Like?"

"Dana was worried about the impact it would have on her family. She wasn't sure her mother would be able to handle it – she's had problems in the past. And Caroline wanted to keep it from her father – she thinks he's a money-grabber. We'd other concerns too. That people would change towards us, that they'd only be interested in us for our money. And if we were in the newspapers then we'd start getting bagfuls of begging letters from strangers pestering us for handouts. I guess we were worried life would get too complicated. But, to be honest, I think it's pretty complicated the way it is."

"But how could you not tell anyone? It must have been hell!"

I shrug. "It's been difficult. All the lying we've had to do and the pretence – it has been hell sometimes."

"I could imagine. I couldn't do it. And you've even kept it from Finn – that can't have been easy."

"Tell me about it!"

"How can you keep up the pretence all the time?" But then she suddenly gives this laugh. "Now I understand. So *that's* where Caroline's getting all the money to buy these houses and apartments!"

"It's not just Caroline. It's all three of us. Me, Dana and Caroline. CKV stands for Connolly, Kiely, Vaughan."

"So I'm living in your house?"

"Well, yes, I own a share."

"I'm living on your charity?"

"It's not like that."

"Isn't it?"

"What's the difference between Caroline letting you stay here or all three of us?"

"I don't know but there is a difference. I wish you'd told me."

"Look, this house would have been standing empty until we managed to find Seán. You're doing us a favour staying here."

"Seán? The father with the two young children? So where is he?"

"That's just it. I can't find him. But until I do, you're welcome to stay here."

Sarah looks baffled. "This is so much to take in." Then she shakes her head again. Then she asks in a tone which is more accusatory than anything. "But how could you have kept all this — your win — everything — a secret? I know I couldn't!"

Suddenly I'm really worried. What have I done?

"Sarah — you *can't* tell anyone. Promise me you won't!"

"But what if I let it slip?"

"There's no *if* about it. You just can't — that's all there is to it."

"All right, all right — I won't."

"Promise me."

"But —"

"Just promise me, *please*."

"I promise."

"And just listen to what else I'm saying — I can afford to pay for a nanny for as long as you need one."

"But, Rosie, I can't let you do that. I don't want you to."

"But I want to do it. I'd be doing it for selfish reasons. You have no idea how glad I am to have you home. I hated it when you were living so far away. I love having you and the kids nearby. Please let me do this, please! Please don't talk about going back to Australia."

"I don't know."

"Please, I'd be doing it as much for myself as for you."

"Let me think about it."

"But what's there to think about? Have you a better alternative? If you let me help, you can get a full-time nanny and the kids will have the continuity of care you talked about — good care, for all of them, in their own home. Then you won't be stressed out worrying about them. You need help, Sarah. I can give it. Please let me." She's looking at me, as if she still can't believe all this. "Sarah, please?"

"Rosie, I —"

"In fact, what am I saying? You could just give up work if you like. I could support you."

"Oh no! That's out of the question!"

"But why, Sarah?"

"Why? *Please* let me retain some dignity."

"But, Sarah!"

"All right!"

"All right – what?"

"All right, about the nanny. Until I get on my feet. The boys have been through a lot. A nanny's help would be brilliant right now."

"Great!"

"I'll start ringing the agencies straight away." And then she suddenly laughs. "I really can't believe it! You won the lotto!"

"Please, Sarah, can you just pretend I never told you, please?"

"But Rosie –"

"Sarah, you can't tell *anyone*."

"Okay, okay, my lips are sealed. Look I'm throwing away the key."

If I thought sharing my secret might relieve some tension, it doesn't. All the way home I have misgivings but I can't undo things now. I tell myself Sarah's not going to tell anyone. Who has she to tell? She's living with three kids, she's so new at work she's not yet had time to make any friends in whom she's likely to confide and, only yesterday, Mum complained that she sees as little of Sarah now as she did when Sarah was living in Australia which is an exaggeration, of course, but it's true she's too busy to be spending much time with her. And anyway, I've asked her not to say a word. But still I can't help but worry.

After Sarah's, I go into town and buy the jeans I was hoping to and, when I do finally get home, I find Caroline in the living-room. She is, I see, in better form than she has been and she looks up and smiles when I come in.

"Rosie, I've been thinking. If Finn goes for the idea of an exhibition —"

"He has."

"Brilliant! Well, what I was thinking was maybe he should get Mick to open it."

"Funny you should say that. Mitch said the very same thing."

"Genii think alike."

"That's weird. He said that too."

"So Finn likes the idea?"

"He's not overly enthusiastic but, between us, Mitch and I have convinced him to go for it."

"Great!"

"And you'd be okay with Mick being there?"

"Sure. Besides . . ." she trails off.

"Besides?"

"Oh, I'm just not right without him. I miss him, Rosie."

"*Finally* you're beginning to see sense."

"It was weird sitting in the cinema the other night, in the dark, and being able to look at him like that on the screen, being able to study his face, to listen to his voice, to his laugh."

"I guess."

"All these memories and feelings just came flooding back." She sighs. "I don't think we should have got married; it was too soon, and too stupid. We — I — wasn't ready for it but I do love him, there's no escaping that fact. I'd like to try and work things out with him. If we could pretend it never happened, to not even try living together but to just be boyfriend and girlfriend again."

"Do you think you could do that?"

She nods. "I think I could but I don't know about Mick. He's older than me. He wanted to be married. But I do think it's time to talk to him."

"And what about the fact he's doing so well? Are you going to let that still bother you?"

She shakes her head. "I know how stupid I've been. Deep down I am really glad things are going so well for Mick. I've just been stupidly jealous. I need to adapt. I need to change the way I think about him – about me – about life. Just because some little madam who used to once bring me my coffee at work now pretends she doesn't even recognise me when we meet at a film premiere says more about her than it does about me. I was good at my job and a good boss to her too. My one failure – our shop – doesn't make me a failure. I need to remind myself of all the success I had before that."

"Exactly."

"And that I will have again."

"Now you're talking."

"And speaking of which, Tom Redmond rang earlier. You know those two apartments we've completed sales on?"

"Yes."

"Well, Tom Redmond has already secured tenants for one."

"Brilliant!"

"Isn't it?"

"Caroline?" Should I tell her about that photo in this morning's paper. Is there any need? It's just a photo. Mick probably doesn't even know that woman. Maybe he just happened to be standing near her when the photographer was going around looking for shots to take.

"What?"

So really, there is nothing to tell. Why upset her?

"What?" she repeats.

"Nothing. Never mind."

"You know, I'll ring Mick straight away about Finn's exhibition. The sooner I can start building bridges the better." She picks up her phone. "Actually no, give me yours – he's more likely to answer a call from you seeing as how upset he was with me after the premiere. I've tried ringing him countless times to apologise but he's now the one who's not picking up."

I hand her my phone and she starts pressing in his number. But if there's nothing to tell, I think, then why don't I just tell her?

"Caroline?"

"Ssh, it's ringing. Oh, hi! Mick? No, no, it's not Rosie. It's me, Caroline. Look I just want to ask you a favour and it's not for me, it's for Finn. He's having an exhibition of his paintings and I want to ask would you open it for him. You would? Fantastic. Yes, yes, sure. When? Well, as soon as possible. Next week hopefully. I'll let you know. Okay thanks. And Mick, if you – Oh!" She looks over to me. "He's already hung up."

She hands me back my phone.

"Caroline – that's fantastic! Well done! Finn will be delighted."

But Caroline looks thoughtful. "Hmm, I wonder where he was? He definitely wasn't at home. It sounded like he was in a pub or a noisy restaurant. I could hardly hear him. There was some silly woman shouting out his name in the background."

Oh, dear!

"Anyway, he says he'll do it, so that's good."

"Caroline, are you serious about next week for the exhibition?"

"Sure, why not. Next Saturday would be perfect. I can start the publicity on Monday and then we have the rest of the week to sort the venue out. Sure it's tight but I already know it's available."

"Well, I guess I'd better go and ring Finn then and tell him."

Divorced, bankrupt, a cramped one-bedroom apartment with two mortgages.

David N. Demarest – $8.8m – US

Remarried to his wife, retired, living in an ocean-front two-storey home . . . with no mortgage.

33

At ten-thirty on Monday, I call into Caroline's office. I've taken to thinking of it as Caroline's office as she's the one who's there most.

"Hi."

She looks up from her computer. "Rosie! I didn't hear you come in. So, to what do we owe this pleasure?"

"I thought we'd make a start on the exhibition."

"I'm ahead of you. The venue, that warehouse I was telling you about, is already nailed down. I'll bring you out to have a look at it this evening if that suits you."

"Great!"

"You can tell Finn to start shifting his paintings down there as soon as he can. I'll give you a key and you can pass it on to him."

"Okay. Mitch and Ashley are going to give him a hand."

"Tom Redmond's just left – I've a full day's work behind me already. I haven't had the chance to start yet but I have lined up the rest of the day for us to work on the publicity. But first, you must take a look at *this*." She picks up a piece of paper from her desk and waves it at me. "Here it is! Our first official rent cheque! The tenants are moving into the apartment today."

"That's fantastic!"

"Isn't it?" She's taken the cheque back now and is studying it. There's a smile playing on her lips. It occurs to me that she looks almost as pleased with this one as with the cheque we got at Lottery Headquarters.

She carefully puts it down again. "*And* I have some other good news."

"What is it?"

"You know Church View?"

"Yes?"

"I think we could soon be the proud owners of a third house there in the not-too-distant-future, the one on the far side of your sister's."

"Oh? I haven't noticed a 'For Sale' sign."

"That's because there isn't one but, the other day, I found out it was up for sale last year but was taken off the market due to lack of interest. However, it seems the owner is still keen to offload it. She's in her late seventies and spends a lot of her time with her sister in England but if she could sell up she'd move over there lock, stock and barrel in the morning. That's where Tom is gone now – to call on her, tell her he has clients who are interested." Suddenly, she gives this little shiver of excitement. "I have a good feeling about this."

"Let us know how he gets on."

"Sure. But that's not all. I also found out that two brothers, two middle-aged bachelors with no family, jointly own the remaining three. They inherited them from an uncle about ten years ago. Both men are based in County Meath. One owns a pub in some small village and lives over it. The other lives with him – I get the impression he may be a little on the slow side. Anyway, they've rented out the houses over the years but they've never put any money back into them so they're in pretty poor repair – inside and out. None of them has central heating and all three need to be re-roofed too. I think only one is occupied at the moment and I doubt there's a queue clamouring to move into either of the other two – you'd want to be pretty desperate. So, right now, they're nothing but a financial liability on these two brothers. It's not beyond the bounds of possibility – I think – that they too might be interested in selling."

I laugh. "How do you know all this?"

"That they may be willing to sell?"

"Well, yes – but all the other stuff too."

"Easiest thing in the world."

"But how?"

"Okay, well, a few days ago I just 'happen' to find myself in the shop across the road from them. So I hang around until I see someone who looks authoritative enough to be the owner of the shop arrive in. I wait for a quiet moment. I go to the counter. I place my newspaper on the counter. I smile. I say, 'Nice day, isn't it?' The owner responds, 'Yes, but it's set to rain later'. Then I say in a casual manner, as I glance out the door, 'Shame how run-down some of those houses have become. You'd have to wonder who'd let them get into such a state.' Fifteen minutes later, as I walk out the door, I'm wondering no longer. The shop owner who's been running the place since 1975 – 'through thick and thin and my father for forty years before me' – has filled me in on every detail I could possibly want to know. Right down to the name of the pub, 'Up there in the County Meath where them two brothers are living'."

I can't help smiling. "You love this, don't you?"

"What?"

"All this scheming, all this property wheeling and dealing?"

She smiles back. "I do." Then she glances down at her watch. "Okay, we need to get down to work on this exhibition. We have loads to do and I'm going to have to leave here at four. I need to book flights to the US."

"You're going to America?"

"Yep. I've had it in the back of my mind since we won the lotto but, until now, the time hasn't been right. I wanted to feel I was accomplishing something first. My mum may have slipped my mind when I won in that raffle as a child and picked a Barbie doll instead of something for her as I'd promised but I haven't forgotten her this time. So, yes, we're going on holiday together the month after next. We're going to hire a car – a soft top, and take a road trip, spend a couple of weeks travelling down along the Californian coast. We'll take in San Francisco, Los Angeles and wherever else takes our fancy."

"Wow!"

"Wow, indeed! It'll be brilliant! Mum has always dreamed of doing something like this. I can just feel it now, the warm Pacific breeze in my hair."

"Won't your mum wonder where the money is coming from?"

"Not my mum. I think after those years with Dad she expects money to come and go easily. She has no problem believing I made it myself. So, like I said, I need to be gone by four to get to the travel agent and I also have to . . ." she pauses for a second. ". . . Before we go to have a look at the warehouse, I want to show you something. I'll meet you back at the house at around seven, is that okay?"

"Sure, what do you want to show me?"

She smiles. "My new post chaise."

"Pardon?"

"'If I had no duties and no reference to futurity, I would spend my life in driving briskly in a post chaise with a pretty woman.'"

"I'm sorry. You've totally lost me."

"I'm quoting Samuel Johnson, or 'wise old Dr Johnson,' as Dad always calls him."

"I'm still not following you."

"After I pick up the plane tickets, I'm going to collect my post chaise, or my modern equivalent – a Saab."

"You've bought a Saab?"

"I sure have. I've had my eye on it for ages, ever since we won, but it never felt like the right time to buy. I guess I wanted to see us making some headway first with CKV but we are now. Things are moving along steadily. We're buying cautiously but well and at very good prices. All the properties are well placed for the rental market. And all this information about Church View is as positive as I could have hoped for. Yep, things are looking mighty good." She pauses for a moment. "Now, all I have to do is get my pretty woman back, or in my case, my handsome man."

At four o'clock, when the time comes for Caroline to pay a visit to the travel agent and collect her new car, both of us leave the office after putting in a very good day's work on organising the exhibition. I offer to go with her but she tells me not to, in case there are any delays. But I get the feeling she's looking forward to pulling up at the house later to unveil her super new car to us all and to bask in her moment of glory.

"I'm a £3 burger and pint girl," said Angela.

Angela Cunningham – £35 million – UK

"The tragedy for Angela," said a neighbour, "is that had she won £50,000, she would have been over the moon. She would have paid off the mortgage, gone on holiday and felt financially secure. Winning £35 million has really ruined her life."

34

Caroline really has got stuck right in and all week has been unstinting in her help in a very hands-on way with Finn's exhibition. She's called up all her old contacts and has given her professional advice in her usual generous and enthusiastic way, and the location she found us is perfect.

I have to admit that first evening – last Monday – when Caroline brought me down the docks to see, in her words, the perfect venue, I was dubious.

"Who's going to want to come all the way out here?" I asked, as we travelled along in her fabulous new car – derelict old buildings on one side, deep, dark murky water on the other.

"But this is exactly what we need," insisted Caroline, "a raw edgy part of town."

"You think?"

"I know."

"Hmm."

"To reflect the raw, edgy nature of Finn's paintings. In fact, we should say exactly that in our press release."

Which she did. And those words go out too on the

hundreds of posters, invitations and fliers Caroline had distributed and on the postings Mitch put on the internet. Plus, of course, mention of the important fact that Mick Boylan would be the special guest on the night.

And whatever doubts I had about the general location, I had no doubts at all about the actual venue. That first time, when Caroline took off the heavy padlock, drew back the big old steel door, flicked on the lights and I saw the vast empty space – five thousand square feet in all – I knew it was perfect. Absolutely perfect. Four blank white walls and one black-painted concrete floor – everything we needed. The ideal backdrop. It's been a hectic week but I haven't enjoyed myself so much in ages.

Now I glance at my watch: it's six-thirty. I take another look around the warehouse. Mentally I go through my checklist to see if there's anything I'm forgetting. I don't think so. In the past few days we have done Trojan work and on those blank white walls now hang Finn's canvases – explosions of colour carefully spaced out around the room. The only piece of furniture is a long trestle table at one end covered in a white cloth, with sparkling wine glasses lined up in rows of military precision and flanked – like colonels to the rank and file – by bottles of red wine. The white wine and the mineral water are yet to come – Mitch and Ashley are going to bring them. Having been here helping all day they, along with the 'artist', have now gone home to shower and change. I look around and give a deep sigh of satisfaction. There is nothing left for me to do but get changed. The evening will officially start at 7.00 pm.

Now I hear the heavy door being pulled back. It's Caroline and Dana back again.

"Wow!" is all I can say when I see them. "You both look incredible."

While I stayed behind to wait for the glasses to be delivered this afternoon, they left here at four, dishevelled and grimy from the efforts they put into helping but now here they are again, utterly transformed: hair and faces all made-up, wearing high heels and short evening dresses – Caroline's heels being typically higher and her dress typically shorter than Dana's more modest one. But both, Dana in black and Caroline in yellow, look fabulous.

"It's easy to look good when you can just go into town and pick out any dress you like and not even bother to look at the tag," laughs Dana. "I can kind of see now why you've become addicted to shopping, Rosie." Then she holds out her nails to me. "Look, I even got a manicure. You may not believe this, but I have never had my nails done before."

"It's quite easy to believe actually," I laugh. "But you did remember to go home and pick up my outfit, didn't you?"

"Actually –" begins Caroline.

"Caroline!"

"Of course we did," she laughs.

"And you remembered my shoes?"

"Yes!"

"Here, before you change, eat this," says Dana, and I register the pizza box she's holding along with a can of Coke. "You don't want to faint from hunger."

I begin eating the pizza while Caroline goes to the car to get my things. I am starving. By the time she comes back, I'm halfway through it and a few more minutes sees me done. Then I begin getting changed. All this time, Dana is wandering around the room, examining the paintings.

"When you see all of Finn's paintings together like this they have such an impact, don't they?"

The big door opens again. It's the two waitresses we've employed for the night to serve the drinks. Mitch and Ashley had volunteered to man the bar but Caroline didn't think they'd present quite the right image and I think she was also concerned they'd put more effort into serving themselves than others.

"Hi, girls!" Caroline calls over to them.

"Hi, Caroline! The place looks great."

They head straight to the trestle table, take off their coats and bundle them and their handbags under it, out of sight.

"Would you like a glass of wine before things kick off?" the older one calls to us.

"I think we deserve it." says Caroline. "Are you ready for a glass, Rosie?"

I glance at my watch. We still have ten minutes. "Most definitely! But will you zip me up first?"

"Sure."

"Hello!"

We spin around. Mick's standing by the big steel door.

"Mick! Hello!"

He gives a quick glance around. "This is amazing! You put all this together in a week?"

"But for Caroline we never would have," I point out.

He looks to Caroline. He doesn't smile exactly but his look isn't hostile either. "Well done," he says.

"Thanks," says Caroline. It occurs to me that she looks a little nervous but I can't be sure. It's not an emotion I usually associate with her.

Now Mick is looking at the paintings more closely. "Finn should be proud."

I laugh. "Should be – but you know what he's like. All modest and humble. But I'm proud. Very proud."

"So, what exactly do you want me to do tonight?"

"Well, if you could just say a few words about Finn, that would be great."

"Sure, sure."

A few early arrivals appear at the door and Caroline, springing into action, goes straight over to them and gives them an effusive welcome.

I glance at Mick. I notice he's watching her closely. Good, I think. Maybe we'll get more than just sales of Finn's paintings out of this evening.

Caroline was right. The location doesn't prove a deterrent and half-an-hour later the place is jammed. Finn's dad is here, of course, looking as pleased as Punch, and Fay is with him, as elegant as ever. But in the main it's a young hip crowd. As the evening goes on, it becomes obvious that the paintings are secondary to the real reasons most of the crowd are here and those reasons are, in no particular order, a) to have this opportunity to mingle with Finn and Ashley and Mitch and talk music with them, rather than art; b) to have this opportunity to mingle with Mick and talk about *Fate Farm* with him rather than art; and, c) to avail of the free wine. There were a few mentions – blink-and-you'd-miss-them kind of mentions – of tonight in a few newspapers but I'm guessing that the majority of people are fans of the band who've learned about this evening through the band's MySpace page – although the higher than expected number of females could be attributed to Mick's presence.

True, I do hear people complimenting Finn on his paintings but what I don't see is them actually buying. An hour into the evening I discreetly go around the room and see that only four of the paintings have little red dots beside them. Dana, who is in charge of sales, tells me that Finn's dad bought one of the four, Fay another, Mick a third and some stranger the fourth.

I begin to seriously worry that we may have misjudged the whole evening. Caroline insisted we should price high as it would make people value Finn's work more and, also, it would generate more money. I agreed with her at the time but now I think we were wrong. The crowd may be hip but they're not well-heeled.

Finn comes over to me. "It's quite a crowd!"

"Sure is."

Then he frowns. "But they're not buying, are they?"

"I think it just takes people a while to commit. There'll probably be a rush towards the end of the evening."

"You think?"

"Sure." But I'm not. "Don't worry!"

"I'm not." But he looks it. "Of course I'm not. Like you say, hopefully there'll be a rush towards the end."

Suddenly I feel terrible. Finn would never have gone through with tonight but for me. I – with Mitch's help – was the one who railroaded him into it. Maybe we priced too high. What if no more paintings sell? There's no way we could dress this evening up, pretend it isn't the horrible, embarrassing failure it's looking like it's going to be if live sales are the marker. What have I done? Finn is going to feel humiliated. But it's still early, I console myself. Things could pick up.

There is one positive. I see Mick and Caroline talking together. But just when I'm feeling happy about this, I see the redheaded model from the newspaper arrive at the door. Oh hell! What's she doing here? I examine her. She's as stunning as she was in the photo but not quite as smiley. In fact, she looks distinctly disgruntled. Maybe this wasn't quite what she was expecting. Maybe she's wondering just what she's doing down here in this draughty warehouse at the exhibition of some unknown painter. But then I see she's spotted her reason – Mick – and her whole face lights up as she makes a beeline for where he's standing, talking with Caroline. I decide I'd better get over there too, and fast.

By the time I get there, Mick is doing the introductions. "Caroline, this is Tammy, Tammy, this is Caroline and – ha – Mitch, where did you spring from? And here's Rosie too. Why, suddenly we're quite a little crowd," Mick finishes, sounding a little puzzled.

"Hi, Tammy." I smile at her and turn to Caroline. "Ah, Caroline, I was just wondering if you could co –"

But Mitch cuts in. "I saw your picture on the paper last Saturday, Tammy. I hope you don't mind me saying but I thought you looked fabulous," he gushes sounding like a smitten teenager. "But you look even better in real life."

Tammy beams. "You mean the photo at the opening of Foxy's Nightclub?"

"That's the one. I've heard great reports about the place. Would you recommend it?"

"Yeah, sure." Tammy looks to Mick. "What do you think, Mick?"

He shrugs. "It's okay, I guess."

"So – ah – how do you two know each other?" asks Mitch.

"Oh, you know, just from around," Tammy lays an affectionate hand on Mick's arm.

Oh damn! I see Caroline has noticed. I see she doesn't look at all pleased. "Excuse me, but I really need to drag

Caroline away for just a moment," I say and I take her arm and firmly guide her across the room.

"What?" demands Caroline crossly. "What's so urgent?"

"Amm . . ." I need to think of something quick. I look towards the painting we're standing in front of. It's one of the biggest, nearly two metres square. "I'm worried this painting isn't secured firmly enough. It might fall and hit someone."

She stares at it for a moment.

"No chance. You saw the guys putting them up. They did a good job. An earthquake wouldn't dislodge these paintings."

A high-pitched laugh comes from across the room. Caroline looks over to the perpetrator.

"Just who is *that* woman? Is she a friend of Mick's?"

"I don't know."

"What was Mitch saying? That she and Mick were in Foxy's Nightclub together?"

"I don't know."

She looks over at them again. "He doesn't lose much time, that's for sure."

"I don't think they're together. In the photo it looked like they just happened to be standing beside one another. At least that's the impression I got."

"Mick was in the photo too?"

"Ah, yeah."

"And you saw this photo?"

Damn! "Amm – yes," I admit.

"Why didn't you tell me?"

"There was nothing to tell."

She eyes me up, then shakes her head. "I'm going off to get another glass of wine."

Another hour later and the crowd is beginning to fall off.

Win Some Love Some

Tammy has left but, unfortunately, so too has Mick. I quiz
Mitch about the exact circumstance of these departures and he
tells me that when Mick announced it was time for him to go,
Tammy promptly told him that she had to go too and offered
him a lift. Now I walk around the room again. I count seven
red dots in total. Seven red dots. Seven paintings sold.

"Do you know who that woman with the – ah – moustache
is?" Dana comes up to me and asks.

I look over. "Oh, that's Big Bertha."

"Is she going out with Mitch?"

"What makes you think that?"

"Well, she came over to me a while ago and just started
talking to me and though she didn't say it directly she kept
implying that she and Mitch were in a relationship."

"Maybe you should ask him then."

"Maybe I will." She shrugs. "I wouldn't have thought he
was her type but you just never know." Then she turns her
attention to other matters. "Anyway, do you think we'll
make any more sales?"

"Caroline said she's going to buy one."

"She already has."

"Have you had any other enquiries?"

She shakes her head. "No."

"Me neither."

"Poor Finn!"

"Don't say that!"

"But, Rosie, I can't help feeling sorry for him."

"Oh God, I don't want people feeling sorry for him."
There's nothing worse. And then the idea comes to me.
"Do you have a sheet of red dots on you now?"

"Ah, yes."

"Okay. Give them to me."

"Why?"

"Just give them to me. On second thoughts, don't. But what I do want you to do is to go around the room and discreetly stick a red dot beside about three-quarters of the unsold paintings."

"But why?"

"Look, the whole purpose of tonight is to raise money for the band but we haven't managed to sell anywhere near enough. But there's no reason I shouldn't buy them. Finn need never know."

"Rosie!"

"Don't 'Rosie' me. Please, Dana, just do it now while there's still people milling about."

"What if Finn finds out?"

"How would he? Will you just go and do it!"

"I don't feel good about this."

"Dana, I'm just trying to do for Finn what you've already done for Doug – I'm trying to help him realise his dreams."

"But, Rosie, what if –"

"Please, Dana, before it's too late."

"All right."

At around eleven, the last of the stragglers depart.

"Well," says Finn, beaming. "You were right. The sales of the paintings really picked up towards the end."

"They sure did."

"I can't believe how many of them sold. Have you the list?"

"List?"

"The list of who bought them."

"Oh, I think Dana took it home with her."

"Pity, I'd have liked to see it. Maybe later. So what happens now?"

"Well, the people who bought the paintings will come back tomorrow afternoon and pick them up."

"Oh, but I'm not going to be able to be here. We've a gig tomorrow night in Sligo."

I already know that. The last thing I want is him hanging around.

"I think it would be better if you weren't here at all," I tell him. "You're the artist. You need to play the part. Let Caroline and me take care of everything. It would look more professional."

"You think?"

"I do. I'm sure Doug and Shane will help."

"You don't mind?"

"Course not."

Finn is smiling at me.

"What?" I say.

"Thanks for all this."

"It was nothing."

"Yes, it was. We made a fortune tonight. It will make such a difference. Without you this would never have happened. And it's not just the money. I know I've always painted for the pleasure of it but it's a good feeling to think that other people get what I do – enough to hand over money for it! So, like I say, thanks."

He leans towards me and kisses me on the lips.

"You're very welcome."

£4m investment in Livingston FC, a Scottish football club.
£3m spent on close family members.
£750,000 gift to ex-wife.
£500,000 on a seafront apartment in Majorca.
£200,000 on a wedding.

A Ferrari Modena Spyder, a Bentley, a Porsche, a Mercedes, a couple of Jaguars, and another couple of BMWs.

Caribbean cruises, five-star ski trips and holidays all around the world.

John McGuinness – £10 million – UK

Eleven years later, deep in debt, looking for a job and applying for a council house.

35

Mum isn't exactly pleased when I turn up with a hired van full of Finn's paintings and ask to stow them in their garage as a temporary measure – until I decide what to do with them in the long term.

"I really don't understand why you have to store all these here," she complains.

"We don't have room in our house."

"Doesn't Finn's dad have room? At his house or in one of his shops? Or why couldn't Finn store them in his own house?"

"Mum, I'm here now. There's lots of room in the garage. Can I just leave them here for the moment, please?"

"But why do you need to store them at all?"

"I just do."

"Did they not sell?"

"Yes, they did!"

"So why are you bringing them here?"

"Does it matter?"

"I'm just asking, Rosie."

"Some of the buyers can't collect immediately."

"Why would anyone buy a painting and then not bother to collect it?"

"I don't know!"

"It seems odd to me. I mean if I had bought a painting I'd be dying to get my hands on it. I'd know exactly where I was going to han—"

"Mum, can I leave them here or not?"

Honestly, if I'd known she was going to ask this many questions I'd have gone straight to a storage depot. I wish I had now. That would have made more sense. "You're right, Mum. It's not fair to fill up your garage with them. I'll take them to a storage depot."

"And pay a fortune! You will not! No, of course you can leave them here. We don't mind. You can tell Finn they'll be perfectly safe here."

"Sure," I lie. Finn can't ever know where they are.

Should I warn Mum not to say a word to him about them? No, I decide, not right now. That would only lead to more questions. Best to keep things simple. Besides, it's not like Finn ever calls here and certainly never without me. I'll soon have found a more permanent home for them. I can make sure to keep Finn away for the moment. I'll only warn Mum and Dad not to say a word when, if, I need to.

With Dad's help I unload the paintings from the van into the garage and, just as we're finishing up, Mum calls us in. In the time it took us to offload the van she's put together a tasty lunch — Quiche Lorraine plus all sorts of salads. I didn't have much of a breakfast and now I find I'm starving.

"So," she says as I'm helping myself to a slice of quiche, "what do you think of Sarah's news?"

"What news?"

"That Rod is coming over."

"Rod is coming over? What? Here?"

"Yes, he's flying in on Friday."

"She never told me. I was on the phone to her just yesterday."

"Didn't she?" But she says this like she already knows.

"No."

"Well, you *can* be very negative."

"Pardon?"

"Yes, Rosie. You're very black and white about Rod."

"Of course I am! He left her!"

"Yes, but he's still her husband and the boys are still his children. If there's a way for them to work things out then they need to try."

"But Mum, you don't even like him!"

"Rosie, I'm not the one married to him."

"Don't you think Sarah would be better off not being married to him?"

"I'm not sure I do. It's very hard for her managing on her own. God only knows how she's paying for that nanny. If there's any chance they might get back together then I, for one, would be happy to see that happen. And so should you. For her sake. For the children's sake."

"But he's a rat! He walked out on her and the children. And if they get back together then she and the kids would go back to Australia. Is that what you want?"

"Rosie, I like having her and the children here too but, just like you, for my own selfish reasons. It would be better for everyone concerned if Rod and Sarah could work out their differences."

"Would it?"

"Yes."

"Even if it meant they all went back to Australia?"

"Yes."

As I'm dropping the van back I think over what Mum said. I guess deep down I know she's right. I might not like Rod but Sarah once did, enough to marry him and have three children with him. And I think she does still love him. Splitting up wasn't her choice. But I was getting used to having Sarah around. It was nice getting to know her all over again. And getting to really know the kids too. I hated when she went away that first time and now to think it might happen again. And not just her this time, but Lachlan and Kyle and Jack too.

Later that evening I'm in my room when I hear Dana calling from the living-room.

"Caroline! Come quickly. Your dad is on TV."

"What?"

"Come on down. You've got to see this!"

Both Caroline and I nearly collide on the landing as we both come rushing out of our bedrooms.

"Why on earth would he be on telly?" Caroline asks as she goes tearing down the stairs in front of me.

She reaches the bottom and hurries into the living-room with me fast on her heels.

"Oh, my God! There he is!" she cries. And, sure enough, there's her dad, standing in the centre of a familiar TV set. "No way! It can't be!"

"Caroline, your father is actually on *The Dragon's Den*!" Then the camera pulls back and I see another figure alongside him. "And Vivienne too! This is amazing! Did you know he was going to be on it?"

"Of course not. I don't believe this!" Caroline is staring at the screen. "Oh, my God! What is she wearing? Would you look at the length of that skirt – if you can even call it a skirt!"

The pair don't really look like business partners, not like the usual pairings I've seen on the programme on the odd occasion I've watched it but more like – I don't know – a natty little magician and his busty blonde assistant? A natty little magician who happens to look terrified. I notice the beads of sweat on his forehead and though he's smiling it's a thin nervous smile – not like his usual wide engaging grin. Now he loosens his tie – certainly not a confidence-inspiring gesture.

"What on earth is he doing on *The Dragon's Den*?" asks Caroline. "Has he said, Dana?"

"I've only just flicked over."

"Hush!" I say. "He's about to say something!"

"Good evening," begins Mr Connolly, confidently enough but then he coughs to clear his throat and then – oh God – he stops talking altogether.

"Oh no!" moans Caroline. "Please don't say he's gone blank!"

The camera stays on him, as he stands there, looking so nervous it's unbearable to watch. I can't imagine what it must be like to actually be him.

"Oh, come on Dad! Say something!"

"I'd never have thought him the nervous type," I say.

"Me neither," says Caroline.

"I'm sorry I'm a little nervous." He gives a nervous little laugh. Caroline gives a groan. "A-hem, well, my name is Eddie Connolly and this is my business partner, Vivienne Ward. We'd – ah – we'd like to introduce to you a revolution

445

in women's footwear which we call the Heel-to-Flat-to-Heel. It's a new concept and one I believe will change the entire shoe industry. If you bear with us, Vivienne will now demonstrate it."

Vivienne, who really is dressed in the tightest little skirt imaginable, now walks across the room in a pair of flats which look peculiar on her – I've only seen her in high heels. Meanwhile, Mr Connolly begins the commentary and – thankfully – he's managing to sound less nervous as he goes on.

"So Vivienne who, let's say, is a hardworking executive has spent the day rushing around the office and it's now six o'clock but still her work isn't finished. Ahead of her is an evening entertaining some corporate clients but she hasn't time to go home and change. So what does she do?"

Vivienne slips off one shoe, clicks a little catch on it – *et, voilá* – a heel descends. She puts the shoe back on, takes off the other and does the same with this one. Then she walks across the room in what are now a pair of high heels. The camera cuts back to Mr Connolly. He's looking more relaxed now, even a little pleased with himself.

The camera shifts to the 'Dragons', all five of them, all in a row, each as grim and stony-faced as the next.

"Oh dear," murmurs Dana, "they don't look very impressed."

"Don't worry. They never do," says Caroline who often watches the programme. "If Graham Alexander Bell were to come on with his new device which allowed people to talk to each other over long distances they'd make sure to appear unimpressed to begin with – it's what they do. It adds to the suspense."

But the 'Dragons' remain silent for what seems like an

age. The camera shifts from one to the other to the other. They really do look so terribly serious. Finally, the first of them speaks.

"Hello, Eddie," he says pleasantly enough.

"Hello," says Eddie.

"Eddie, I have a question."

"Sure, fire ahead."

"Why couldn't the lady bring a spare pair of shoes to the office?"

"Well, you know ladies' handbags. They're usually quite small," Mr Connolly answers.

"Not in my experience," laughs the Dragon. "Anyway, you said this lady is an executive. Where's her briefcase then? Couldn't she keep them in that? Or couldn't she keep a spare pair in her office?"

"What's with all this nit-picking?" asks Dana.

"I'm using a female executive as an example," Mr Connolly answers. "These shoes would do for all sorts of women in all kinds of situations. I believe the market for them is enormous."

This particular Dragon doesn't look overly impressed. "Eddie," he says, after a suspenseful pause, "tell me, what exactly do you want from us?"

"What I want is an investment of fifty thousand and for that I'm willing to give over twenty per cent of the business."

"And you would use this investment for what?"

"To perfect the mechanism that turns the shoe from flat to heel and vice versa."

"So that's still in the development stage?"

"The mechanism does work but it tends to stick from time to time – I need to perfect that and I need to develop it so that it will stand up to repeated and robust use."

"Have you managed to interest any shoe companies?"

"I haven't approached any yet."

"Can I ask why? Don't you think the proper order of things would be to approach a shoe company and let them finance you?"

"I want to perfect the mechanism first. And, when I do, I want to make it available universally. I don't want to be tied to one company. I think that would limit my potential market."

"Hmm."

Still the Dragon doesn't look entirely convinced but he doesn't dismiss the idea out of hand either. The camera moves on to the next Dragon.

"I like your idea," he tells Eddie.

"Thank you."

"It shows promise. But it's still at a very early stage, isn't it? I hope you haven't given up the day job."

"I don't have a day job at present."

"Oh?"

"I gave it up to spend more time on my inventions. The Heel-to-Flat-to-Heel is just one of many."

"What is it you used to do?"

"I've had a lot of jobs – mainly in sales and in property."

"And what was your last job?"

"I worked in a carpark."

"In a carpark?"

"Yes."

"So you've no background in design?"

"No formal background."

"Can you tell us about some of your inventions?"

"Pending patents I'd prefer not to."

"Have any of your inventions been put into production?"

Mr Connolly shakes his head. "No."

"Hmm, I see."

The camera moves now to another of the Dragons.

"Eddie, can I ask what age you are?"

"Can I ask how that's relevant?"

"Of course. I'm guessing you're about – maybe – sixty? And you've been working on your – what do you call it again?"

"Heel-to-Flat-to-Heel."

"Your Heel-to-Flat-to-Heel for quite some time – for how long exactly?"

"A couple of years, on and off."

"Yet you haven't yet perfected it sufficiently to make it a commercial proposition."

"But with funding I will."

The Dragon looks thoughtful. "You know, I like you, the two of you. I do, but as business people you don't convince me. Eddie, you mentioned other inventions but you can't say what they are because none of them have been patented. That makes me think I can't take you seriously. You've been inventing for what – twenty, thirty years, your whole life – but you haven't managed to make money out of any of these, am I right?"

"Yes, but –"

"I just don't buy you as a serious business person. I'm sorry but you're a daydreamer and business is no place for daydreamers. You're like the father in *Chitty Chitty Bang Bang*, full of crazy ideas – all whistle sweets and automatic haircutting machines – crazy ideas that never quite work as they're supposed to. And, Vivienne, I'm not sure what your role in all this is. Eddie introduces you as his business partner but, quite frankly, given how you're dressed here today I wonder just what kind of business you're in."

"Hey, that's way out of order!" Caroline shouts at the screen.

"Relax, Caroline," I say. "Maybe he didn't mean it the way it sounded."

The Dragon goes on. "It seems to me there *is* no business. I'm afraid you'll have to count me out."

The camera doesn't show Eddie or Vivienne but reverts to the first Dragon. He's dolefully shaking his head.

"Count me out too. I like you both too and I quite like the idea but I think you're coming to us too early. I'm afraid I have to pass."

The third Dragon shakes his head. "I'm out."

The fourth Dragon shakes his head. "And me."

Now there is only one Dragon left, the sole woman who, so far, hasn't said a word. The camera closes in on this final Dragon. She looks pensive – her eyes are squinted, her lips pursed. This is agonising. If I feel this way, I can't imagine how Caroline must feel. Even more so her dad and Vivienne.

"You look like a shoe lady, Vivienne?" begins this final Dragon.

"I am."

"A high-shoe lady?"

Vivienne laughs. "I guess."

"Do you ever wear flats?"

"Well, no, but sometimes when I'm rushing for a taxi I wish I had a pair with me. Or a pair of these."

"I don't buy that!"

"Pardon?" stammers Vivienne.

Unheeding, the female Dragon continues. "You know what, I just can't see these being popular because women are either one or the other. Heels or flats."

"That's rubbish!" shouts Caroline at the screen. "If she's going to reject it too, at least let it be for a proper reason!"

But the woman is shaking her head. "I'm sorry but I'm out. I can't invest. I just don't see it ever catching on. To me, this is a male idea that simply will never be popular amongst women."

"Oh, for crying out loud!" shouts Caroline.

Now Mr Connolly and Vivienne stand there, looking like they can't quite believe that that's it, their opportunity is over. They glance at one another. They both look shell-shocked and unsure of what they should do now.

Then Mr Connolly gives a dignified smile. "Thank you very much for your time." He takes Vivienne's hand and together they walk off.

"What idiots!" cries Dana.

"How dare you!" shouts Caroline.

Dana looks startled, then puzzled. "God, no, Caroline, I didn't mean your dad and Vivienne. I meant the Dragons."

"Oh, right."

"I actually think their idea is a great one."

"And so do I."

"Your dad and Vivienne really handled the whole thing very well," I say.

"You should be proud, Caroline," adds Dana.

Caroline looks confused for a moment. Then she laughs. "Yes, yes I am," she says, sounding more than a little surprised. Then she goes on. "Okay, you know what? I'm going to need a cheque for . . ." She mumbles something I don't quite get. But Dana does.

"Did you just say for your dad?" she asks.

"Yes, I did," Caroline responds defensively. "Is there something wrong with that? You're both writing cheques, helping out your friends and family, so why shouldn't I help my dad?"

"Are you sure about this?" I ask. "The Dragons just turned him down."

"Yes, and they're making a big mistake."

"But, Caroline," I say, "one of your reasons for keeping our lotto win a secret was because you didn't want to give him money."

"I know. And now I've changed my mind."

"But you think he's a crook," I point out. "That he can't be trusted."

She shrugs. "Well, maybe his past isn't exactly blemish-free but we can't all be blessed with perfect parents like you, Rosie. And I happen to think his idea is fantastic. It just needs some more work. Like he said, with its present mechanism it tends to stick so he needs to look at ways of perfecting it. Maybe he should engage an industrial engineer. And that's just the short term. In the long term, he's going to need money to present it professionally enough to attract a client, hopefully some international shoe manufacturer, some big name in the business."

"And you want to finance all this?" I ask.

"In a word, yes."

I'm confused. "The Dragons *and* you yourself have said that your father has poured money into his inventions over the years without ever really getting anywhere and now you want to throw your money in as well?"

Caroline shrugs. "Maybe all he's been missing is that lucky break."

"I don't understand. How come you've changed your mind all of a sudden?"

She thinks for a moment, "Okay, remember when he called around out of the blue a while back after so long?"

"Yeah?" Both Dana and I nod our heads.

"Well, I assumed he was after something – money most like – but he wasn't. I know now he genuinely just wanted me to meet his new wife. He didn't ask me for a penny. Nor has he asked Donald. Maybe I'm just too suspicious. I don't give him a chance. Maybe he has really changed. Maybe it's time I gave him a break."

"Just *maybe,*" I say, thinking aloud, "the reason he didn't ask for money was because he knew he was going on this show. Maybe now that he's got nothing out of it, he'll be back asking you and Donald for money."

"And so what if he does? I have the money to give him and that's what I'm going to do. But without him even asking. I want to help him. For the first time in my life I felt really proud of him. You know, he's sixty and he still has that optimism, that belief that things will work out for him, that one of his ideas will make him a fortune. Sure, a smarter man might have got there years ago but a less tenacious man would have long since thrown in the towel. But there's my dad, still working away at one idea after another, hoping that one day he'll hit the jackpot."

"So how much are you going to give him?" Dana asks.

"Well, he told the Dragons he wanted fifty grand. So," she thinks for a second, "I'm going to give him double that."

"What are you going to tell him when he asks where you got the money from?"

"Why should he know it's from me? Thousands of people will have watched him tonight. It's not beyond belief that one of them would have been prompted to fund him anonymously. Like some eccentric millionaire who's taken a shine to him."

"Like you?" I ask.

Caroline grins. "Yeah, like me."

Even the rich can be slow to pay their taxes.

Phillip W. Cappella - $2.7 million - US

On his tax return the following year, Cappella claimed $65,000 in gambling losses against his winnings, in a bid to save over $20,000 in federal taxes.

When auditors asked for proof of these losses, he produced 200,000 losing scratch-off lottery tickets - tickets he'd rented for the audit for just $500.

36

Sarah answers the door. "Hi!"

The first thing I notice is how well she looks. She's wearing a pink skirt, white T-shirt, and a pair of flat pumps. Her hair, which she's wearing down, looks newly-washed – all bounce and shine. For the first time I notice she's wearing make-up. She never wears make-up.

"So, did he arrive?"

"Rosie, *he* has a name."

"Sorry. Did Rod arrive?"

"He's out the back with the boys. Come on in."

I follow her down the hall and into the kitchen. The place is spotless. The table is set. And there's a lovely smell of cooking. I hear someone – Kyle? – give a high-pitched laugh and, going to the window I see him and Lachlan in the garden with Rod. Both boys are chasing their dad but they haven't a chance of catching him – he's weaving this way and that with surprising agility. I look at him. Tall, tanned, with wavy chestnut-coloured hair. It's easy to see why Sarah was attracted to him. He is a very handsome man.

"They look pleased to see him."

Sarah joins me at the window. "They are. Of course, they are. Thrilled."

I look over at her. She's smiling at the scene before her.

She gives a contented sigh. "I hate to interrupt their fun but I'd better call them in for lunch. Rod wants to take them to the zoo afterwards though they don't know yet." She leans out the window and shouts out. "Hey, guys, come in! Rosie's here! Lunch is ready!"

"Ah, Muuuumm!" moans Lachlan, "do we have to?"

"Yes!"

Kyle shouts out, "Come on, Dad. Race you in!"

The two boys come running in first and Rod follows after at a more sedate pace.

I can't say Rod and I know each other well. We've met so seldom but it isn't just that. Our relationship – if that's what you can call it – is based entirely on the fact that he's married to my sister and that suits us fine. Such superficiality works for both of us. I think we both know that getting to know one another more wouldn't make us like each other any better. That said, Rod has always been one for an over-effusive greeting – hugs, kisses, exclamations of how well I'm looking – but today it's even more over the top than usual.

"Hi, Rod."

"Well hello, Rosie – long time no see. Wow! Look at you! You're looking more fabulous than ever! It's fantastic to see you again. Here, give your old brother-in-law a hug!"

And suddenly I find myself engulfed in a bear hug which I'm not entirely comfortable with.

"Mum! Mum! Can I sit beside Dad," I hear Lachlan calling through my muffled ears.

"No, I want to!" shouts Kyle.

Finally, thankfully, Rod lets me go.

"Guys! Stop shouting!" shouts Sarah. "Relax – you can sit on either side of him."

The food – a shepherd's pie – is surprisingly delicious. I didn't know Sarah could cook so well. Up to now all I've seen her serve up is pasta or takeaways. And though I've little experience of them as a family, with both Mum and Dad present, I guess I'm surprised to see how hands-on Rod is today. He's really involved – coaxing the older two boys to eat, filling up their glasses, responding to their every question while all the time feeding little Jack.

"Is shepherd's pie made of shepherds?" Kyle suddenly asks, causing us all to laugh.

"Well, what do you think?" asks Rod.

"Ah, yeah?"

"No, it's made of lamb."

"You mean like a baby sheep?"

"Yes."

"A poor little baby sheep?"

"That's right." Rod looks over at Sarah and does this, 'Yikes – *what* have I started?' expression and she laughs, shrugs her shoulders but doesn't get involved.

But Kyle doesn't seem perturbed by this knowledge. He has another question: "Why isn't it called lamb's pie so?"

"Maybe it's called shepherd's pie because shepherds used to eat it long, long ago when they were up on the mountains minding their sheep."

"And minding their lambs?"

"Yes, and their lambs too," answers Rod.

"But if they were meant to be minding the lambs then they really shouldn't have been eating them," reasons Kyle.

"And how did they even cook them anyway if they were up on the mountains?"

All the time, Sarah remains sitting back, relaxed, a happy look on her face. I notice Rod glance over at her again. This time he gives her a fond private little wink.

Would Sarah go back with him if he asked her? In a heartbeat, I think. Would he want her back? He was the one who walked out on them. Maybe Sarah moving so far away with the boys was enough to bring him to his senses. Still, I don't get how she can sit there, letting him play happy families when, so recently, he blew that happy family right apart.

"That was delicious!" says Rod now when, despite all the interruptions, he finally finishes his dinner.

"Do you want some more?" asks Sarah.

"No, I couldn't eat another bite. Anyway, look at the time. If we want to get to the zoo we should go now."

"The zoo!" cries Kyle. "We're going to the zoo?"

"Unless you don't want to," jokes Rod.

"Of course we do," insists Lachlan.

"Are you sure? Because if you don't we can stay here and help Mum tidy up after lunch. Maybe you'd prefer that!"

"No way!"

"Well then, go on, get your coats! The sooner we go, the more time we'll have."

The boys scoot off.

I get up. "I'd better go too. I have some things to do."

"See you again, Rosie," says Rod. "I'm sure we'll have other chances to meet before I go. Maybe we could all go out to dinner? I'd like to meet this boyfriend of yours."

"Yeah, sure."

"Are you certain you won't stay for coffee?" asks Sarah.

"Ah, no thanks."

"I'll walk you out."

"Bye, Rod," I say.

He's cooing at Baby Jack now but he calls out cheerily, "Bye, Rosie. See you soon."

"You didn't tell him about the lotto, did you?" I ask when we reach the front door.

"No."

"Well, don't, okay?"

"Okay. And even if I did, he's not going to tell anyone."

"Sarah! What do you mean, *even* if you did? Either you told him or you didn't."

"Relax, Rosie."

"So you didn't?"

"No."

"Good. Apart from Dana and Caroline you're the only person who knows. You can't say a word."

"I know! Now stop going on about it!"

They were on welfare when they won it.

Donna Lynden and Allan Taylor –
$800,000 – Australia

And they were on welfare when they lost it. With so many people coming around, looking for handouts, they were just too busy to cancel it.

In seven – seven – weeks their winnings had run out, and the couple were charged with receiving $29,000 in welfare payments.

37

It's a Sunday afternoon and Finn and I are round at Mum and Dad's. Sarah, Rod and the kids are here too. Ever since we got here, I've been on edge. This is the last place on earth I want to be and, had it been up to me, we wouldn't be here now but, through an unfortunate set of circumstances, this is where I find myself. Finn stayed over at my house last night and, while I was showering this morning, he happened to answer the phone when Mum rang to ask us to lunch. Of course, he jumped at the invitation. "Sure, we'd love to come, Mrs Kiely. We're not doing a thing today. Not a thing. We've no plans at all, none whatsoever. In fact, we were wondering earlier how we were going to spend the day. Yep, count us in for sure," he said, or some such words to that effect. Needless to say, as soon as he told me I called back to cancel but Mum was having none of it. "But, Rosie, you've nothing else on. Finn told me so." But still I protested which prompted her to play the family obligation card. "Sarah and Rod are coming too. It's a hard time for her. She needs to see that we're all there for her." When I protested further she threw down the guilt card. "God knows, Rosie, I don't ask much from you but I'm asking you to come today. It's the one thing I really want you to do for your dad and me. For Sarah."

At least I managed to warn her not to say a word to Finn about the paintings in the garage, and to tell Dad not to either. I told her that Finn would be disappointed if he knew they still hadn't been collected and, though she didn't really get why, she agreed to keep quiet. So far she and Dad haven't spilled the beans but that doesn't stop me from being seriously worried and itching to get out of here.

We've just finished an enormous lunch and now Kyle and Lachlan have gone out into the garden to play. We're on our second coffee and though I've mentioned we should think about going several times, there's no moving Finn. Away all week, he only got back last night. With the money raised from his art exhibition he and the band hired out a recording studio down in Cork plus the services of one of the best sound engineers in the business. Now, ignoring my restlessness, he's telling everyone about the experience.

"The studio really was state of the art. And the setting was amazing – this big old country house in the middle of nowhere. We were in the lap of luxury." He looks to Mum. "You'd have loved the grounds, Mrs Kiely." Then he turns to me. "Oh, and do you know what we found out? Lily Allen recorded her last album there!"

Rod laughs. "You know, Lily Allen is also the name of our next-door neighbour in Melbourne?"

"What? Is your Lily's second name really Allen?" I ask Sarah.

Sarah nods. "Funny, isn't it?"

"Does she know she has a famous namesake?" Mum asks.

"Yeah, the other Lily Allen toured Australia last year. Remember, Rod, you cut out that newspaper headline. '*Lily Allen Parties Until Dawn – Again!*' You even stuck it up on the fridge. I think our Lily was quite tickled by the idea."

"Knowing Lily, I can imagine," I laugh but immediately realise what I've just said and I look over to Finn to see if he's noticed my slip but, right at that moment, there's a distraction when a little head comes running past the window.

"Hush," says Sarah, "here comes one of the boys. I don't want him to hear us talking about Lily. It will only upset him."

Lachlan comes running in now and, boy, am I glad to see him! I was so preoccupied with the paintings in the garage I'd completely forgotten the other danger – that Sarah or someone might mention my trip to Australia. I have *got* to get Finn out of here.

"What's up, Locky?" asks Rod.

"I can't get the ball! It's rolled in under some stuff."

Rod sighs. "All right, all right, I'm coming. Can you not stay out for more than five minutes?"

But Finn gets to his feet first. "You stay there, Rod. I'll get it."

"Finn, we should really be going."

"Relax, Rosie, where's the fire? Come on, Lachlan, show me where the ball is."

And before I can think how to stop him, he's gone. "Mum, is the garage locked?"

"Of course, it's been locked ever since you put the paintings in there."

"What paintings?" asks Sarah.

"Paintings from Finn's exhibition that the buyers haven't

collected yet," Mum explains. "But just don't say anything to Finn about them or Rosie will go mad."

"But why?" Sarah asks me.

"I'll explain later. You are sure the garage is locked, Mum?"

"Yes, didn't I just say it was?"

"Actually," interrupts Dad, "I'm not sure if I did lock it after I put the lawnmower back this morning. I think I did but I just can't be a hundred per cent certain."

"Dad!"

I jump up from my seat and hurry out.

"Rosie!" I hear Mum calling after me.

Outside I see Lachlan and Kyle are already playing with their ball again so Finn was successful then, but where is he?

"Lachlan, where's Finn?" But I don't wait for an answer. "Finn!" I call out. I run around the side of the house. "Finn!"

I see the garage door wide open. Oh God! Oh no!

"Finn?" I call out tentatively and as tentatively put my head around the door hoping against hope but already I know, I just know, I'm going to find him there.

And I do. He's standing stock-still, surrounded by all his paintings. I see he's unwrapped a few of them. His back is turned to me. He doesn't look around.

How could I have been such a fool! I should have moved the paintings. I should have withstood Mum's guilt trip and never, ever have come here with Finn today. What am I going to do now? How am I going to explain this? But has he heard me? Does he even know I'm here? Could I scurry away and give myself a chance to think up some plausible explanation?

But, too late. "I came in after Lachlan's ball," says Finn suddenly, his back still to me.

I don't say anything. I don't know what *to* say. Of all the awful, filthy, rotten, bloody, bad luck!

"And look what I found! My paintings!"

"Finn – I –"

Now he finally turns around. He looks calm. *Too* calm. Before-the-storm kind of calm.

"I'm confused, Rosie. Maybe you can tell me what's going on because I sure can't figure it out. You see, I thought all these paintings had been sold but then I find them here. How is that? How can that be? Have they been sold or haven't they? If they have, then what are they doing here when you told me the purchasers had collected them the day after the exhibition? But if they haven't been sold then where did all the money that paid for the last week come from?"

"I can explain."

"Good."

But I have no idea what I'm going to say. I wish I could close my eyes, that this would all go away. The seconds tick by ever so slowly. I can feel a vein throbbing in my temple.

"So?" prompts Finn.

"Well –" What plausible explanation can I possibly give?

"Go on."

"Finn –"

"Yes?"

"You see –"

"Yes?"

"You see, CKV decided to invest in some of your paintings," I blurt out.

"CKV?"

"Yes. The way the property market is going at the moment it was decided to diversify and invest in art too."

"CKV?"

I nod.

"As in Connolly, Kiely, Vaughan?"

I nod again.

He doesn't respond immediately.

"I'm confused. You talk like CKV is some separate entity but it isn't, it's just you and Dana working for Caroline. So what you're really saying is that my girlfriend's friend bought all my paintings?"

"Not just yours – others too," I add impulsively.

"Others?" He looks around. "Where are they? Are they here? I only see mine."

"Well, she hasn't bought any others yet, but she's going to."

He doesn't look convinced but he doesn't press the matter. "Was even a single one of my paintings sold to anyone I don't know?"

"Yes, of course."

"So, other than those that Caroline bought, how many of my paintings were sold?"

"What?"

"How many were sold to other people that night?"

"I don't remember exactly."

"How many?"

"Finn –"

"How many, Rosie!"

"Seven."

"Seven? One of which was to my father, another to Fay, another to Mick, and I knew Caroline had bought one earlier on or are you including that? If you are then that leaves a total of three. Three paintings were bought by strangers. I wouldn't have thought I was egotistical but that, well, that really is a little humbling. Maybe I'm thick but I still can't work all this out. Why did you put me through all the bother, all the expense of holding an exhibition when Caroline was so interested in them?" He thinks for a moment. "It's odd that she brought one first and then decided to buy the rest. When did she decide to buy the rest?"

"Pardon?"

"When it was obvious nobody else was going to buy them?"

"No, of course not. She decided to buy them when she saw them all on display and realised how fantastic they were."

"Fantastic?"

"Yes."

"And this was after she'd bought the one she'd told me about?"

"I don't know."

"How come they're here?"

"There was the space."

"How come you didn't tell me they were here, or about any of this?"

I shrug. "I forgot." Oh God, I'm not handling this well. I've never seen Finn so mad. I wish he'd stop firing all these questions at me. I can't think.

"You forgot?"

Now he laughs but it's not a happy laugh. "I don't really understand this. You know what I've been doing since the exhibition? Whenever I've had a quiet moment, I've pictured my paintings hanging up in people's living-rooms throughout the city. I imagined people – strangers – showing theirs to friends. I imagined them telling how they'd bought theirs recently at an exhibition by an up-and-coming young artist. I feel quite foolish now. Actually, humiliated would be a better way of putting it. Here they were all along, in my girlfriend's garage after her friend bought them." Then he demands sharply "Where did she get the money to buy them?"

"The money?"

"Just tell me where it came from."

Oh God! I wish this would stop. Should I just come clean and tell him about the lotto? Could that really make things any worse? I try to think. Okay. If he's this mad over how I deceived him with regard to the exhibition, how much madder would he be if he knew the rest? Would he ever forgive me? Oh God! Maybe this just isn't the time. I need to work this out.

"Where did Caroline get the money from?"

"I told you – from the business."

"The business! Again you say that like it explains things but it explains nothing! Where did the business – where did *Caroline* – get the money?"

"From . . ."

"From?"

"From . . . from other investments."

He looks at me like I'm stark raving mad. "Let me get this straight. She's *somehow* managed to make money though she's barely been in business a wet weekend *and* at a time when the property market is in freefall. I might know nothing about property but I know that is bullshit! I don't buy it!"

He's right, of course. "No, you're wrong, Finn."

"Rosie, are you hiding something from me?"

"Like what?"

"If I knew I wouldn't be asking. Where did the money to buy my paintings come from?"

"I told you already."

He sighs. He shakes his head. He looks around at the paintings again. "You know what I'd really like to do? I'd like to get a van and take all these away but I can't. Caroline owns them now. What she paid for them financed our week's recording. I feel such a fool. I've been going around telling anyone who'll listen how successful the exhibition was."

"It was. Does it matter who bought them?"

"Of course, it matters."

And, then, out of the blue he suddenly asks, "Were you ever in Australia?"

"Pardon?"

"Were you ever in Australia? What part of the question don't you understand?"

"No, no, I wasn't."

"Then how come Mitch is under the impression you were?"

"Mitch?"

"Yes."

I'm puzzled. "I don't know."

"When we were down the country recording he happened to mention a conversation you had recently, about some indie band from Australia that you told him you'd discovered while you were there."

I can't remember any such conversation. "I haven't a clue what Mitch is talking about. He must be mixing me up with someone else."

But then I remember. A while ago, when Mitch and I were discussing bands who'd successfully used the internet to promote themselves, I mentioned a band from Australia. Did I say I'd heard of them when I was there?

Finn goes on. "I thought I'd got it wrong, that I'd misunderstood him, I'd more or less forgotten about it. But when we were talking about Lily Allen inside just now you sounded like you'd met Sarah's neighbour, that other Lily Allen."

Now I shrug as casually as I can manage. "Did I?"

"Yes!"

"I guess it was because Sarah talks about her so much."

Finn shakes his head. "No, it was more than that. You definitely gave the impression you'd met her."

He's staring at me. I don't know what to say. If I tell him I was in Australia, then what else will I have to tell him?

"But you're not going to tell me the truth, no more than you're going to tell me where the money to buy these paintings came from. Well then, fine. Don't. Treat me like an idiot. Have your secrets. I don't know what's going on, but something definitely is. I just hope for your sake it's not illegal."

"I swear it's not, Finn!"

"So something is going on?"

"No, no, it's not."

"Have it your way. I just wish you and Caroline had stayed out of my affairs. It might have taken a little longer but we'd have raised the money ourselves somehow, in our own time." He brushes past me. "See you around, Rosie."

"Finn! Come back! Please!"

But Finn didn't leave immediately as I find out when I finally pull myself together and leave the garage and go back into the house.

Everyone – bar Finn of course – is still sitting around.

"What's going on with you and Finn?" asks Mum. "How come he had to leave so suddenly?"

"Sorry about that. He had – um – things to do."

"So he said."

"Why is he so interested in our neighbour Lily all of a

sudden?" asks Sarah. "Before he went he asked had you ever met her?"

"And what did you say?"

"I told him you had, when you visited."

Damn! I should have thought to warn Sarah not to say anything about me and Australia before I went out to find Finn but I was in such a state.

The house is empty when I get home and I sit down at the kitchen table and try to figure things out. There are three parts to this problem with Finn, or even three separate problems. One, how to make him feel okay about the fact that CKV bought his paintings. Two, to give him an explanation he can accept as to how Caroline came up with the money. Three, how to explain why I went to Australia and never told him. Even though I don't have a solution to any of these, I almost ring him several times but I stop myself. What can I say that won't make matters worse? I consider calling over to his house but I put that off too. Again, if – when – he asks questions I just don't know what answers I would give. Maybe I'd end up blurting out the truth but would now – when he's already so mad – really be the right time to do that?

But if I don't tell him now, are things just going to keep on getting more and more complicated? Am I prepared never to tell him? Can I really live for the rest of my life like this, always having secrets? I'm not sure that I can.

But, in the end, the decision is taken out of my hands when our house of cards comes crashing down around us so suddenly.

What do you do when the shop assistant mistakenly sells you a ticket for the wrong draw?

Pamela Fitch – $1 million – US

Fitch was about to ask for an exchange but changed her mind and decided to keep it. It was the best mistake of her life.

38

The following morning started out in a normal fashion, a usual sort of morning really, nothing to indicate what lay ahead. Caroline, Dana and I were having breakfast, the usual – bowls of cereal. The radio was on in the background but nobody was paying it much attention but neither were we talking much. Caroline was reading a newspaper, Dana was going over some notes from college and, my mind was still on Finn and how I could sort all that out. I hadn't told the others for the simple reason I didn't want to be confused by what they thought, or persuaded to do what they felt I should do. This time I wanted to figure it out myself. On my own.

Anyway, I'd a fair idea what advice they'd give without even asking. Led by Caroline, they'd probably tell me to stick to my story as regards the paintings. And, as for Australia, it was likely they'd tell me to invent some plausible reason for my visit. To say, perhaps, that I flew out on a mercy mission at Sarah's behest because of her marital problems and, because Sarah didn't want Mum knowing, I'd been sworn to secrecy. Something along those lines.

So, apart from my preoccupation, a regular enough morning. But then Shane came down for breakfast.

"Morning."

"Oh hi," says Caroline looking up from her paper.

"Hi, Shane," echoes Dana. "I didn't know you were still here. How come you haven't gone to work yet?"

"I arranged not to go in until ten. I figured I'd need a late start after the wedding."

"Oh yeah, I forgot you were at a wedding this weekend," said Dana. "How did it go? Did you and Loretta have a good time?"

"Brilliant. It was fantastic."

"Remind me who was getting married?" asks Dana.

"An old classmate of mine."

"Was it a late night?" Caroline wants to know.

Shane laughs. "Early morning, you mean."

"What was the bride like?" asks Dana.

"Oh you know, big white dress, veil, shoes, et cetera, et cetera."

"Ah, Shane!" groans Dana.

"What?"

"Et cetera, et cetera! Can't you do any better than that? Was she beautiful?"

"Yes, of course, she was. Aren't all brides?"

He takes a couple of slices of bread from the bread bin and puts them into the toaster, then puts the kettle on to boil. Caroline returns to her newspaper and Dana to her bowl of cereal. But I notice Shane is just standing there, leaning with his back to the counter and he seems to be eyeing us up somewhat curiously.

"What?" I ask.

"What, what?"

"Why are you looking at us like that?"

"Like what?"

"I don't know exactly. Like you're trying to figure something out?"

He shrugs. "I'm just waiting for my toast to pop."

But despite what he says, there does seem to be something on his mind and, as I go on with my cereal, I can feel his interest.

Then, just as I'm about to ask him again what *is* up with him, he suddenly announces:

"I met a mutual acquaintance at the wedding."

"Of mine?" I ask.

"Of all of you. Tom Redmond?"

"Tom Redmond? Oh, Tom Redmond. Is that right?" I glance over at Dana. She suddenly looks as uneasy as I feel. I glance at Caroline. She's managing to look completely unconcerned.

"He tells me he's working for you now."

"Tom Redmond? Yes, he has done a few bits and pieces," answers Caroline.

"Bits and pieces." Shane mulls this over. "So he said. I have to say I was taken aback when he told me. Not least because most solicitors don't go around divulging the names of their clients quite so freely."

"He shouldn't have," says Caroline. "I'm surprised."

"Are you? Knowing Redmond from his college days I guess I wasn't. But then you knew him too. And here's what I do find surprising, that you took him on. You must remember what he was like?"

"Sure, he was wild back then but he has his own firm now."

"True. But it's only by the skin of his teeth he's still

practising. You do know he's been up before the Solicitors Disciplinary Tribunal?"

"Really?"

"Yes. More than once. And also he's not even based in Dublin – that can't be convenient for you. Can I ask why you hired him?"

"I don't exactly remember now. I think someone recommended him," says Caroline.

"I can't imagine who. If you were looking for a solicitor, why didn't you ask me? I could have given you the names of any number of good people."

"We didn't think of that."

Shane's toast pops and he turns and takes it from the toaster. His back is to us now as he butters it and we all look to each other. I guess we're all wondering the same – just how much Redmond has told Shane. Poor Dana looks very worried.

"Does anyone else want tea or coffee?" Shane asks, looking over his shoulder.

We all shake our heads and tell him we don't.

Shane takes his cup and his plate and joins us at the table. He picks up a section of Caroline's paper. I relax a little. I breathe out. I realise I've been holding my breath, waiting in case there's more. But maybe that's all there is. But then, Shane puts the paper down again.

"One other thing. Tom was always a drinker, you may remember that. And nothing's changed there. And the thing about Tom is that drink loosens his tongue. To be honest, I think you might be better off changing to another solicitor."

"Why?" asks Caroline evenly. "What exactly did he say to you?"

Shane doesn't answer immediately. He picks his cup up

and takes a sip. He looks from me, to Caroline, to Dana. When he does respond, he ignores Caroline's question. "Like I say, he's neither reliable nor discreet and nobody wants a solicitor like that . . ." now he drains his tea in one long swallow ". . . even when there's nothing to hide." He stands up and picks up his slices of toast to go. "Anyway, I'd better be off if I want to be in time for my first appointment. See you later."

"Shane!" Caroline calls after him, but he's gone.

"Oh, my God," says Dana quietly. "He knows."

"Knows what exactly?" demands Caroline.

"He probably knows everything. All our business. That we're buying up properties. That we're giving away money. That . . . that we've won the lotto!"

"Get a grip, Dana. How could he? Redmond doesn't even know. He thinks we're self-made millionaires."

"Yes, and if Redmond has said as much to Shane, Shane will be asking where those self-made millions came from."

"And so? Even if he does, we don't have to tell him anything. Deny. Deny. Deny. If we have to, we'll just say that Redmond has foolishly overestimated or misunderstood how much money we have. Dana, Shane will believe that – he thinks Redmond is a fool."

Dana is quiet for a moment, and then: "Do you think it's never come to his notice how the pair of you have been throwing money around like confetti these past months? What do you think he thinks when he looks around this house? When he listens to that state-of-the-art sound system? Or passes by those exercise machines in the hall that haven't yet been taken out of their cardboard boxes? Or when he switches on that whopper of a TV in the living-room? Or says hello to Yvonne as she goes about the place with that brand-new Dyson? Or when he trips over the shopping bags full of clothes that Rosie hasn't yet even hung in her wardrobe because there simply isn't any room? Or when he opens the door to the DSL guy as he delivers yet another parcel – another BlackBerry, another laptop, another digital camera that contribute further to the electronic gadgetry that now litters this place. Can you not see how – little by little – things have changed? Do you not think he sees that?"

"Look –" begins Caroline.

"And that's just the little stuff."

"– look, Dana, all Shane actually knows for definite is that Tom Redmond is our solicitor. That's all."

Dana doesn't look convinced. And I'm not sure I am either. But just then we hear a noise in the hall.

Dana's eyes open wide in horror. "Is he still here?" she demands. "Did either of you actually hear him leaving the house?"

And then he's back again. He doesn't come into the kitchen, but just stands in the doorway. His expression is neutral, there's no knowing what he's heard, or how much.

"One other thing. Redmond mentioned you were buying – amongst many other properties he's negotiating for you – this house. I presume he's talking nonsense. You'd hardly do something like that without telling me. After all, we are meant to be friends."

"Shane –" Caroline begins.

"I've got to go now – I'm already late. Will you all be in later this evening?"

"Ah – yeah," says Caroline hesitantly.

"Good, maybe we can talk then."

"Shane –" calls Dana, but he's gone.

Caroline looks to Dana. "Well, if he knows it'll be because of you!"

"Look —" Dana begins defensively but Caroline ignores her.

"Okay, there's no point in speculating. We need to talk to Redmond."

Immediately she tries Tom Redmond's mobile and Dana and I sit there anxiously waiting.

"He's not answering," Caroline tells us. "I'll try his office."

Caroline makes another call and gets through to his secretary and we listen to her side of the conversation and, when she hangs up, Caroline tells us the full extent of it. "She says he's preparing for court so he's not taking calls but she's going to get him to ring us back as soon as she hears from him."

"When does she think that will be?" asks Dana.

"She expects sometime this morning"

Just then, Caroline's phone beeps. She looks at it. "It's from Tom Redmond. She reads it out to us: 'Got your call. Can't talk right now. Am in Dublin on High Court business. Am keen to meet up.'"

"Why is he so anxious to meet all of a sudden?" worries Dana. "Maybe he's concerned about what he let slip to Shane. Or maybe he knows too."

"Of course, he doesn't!" insists Caroline.

I see she's already texting him back. "What are you saying?" I ask.

"I'm asking can he meet us as soon as he's finished."

Almost immediately she gets a response. "He figures he can meet us in an hour. He's suggesting a coffee shop around the corner from the courthouse." She begins texting again. "I'm telling him we're going straight there to wait for him." Then she stands up. "I'll drive. Go and get your coats."

But now the doorbell rings.

"Oh, for crying out loud! What now!" mutters Caroline.

Dana goes to answer it and, moments later, she comes back in with just about the last person in the world I might expect to see following behind her – Rod.

"Rosie, there's someone here to see you."

"Hi, Rod!" I say, no doubt sounding as surprised as I am.

"Hi, Rosie," he answers jovially, and as if his sudden appearance here this morning is the most normal thing in the world, as if he calls around like this all the time. "Sorry to drop by like this but I was wondering if we could talk."

"Well, we are on the way out."

"It's about Sarah."

"Oh!"

I look to the others.

"Why don't you get a taxi and follow us in?" suggests Caroline.

"Are you sure?"

"Of course."

As soon as they're gone, I turn to Rod to find him just standing there, staring coldly at me. "Would you like a tea or a coffee?" I fluster.

"Neither, you're in a hurry and what I have to say won't take long."

But I could do with a quick shot of strong coffee. I put the kettle on and I stand by it waiting impatiently for it to boil. I'm not in the mood for chat. I really have nothing to say to Rod, I just want to know what he has to say yet he doesn't seem in any hurry. I make my coffee, take a sip, then ask,

"So you came to talk about Sarah?"

"Yes. Amongst other things."

Another pause.

"What about her?"

"She tells me you've been very good to her."

"Does she?"

"Yes. In all sorts of ways."

I shrug. "I've only done what I can to help her out."

"No, no, you've gone way beyond what anyone could expect. If it wasn't for you she'd never manage. She'd probably have to come home with me. But, then, I guess you must be delighted to have her here."

"Yes, I am."

"You certainly did a lot to bring it about."

"I don't think I brought it about. It was her own choice. It's not like I'm making her stay here."

"You never liked me, did you, Rosie?"

I'm taken aback by this abrupt change. "Like you? I hardly know you."

"No, I guess you don't. We never really had the opportunity to get to know one another. What can I tell you now about myself so that you'll understand me a little better?"

What makes him think I want to understand him any better? "I'm sorry, Rod, but could you just tell me what the problem is – why you're here?"

But he ignores me. "Let me see. Well, the first thing you should understand is that I love Sarah and the kids."

I give a disbelieving grunt.

"I do, you know. As families go, I couldn't have done better. Three clever, handsome, lovely sons, a beautiful, adoring wife. The perfect family. But the problem is, the whole family thing, well, it's just not for me. Shocking maybe but I am who I am. I can't change facts. Don't get me wrong, I do love them but the family situation just doesn't suit me."

"It's a pity you didn't realise that a little earlier."

"Hmm. I hear what you're saying and you have a point. But life has a way of shoving us along in a particular direction without us realising until it's too late."

"And just when did you realise that? When you were standing at the altar? Or on the way to the hospital for the birth of your first baby? Or your second? Or your third?"

"Probably the first – or even more so the weeks that followed. You'd never think it now but Lachlan was a terribly difficult baby. But you know Sarah – that didn't put her off wanting more children. All she ever wanted was her own happy family and I could never say no to her."

"You did in the end. You gave her the happy family she wanted, then you turned around and said, 'Ah no, actually I don't want this,' and so you blew it all apart."

"I can see how it might look like that from the outside."

"Why? Because that's how it is?"

"She wants to come home, you know."

"She *is* home."

"No, I mean home to Australia with me. Deep down that's what she really wants. You know, the thing about Sarah is she's an optimist. Despite all the evidence to the contrary she still thinks we can work things out. But me? I'm a realist. I know it wouldn't work. Still, I don't like the idea of my family being so far away. It's quite a quandary for me really. What do I do? Tell her to come home even if I know things won't work out between us? Or do the right thing, encourage her to stay here – where she has the help and support of all of you?"

"You really think a lot of yourself, don't you? You think her decision is entirely dependent on what you say."

"I know so. I've been married long enough to her. I know her inside out. I know she'd do anything if she thought she could have us all back together again."

"And so, what? You're going to ask her to come home with you?"

He doesn't answer immediately. He just stands there, eyeing me up coolly. "Well," he says finally, "that rather depends on you, Rosie."

"What?"

"Like I said you've done everything you can for her. The air fares, the house, the nanny fees."

"Excuse me. I —"

"So perhaps you might consider doing one last thing for her?"

"Pardon?"

"She's told me about your good luck."

"What good luck?" I ask, but I know. Sarah's told him. What an idiot I've been!

Rod laughs. He's enjoying this. "Ooops, she'll kill me — she warned me not to say a thing."

"I'm sorry, Rod. I don't know what you're talking about."

"You know exactly what I'm taking about. You think Sarah could ever keep something that big from me? You're just her sister; I'm her husband. You may not know me so well but I don't think you know Sarah that well either otherwise you'd know that she could never keep a secret, at least not from me. And the other thing you don't know about Sarah is how she feels about me. She adores the ground I walk on. Always has. That's why she put up with all my faults, tried to see the best in me, to see the best in her situation. Any sane woman would have left long ago but not my faithful, loving Sarah. Not my loyal little Labrador."

"Don't you talk about her like that!"

He ignores my interruption. "But like I said, you don't know her but then how could you? You were only a kid when she moved to Australia. But I'm not an unreasonable man. In fact, I like to think I'm very reasonable. Like you, I think staying here is the best thing for Sarah and the boys in the long run. If she comes back to Australia then think how isolated she'll be. Especially if – or when rather – she has to bring up the kids on her own, for that's what will happen. Like I say, I'm a realist. I know what the outcome will be no matter how she might like to think otherwise. I might try for a while to make things work but, in the end, I'll leave them again. But I do love my kids, and Sarah too, and I can see staying here is the best option for them."

"Good."

"Even if it's not for me. I might not want to live with them but I would like to see them regularly – giving up that opportunity would be a real hardship. So, here's what I was thinking: you could make things a little easier for me."

"What are you saying exactly?"

"What I'm saying exactly, Rosie, is a quarter of a million euros."

"You want me to give you a quarter of a million euros?"

"Yes. In the circumstances, I don't think that's unreasonable. And don't worry. I wouldn't tell anyone. Your secret would be safe with me."

"You want me to give you a quarter of a million?"

"Yes. You get to have your sister near you. She gets to have her parents and you nearby and, for doing what's right

by them, for making such a big sacrifice, I get a little
monetary compensation to ease my loss. Plus the money
would allow me to travel back and forth and see them when
I want. You wouldn't like your nephews growing up without
ever knowing their father, now would you? Not when you
have the means to make sure that doesn't happen."

"You're disgusting!"

"Pardon?"

"You're practically selling your family!"

"Oh, what a crude way to put it. I don't see it like that.
The way I see it is I'm making a big sacrifice for their
benefit. Really it's a win-win situation for everyone. What's
not to like about that?"

"Get out!"

"I didn't expect you to say yes straight away. Take your
time. Get used to the idea."

"I don't need to get used to the idea. The answer is no!"

"Now, now, Rosie, I think you're being a little hasty. You
really need to −"

"Excuse me! Are you deaf? I said no! No! No! No!"

"Rosie, I think you should consid −"

"And the answer will always be no! Understand? Now
this conversation is finished − get the hell out of my house!"

"Rosie, I'm warning you −"

"You lowlife scumbag!"

"Don't you get it, Rosie? I mean it when I −"

"Just get out!"

I'm left reeling when he's gone. I sit at the table not quite
believing what's just happened. I could kill him. I'm so angry.
I could kill Sarah. Why did she have to tell him? I was so
stupid to trust her! What the hell am I going to do now?
Should I tell her about Rod's visit? Would Sarah even believe

me? Would she think I was making it up? If I say anything he's sure to deny it. When it comes to believing me or Rod, who would Sarah choose? I've a worrying feeling it would be Rod and then, how would that leave things between me and her?

My phone rings. Oh God! What now? What fresh hell is this? I look to see who it is. But it's only Caroline.

"Rosie, Tom Redmond sent a text to say he'll be here in five minutes. You need to get down here."

"No. I can't."

"What? Is it Sarah?"

"Yes and no."

"Rosie, I don't have time for —"

"We have another problem."

"What?"

"Rod knows."

"Knows what?"

He knows about the money."

"Jeez, Rosie! How? Did you tell him?"

"No, of course not!"

"Well then, how does he know?"

"I told Sarah — a while ago, and she's after telling him."

"*Rosie!*"

"I'm sorry! There's worse. He wants . . . well, you can guess."

"What? He wants what?"

"Money!"

"You're kidding!"

"You think?"

"How much?"

"A quarter of a million. If I give it to him he'll go back to Australia and leave Sarah and the boys here. If I don't then he says he'll persuade Sarah to come back with him."

"But she wouldn't!"

"I think she would."

"Not if you told her everything."

"Even if I did I don't think she'd believe me."

"Okay, stay there. I see Tom Redmond's just arrived. I'll find out everything he said to Shane and then we'll come straight back to you and we'll all sit down and talk everything through."

"Maybe I should call around to Sarah, talk to her."

"No! Stay where you are. Don't do anything yet."

I look at the clock on the wall. Where are they? It's been over an hour. This is crazy! But then my phone rings again and I pick it up thinking it's them, ringing so explain what's keeping them or to say that they're nearly here but, then, I see it's Mum's number. I answer it.

"Hi, Rosie. Has Sarah been on to you?"

"No."

My mother takes a sharp intake of breath and even before she utters another word I know, I just know, exactly what she's going to tell me.

"She's just rung me. She's decided she's going to go back to Australia with Rod."

"Oh."

"I guess it's for the best."

I don't answer straightaway. Maybe he's bluffing. But maybe he isn't.

"Rosie, are you still there?"

"How, Mum? Tell me how it is for the best."

"Rosie, please! Sarah said you'd react like this. Of course, you're disappointed she won't be around any more, we all are. But if there's a chance she and Rod can work things out, then she's right to go home."

"But Mum, you don't know what Rod is like!"

"Rosie, Rod is your brother-in-law – don't talk about him like that."

"Mum, really you have no –"

"Rosie! Stop! I know you're disappointed, but you have to understand that it's for the best!"

"But that's the thing, it's not for the best. Rod is –"

"Rosie, I really don't have time for your theatrics!"

"Mum, can't you just listen to me?"

"And you listen to me! It's good that Sarah and Rod and the boys will be back together again and –"

"But it's not!"

"Okay, Rosie, I'm not listening any more. You really need to grow up. I'm going to hang up now!"

"Mum!"

The phone goes dead.

The chance of being killed in the bathtub is five times greater than that of winning the Irish National Lottery.

39

Okay, things were falling down around us but maybe we'd have been able to sort them out but, when the final card fell onto the table, I lost the will to even try.

And so, the final card:

Ten minutes after Mum's phone call, I hear a car pulling up and hurry to the front door assuming it's Caroline and Dana but it's not. What I do see is an unfamiliar car parked on the road outside. When a man climbs out I recognise him as Caroline's brother, Donald.

"Hi, Rosie,"

"Oh, hi, Donald."

Like Caroline and her father too, Donald is a larger-than-life character but now I can't help noticing that he seems unusually downbeat. I wonder what's wrong. I wonder what he's doing here.

"Caroline isn't here, Donald," I tell him as he walks up the path towards me.

Maybe it's something to do with the sale of this house but then he doesn't know it's us trying to buy it from him.

Maybe he's found out. It wouldn't surprise me, given all that has gone on today.

"Actually it's you I've come to see, Rosie."

"Oh?"

"Part of the roof collapsed on one of my buildings."

I'm staring at him, trying to figure just why he's telling me this. I know Caroline says he's been under a huge strain lately. He has so many businesses and they're not doing as well as they were. Has he simply cracked up?

"It fell into the building."

I'm still staring at him blankly. He sees I'm not following him.

"Remember you were asking me about that guy who was squatting in the building I own down in Wicklow. It was that building."

Realisation suddenly dawns. "Oh, no!"

"They found a body. A young man."

"Oh, no."

"It's the man you've been looking for."

"How do you know?"

"Seán Blake?"

I nod but find I can't answer.

"His mother identified him."

"His mother? But she's a dope-head. She could hardly identify herself. As far as I know she hasn't seen Seán in years."

"Rosie, they also used dental records They're absolutely sure."

I try to make sense of this but I can't. "I don't believe you!"

"I'm sorry to have to tell you."

"But it was all boarded up. I went down myself to check. No one could get in. You said so yourself "

"I was wrong. He may have been living there for some time. We think he managed to lever off a sheet of wood covering one of the windows on the second floor but he always replaced it carefully so the place always looked undisturbed. The security firm I employed never noticed – bloody fools. I figure he used to climb up on to one of the flat roofs to get in – don't ask me how exactly. It's quite a way up. And there was never any sign of him inside, he never left his gear around. Nobody ever suspected he was using the place. He always left things in order."

After Donald leaves, I go back inside and sit down once again at the kitchen table. I think of how my plan to help Seán has come to nothing. Now it's too late. Bloody hell! Life is so bloody unfair! He's so young and now he's dead. And those two little girls are left without mother or father. How crap is that! It puts all my stupid problems in perspective. I hear the front door open. I hear Caroline and Dana talking as they come down the hall though I can't hear what they're saying. They come into the kitchen.

"Sorry we were so long but you won't believe this! All the time we were worried about Shane figuring things out after he'd had that conversation with Tom Redmond at the wedding and we barely even considered that it might happen the other way around but it has. Redmond has worked everything out. It seems Shane told him the only business we'd ever been involved in was our shop and how that folded, and it got Redmond thinking. He did some snooping. He figured out where the money came from. He even pinpointed the weekend we won – there has been only one large prize paid out anonymously in the Dublin area in the last few months. Seems he isn't so thick after all." Caroline goes on and on but I hardly hear her. "Of course, he says he's not going to tell anyone. First your brother-in-law and now Tom Redmond. We're going to have to sit down and –"

But then Dana notices.

"Oh, Rosie, don't cry. We'll figure some –"

"Who cares about any of that?" I interrupt.

But Caroline doesn't hear what I say.

"We told Tom Redmond he was crazy! That he was talking nonsense."

"I *don't* care! At all! Can't you hear me? What does it matter?"

"Rosie, come on. Look –"

"Seán is dead!"

Both of them stare at me.

"Your Seán?"

"Yes."

"Oh, Rosie!"

"But how?" asks Caroline.

"He was squatting in that derelict youth hostel Donald has in Wicklow. The roof collapsed in on him."

"Oh, God!"

I stand up. "You know, I've had enough of all this, this stupid pretence. Keeping our win a secret is idiotic. I want to come clean with everyone. I'm sick of all the lies. We should be sharing our win, enjoying it, not doling it out meanly when and where we see fit. We're at odds with almost everyone. Finn isn't talking to me because of those paintings – I didn't tell you but he found them in my parents' garage. Rod is trying to blackmail me. And look at you, Dana – you're barely talking to Doug. As for your mum, she's never been happier or more engaged since she started looking after Cathy – where's the need to keep it from her any longer? And you – you – Caroline didn't want to go public because of your dad but you've given him what he wants anyway. And Mick is your husband, Caroline! Half of your money belongs to him. What gives you the right to keep it? You know, I don't care what you want to do but I'm not having any more pretence." I think of Seán again. "Life is too precious and too bloody short!"

One year later . . .

When I get out of the car, I breathe in deeply and catch the smell of the sea on the breeze.

"What a peach of a day," Finn murmurs, coming around to my side.

"Just perfect."

"Are you happy?" he asks.

"Very."

"Good."

He takes my hand in both of his, brings it to his lips and kisses it.

"Rosie! Finn! Over here!" Our tender moment is sharply interrupted.

I look over to the crowd already seated in chairs laid out in rows and spot Mum towards the front, with Dad sitting alongside her. Both of them are looking in our direction, big smiles on their faces, and she's frantically beckoning us over with one hand while holding onto her hat with the other.

"Wow! That's some hat!" laughs Finn.

It is enormous and quite probably a little-over-the-top for the occasion but, then, what do I know? I've never been to something like this before. Anyway, it suits her. She looks fabulous. Fabulously over-the-top.

"Come on." I take Finn's hand and we cross the carpark, go along the gravel path, and over the grass to where Mum and Dad are sitting.

"Hi there, you got here in good time."

"Of course." Mum is smiling. She looks so happy. "You know, in the car on the way down your dad was saying that this is one of the proudest days of his life, weren't you, Will?"

"I most certainly was," Dad says, ever so proudly.

Damn! I told myself I wasn't going to cry today but already I can feel my resolve wavering and we've only just got here. I'll have to do better than this. I try to remember: did I put that packet of tissues in my handbag? I think so. I hope so. In any case, Caroline probably has some – her emotions are all over the place these days.

"Is Sarah here?" I ask.

"She should be, or else very nearly. She rang when she was leaving."

I notice Mum is unsubtly giving my dress the once-over.

"Like it?" I ask.

She nods. "Gorgeous. I won't even ask how much it cost you."

"Best not. I wouldn't like to shock you!"

"Oh, Rosie!" But it's an indulgent, 'Oh, Rosie!'

"I see," says Dad to Finn, "you've managed to drag yourself away from your easel."

Finn laughs. "Well, I do have to take a break every now and then."

By his presence at my side today, you'll have figured that Finn – eventually – forgave me for that whole business with the exhibition and its messy aftermath. My confession to him about our lotto win certainly didn't help. If anything it set us back even further, so far back I feared we'd gone beyond the point of no return. That I had kept something so big from him, that I was *capable* of keeping something so big really bothered him. There were – as Dana, or indeed Doug might say – trust issues. But all has finally been forgiven.

What helped in part, I think, was how well everything worked out for Finn. It put him in more of a forgiving mood than he might otherwise have been. You see, as luck would have it, one of the few paintings purchased by a stranger at Finn's exhibition was bought by a fan whose father just so happened to be the owner of a major gallery in town. When this man saw the painting, he was so impressed he contacted Finn and asked to see the rest. Since Finn no longer owned most of his work, he put the man onto me and when we met up I brought Caroline to help in the negotiations, i.e. to broker the best possible price. Anyway, the man ended up buying a dozen for his gallery on the spot and, ever since, there's been a constant demand for them. A stroke of luck for sure but then, don't we all depend upon that in life? So Finn's art has taken off and his music will too one day. I'm sure. *Dove* are still playing to loyal and full houses every weekend, steadily building upon their fan base. They haven't managed to attract the interest of any big record company yet but it's just a matter of time. I'm sure. They just need another lucky break.

"So," says Mum looking around, "where are all the others?"

"Dana and Doug should be here somewhere. They left before us. Look, there they are." I point to the far side of the crowd.

Mum stares. "What? Is that really Doug? Since when did he start wearing glasses?"

"About six months ago."

"Hmm," says Mum approvingly. "You know, they suit him. He looks very scholarly indeed. I like the beard too. And Dana's looking absolutely lovely."

I have to agree. She's all dressed up today but on a normal day she still wears sweaters and jeans that are years old. Ages ago, Caroline said that Dana was probably one of those rare people who'd remain unchanged by her lotto win and it's true. She's still taking the bus to college. She still prepares a packed lunch each morning.

But one thing that has changed is her attitude to Doug. When Doug learned it was Dana who was paying for his education, and not a dead teacher who'd held him in high regard, he had a serious wobble of self-confidence. But, by then, it was obvious to Dana that Doug was made for his studies and, instead of worrying about how he was outshining her, she suddenly found she had to convince him that he really was up to it and to not chuck it all in as he was threatening to do. So, with her encouragement, he stuck at the books and – no surprise! no surprise! – came top in his exams. It wasn't long after that he started wearing glasses. He's now halfway through the first year of his degree course and loving every minute of it.

"Are they Dana's parents sitting alongside her?"

"Yep. And that's her little sister, Cathy, on Mrs Vaughan's lap."

"The father's love-child?"

"Mum!"

"The autistic girl?"

I sigh at her description. "You mean she *has* autism."

"Isn't that what I just said? Is her mother here?"

"Mrs Vaughan may have taken Cathy to her heart but there are limits."

Mum looks over at Mrs Vaughan contemplatively. "I'm not sure I could be so big-hearted if I found myself in her situation."

"You're safe enough, Nora," mutters Dad.

"And tell me, do you know who that man over there is? Yes, there."

"Oh, that's my dad," Finn tells Mum.

"Well, there's no denying you're related. That's for sure."

"And that's Fay," I tell her.

"My! So it is. I'd hardly recognise her. Doesn't she look fabulous?" says Mum.

They both see us looking and give a wave. "I told you they got engaged, didn't I?"

Now Mum is waving at them too. "Such a lovely couple. And, Rosie, who's that very distinguished gentleman sitting in the row behind?"

I look. "Eddie Connolly, Caroline's dad."

"Oh, the Heel-to-Flat-to-Heel man. You know, I'm wearing a pair right now – they're marvellous."

Yes, Mr Connolly's invention is doing fantastically well. One of the big shoe manufacturers is using it. I even have a couple of pairs myself but then, who hasn't?

"And is that his wife?" asks Mum.

I nod.

Mum is silent for a moment. I can see her eyes scanning over every showy detail of Vivienne's appearance – the brassy blonde hair, the heavy make-up, the necklace of colourful beads the size of golf balls nestling in her ample cleavage.

"Hmm, she is *very* young for him, isn't she?" says Mum, not even attempting to keep the disapproval from her voice. But then her tone softens when she notices the pram parked alongside Vivienne's seat. "Ahh, look, she has the baby with her! You must bring me over to them later. Tell me again, is it a boy or a girl?"

"A boy."

"What did they call him?"

"Triton."

"What?" My dad's ears prick up. "After the shower people?"

"No! After the son of the Greek god of the sea."

Dad raises his eyes to heaven. "Like anyone is going to know that? They hear Triton; they'll think showers. Poor little fellow."

That 'poor little fellow' is Caroline's half-brother born just over a month ago. And does it bother Caroline? Actually no, she isn't at all put out, nor is she put out by the fact that her own child is going to be a few months younger than his Uncle Triton. That's right too. Caroline is pregnant. I don't think it was planned, I *know* it wasn't planned but Caroline is very pleased. We'd never have suspected it – nor did she, I imagine – but it turns out she has a very strong maternal streak. Happily too Caroline has seen sense and is back with Mick so the child will be born with parents who are still married to one another.

Caroline likes to say her pregnancy is the reason she dropped her plans to divorce Mick but we all know that's a big fat lie. The evidence is plain to see – relations were on a better footing even before that – or how else would the baby have been conceived?

As far as I can work out, things started improving between them when Caroline called around to tell Mick she had 1.8 million euros that belonged to him. A lot to most people, even Mick, but what meant more to him was the fact that she was prepared to give it to him. Of course, those pesky trust issues raised their tedious heads once again, but, those aside, Mick, somewhat amazingly and to his credit (or in this case not), held the same opinion as Caroline: that one day's marriage did not merit such a whopper of a payout. So, while Caroline went there with a cheque, all he took was her affection back again. His only real interest was in her, of course, as always. For some people there's no escaping their fate no matter how they might mess up along the way or thwart it at every turn. Mick and Caroline were always meant to be. Any one of us could have told her that – did tell her – even if she didn't always listen.

But don't think for a moment Caroline is sitting at home, a box of chocolates resting on her pregnant belly as she watches *Home and Away*, nostalgically thinking back on the good parts of her trip down under. This is Caroline we're talking about. Despite her encumbered state and – hankies aside or even included – Caroline's become more herself than ever – and the lotto money has allowed that to happen. Dana's and my input into CKV is purely monetary now. We leave all the running of it in Caroline's capable hands and she's enjoying every minute of it. True, she hasn't started turning a profit for us yet but we are in the fortunate position of being able to wait out this current slump; she – we, at her direction – are in the property game for the long-term. Amongst other deals, she has managed to buy all the rest of Church View, that inner city terrace. Their location means they're easy to rent out now we've carried out all necessary repairs and, though there's an income from them and our other properties, that's not where Caroline expects the real money is going to come from. She put in for planning and has got permission to build a block of twenty-eight good-sized quality apartments on the footprint of Church View. Caroline's not planning to build them any time soon – there's not the demand right now but she figures the day will come when the market improves again and she'll be there, ready and waiting.

It helps too that she, we, have a good solicitor now, someone we can trust, someone who looks out for us – Shane, of course. Tom Redmond has bit the dust – all we've heard about him since is that, once again, he's been up before that disciplinary tribunal. Despite our fears, Shane hadn't worked out that we were lotto millionaires and happily he wasn't put out when we told him. Well, okay, yes, he was at first. Trust issues again. But the three-week Caribbean holiday we bought him and Loretta as a softener before we told him acted as just that. He's still living with us in the house we now own, and paying rent too – we're a little more savvy these days and times are a little tighter but what he pays to us he gets back and much more besides in the fees we pay him. When I say he's living with us, I mean with Dana and me. Caroline has moved in with Mick in the beautiful house he bought up in County Meath. Mick's career is really going from strength to strength – but whatever it is – hormones, renewed confidence, maturity – Caroline is happy to enjoy Mick's success. Bask in it even.

I found the cheque from my old colleagues in SciÉire in an old handbag the other day, the cheque they gave me on my last day there. I'd forgotten all about it but I took it into town to have it framed. It's a reminder. A reminder of just how lucky I am. In any case, I could never have cashed it in. It would have been wrong. SciÉire folded a few months back, leaving everyone out of a job. If I could give them all their jobs back I would, but I can't. What I did do was have Shane send an anonymous bank draft to every single person who worked there – everyone, all one-hundred-and-seven – even those I'd never so much as bumped into in the lift. € 1,000 isn't going to dramatically change their lives or turn their fortunes around, but it will, I hope, give them a little boost *and* also something to talk about when they meet up. There's no way they'll ever work out it came from me.

Of course, any journalist with the slightest bit of interest could figure out our win but we're old news now. Others have won the lotto since, and bigger amounts too. Nobody is interested any more and that suits us just fine.

Given the plight of my old colleagues, I do understand that it's a privilege not to have to worry about how we're going to pay the bills but perhaps, corny as it may seem, money isn't the only valuable thing we gained from our win. Having said that, the syndicate is going strong. We stopped it for a while but it's up and running again. Shane has even deigned to be in it – actually it was his idea. I think he hopes some of our good luck might rub off on him, and on Loretta, Doug, Mick, Finn, Mitch and Ashley too – they're all in it this time. Shane still thinks it's a tax on morons, but sometimes, as he says, even morons get lucky. His little joke, I think.

Pending their long-term development, Sarah is still living in the house in Church View – rent-free, despite her protests. But I have managed to persuade her to let me help her buy a new house and she's looking around for something suitable.

When I told Mum about the win I also told her about Rod and his attempt to bribe me and then, with her to support me, I went to break the news to Sarah. Understandably Sarah found it hard to comprehend at first but I think she's come to terms with it now. I know the boys talk to Rod on the phone all the time – no surprise he went back to Australia. Once I might have said good riddance to bad rubbish but I understand that the rubbish in question was the love of Sarah's life and I think I have an idea of how much he and the end of their marriage broke her heart. I am just full of admiration of how she's making a new life for herself and the boys here.

After our win, Caroline just became more resolutely herself. Dana didn't change a bit so, of the three of us, I think our win changed me the most, or allowed me to change the most. Yes, it turned me into a shopping addict for a while. But you know, there really is a limit to how many shoes one person can wear and, after a time, shopping just becomes monotonous. And life was boring when everyone else – Caroline, Mick, Finn, Doug, Dana, Shane, Loretta – were all so engaged in their own lives.

Of course, Mum was pleased for me when I did tell her but I think she was worried I'd never bother working again when I didn't need to, that I'd never find my own niche in life. I can see where her worries stemmed from – I did have more jobs and more career changes in my short life than most do in a whole life. But, here's the thing, I'm back in college. I know. I know. Sometimes I find it hard to believe myself after my lack-lustre performance the first time. But this second time I know what I'm doing, I have a plan. And my plan is this: to one day become a children's welfare officer. *How*, you may ask, did that come about? Like I said, I've changed. But just how did it come about exactly?

After Seán's death I finally managed to track down his two daughters. It was something I needed to do. I enlisted the help of a detective agency again and this time they were more successful. It turns out they're both together, living with a lovely foster family so now they're growing up as the youngest of a family of six kids and with parents who are just the nicest, kindest people ever, and who are in the process of adopting them. They're beautiful, healthy, happy, and much doted-upon little girls – Seán and Hilda would be very proud of them. Oh, God, I'll be in need of a tissue soon. But it's so wonderful to see them getting a chance of a life that neither Seán or Hilda ever had. It's they – the girls – who got me thinking that I wanted to work at something that would make a difference in other people's lives – people who aren't as fortunate as me, people like Seán.

Apart from Sarah, we dropped the idea of giving houses rent-free to people and instead put money into buying Donald's old youth hostel for a good price – thanks to Caroline's clever negotiations, Shane's help, and the economic climate. Renovating it was a more costly process but it's complete now and is about to be turned over to the professionals to run as a home for homeless teenagers.

And that's the reason we're all gathered. We're here for the official opening. And now it's soon to begin.

But, as us adults patiently sit and wait, I spot two little girls in matching white dresses running around in the grass in front of the podium, two little girls called Julia and Queenie. At this moment their only concern in the world is to avoid being caught by my three nephews chasing them, and Dana's little sister Cathy who's following behind.

Queenie and Julia have no real idea now but, one day, their loving adoptive parents will tell them. Tell them that their dad — Seán — is the reason all of us are gathered here on this sunny, breezy day.

THE END

If you enjoyed *Win Some Love Some* by
Anne Marie Forrest, why not try
Love Potions also published by Poolbeg?

Here's a sneak preview of Chapter One.

Love

Potions

Anne Marie Forrest

POOLBEG

"Fetch me that flower, the herb I show'd thee once;
The juice of it on sleeping eyelids laid
Will make or man or woman madly dote
Upon the next live creature that it sees."

From Shakespeare's, A Midsummer Night's Dream.

1

The thing is, I don't feel comfortable. I should have known better. I should never have allowed Caroline persuade me. I should never have let her talk me into wearing her navy Paul Costello suit. For starters, it's too big, the skirt especially, and despite her assurances (and the presence of a couple of discreet safety pins) I worry it might go sliding down over my hips without notice – most likely at some inopportune moment, like when I'm crossing the room to shake hands with the interviewers. I did try voicing my worries to Caroline last night when she was doing her Trinny and Susannah on me but she just waved my concerns aside and told me the suit could have been made for me. Made for me? Why, yes – *if* I were a stone or two heavier, a couple of inches shorter and was shaped and proportioned altogether differently. Made for me? No, but the sad truth is, it is so much better than anything I own.

And, because it is so much better, I've been terrified all morning that I'll spill a cup of coffee on it or rip it on something sharp. Caroline must have mentioned a dozen times how very expensive it was and how privileged I am to be getting a loan of it. What with the prospect of being humiliated by a panel of interviewers hanging over me, this additional worry of doing hundreds of euros' worth of damage is one I could do without.

Another reason I don't feel comfortable is because I simply don't feel like me. This power-suit-wearing me is a false me; it's me playing at being a Caroline type – sharp, in control, the kind that looks like she could juggle a budget of millions with one hand while applying blood-red lipstick with the other.

And that's another thing. I should never have let her persuade me to wear her blood-red lipstick. It makes me feel like a hooker which isn't quite the look I was aiming for and, now, even at this late stage, I have the urge to find the Ladies' and go wipe the scarlet gash from my face. Only the worry of having my name called out in my absence keeps me in my seat.

Despite my preoccupation with my too-loose skirt and my too-tarty lipstick, I get the feeling that someone is staring at me and I look up to be met by the haughty gaze of a haughty-looking woman, early twenties I'd guess, who's sitting across the waiting-room and who heretofore has been at pains to haughtily ignore me. Now that she's caught my eye, she arches one of her thinly plucked eyebrows and stares pointedly at my foot. I follow her gaze and look down. My foot is tapping like crazy, powered by my nervousness.

"Nerves," I explain, smile apologetically and force myself to still that errant foot. She looks at me stony-faced, like she has no comprehension of this word. "What is this 'nerves', you speak of?" I half-expect her to ask in (for some reason) a heavily accented voice. I struggle to keep my foot still while she sits there, coolly studying me, deciding whether I'm a worthy opponent, all the while managing to look utterly composed as if being here in this sterile room, waiting for a head to pop around the door, call out a name and then the owner of that head to lead one of us candidates, one of us condemned, down a corridor to face a panel who'll look us up and down, judge us, ask us to explain our life, or at least that portion and version of it outlined in our CV and then, most likely, reject us – *me* – is, well, no big deal. No big deal! Oh God! God!!!!!!!! My stomach lurches. I think I'm going to get sick. I think about making a dash for the toilets but again the fear of being called in my absence keeps me where I am.

Across the room, Ms Cool, Calm and Collected, having now dropped me from her stare in the manner a child might drop some bug after examining it to his or her satisfaction, picks up her expensive-looking leather satchel. She unfastens it, extracts what I guess is a copy of her CV, then relaxes back in her chair, opens it, and begins to read. Maybe I should take my lead from her and study my own CV but no, I would find no comfort there – it would make me even more anxious: the poor science degree that took longer than it should, the lack of any relevant work experience, and – yes – the lies. Was I right to listen to Caroline? Was I right to take her advice and omit the fact that I'd spent my time since graduating working in the unrelated area of fashion to put it in lofty terms or, more prosaically, as a shop assistant in a Dublin city centre boutique? I'd probably still be there but for the fact that months back it closed its doors permanently to the city's shoppers who failed to come through those doors in numbers sufficient to keep it viable, lured as they were by trendier, brighter, brasher and much cheaper shopping opportunities in the city. All that I left out. Caroline argued that to tell the truth would show a lack of interest in my field. Far better, she maintained, to say I'd been travelling. They'd like that, Caroline said. They'd like the idea that I'd wanted to broaden my mind and now that it was sufficiently broadened, I was ready to settle down and apply myself to this new job, ready to become a productive member of their team and society at large.

Now the door slowly opens. I look towards it, holding my breath – has my time finally come? But no, instead a nervous-looking human beanpole sidles in, eyes firmly focused on the ground. His fresh-from-the-shop suit but even more so his nervousness suggest he's here for the same reason I am. But how can this be? He looks fifteen – tops. Nervously he glances around the room but manages to avoid eye contact with either me or Ms Cool, Calm and Collected. Then he takes a seat exactly equidistant from me and Ms CCC so that we're like three magnets repelling one another. For what seems like an age he sits there, head bent, not daring to look up until, finally, he garners the courage, raises his eyes nervously, catches mine and, when he does, I smile, hoping to put him at ease but instead I guess I startle him, my own nerves having strangulated my facial muscles, doubtlessly making my smile more like a wolf-like grimace. He promptly drops the A4 pages he's been clutching – his CV? – and, unstapled, they flutter to the floor.

Both he and I jump from our seats and bend down to pick them up.

"Ms Rosie Kiely?" a voice calls out from behind my back.

From my disadvantaged squatting position, I turn my

head around and look up to see a friendly, bubbly young woman looking down.

"Yes, that's me."

"Can you please come with me, Ms Kiely?" She beckons with a nicely manicured nail but to me it's as menacing as the long gnarled finger of the Grim Reaper.

I get up from my haunches. My time has come.

The Love Detective
by Anne Marie Forrest

Beautiful Rosie Kiely presumes that one day she will fall in love, marry and live happily ever after. Until she does, she enjoys a stream of handsome boyfriends whom she treats carelessly but, after a heart-to-heart with her friend Caroline, she begins to doubt her presumptions.

Is she – Rosie – even capable of falling in love? Does true love really exist? Or is love just a myth we all buy into?

In a bid to find out, Rosie begins nosing into the romantic affairs of those closest to her: her parents whose marriage has survived through thick and thin; her work colleague, Fay, and the man who hurt her so badly all those years ago; her childhood friend, Shane, and his girlfriend, Loretta, whose bond is unfathomable to Rosie; her friends, Caroline and Mick – utterly unsuitable but increasingly drawn to one another; and her friend, Dana, who falls for the monosyllabic Doug.

Violence, infidelity, lust, but friendship and loyalty too – Rosie finds a whole lot more than she expected. For love – like life – can be a messy business with a habit of making fools of us all as Rosie – self-appointed love detective – discovers.

And when Rosie does find her own true love, does she realise her good fortune? And is she now ready to grab it with both hands?

ISBN 978-1-84223-119-7

Dancing Days

by Anne Marie Forrest

Ana: a little girl intently dressing up in her old friend Celia's jewels . . . a young woman walking alone to church in her bridal gown . . . a loving wife who suffers tragic loss but survives to travel to Africa and fall in love . . . an aging woman who still has an eye for form and likes to take risk, ride pillion on a motorbike, sing in a woodland glade with a handsome gardener . . .

Ana: who always depends on life's unexpectedness . . .

When such a woman at last comes to retire, do we believe for a moment that her dancing days are over?

An upbeat, hilarious and tender novel from the author of the bestselling *Who Will Love Polly Odlum?*

ISBN 978-1-84223-045-9